Chart of *Catastrophic Events* Characteristics

©2012 AFOC LLC

Catastrophic Event List	Probability of the Event	Probability of *A Failure of Civility*	Likelihood of a Long Term Crisis	Food Supply disruption or shortage	Potable Water disruption or shortage	Geographical area most likely affected	Probability of Global Expansion	Electrical disruption	Communications disruption	Transportation disruption	Medical Services disruption	Civil Unrest in Area	Probability Martial Law in Area
A. Financial collapse of the United States and world economies-Depression, mass unemployment and hyperinflation	Highly Possible	Yes	Yes	Shortage	No effect	Worldwide	Worldwide	No	No	No	Yes	Yes	Yes
B. Cyber hacking and viruses damaging the infrastructure control computers creating *Critical Life Supplies and Services* shortages or disruption	Highly Possible	Yes	Yes	Shortage	Shortage	Industrialized World	Yes	Yes	Yes	Yes	Yes	Yes	Yes
C. Electromagnetic Pulse E1/E2/E3 component – Nuclear Weapon generated destroying computers and or the electrical power grid.	Highly Possible	Yes	Yes	Shortage	Shortage	Industrialized World	No	Yes	Yes	Yes	Yes	Yes	Yes
D. Class Warfare in American and or European countries or Racial/Ethnic Wars or Federal versus State disputes over 'States Rights' autonomy causing civil conflict	Highly Possible	No	Yes	Disruption	No effect	America, Europe	No	No	No	No	Yes	Yes	Yes
E. Solar Electromagnetic Pulse E3 component–Extreme X-Class Solar Coronal Mass Ejection (CME) striking Earth destroying computers and or the electrical power grid.	Possible	Yes	Yes	Shortage	Shortage	Industrialized World	No	Yes	Yes	Yes	Yes	Yes	Yes
F. Worldwide famine from crop failures-Wide spread drought or Natural fungal/blight problems.	Possible	Yes	Yes	Shortage	No effect	Worldwide	Worldwide	No	No	No	No	Yes	Yes
G. Massive ash ejection from volcanoes and the resulting cold summer-Crop failures	Possible	Yes	Yes	Shortage	No effect	Worldwide	No	No	No	Yes	Yes	Yes	Yes
H. Worldwide shortage or long term loss of potable water	Possible	Yes	Yes	Disruption	Shortage	Worldwide	Worldwide	No	No	No	No	Yes	Yes
I. Nuclear 'dirty bomb' explosion or biological terrorist attack or chemical terrorist attack	Possible	No	Yes	Disruption	No effect	Non-Muslim Countries	Yes	No	No	No	Yes	No	Yes
J. Worldwide pandemic of disease or bio-engineered disaster	Possible	No	Yes	Disruption	No effect	Worldwide	Yes	No	No	No	Yes	No	Yes
K. Fuel shortage or union strikes disrupting trucking and railroad distribution of *Critical Life Supplies and Services*	Possible	No	No	Disruption	Disruption	Industrialized World	Yes	Yes	No	Yes	Yes	No	No
L. Earthquake	Possible	No	No	No effect	Disruption	Localized	No	Yes	No	Yes	No	No	No
M. Tornado	Possible	No	No	No effect	No effect	Localized	No	No	No	No	No	No	No
N. Hurricane	Possible	No	No	No effect	No effect	Localized	No	No	No	No	No	No	No
O. Prairie or Forest fire	Possible	No	No	No effect	No effect	Localized	No	Yes	No	No	No	No	No
P. Asteroid strike causing a 'Nuclear Winter'	Little Possibility	Yes	Yes	Shortage	Disruption	Worldwide	Worldwide	No	No	Yes	Yes	Yes	Yes
Q. Magnetic pole shift causing long term disruption	Little Possibility	Yes	Yes	Shortage	Disruption	Worldwide	Worldwide	Yes	Yes	Yes	Yes	Yes	Yes
R. Nuclear detonations severe enough to cause a 'Nuclear Winter'	Little Possibility	Yes	Yes	Shortage	Disruption	Worldwide	Worldwide	No	No	Yes	Yes	Yes	Yes
S. Conventional World War Three	Little Possibility	No	No	Disruption	No effect	Worldwide	Worldwide	No	Yes	Yes	Yes	Yes	Yes
T. Tsunami or costal damage from open water waves	Little Possibility	No	No	No effect	No effect	Localized	No	No	No	No	No	No	No
U. Pandemic of food borne illnesses	Little Possibility	No	No	Disruption	No effect	Localized	No	No	No	No	No	No	No
V. Nuclear power plant meltdown and radiation leak	Little Possibility	No	No	No effect	No effect	Localized	No	No	No	Yes	Yes	No	No

A Failure of Civility

First Edition

© 2012 AFOC LLC

The information in this book may not be duplicated or disseminated by any means or in any form without the previous written permission of the copyright holders.

ISBN Number: 978-0-615-67010-2

Cover Illustration by Ken Meyer, Jr.
at www.KenMeyerJr.com/port

Our Website… **www.AFAILUREOFCIVILITY.com**

AFOC LLC

Printed and bound in the United States of America

First Edition 120825

Content Index by Chapter and Section

- 12-Communications
- 12-Sanitation and Hygiene
- 12-Centralized area for medical aid
- 12-Get a *Ring Bound* version of the *Special Operations Forces Medical Handbook*
- 12-Medical aid and medicines
- 12- *Jointly...* what your Group Members will have to buy for the *Communal NPP equipment and supplies...*
- 12-*Individually...* what each Group Member must have... per each Group Member...
- 12-Alternative electrical power
- 12-Specialized Items needed for certain *Catastrophic Events*
- 12-What will happen if *A Failure of Civility* is prolonged or permanent?
- 12-Vehicles and fuel
- 12-Preparing your *NPP* with supplies and equipment.
- 12-Sharing food and provisions to maintain cohesion of *NPP*
- 12-After the storm

Conclusion

Check Lists, Forms and Supplemental Information

- Map of one million plus Metropolitan Areas
- Emergency Radio Frequencies
- The Military Phonetic Alphabet
- Calculation of food, water and provisions for EACH PERSON
- *Neighborhood Protection Plan* Survey Questionnaire and Address Checklist
- Our *Neighborhood Protection Plan (NPP)* Statement of Purpose
- *NPP* Group Member Information Form

"A Failure of Civility"

How to Defend and Protect

You, your family, friends, neighborhood and **America**

during a disaster or crisis.

A few notes to our Readers...

Consider reading this book as if the Authors have parachuted into your backyard as Special Operations Soldiers to assist you in forming a cooperative protection of your neighborhood. That's one of the things Special Operations Soldiers, or 'Special Ops', are best at... covert insertion into isolated areas to train people how to defend themselves against inequitable justice and malicious aggression.

The Authors' combined life experiences, military and law enforcement span 80 years. With this book, we give you *the tools of knowledge* ***to enable you to teach you and others*** how to defend yourselves, family and neighbors. We want you to help save lives and to keep America strong.

We have printed this book in large 14 point font and broken up the paragraphs so it is easier for our Readers. We have tried to limit the paragraphs to no more than 6 lines between breaks as most military, law enforcement and technical manuals are one continuous mass of words and consequently very difficult and taxing to focus on and comprehend.

We also decided early on in this writing to make the book a full sized 8.5" by 11" book with as many diagrams, depictions, charts and color photographs to convey the content and make the book as visually pleasant as a technical manual can be. This consequentially cost us much more to produce this book... but we hope the ease of reading and understanding is much better.

If we repeat issues in this book or sound like we're reiterating the same thing... read these areas carefully. This is not to take up space or see our words in print again and again... that costs us a lot of extra money to print this book. *It is to ensure that you, the Reader, understand the importance of the subject.*

As with all explanations of diagrams and examples of tactics in this book... read them... learn the terminology and meaning of each. If you go back and review the diagrams and explanations again... multiple times if necessary... your understanding of tactical application will begin to become logical and make sense to you.

You must understand, as difficult as some of these concepts are to learn, professional soldiers undergo years of study and practical application to be able to utilize tactics properly. Do not get disenchanted while learning these concepts.

We are not promoting collectivism or shared interest of group activity except for common defense, providing shelter and food to those in need to the extent possible, providing communications, maintaining hygiene and giving medical aid to those in need *only during an emergency until the Crisis passes*. Rather we promote cooperation and consideration for others.... just like all good neighbors should do always.

In the spirit of all compassionate beliefs, decency and common sense, it is the wish of both Authors that people maintain their civility towards each other as much as possible should adversity arise. People should conduct themselves by the rule of law, respect other's rights, hold life reverent and do everything to cooperate with local law enforcement to the greatest extent possible.

Readers should totally prevent, or in a worst case scenario, attempt to minimize the loss of life resulting from the application of information in this book should *A Failure of Civility* occur.

The Authors inform the Reader that any reference to a religion or religions is not necessarily the religion of the Authors nor is this intended to promote that religion, even though names of beliefs and certain religious disciplines may be made throughout this book.

Each of the Authors has their beliefs, however, they believe most deeply in Freedom of Religion as the Constitution of the United States of America proclaims. The Authors are not judgmental on how people come to their God.

We respect the religions of all... as long as that religion *does not harm others...* if the spirit of those beliefs is *for the good and beneficial interest of mankind...* and if each person professing that belief *can be truly humble before their God.*

The Authors do believe that Americans are abandoning their belief in God. There is no doubt that organized religion has harmed humanity many times over past thousands of years.

However, we believe that *much more good* has come to our society when people are humble before and believe in a benevolent, immortal spirit much larger than themselves.

America was founded on the principles of Judeo-Christianity and these beliefs have had a major impact on creating the tough, resilient and durable fabric that holds our society together.

Although imperfect and unjust at times, our founding Father's vision of this country based on Judeo-Christian principles has been far more beneficial to Americans and the country than the grandiose egos that some leaders would have solely represent the aggregate value of a country.

That is measured by America's successful tenure amongst other forms of government and 'republics' that have come and gone like summer rains during the past two centuries plus of our country's existence.

We know that people should conduct themselves and treat each other by the Biblical saying *"Do unto others... as you would have others do unto you."* However, to protect yourself, your family and your neighbors, you must also be ready to *"Do unto those first, the harm that they undoubtedly intend to do unto you... without blinking and eye."*

About the Authors

Mike Garand and Jack Lawson are former Special Operations unit combat veterans who were involved with rapid response Airborne and Heliborne Counter Insurgency Units, overseeing perimeter protection, training and providing bodyguard services in conflicts of Africa, Iraq and Afghanistan.

Mike Garand holds a Bachelor of Arts Degree and a Master of Science Degree in Urban Studies with an emphasis on Criminal Justice. He has spent much of his life in the U.S. Military as a Marine and Special Forces Soldier and is retired from the U.S. Army Reserve. He is also a retired Detective from a major metropolitan police department.

He has worked for years as a private security contractor for the largest and most well known of the American private military companies, providing training and security services worldwide. He has seen service numerous times during the conflicts in Iraq and Afghanistan. Mike is a member of a U.S. Army Special Forces Association chapter.

Jack Lawson served in the United States Air Force and was also a member of a Foreign Legion counter insurgency unit during an anti-communist guerilla war in Africa. He was trained by British Commonwealth SAS and Israeli commando instructors and took part in counter insurgency operations and commando raids on communist training camps in a number of African countries. While there he became a bodyguard for a farmer's cooperative association in his off duty time.

Jack is an Honorary Member of a U.S. Army Special Forces Association chapter and for seven years served on a metropolitan police department Review Board that judged Officer Involved Shootings and use of deadly force incidents. He was also a consultant to the United States Marine Corps on heliborne vertical envelopment and anti-terrorist tactics. He has authored two other books.

The Intent of this Book

This is a manual for the American citizen to use to assist them in protecting themselves and maintaining *Normal Civility* in their neighborhood during the time of an emergency that would lead to a *Crisis*. It is compiled from the view of Special Operations soldiers.

Most well-to-do people concerned with survival are ready for a disaster. They have the best that money can buy. This book is written for the John and Joan Q Citizens and their families in neighborhoods across America.

We write this book for those Americans who don't have the financial resources to build or buy space in a bunker, have a house or compound out in the woods to leave the city for, or much money to spend for disaster preparation. Maybe this describes you... maybe it doesn't.

But if this does describe you... this book will show you how to survive in your home and with the cooperation of your neighbors... in your neighborhood if *A Failure of Civility* occurs. There just isn't much in print that will instruct you how to organize and cooperate to achieve a total concept of *Safety and Protection* for survival.

John and Joan want to survive with their children to carry on life when it returns to *Normal Civility* like everyone else... and they need to... because *they* are the core of what makes America.

The Authors inform the Reader that the Authors are not attorneys and some recommendations or actions in this book that the Reader takes may lead to loss of life, injury to them or others or violations of the rights of others. Even though the Reader may determine that action to be in the spirit of simple self defense, it may not be viewed that way by authorities in some States and Locales.

The Authors further advise the Reader that the Authors will not be liable for situations that arise from the Reader's interpretations of material in this book, the Reader's instructions to others, the Reader's actions or implementation of recommendations and information from this book... that leads to the violations of rights of others, injury or loss of life. You're all adults, behave as responsible adults and verify your Federal, State and Local laws and ordinances.

Dictionary Definition
Civility *(Old French* civilite) *from* (Latin *civilitas*)
(Noun) In early use the term denoted the state of being a citizen and hence good citizenship or orderly behavior... The sense 'politeness' arose in the mid 16th century.

In the context of this book, a *Catastrophic Event* is a disaster that could lead to *A Failure of Civility. A Failure of Civility* would be the crudest, most barbarous and brutal deviation from *Normal Civility* that society can get. In short... *A Failure of Civility* would be a *"New Dark Ages"*.

The types of possible *Catastrophic Events* are listed and explained in *Chapter 3, Catastrophic Events* and their characteristics are listed in the *Chart of Catastrophic Events*.

However, before you turn to read *Chapter 3,* the following will give you an overview. The term *Area Emergency* refers to the interruption that society will experience after a *Catastrophic Event.* This *Area Emergency* can lead to a *Crisis* which can turn into a *Long Term Crisis*.

A *Long Term Crisis* is the stage which will precede *A Failure of Civility* if *Critical Life Supplies and Services* are exhausted... primarily food and water. Civil order will not be able to be maintained without these two items of *Critical Life Supplies and Services* being available to all people.

By the term *Normal Civility*, the Authors describe the way Americans live day to day without killing or brutalizing each other for *Critical Life Supplies and Services*, of which again... the two most necessary are... *food and water.*

Normal Civility also embraces government services such as law enforcement and a judicial system through which disputes are resolved. But without food or water... people cannot live for long and society will face *A Failure of Civility.*

America's *Normal Civility* has become increasingly fragile because of one item in the list of *Critical Life Supplies and Services...* food. Americans today have moved further away from the *"Garden to Table"* existence of past generations than ever before in the history of this nation. We now rely on a food system that is extremely complex and *fragile.*

A *"Garden to Table"* existence is how families used to live. Like the next diagram shows... families and local farmers... grew much of what they consumed and it was locally processed. In the past, food was widely produced by many people on a low level technical and localized basis.

Food was fresh and immediately available. The food went literarily from 'the garden to their table' making them *Self Dependent* regarding food. In addition, food stocks were stored to live on during bad growing seasons, difficult financial times and for the off growing seasons.

Our present food supply system is, for the most part, a result of the past *"Age of Abundance"* and our lifestyle. It has allowed us to choose to eat the cuisine of the world wherever we live in America and most of the world and after only a simple trip to the store.

However, this food supply system is extremely concentrated, complex, cluttered with packaging, chemicals and preservatives moving through production lines and is wholly dependent on an extensive transportation and storage system.

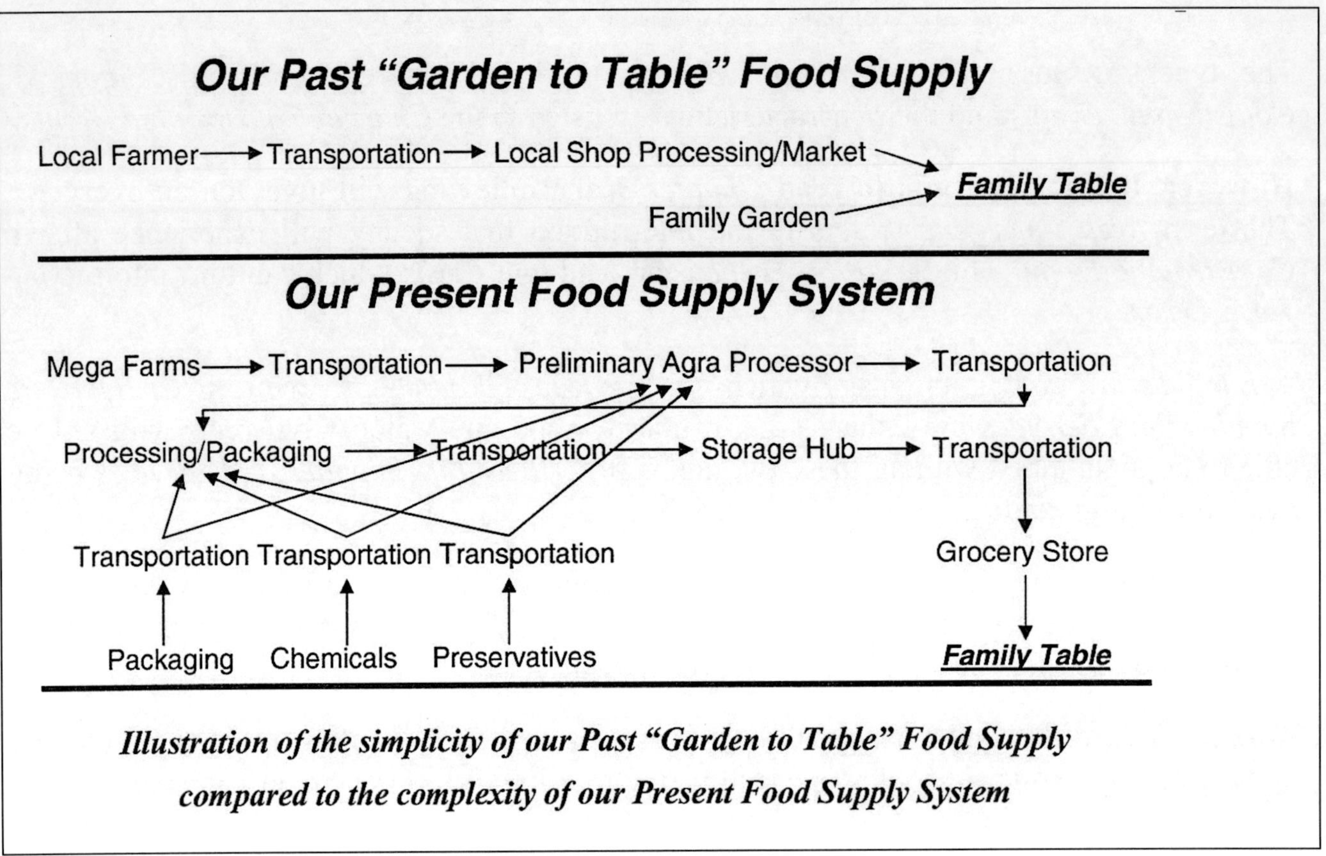

Illustration of the simplicity of our Past "Garden to Table" Food Supply compared to the complexity of our Present Food Supply System

The growing and processing of each food item is dependent on not only transportation and proper storage… but each item is totally dependent upon packaging, chemicals and preservatives usually produced thousands of miles away from the processing facilities. Without these processing items the food production line comes to a standstill.

It is necessary that food in this system be processed with chemicals and treated with preservatives because of this time-intensive processing, storage and transportation system. Each item in your grocery store endures weeks of processing and an average 1400 mile trip to get to your table. Unfortunately, as a side effect, food is less fresh and has far from the nutritional content it used to have.

If one minor link in this food system production-line chain breaks… the system stops. It's totally reliant on computers, electricity and electronics.

This movement away from the *"Garden to Table"* existence is compounded further by our reliance on electricity and an electronic digital infrastructure that virtually controls every facet of our food production line, yet is susceptible to disruption and in some cases even protracted disruption or destruction. Even though we eat foods now that in the past would have been a great delicacy… few people now stockpile food reserves. We live a 'hand to mouth' existence.

This system is the caretaker of virtually *everything* we use or consume… but most critically our food supply… the growing, processing, storage and distribution of it.

After some *Catastrophic Events… nothing will move... no transportation system will function. All vehicles... including trucks... railroads, aircraft and even ships will cease to operate.* Our *Present Food Supply System* will not only break down in the transportation of food stocks… but the growing, the storage… including refrigeration and processing… will stop.

Even the manufacture of packaging and chemicals to process foods with will cease to function… let alone be able to be transported from their manufacture point to the processing facilities, usually thousands of miles away. This goes for medicines and almost everything else we depend on daily for our existence and well being.

In a worst case *Catastrophic Event,* an example of such, a powerful man made nuclear generated Electromagnetic Pulse (an EMP with E1, E2 and E3 components) or an extremely high intensity 'X Class' Coronal Mass Ejection (CME) from a Solar Flare causing an Electromagnetic Pulse (an EMP with E3 component similar to that of the nuclear generated pulse) that directly strikes the earth, the world as we know it could take a giant leap backwards to a *New Dark Ages.*

After an EMP *Catastrophic Event... A Failure of Civility* would eventually occur. The *Critical Life Supplies and Services* which we take for granted during our *Normal Civility* would become scarce or non-existent and money would generally become replaced by food, water and other life sustainable items as a 'new currency'.

A Failure of Civility would be a total lack of concern for others and it would be everyone for themselves. Life would be survival by brutality and use of force… survival at the point of a gun.

People would soon find that normal societal controls of the rights of others and sanctity of life would disappear. People would not be held accountable by their peers nor the judicial system and consequently would not have inhibitions against violating these constraints in an environment of desperation.

The Authors believe death from starvation and indiscriminate killing would abound if *A Failure of Civility* was long term or permanent. It would not be an environment that anyone would enjoy being in.

It would be a struggle between good and evil and a great effort would have to be made to maintain or reinstitute the most basic civilization.

Successfully defending your neighborhood as a group if *A Failure of Civility* occurs is an extremely complicated task… but not impossible… it can be done.

The alternative is unthinkable… unless you consider the suffering, starvation and death that you, your family and friends, neighbors and America will face if you do nothing.

Since the end of the American Military Draft in 1973, fewer of the younger generations have seen military service than ever before in this country.

That means a greater percentage of the American people have never been exposed to military training and tactics… and many more have never fired a weapon.

We can't give you the 'real life' experience of shooting firearms through this book, but we can give you *our* experiences and knowledge to help you with firearms and help you formulate your *Area Tactical Protection.*

The American Fighting Spirit

We know you can do it because we American people still have the American Fighting Spirit.

We hope sharing *our* experiences and *our* advice on safety and techniques on tactics, how to use firearms safely and effectively and giving you the greatest chance of survival in a gun fight… will provide you with an 'edge' over others if a *Crisis* occurs and it comes to that.

What is an *Area Tactical Defense…* or what we recommend… *Area Tactical Protection?* Well first, we'll mention a statement by an old Special Forces Instructor long ago that left an indelible impression… *"Tactics are like @$$holes… everybody has one!"*

We think you get the meaning of what this Special Forces Instructor insinuated by the above phrase. As crude as it sounds his statement is remembered. *Tactics are not cast in stone.*

Everyone has their *own concept* of tactics and how they should be employed. We give you *our* concept of tactics in this book… and *you* can adapt them to *your* circumstances and create *your* own concepts.

We'll explain the difference between a Defense, an Area Tactical Defense and Area Tactical Protection by what George and Tom do…

A Defense… *George sits in his home with a shotgun ready to shoot the robber who's kicking in the front door of his home intent on beating or killing and robbing George and his family.*

Tom, who lives across the street from George, is sitting in his house with his shotgun waiting for robbers to break into his house also. George and Tom haven't talked to each other for years. They're both scared... but they're each acting alone to defend their own houses.

George moves from sitting in his chair to crouching behind it waiting nervously for the assailant to come through the door. The robber may shoot George before George can stop the threat by shooting the robber. The door of George's house comes crashing in, the robber comes in and gunfire erupts. George... We'll let your imagination decide what happened to George.

A Tactical Defense… *George sits in his home with a shotgun ready to shoot the robber who's kicking in the front door of his home intent on beating or killing and robbing George and his family. George moves from sitting in his chair to crouching behind it waiting nervously for the assailant to come through the door. The robber may shoot George before George can stop the threat by shooting the robber.*

But George is not alone. George's neighbor Tom lives across the street and is walking guard in the neighborhood with his shotgun. ***George and Tom have a Tactical Defense Plan.*** *When the thief begins to kick in George's front door Tom hears the noise and Tom comes around from the side of George's house to confront the robber just as the robber kicks George's door open. Tom shoots the robber from the side and George shoots the robber from the front while both Tom and George are being careful not to shoot each other.*

The robber never had a chance to shoot George ***or*** *Tom because of their* ***tactics,*** which were their ***Tactical Defense plan.***

Tactical Protection… *George sits outside protecting his home with a shotgun and his neighbor Tom is walking guard in the neighborhood with his shotgun. It's lawless in the city and looters and robbers have broken into houses and have killed and robbed many homeowners in their area.*

George hears shots and walks out to the street in front of his house. He sees a robber come running out of a house down the street with a shotgun. The homeowner follows out into the street yelling at the robber. The robber shoots the homeowner. Tom hears the sound of shooting also and joins George. Both Tom and George watch the robber in the distance walk towards their houses.

George and Tom decide to be proactive and stop this threat before the robber can attack them. George and Tom move along the road behind the houses on each side of the road towards this killer but out of view of him. George and Tom come to an area with a huge rock on one side and a big tree on the other side of the road that they can use as Cover from this killer.

Both George and Tom will stand behind their Cover on each side of the road while pointing their shotguns at this killer being careful that neither George or Tom are in the line of fire of the other. The rock and tree will give George and Tom 'Cover' and Concealment'. George and Tom will make a citizen's arrest and turn the killer over to law enforcement.

George and Tom both peer out from behind their Cover by the road at the same time and order the killer to put his weapon down. The killer, counting money from the homeowner he has just killed and robbed is taken by surprise. He drops the money, turns and fires at Tom but instead hits the Cover Tom is standing behind. George shoots the robber dead. George calls the police. The police tell them they aren't able to respond. The police show up two days later and radio the Coroner's Office for the meat wagon.

George and Tom had a Tactical Protection plan… a Proactive Defense plan. They acted aggressively towards their threat in defending both their homes by using tactics of 'Enfilade' or 'Flanking' plus the Element of Surprise.

Now put the geographical dimension of *Area* in front of this term *Tactical Protection* and you have the *Area Tactical Protection* theory… which includes *Flanking Attacks*, *Defense in Depth*, *Skipping Rounds, Kill Zones, etc.* This is the Authors' concept of *Area Tactical Protection.*

The difference between an *Area Tactical Defense* and *Area Tactical Protection* is being ***proactive*** *towards the threat* and ***aggressive in your defense*** by utilizing *Flanking Attacks, Fatal Funnels, etc.* The *Area Tactical Protection* is a *Proactive Defense.*

What in blazes!? *Fatal Funnels... what the heck are those!?* We'll cover that later…

Criminal gangs in America have actually encouraged members to enlist in the military for *tactical training*. Some of these former gang members are seasoned military combat veterans of Iraq and Afghanistan and are now back with their gangs.

Others are gang youth with clean police records who enlist in National Guard Units at the direction of their gang leadership, attend basic training and then the School of Infantry. After that period, most of them fail to show up for the remainder of their enlistment. They could care less about an dishonorable discharge. The activities of most gangs are unlawful and being intent on becoming career criminals… they have achieved the gang's goal.

It is suspected that this goal is two fold. *First,* to gain tactical training for gang members and *second,* to have knowledge of where National Guard Armories are and what weapons are in them. It is further suspected that if there is a disaster, social and law enforcement breakdown that they will seize these weapons for their gang's use and they will have the people in their gangs with training that know how to use these weapons and military tactics.

A curious note is that one of the older well established Hispanic gangs is recruiting across racial and ethnic lines for combat veterans. This gang now has whites, Orientals and blacks as members in addition to Hispanic combat veterans. It is not hard to visualize what their actions will be if there is *A Failure of Civility.* They will become the authority and control in their areas. These people are actively pursuing knowledge of tactics and firearms training... *so shouldn't you?*

We understand that you're not Army Rangers, Special Forces, Navy SEALS or even regular Army Combat Infantrymen. We also know that many of you have never been in law enforcement, the regular army, had any military service or have even fired a weapon. A U.S. Army Combat Infantryman goes through 12 weeks of schooling on tactical training, over half of which is physical training exercises with tactics.

But the tactical plans and information in this book, coupled with basic competent leadership and your initiative, can make a group of able bodied people with a *Survival Mentality* a formidable force in defending a neighborhood.

The American Military is the best equipped, trained and the most sophisticated military force in the world. They have many, many tools that we will not even mention here that would help you immensely in the defense of your neighborhood. Their sophisticated weapons, body armor, electronics, alert, surveillance and explosives are the best in existence.

However, the Authors have had to remove from their thought the sophisticated equipment they have used and create and provide you simple known methods and equipment of basic protection for the intent of this book. The items we describe here are practical and easy for the *citizen trained Guardians you will become* to use in protecting your neighborhood.

In addition, we have had to evaluate those methods and equipment for cost. What we present here are methods and equipment that are relatively cheap to use and implement for the average John and Joan Q Citizen in the thousands of neighborhoods across America. We will tell you what you need… most of which you can make or buy where you live now.

We have attempted to avoid military terminology and keep the wording of this book as simple and as much in layman terms as possible. Just as there are infinite combinations of words to write this book, there are countless methods and items that can be used to defend a fortified area and an almost infinite number of scenarios of what could happen during a *Crisis* around a Protective Perimeter... too many to go into detail with in this book.

We will give you the basic scenarios, tactics, tools and knowledge… and as Americans, we know that you will adapt and improvise to your situation. Americans are a unique strain of people and have been a most remarkable people in doing just that over the last two centuries plus… fighting for their nation and their individual rights by adapting and improvising.

Since firearms are the preeminent and most efficient means of defense, to start with you must have at least one firearm. If you don't have a firearm, have an NRA Certified Instructor advise you on what to purchase *by our description of what you need* from this book and teach you how to use them *safely* and properly. Then employ some of the techniques we illustrate in *Chapter 10,* ***keeping safe firearms handling foremost in your mind.***

If you join together with your neighbors, this book will give you an 'edge' over most threats. Such a plan will drastically increase your chances of surviving a *Long Term Crisis* or *A Failure of Civility* if it comes to that.

Many books about survival are on the market, however this book is different. Some of these books have become 'Bibles' for preparedness minded persons. Most all of them encourage people to leave populated areas to survive. Having the equipment, location, retreat and resources as some people have would be reassuring… getting out of the city to these retreats would be another issue.

However, considering the income of the average American and due to the fact that the economic "*Age of Abundance*" is gone, for the majority of Americans… the equipment, location, retreat and resources such as some preparedness minded people of financial means have is beyond the possibility of most individual's financial means. This is who we've written this book for.

This book is the antithesis of other books that advocate people should quickly leave cities and populated areas for remote and unpopulated areas with the minimum of necessities in a *"Bug Out Bag."*

The Authors *do not* believe in the *"Bugging Out"* or *"Going Remote"* mentality of leaving populated, strife torn areas for remote areas to try to live off 'Bugs, Berries and tree Bark' as the primary strategy for survival in a *Crisis*.

The Authors have lived like this for days and it was not an enjoyable existence nor will it be for longer periods of time. You have way more resources in your neighborhood and are better off there. Further, you will not be well received by the people living in these areas that you leave the city for.

Leaving the chaos of a populated area does have some distinct advantages, but in our opinion the disadvantages far outweigh the advantages for all but the most well established, equipped and prepared citizen.

The Authors question the feasibility of most people being able to travel from a populated area to a remote area after some *Catastrophic Events* have occurred. We don't believe this will be possible for most people of a city and the majority of metropolitan areas.

In addition to a most probable miserable existence from *"Going Remote",* a single person or small group in a remote area will not last long by themselves in our opinion. Unless these people are exceedingly mentally disciplined, the 'Solitary Confinement' mentality of living alone, remotely will cause them to seek human contact for medical attention, food and provisions, conversation, comfort and current situational information and news.

Even 'Jeremiah Johnson' of the movie by the same name needed human contact periodically. Eventually, that single person or small group will encounter a larger group of people who will be desperate for what they have and will overwhelm even the best trained and armed person or small group. That is if the that individual or small group hasn't become as destitute and desperate as those they're trying to evade.

Most Americans are armed. This is a rarity in the modern world even in most 'Democracies' of the world. Most governments have little trust in their citizens having the abundance of firearms Americans do.

The American

Most government entities in America have so far voluntarily or have been mandated by the judicial system to respect our Constitutional Right under the Second Amendment to possess and use firearms.

Regardless of the push-pull battle that goes on constantly over the 2nd Amendment Right, we have the right to defend ourselves and to possess and use firearms to do so.

In your hands... the hunting rifle, shotgun or home defense handgun and the implementation of your Neighborhood Protection Plan will make America strong!

This book will encourage people to *"Stand in Place"* to protect their neighborhood. By maintaining *Normal Civility* in their neighborhood… citizens can aid local government and law enforcement in managing the *Crisis* until society can hopefully be restored to *Normal Civility.*

In a worst case scenario, should a Long Term Crisis deteriorate into A Failure of Civility, implementation of the Neighborhood Protection Plan (NPP), which we will abbreviate as NPP, outlined in this book in neighborhoods across this nation will help maintain America as a civilized power and an oasis of freedom forever. Street by Street.

Under certain circumstances, you may have to cooperate with local law enforcement to evacuate your *Neighborhood Protection Plan (NPP)* area or conduct an evacuation yourself. New Orleans and the metropolitan areas around there were a case in point after Hurricane Katrina in 2004. Much of this area became indefensible and unsustainable for a *Neighborhood Protection Plan (NPP).*

Because of this, we provide information on SERE (Survival, Evasion, Resistance and Escape) procedures in *Chapter 11,* which you will need if your *Primary Neighborhood Protection Plan (NPP) Location* fails or for whatever reason you cannot stay in your neighborhood and you *must* relocate to a more sustainable or safer area.

Americans *are* the core of this country's freedoms and are critical in maintaining those freedoms. Americans need to protect themselves, their families, their homes, their neighborhoods and their country *where they live.* If Americans do not *Stand in Place* during time of *Crisis* and assist in maintaining law and order, *each and every one* of them is *weakening this country.*

What we will outline in this book *is the necessity and advantage of the cooperation of a group of people, over the individual efforts* of the citizen, should a *Crisis* or *Failure of Civility* occur. The basics of survival are at your fingertips and with little individual expense you can provide your neighborhood with the means to survive almost any *Catastrophic Event.*

Dictionary Definition
Community *(Old French)*
(Noun) All the people who live in a particular area... or a group of people who are considered as a unit because of their shared interests

With the cooperation of your neighbors you can greatly aid the efforts of local law enforcement to maintain order and save lives in your neighborhood. This means that you become part of the solution… not part of the problem. Not being part of the problem means being prepared. This includes having sufficient supplies of food and a water source.

We do not wish that the Reader obsesses with 'Doom and Gloom' because of current events or the prospect of disaster... rather that each family concentrate on having food stocks and prepares for an emergency. The main expense for each involved will be a stockpile of food, water storage, a water source and the means to protect your neighborhood... firearms and training in using them.

A book that will greatly expand your thinking and broaden your horizons in understanding just how frail our society is... how dependent we are on technology... how thin the veneer of civilization is and the extent of the *Catastrophic Event* and *A Failure of Civility* that follows is outlined in the book *"One Second After"* by William R. Forstchen. It focuses on an EMP disaster.

As Forstchen states something similar to this... *"What if you flipped a light switch in your house and nothing happened... turned on the ignition of your vehicle with no response?"* Our *Normal Civility* as we know it would be turned off like a light switch! We recommend that you read "*One Second After"* also.

Forstchen's book outlines the collapse of society after an Electromagnetic Pulse or EMP *Catastrophic Event.* These can be man made or natural. The book illustrates just how sophisticated and dependent our society has become on *everything* due to electricity and computers.

To a greater degree Forstchen's book describes just how fragile this has made our manufacture and delivery systems of *Critical Life Supplies and Services*. The *Catastrophic Event* portrayed in this book, an EMP, is more frightening in the fact that even experts conclude that this *Catastrophic Event* is not *"**If** it will happen... but **when** it will happen".*

Our book is meant to be separate from ideology and politics. We write it on the assumption that The American People obey the Law of the Land as set down in the United States Constitution and Bill of Rights by the Founding Father's visions... and that people will tolerate and respect each other regardless of race, creed, religion or sexuality... and that free enterprise prevails and endures in America.

Even though the Authors may insinuate by some statements in this book their doubt of their government and its agencies... to the contrary, the Authors *love* their country and know that the majority of Americans in government want to do the right thing. The Authors have been in many countries and know that this is still the greatest country on earth and the best to be a citizen of.

However we are realists and know that government is comprised of agencies... and government agencies... act like government agencies... no matter where they are, what acronym by which a government agency abbreviates itself, regardless of whatever promises the people directing these organizations make or how they propagandize the agency.

The Authors believe deeply in the American Spirit and know that American citizens are much more capable of providing for themselves, even with much less in resources, than our government. Americans are innovative and resilient.

Stockpiling food is protection against inflation and is simply common sense logic. Most every American has a firearm and additional ammunition is not an unbearable expense. This is just a common sense lifestyle.

We base the supply requirements stated in this book for a Neighborhood Protection Plan... on a ***Crisis lasting 6 months.*** *We recommend enough food for at least a 6 month period of time* ***per person...*** *more food for a longer period of time if you're able to.*

If there is a *Long Term Crisis*, you may have enough food. If there is *A Failure of Civility*, you will never have enough food, water or ammunition. You'll find that buying two extra cans of each type of food every time you shop will build you a food stockpile quicker than you can believe *without creating a financial hardship.*

Starvation Insurance. People spend a lot of money on all kinds of insurance... life, health and medical, vehicle, property, liability, home, flood, malpractice and business insurance. Unless you have a loss... the money spent for insurance has disappeared at the end of the year and you have nothing to show for it.

What about *starvation insurance?* Ask yourself this question... *"Can my family survive on the food I have in my house? How long will that food last if the grocery stores close?"*

Food is the only way to insure that you and your family do not starve... and if you have food put away... unlike insurance... at the end of the year you can eat it or it still has the same or greater value.

Starvation Insurance

Look at emergency food supplies, firearms, ammunition, preparedness equipment and supplies as a bank account... these will be more valuable than gold if a *Long Term Crisis* or *A Failure of Civility* strikes and they will be worth more than the last time you purchased any of these items.

When have you last seen food go down in price? Regardless, you can't eat money and practicing food storage and preparation is sensible *Self Dependence...* especially in light of *A Failure of Civility.*

The Authors believe that moderate to extreme inflation, unlike this country has ever seen, will come to America in the next few years. Your money is far better invested in

food supplies, firearms, ammunition, preparedness equipment and other provisions than almost anything else.

Go back 20 years, 40 years, 60 years or more and price anyone of these food or preparedness items. Their value in the dollar's buying power at that time compared to now is far better than virtually anything other investment or expenditure of money. You can always create cash by selling some of these items at their new, higher price.

We defy anyone to show us where any of these items have decreased in price in relation to the buying power of the American Dollar. This is not true of the real estate market, the stock market and most like financial instruments.

Like the Authors say … "We've known too many people who would have been much further ahead investing in preparedness items than investing in the hundreds of thousands of dollars of real estate they had for years before the crash of 2008!"

Chapter 1
In the Beginning…

In this Chapter we describe…

- **1-Neighborhoods**
- **1-Story-*"Nobody wins… we just survived… with a lot of bad dreams."***
- **1-*Strength through Numbers***
- **1-Reliance on the government for help**
- **1-The 'Bunker Mentality'**
- **1-Practical *Self Dependence***
- **1-You're *not* a Militia or law enforcement**

1-Neighborhoods

Dictionary Definitions
***Neighborhood** (Old English)*
(Noun) A division of a municipality or region, formally or informally divided...
A modern sense of "community of people who live close together."

Since the beginning of recorded history, man has formed communities and neighborhoods as groups of family homes. The origin of the city was not just as a central gathering place or for shared commerce, but as much for the protection of its inhabitants against other villages, bandits, armies and marauding groups.

Strength through Numbers

This is evidenced by older surviving cities being walled in and the many archeological finds that show walls and fortifications around groups of homes during times of unrecorded history.

Whether these groups of people formed along family blood lines, tribes, clans, religious doctrine, common language, race, ethnicity, geographical boundaries, political beliefs, customs or a combination of these reasons… groups of people formed communities for the common purpose of defending the intentions, possessions, rights and securing the survival of the inhabitants.

They understood that *Strength through Numbers is superior and preferable to the strength and capabilities of the individual.* Within these communities, neighborhoods formed… and flourished.

The time proven advantage of a group being far superior to an individual defending themselves for whatever reason can not be disputed. A case in point is the growing pestilence of modern day 'Gangs'. Even though most of them operate contrary to the law, they are proliferating and through their common interests, whatever those may be, they are a classic example of *Strength through Numbers*.

Gangs in America have, in fact, become separate societies and cultures within our society. Even though their pursuits are mostly unlawful, it's been found almost impossible to eradicate them.

Most of them will not only survive *A Failure of Civility* in the Authors' opinion… they will thrive. Why? …because they already know how to use deadly force… *without blinking an eye… they have the* ***Survival Mentality***.

Read the following…

1-Story-*"Nobody wins… we just survived… with a lot of bad dreams."*

When the catastrophe struck, the electrical grid, water, sewer and utilities stopped functioning. Thus there was no sanitation, no heat in the winter and no water available for drinking or bathing. The currency and banking system quickly collapsed and commerce in its traditional form came to a standstill, leaving only barter and violence as a way to acquire necessities.

The food supply and transportation systems fell apart. Police, fire, and medical services disintegrated and eventually vanished. Violence, disease and death spread throughout the region. *Few were prepared for the months that would follow…*

"Nobody wins… we just survived, with a lot of bad dreams."

*"**For** one whole year I lived and survived in a city of approximately 50,000 residents without electricity, fuel, running water, food distribution, or delivery of any goods and without any kind of organized law or government. When this happened, it happened so fast that we couldn't get out of the city."*

"Grocery stores and gas stations were robbed and everything of value was taken as soon as the chaos started. It happened very, very fast. There was some effort by law enforcement to keep things under control, but everything fell apart in just the first weeks… and then the police force vanished."

"After about a month, gangs started attacking anyone with anything. There were organized groups of gangs of 10 to 15 people, sometimes up to 50 people."

*"**But** there were also normal people like you and me... fathers, mothers, daughters, grandfathers, sons... decent folks, who robbed and killed. There were no good guys wearing white hats and bad guys wearing black hats. Most of us wore gray hats. This was not like in the movies... when it took place it was ugly, dirty, smelly and we did what we had to do to survive."*

"Most people turned into monsters and the city turned into a hell beyond belief. Strength was in the numbers. If you were alone in a house, no matter how well armed, you would have probably been robbed and killed in the first months."

"Most of the time you were not able to determine who was an enemy or who was a friend. Except for my family and few real close friends, everybody was a potential enemy. But when your friend had to choose between his child's life and your life, you can guess who he was going to choose."

"In the first months weak people vanished, others fought and survived. You could stay home and die of hunger and cold or even from the infection of some small wound, or go out and risk your life to try to find anything useful or trade for what you needed. Those with the will to live... lived... and those who couldn't cope with the way life had become... died."

"A one man survivor had little chance no matter how well armed and prepared he was. At the end most of them died. I saw that many times. But some survived."

"We quickly organized neighborhood defense groups. On my street of 20 houses, we organized 5 armed men who patrolled our street every night defending against gangs and looters."

*"**My** group was only my family. My blood relatives like uncles, grandmother moved into my street. I also had some close friends, but my best friends were my family. I never brought a stranger into my close group. During this time, my family was big and in one large house."*

"In the beginning we had only one antique gun, but later on we had 5 pistols and 3 rifles and because of these weapons, most of us survived. I did not see my big family and good friends as more mouths to feed... I saw them as more people to shoot guns and in that... strength for survival in numbers."

"Our defenses were primitive. Brick walls around the house, sandbags on windows and over the outside doorways. We covered the sandbags with whatever we could find, big pieces of metal and stones. Inside the house we put all kind of things on the windows leaving only a small opening to shoot out of. There were always 5 members of my family ready to fight and one was always outside on the street hidden to alert us to Intruders."

"A small family trying to defend themselves didn't last even if they kept a low profile and were hidden in their house with a lot of food. Sooner or later a mob would come and regardless of their guns they were usually killed and their possessions taken. So smaller families got together in a bigger house and if they stayed together they survived the mobs."

*"**When** somebody came to attack our family we showed them that we were ready to fight to the death and that they would probably die if they attacked. If they did attack, our gunfire was so intense that those who survived never came back. We also had our street watch, which the people from my street organized, which alerted us in time to repel attacks. You need as much ammo as you can buy. How much... lots. There is never enough."*

"The most secured houses were attacked by the mobs and gangs first. We had some very nice houses in our neighborhood with walls, dogs, steel bars on the windows and alarms. Mobs attacked those houses first. Some were well defended and others were not. The best defense was to have an uninteresting looking house or even something that looked like a ruins. It had to look as bad as or worse than the others or it would be attacked."

"We used what we had when this started as we were not prepared for the situation. We did not know what 'Prepping' was. Some of us were better prepared than others, but most families had food for only a couple of days. So we went back into the Stone Age, actually that described almost everything."

"Most of the time I collected my water from our roof in four big barrels, then boiled it to disinfect it. But if it didn't rain, there was no water. The river water was too polluted to use, but sometimes you had to choose that. I guess it depends how on desperate you are to survive. Some houses had little gardens with vegetables, but most did not."

*"**Some** people would go miles during the night just to find a fire so they could light a piece of wood and bring the fire back to their home to start their own cooking or heating fire. Lighters and matches were precious and most people did not have enough firewood to keep their fire constantly burning. For most people... life was a continuous search for firewood, food, medicine and ammo."*

"During the summer I cooked in my backyard as it was luckily walled in with brick. As far as the smell of the food attracting starving people, try to picture this situation... no electricity, no running water, the sewers didn't work for months, dead bodies in ruined houses and lying where they fell, grime, dirt and a great mess. It was very hard to smell anything nice."

"Winter came early that year. Three months after this started the rumors began to circulate about the first deaths from starvation and from freezing temperatures. We stripped every wood door and window frame from abandoned stone houses and buildings, which we burned for heating. I burned all my own furniture for heating."

"We had some trees in the city parks, but most of the city consisted of brick and stone buildings and houses. You have no idea how fast the trees in the city disappeared... cut down for firewood and burned. Next went the furniture, doors, wooden floors... those didn't last very long either."

*"**Hospitals** looked like butcher shops and over three fourths of the hospital staff went home concerned about their families. Many people died from diseases, but mostly from bad water. Bad water killed two of my family. People ate pigeons, birds and rats. Pets were eaten."*

"Lack of hygiene supplies killed a lot of people. Most of the time we did not have toilet paper and even when I had it was too valuable, so I traded it. For our toilet we used a shovel and any piece of land close to the house. It sounds dirty and it is dirty, washing with small amounts of collected rainwater. It was a filthy situation all the time even though we did our best to keep clean."

"Wounds were mostly gunshot wounds. Without specialists like surgeons and what they need for their operations, a wounded person had like a 30 % chance of survival. Most people who were wounded or injured and needed medications died. People died from the infection of a minor cut. I had antibiotics enough for maybe three treatments and these of course were for my family only."

"Simple things killed people. Civilization has forgotten that diarrhea can kill in a few days, especially small kids, without medicines and rehydration such as fluid therapy and Intravenous administered fluids. All kinds of fungal skin diseases appeared on people and food poisoning killed many."

"There was little we could do. Basically we treated diseases mostly with local herbs, and wounds were disinfected with whiskey until we could find antibiotics to treat it with."

*"**Money** became worthless. Trading became the normal way of to get what you didn't have in addition to a thriving black market. I gave all my gold for ammunition during that time, but gold wasn't worth that much. Food was worth more than gold."*

"We mostly traded things. Salt was valuable but coffee and cigarettes were worth much more. Consumption of strong liquor was probably 10 times greater than in normal times, not to mention the use of it for cleaning and disinfection. Strong liquor was very valuable."

"I'll give you an example of a trade during the worst of times... for one can of corned beef you could have a woman for a couple of hours. It may sound horrible, but it was our reality. Most women were just desperate mothers trying to get candles, lighters, antibiotics, fuel, batteries, rifle ammo and of course food to feed their family and children. We would do almost anything for food and fought like animals for it."

*"**Goods** are exhausted eventually, but if you knew how to fix something people needed, that was a valuable skill. For those who knew medicine or how to fix shoes, their specific knowledge was their food."*

"There were almost no vehicles operating because the roads and streets were jammed with rubble, abandoned cars, destroyed houses and petrol was like food, very scarce."

"People looked desperate, poor and dirty and we made sure we looked the same when we moved outside our house. We looked and acted like everybody else. If I needed to go somewhere I almost always used the dark of night."

"I never went alone but also never went in a big group, no more than 2 to 3 men, always armed. We moved very fast, always traveled in the shadows or through ruins that gave us Cover and we rarely moved openly on the street."

"After the catastrophe was over, everyone had a weapon. The police conducted some operations to take illegal weapons from citizens, but most people found ways to hide their weapons somewhere."

"The first days of a catastrophe are the worst in terms of chaos and panic and to be unarmed in chaos, panic and riots can mean your death."

"Whoever died or got killed during this period did not get a proper funeral. The dead were buried in every piece of spare land, close to the house and sometimes even in the garden. Two or three of the city parks turned into graveyards at this time."

One of the Authors heard another account from two beautiful young women…

***Their** father was killed at the onset of their disaster so their mother prostitutes herself for food, while hiding her two beautiful and formerly outgoing daughters in the basement of a destroyed and abandoned house. They live not much better than the rats scurrying about in that dark ruble strewn basement.*

The mother conceals the fact that her 11 and 13 year old daughters are even with her, fearful that she will be forced to make them part of the way she is earning her life sustaining necessities.

One of the young women, now an incredibly beautiful 26 year old, speaks softly and at first reluctantly to me. But I see in her eyes the haunting memories she has as she begins to open up and describe to me for twenty minutes her life back then.

The scar running down her cheek to her neck is mute testimony to the horrors she went through while she recalled those 14 months… the scar is from an artillery shell explosion, she tells me. As she finishes telling me her story, a tear follows the furrow of that scar as it flows down her face… and she becomes silent.

1-*Strength through Numbers*

Does this sound far fetched or like a fantasy story!? You'll read other stories in this book… some based on actual events and others on fiction… but the above story *is* an actual event. Most of the account above is from 'Selco'… who lived through it to survive and write about it.

Selco has a school on the internet called *SHTFSchool.com* through which he gives advice on urban survival… and his advice is cheap. The Authors have found his information to be very realistic and informative. Go to his website and read his story *"One Year in Hell."*

The Authors also have friends and contacts in the Military and Intelligence Services and through interpreters hundreds of these accounts were compiled that verify the above.

The above stories are true. These accounts are from survivors of the horrors of living in the former Yugoslavia in the early 1990s where virtually everyone was fighting everyone else.

Situations like these were happening all over the former communist country in the early 1990s. Communism had gone by the wayside with the fall of the Soviet Union and nationalistic fevers ran high and eventually turned into violence. Was this a religious or ethnic war? Not really.

It became a land grab of one nationalistic group against the others as to who would end up with the largest land mass to call their country, by their respective name. Cities were surrounded and besieged by one army or another… just like in medieval times.

The aftermath of the Yugoslavian Civil War

Religious beliefs, nationality interests and ideology soon blurred, then disappeared and had little meaning to anyone. Especially to those trapped in a city. Survival was the only thing that occupied anyone's mind… *animal survival.*

This story points out a number of 'real life' experiences that re-enforce the Authors statements and recommendations in this book. *The above compilation of stories describe exactly what the Authors mean by* ***A Failure of Civility***.

Many theories and opinions flourish on how to survive when it comes to a time of *Crisis* and especially if it leads to *A Failure of Civility.*

The *main point emphasized in our book and from the Authors' experience, through the above stories and common sense* for successful protection is that of *"Strength through Numbers"*... and that being through a ***Neighborhood Protection Plan (NPP)***.

1-Reliance on the government for help

Next to the point of *Strength through Numbers* was how these people's *reliance on their government lulled them into this predicament.*

Their misfortune was the result of these people being born and raised in a communist country... a 'collectivist society.' Their world was that of *a cradle to grave society... a 'nanny state' where they depended on the government to provide their* ***every*** *need.*

Consequently, they had no concept of being prepared for a disaster... one they didn't think possible. Few had food or medicines stored in their homes. Water, which we take for granted as being simply a turn of the tap away in the kitchen... disappeared overnight.

Americans are still *Self Dependent* but are progressively being lulled into the state of mind of expecting the government to do and to provide everything for them... even in time of disaster. You can see by the above story and the aftermath of Hurricane Katrina what that will lead us to.

President John F. Kennedy probably said it best in his inaugural address to America... *"Ask not what your country can do for you... ask what you can do for your country!"*

Be *Self Dependent*... rely only on yourself and neighborhood... in doing that during disaster... you will be helping your community and your country to remain strong.

Because Yugoslavia was a communist state, a 'collectivist society'... firearms were outlawed *"For the greater good of the people."* Few had them and those that did, had precious little ammunition. Medical aid, available for almost anyone prior to this *Catastrophic Event*, became ever more critical during this disaster and yet at the same time almost non-existent.

It was interesting to hear the warnings from many of these people. They each basically said... *"If the authorities confiscate firearms, have others hidden that they can never find."*

The Authors believe that you must... *never, ever,* ***ever*** *give up your firearms!*

Don't think for a minute that America would be any different if a *Long Term Crisis* led to *A Failure of Civility*. Don't think for a second that Americans would not react like the Yugoslavians did.

People are people the world 'round and all people need food, water, shelter and security and when without, they will go to any length to get two of them... food and water. The Yugoslavians had a 'refresher course'... and now know this... Americans don't.

1-The 'Bunker Mentality'

When most people become fearful of a *Catastrophic Event* and *A Failure of Civility*, they think of hunkering down in the basement with their family, weapons, food and water. Some even have elaborate bunkers built stocked with months of supplies where they think they can *"lock themselves away from the world until the craziness passes."*

We've found this thought process begins to consume people to the point that they *"Eat, Sleep and Breathe the thought of survival"*.

Many live in a world of fear and have a *"Gloom and Doom"* mentality that we call *"The Bunker Mentality"*. This is not a healthy way to live, in our opinion.

We've seen people accumulate huge stockpiles of weapons, food, water and in one instance, a person who has a virtual emergency 'hospital' in their home in addition to all else. To us, this is unbalanced living which will interfere with and destroy interpersonal relationships and positive function in society.

In addition, we consider most of these people 'collectors' of survival gear... most do not have any comprehensive plan for protection and practical survival should the world go bad, nor do they train for it with actual exercises.

Underground Survival Bunker

Many of these people *"Talk the Talk,"* but can't *"Walk the Walk."* There are exceptions to this, but they are generally individuals and loners intent on hunkering down and defending themselves and their family where they are or by 'Going Remote'.

We can't fault them for that motivation but we can predict their probable outcome during *A Failure of Civility* by what happened to such individuals and small groups in the stories about the catastrophe in Yugoslavia.

We'll give you a good example of practical *Self Dependence* geared towards survival that incorporates living a normal life and being prepared for disasters at the same time.

It just happens to be that of a church organization and is the only organization of significant size whose members live worldwide that advocates being *Self Dependent.*

1-Practical *Self Dependence*

The Amish advocate *Self Dependence,* but they're very segregated from mainstream America and concentrated in specific areas of the country. The Amish live a life that is a very 'Spartan life' that is impractical and unattractive to most Americans living a modern lifestyle.

The Amish forbid most modern conveniences or technology. So compared to other Americans they are prepared for an Electromagnetic Pulse event as well as many other types of *Catastrophic Events*. They are totally *Self Dependent...* but for most Americans their lifestyle would be unlivable.

The Authors believe that the Amish would initially survive most *Catastrophic Events*. But they would be doomed to extinction if civil unrest reached epic proportions because of their anti-violent and passive religious doctrine. What they've grown and stored would be violently taken from them by hungry *Outsiders* turned *Intruders* invading their areas.

Outside of the Amish, no other group exemplifies the Boy Scouts of America motto *"Be Prepared!"* more than *The Church of Jesus Christ of Latter Day Saints*. Although the Authors are not members of this church, these people have fine tuned living an ordinary and normal modern lifestyle... coupled with being totally *Self Dependent.*

Probably no organization with members as widespread throughout America and the world practice what they preach for *Self Dependence* more than the people of this church. By the most time tested and logical of thought processes, members of *The Church of Jesus Christ of Latter Day Saints*, most commonly referred to by the slang name of 'Mormons'... have food, water, hygiene items and health critical medicine reserves.

We'll refer to them by their proper acronym here which is *LDS* and stands for *"Latter Day Saints."* These people are counseled to be *Self Dependent* by their church and that teaching focuses on reserves of food, water, hygiene items and critical health medicines.

The experiences of the ancestry of this church determined this doctrine for their members over almost two centuries. The early years of the *LDS* were that of the *Catastrophic Events* of upheaval, forced relocation, crop failures from the Midwest... to the hardship and drought of the arid landscapes of Utah, Nevada, Colorado, Wyoming and Idaho from the early to latter 1800s.

They were thousands of miles away from food sources. Without a reserve of food or water, they were doomed to a death of starvation or thirst... so they quickly learned to have reserves. If a family encountered problems that kept them from raising their yearly harvest, those reserves would sustain them without causing a burden on other church members and community.

The *LDS* Church Leadership knew that to keep your family alive, you must have individual reserves of food or water. The *Crisis* of localized drought and crop failure causing the threat of starvation is not a current problem today and these reserves have somewhat changed in purpose to that of their members more being able to deal with food shortages from financial 'hard times' due to unemployment or sickness.

Their preparedness mentality has evolved to some extent more into the present day belief that if a family breadwinner loses his job or the family has health problems that keep them from working for a period of time they can eat.

But in the back of their minds there is always the thought that if there is a recurrent or different *Catastrophic Event*, the family can turn to their food reserves to live on. The reasons may vary but the principle is the same… *Self Dependence.*

The *LDS* are not 'Collectivist' but rather 'Cooperative' in sharing food storage. Even though the *LDS* have central food storage depots known as *"The Bishop's Storehouse,"* the *LDS* Church counsels each family to keep food, water, hygiene items and health critical medicine reserves in each family home for each member of the household. Church Members draw on the food reserve of The Bishop's Storehouse *only* if their individual family food reserves become depleted.

The logic is simple and enduring… there weren't grocery stores 'just around the corner' in the early years of their church. Even if there had been grocery stores as we know them now, the *LDS* hierarchy knew that if their entire membership ate out of central stores in time of shortage, be it a 'grocery store' like today or The Bishop's Storehouse, it would quickly deplete *all* food stocks leaving everyone without. So came about the encouragement that each home has food reserves.

The Authors were astonished and surprised by the organization that the *LDS* Church has created after being taken on a tour of one of their food processing facilities. They are experts on long term food preservation and storage procedures.

However, not only were we impressed with their centralized food processing and storage, but with the *"Emergency Response System"* they have throughout their communities. They *do not rely* on any government's emergency services.

The *LDS* rely only on their cooperative membership to take care of their problems. They encourage each family to garden. In areas of past disasters where the *LDS* live, State and Federal Government Emergency response teams and supplies have shown up days later only to find almost everything taken care of by the *LDS* Church. People were fed, clothed and sheltered before these government emergency response teams could even finish mobilizing.

We know that *LDS* Members are generally people who own firearms, mostly for hunting. This is another source of their daily food supply for those of them who live rurally. They enjoy and practice hunting and fishing. They take advantage of these sources of protein as another means of being *Self Dependent.*

Where the *LDS* members are unprepared, to our knowledge, is that they don't have *Area Tactical Protection Plans* for their neighborhoods. They do have an emergency response system plan and have an extensive HAM Radio and two-way radio communications system.

Each family also has what they term a *"72 Hour Bag"* similar to a *"Bug Out Bag."* This bag holds enough food, water, hygiene items and health critical medicine reserves to last them for three days. Their intent is not to 'Bug Out' to the woods with this bag, rather to seek shelter in their area churches or other member's homes should they have to vacate their own house during an emergency.

Their most probable *Area Tactical Protection* would be in areas that the *LDS* Church has such a heavy influence on local government. In those areas their *Area Tactical Protection* would probably be more like an Area Tactical Defense and would encompass the entire community. This would take place in the form of responsible ex-military and former law enforcement citizens bolstering Local Law Enforcement.

Typical LDS home food pantry

The *LDS* Church has *Strength through Numbers* in areas where there are numerous *LDS* members, but otherwise for tactical protection, they are untrained for *A Failure of Civility*. Our gut feeling is that they would hold their areas together and maintain law and order until *Normal Civility* could be restored.

Another issue we regard as an 'Achilles Heel' to the *LDS* Church preparedness is that they have a very Christian viewpoint in caring for others in time of need, including those outside their church.

We do not fault them for this attitude… quite to the contrary, we admire them for this. However, if *A Failure of Civility* does occur, at some point they will have to turn others away or risk everyone starving.

Whatever happens… the members of *The Church of Jesus Christ of Latter Day Saints* are prepared… *unlike most of the American people.*

The way they live is an example of the way everyone should live today and this is the way most people used to live in America. Up to the 1960s, most of our Parents and Grand Parents had gardens, canned goods and food in the basement… and a pantry that would feed the family for months on end.

We have since become hypnotized and seduced by the *Age of Abundance* and have abandoned the *Self Dependence* and food stockpiles we once had.

1-You're *not* a Militia or law enforcement

Dictionary Definitions
Militia
(Noun) A group of ordinary people… generally citizens of a country… who are trained as ***soldiers*** *to fight in an emergency*

The *Neighborhood Protection Plan (NPP)* ***should not*** be interpreted by you as your Neighborhood Militia, forming a Militia or acting as law enforcement. You are simply citizens protecting against fire and maintaining civility, law and order *in your neighborhood* and protecting yourself, your family and property *within your neighborhood. You are not citizen soldiers… you are your* ***Neighborhood Guardians.***

Since you are mostly stationary in your *Neighborhood Protection Plan*, you are only attempting to enforce the law in areas around your *NPP that are relative to your NPP's defense*. You and your *Neighborhood Protection Plan 'Group Members', those neighbors involved in your NPP*, do not have government vested authority as a Militia.

Your *NPP* is not acting by an accepted characterization of a Militia, which includes the component of far-reaching maneuverability just as a State sanctioned Army does. What we describe in this book for use with your *Neighborhood Protection Plan* is very much different to a Militia. You are your ***Neighborhood Guardians.***

You have the right and the duty to defend yourself, your family members, your friends and your neighbors *anytime* you or they are confronted with an *immediate threat.* That is *your duty* whether law enforcement is available to respond or not *during Normal Civility,* a *Crisis* or *A Failure of Civility.*

If you are one of the growing number of Americans who don't believe you have the right to defend yourself against the threat of physical attack… don't believe in the citizen's right to be armed… or think you can reason or negotiate with everyone in all situations or if the tactical descriptions and the reality of the term 'Kill Zone' upsets you… read no further. Put this book down… and good luck to you!

For all the rest of you... you have the right of the Use of Deadly Force against a person or persons *to stop the threat of death or great bodily harm against yourself, your family members, your friends and your neighbors.* This is your right at the immediate time of that threat to you if law enforcement is present or not.

If a *Crisis*, *Long Term Crisis* or *A Failure of Civility* occurs you will definitely hear the 'Sound of Gunfire.' Your response to help people in other areas should be very measured. As much as you will want to help neighbors in other areas… *realize that you may be mistaken for an armed looter or rioter and shot by the people you're attempting to assist, the police or National Guard or you may be disarmed and arrested.*

Neither law enforcement nor the National Guard can read minds and you don't have 'Good Guy' tattooed on your forehead. If they're in the mode of firing at people because of rioting and looting, be aware that your simple presence with a firearm, whether your intent is to assist others in need or not, may get you shot.

Also, if you and other Group Members leave your *NPP*, you are weakening your defense.

You need to help others as much as possible… but let's continue on with preparing to help yourself, your family and your neighbors… *first.* Once you're capable of helping yourself… you can then help others

---

Chapter 2
Why you need Neighborhood Cooperation

In this Chapter we describe…

- **2-Story-"*It's the year 1933…*"**
- **2-Story-"*Present Day…*"**
- **2-The *Age of Abundance***
- **2-The anger in America**
- **2-The failure of government emergency services and FEMA**
- **2-Have a *Weekend Dark Ages***

After reading the story about Yugoslavia, little should have to be said about the benefits of *Strength through Numbers*, forming a *Neighborhood Protection Plan* and the cooperation needed between people in a *Crisis*. However, all must know something that makes it much more necessary now… that is the anger that exists in most Americans today.

Get out of the mindset that a situation like the one that happened in Yugoslavia can never happen in the 'good old US of A'. People are people, no matter where they live. When their survival mode kicks in, they will do *exactly the same things, if not worse,* than what the Yugoslavian people did to survive.

We've entered this 'Great Recession' with a new and very different mentality, compared to the mentality of people decades ago during the 'Great Depression.' We're a different people now than we were decades ago during the last depression. There is an 'Anger in America' as the following information and stories illustrate…

2-Story-"*It's the year 1933…*"

The sound was a soft, almost barely discernable knock on the front door that caught fifteen year old Maxine's attention. It was a hot summer's day in Minnesota almost four years after the Great Stock Market crash of 1929. A quiet day in this small town, but it was quiet all over the country.

The most memorable large scale violence that had occurred since the Stock Market crash was that of the people jumping out of windows to their deaths on Wall Street and the shameful enthusiasm of General Douglas Mac Arthur… violently putting down the Bonus March of World War I veterans insisting on their promised payment from the government.

But, there was still no work as a result of this greatest economic disaster to hit America in decades. Even though the economy was very bad, the government had billions of dollars in surplus and no debt. The economic problems would work themselves out and people would get along with each other until that happened.

Even *with so many people out of work, there was plenty of food around. Maxine's parents farmed crops and raised livestock, but their house was in a small railroad town in Minnesota.*

The fact that their house was directly behind one of the local churches made the unemployed families and men who rode the trains and wandered from town to town in search of work think their home was the church parsonage.

The townspeople called the out of work men that rode the trains town to town 'hobos' and these homeless, out of work and hungry people were constantly knocking on their door.

Maxine opened the door *that late afternoon to set her eyes on a rough and mean looking man dressed in a tattered suit jacket covering denim blue bib overalls. The man tipped his broad brimmed hat to her.*

"Ma am, could you spare a plate of food for a hungry man? I'm willin' to work for it in exchange. I'd be mighty grateful!"

Depression Era Soup Line

"Well mister, I don't think we have any work, but you wait right here. Let me talk to my mother".

"Yes ma am."

Maxine closed the door and went into the kitchen where her mother was making supper.

"Mom, there's another hobo at the door. He's begging for a meal"

"Good Lord Maxine, we can't feed everyone. He's the third person today."

***Seeing the look of disappointment in Maxine's eyes**, she said, "Oh, I'll go tell him."*

Maxine's mother opened the door, "I'm sorry mister. We can't feed you. We've fed two others today that came before you. I'm sorry."

"I'm good and strong ma am, I'm willing to do some hard work for a plate." He looked at her with desperate eyes.

"I'm sorry sir. We just can't. Maybe you can try another house."

"Well then thank you ma am." The man said as he tipped his hat to her out of courtesy. "I'll be movin' on then."

Maxine moved to her mother's side, her eyes begging her mom to reconsider.

"Mom, I'll give some off my plate, and maybe Bob and Dad would do the same. That would be enough to put some food in his belly. We'll still have enough to eat."

"Oh shoot, we're butchering a hog tomorrow and I guess we won't starve between now and then. We've got some extra bacon left until then. I guess we can handle one more mouth to feed today. You go tell him to come back, but make sure he washes up outside and he'll have to eat on the front steps."

At that Maxine smiled at her mother and ran after the man to bring him back to their house.

After finishing his meal on the front steps of their home, Maxine's family gathered around the hobo and heard another of the countless stories of heartbreak and despair happening in America at this time.

***The man had been in the Great War,** World War I as it would be later called, and had been badly wounded in France. He was still waiting for his promised 'Bonus' from the War Department. After recovering from his wounds, he landed a job at the Ford Motor Company River Rouge Plant in Michigan.*

He worked his way up to a supervisor position before long and had invested all his savings in the stock market. He had been going to school at night to study engineering and was about half way through when the crash hit. He lost everything when it crashed, including his house… and soon his job.

His wife and children were staying with his parents in Michigan and he said he was going to send for them when he found work. He'd been all over the country by hitching train rides and hadn't talked to them for eight months.

He asked if he could get a piece of paper and an envelope to write a letter to them telling them where he was going and that he was alright. He was sure they were worried about him.

"You've been good enough to share a meal with me, now I need to do something for you. What do you need done around here?"

"Well, there's some garden work that needs to be done. I guess you can do some hoeing if you want." Maxine's father told him.

He hoed until it got so dark that Maxine's father and mother, concerned, went out to get him.

***"Fella, that's enough.** You'd better be on your way now" Said Maxine's father.*

The man came out of the garden and leaned the hoe up against the garden shed.

"Understand we can't feed you breakfast if that's what your aiming for," said Maxine's mother suspiciously.

"Oh, I'm not angling at another meal ma am. I just as soon spend time here than down by the rail tracks. There's a lot of drinking and trouble there. I'll sleep away from that bunch tonight but I need to be close enough to make sure I catch the train going west… the one to Seattle, Washington. Heard there's work out there in aircraft factories.

They walked to the front of the house. Maxine gave her father a paper bag that he handed the man. It had a couple pieces of bread with some raw bacon in between and a few carrots from the garden.

"What's this?" the man asked as he took the bag.

"Just something help keep you fed on your way to Seattle" replied Maxine's father.

***"I'll never forget you!"** he said as he tipped his hat to them, lifting it fully off his head by the crown, then turned and walked off.*

In the dim light from the porch bulb, Maxine thought she'd seen his eyes well up and a tear run down the man's face.

2-Story-"*Present Day…*"

The failure of the European Union Euro currency had dragged the stock market down to new lows that hadn't been seen for decades. Their problems quickly jumped the Atlantic Ocean to America. Actually they were intertwined and the great Atlantic had little to do with isolating America from Europe.

Overnight, the panic of 2008 was dwarfed by this new disaster. Money, most of which had already gone to 'Money Heaven' in the 2008 collapse… was suddenly everywhere after the Euro disaster.

The Federal Reserve Bank had been making money by printing it and digitally entering it into the monetary system by the trillions of dollars. At this new Crisis, the Federal Reserve Bank began immediately infusing more… but now printing and distributing it. The government was deeply in debt and going further in debt with no end in sight. Everyone who had warned of high inflation was now pointing their finger and saying… "I told you!"

***Even though 'Contractual' payments** of pensions, social security and other benefits, along with 'Entitlement' payments continued to infuse money into the economy and people's hands, the cost of everything had been rising at a much faster pace than expected.*

The BRICS nations… Brazil, Russia, India, China and South Africa were conducting trade based on their own currencies fixed to their own gold index… not the American dollar. The American Dollar had lost the confidence of the world as the world's Reserve Currency and the 'Cows had come Home'… as they were never supposed to. America could no longer keep writing checks from a bank account it had no money in… it no longer owned the bank.

The Great Recession had become 'The Great Collapse' within days. Pensions, dependent heavily on municipal bonds, were drastically reduced or entirely disappeared within a month and panic set in. Grocery store shelves were empty within minutes of being stocked.

***People wanted** to be sure they had food, and the demand far exceeded the ability to replenish it. Stores that tried to raise their prices or limit the amount purchased by individuals, found customers turning into ugly mobs, simply looting the store and walking out without paying.*

Within weeks people began to run out of food. The hoarding of food by people far exceeded production capacity, an anomaly of supply and demand that even American productivity could not quench.

To complicate this, even with stores restocking their shelves, by the end of the month, the dwindling purchase power of money that Americans depended on to live would buy much less. Almost one third of the population could no longer afford food and the people that did have were buying all groceries in sight.

***Food was no longer grown in a garden** in the back yard or brought in by a farmer close to town as it had been during the last Great Depression. Food was trucked in from hundreds of miles... and there wasn't enough.*

A ripple effect soon took place as frightened people emptied their savings accounts. The Federal Reserve delivered truck loads of money to keep the banks open but the entire financial system quickly ground to a halt. Soon the delivery trucks stopped running and the grocery stores closed their doors... the system had broken down.

The Federal Government eventually geared up to get emergency food supplies to cities, but they were so disorganized and hampered by their own incompetence and regulations, they got very little food from warehouses to the starving public. When they did the trucks were stripped bare by mobs before the food could be fairly distributed.

The National Guard was ordered in but despite their help, local law enforcement couldn't keep masses of hungry people off the streets looking for something to eat. Groups of armed people had begun to fire on police, National Guardsmen and firemen.

***Police, assisted by National Guard members** began to have daily shootouts with gangs of people. Hampered by their ability to patrol and maintain order, police and guardsmen, concerned for the safety of their own families, drove off to their homes with their weapons and as much food as they could find. A 'Failure of Civility' was in high gear.*

The resultant rioting, looting and killing had virtually destroyed this city over the last two weeks and was doing the same across the country. Smoke from burning buildings and fires gave an eerie picture across every metropolitan area in America. The grocery stores were empty in their city, but Bill and Jeanie had enough food and water to last another couple of weeks if they were careful.

As he sat in his chair, veteran police officer Bill Schorn's conscience assaulted him again. "Damn it! Maybe I should go in. I just can't keep doing this. I'm sitting at home letting the other guys and the city down... I feel so selfish!"

***Then he thought** of his precious wife and their three beautiful children. He'd waited almost too late in life for them but he knew he'd die for them if he had to.*

Jeanie was a stay at home mom. She had decided to put her dental practice on hold and spend the time personally raising her kids. She was an avid vegetable gardener and with that garden, Bill, her and the kids would have had food for months. But, last week she called Bill in a panic while he was out on patrol.

Strangers began to strip the garden bare and when she tried to stop them, one fired a pistol at her. She fled to the house and locked the door. By the time Bill got the message and raced home the raiders were gone and so was everything edible in their garden.

Like many of the police force, especially the married people, Bill quit going to his job as a patrolman for this metropolitan city, he was now more concerned with protecting his wife and three little children.

***His guilty flash and sense of frustration was interrupted** by a knock on the door. Bill told Jeanie once again to take his service pistol and move the kids into the bedroom. He picked up his shotgun and moved to the side window.*

Peering out through the blinds he could see a young man, medium height with close cropped hair standing with his hands in his pockets and looking down dejectedly. He was alone and looked harmless.

"Another beggar!" Bill exclaimed with irritation and yet a sense of fear as he moved over and cautiously opened the door just wide enough open to have conversation but yet make certain the guy saw the barrel of his shotgun pointed at him.

"Mister, don't shoot!" the kid yelled as his hands shot up in the air.

"What do you want?" growled Bill.

"I'm hungry and thirsty. I haven't eaten for three days. Can you give me something, anything, a piece of bread?"

"We don't have enough to feed you. Go away!" snapped Bill.

"You won't give me anything!?" The kid said, in an almost indignant tone bordering on nasty, "Then, how about some water or soda... please mister?" the kid said in a pleading tone as he held out his water bottle to Bill.

***Bill's first reaction was to stick his shotgun in the kid's face.** "Get the hell away from my house!" he threatened.*

The startled kid blurted out, "Hey, I'm just hungry and thirsty!" as he lurched back then turned and walked away muttering out loud, "Jeez guy, I wouldn't do this to you!"

Bill suddenly felt bad. He knew his reaction towards this kid was partly from the guilt and frustration he felt not reporting to work... and he was now taking it all out on him.

Bill yelled after the kid, "Kid, come here. I guess I'm over reacting a little bit. I'm sorry but there's so much shit going on out there. Wait right here, I'll fill your water bottle and get you something to eat. You'll have to drink water."

Bill closed and locked the door, leaned his shotgun against the wall, then went to the kitchen.

"What's going on?" asked Jeanie from the bedroom door in a hushed tone.

"Just go back in with the kids and stay there until I tell you to come out!" Bill snapped back at her.

Bill wasn't going to tell her he was giving food to another stranger *because she'd get pissed off at him again. He stuffed a piece of cold meat between two slices of bread. As he filled the kid's water bottle the thought of the water system and electric functioning still amazed him. He wondered for how long.*

He thought about his own kids and then muttered to himself "He seems like a nice kid, I guess this is the least I can do".

Bill returned to the front door, opened it and as he looked up to hand the bottle and sandwich to the kid, Bill was instantly hit dead center in his chest by a large caliber handgun round. The blast knocked him backwards into his front room almost before it registered in his mind that two dozen armed youth were standing there behind the kid.

They'd been hiding out of view by the garage door just off to the end of the sidewalk and had used this ruse to get the Bill's guard down. This ploy had worked impressively well over and over for the last few days. The kid, younger than the rest, was their leader because of his ruthlessness and cunning.

The others piled into his house armed with everything from baseball bats to handguns, shotguns and rifles. As the last of them came through the door, the kid sauntered in and walked over to where Bill Schorn lay dying.

The kid looked down into Bill's eyes and said, "I can't believe you fell for that, dude... you're a cop! We saw your patrol car parked in the driveway. I play video games man. I'm a gamer and I took you out, you fool!"

Jeanie screamed as she fired Bill's pistol *at the first Intruders coming through the bedroom door. She knew as she pulled the trigger repeatedly, that something had happened to Bill. Jeanie killed two of them before a number of blasts from a shotgun killed her and the children. It was all over in less than thirty seconds. It was suddenly very quiet.*

The Intruders dumped Bill, Jeanie and the children's bodies in the barren garden along with the two of their own killed. No problem losing two members. Another marauding group joined them that week.

They were now twice as big, better fed and growing stronger by the week. While people began to run out of food around the city and enter the first stages of starvation, they were eating better than they ever had.

They partied there that night, *eating Bill and Jeanie's remaining food and drinking what beer and liquor they had. They didn't care if the house belonged to a cop. If any other cops showed up, they'd ambush them too and take their guns.*

That week, within days of each other, the lights went out and the water stopped flowing, so they left. The gang had robbed and killed almost every resident in the houses on this street this week and there would be no one to stop them on the next street over.

If you think the last of the above stories won't happen, think again. Sounds negative or frightening? It's a realistic representation of the mentality of people now. In fact, these types of crimes *are happening this very day* during *Normal Civility…* watch the news and read the papers. Buckle your seat belt if America has a *Catastrophic Event.*

If people will fight over toys for their children at Christmas time, turn into a mob over the newest footwear's first release, it takes little imagination as to what they'll do for food and water.

The Authors don't have to imagine, because they've seen the *beast in the human* many times. Most people haven't, so they have little to go by. Civilization is a very thin veneer on mankind and most people can't visualize the desperation people will have.

Strength through Numbers is the only viable means of protection if law enforcement cannot maintain order. If you're counting on the National Guard or the military, put yourself in their shoes and think of how concerned they will be for their own family if the *Crisis* from a *Catastrophic Event* leads to *A Failure of Civility*. If there is an EMP… would they do their duty and man their posts… or go home to protect their wives and children?

2-The *Age of Abundance*

For the last 30 years, since about 1980, Americans have experienced the *Age of Abundance.* For the 30 years prior to that, back to the 1950s, few Americans have experienced extreme hardship in their daily life, let alone hunger. It did not exist for most Americans.

If you're hungry and feel like eating a hamburger and fries you simply drive to the fast food restaurant that's in almost any town of size. Or if you're home, just pop a frozen meal in the microwave… as soon as your reality show sputters into the commercials.

If your pants have holes in them and you need a new pair, virtually every town and city has a Walmart, Target, Family Dollar or clothing store.

Money!? No problem! If you don't have it, there's plenty around to borrow… from family, friends or credit card companies.

What if these items just weren't there… or the money to buy them was gone?

Along with this *Age of Abundance* came cheap goods and services. For the last 60 years Americans never went without.

Rockwell American Thanksgiving

Clothes are cheap… cheaper than what it costs to have them sewn or repaired. Water!? It's in bottles in every convenience store in America or at the turn of a tap, however, few people drink tap water anymore. We spend money to buy a bottle of water, unheard of in past times.

When have you ever seen so much discretionary spending money in the hands of teenagers of school age who for the most part don't have jobs?

The above has bred at least two generations of adults that think that they come first and have a 'Birth Right' to necessities.

They are imposing their attitude on everyone, even forcing some of their employers to change the hours they work and the company rules to accommodate them.

When it comes to the *Age of Abundance* we're all spoiled. We're accustomed to endless credit card limits, huge housing equity gains that made the average American family a bonus income yearly. Every one of us who wanted to work had a job during the last 60 years. But… most of this has disappeared or is disappearing.

Count on much more of this going away in the near future… for a long, long time. With money tight or gone for families, the ability to have luxuries… or even some necessities… has disappeared for many and will disappear for many more of us in the near future. But what will take longer to disappear is our attitude that we deserve it and expect the necessities!

We are also an *'Instant Gratification'* society and many of us haven't experienced the hunger pangs from an empty stomach for more than a few hours. We expect food to be there when we want it. We get irritable and angry when food… and even items not necessary to our survival… aren't there immediately.

This has bred a new attitude in people of impatience and resentment that is turning into anger lurking just beneath our veneer of civility. There is a potential for problems that the Authors know will come to the surface if there is a *Crisis* that denies necessities to people.

People will not behave the same as they did decades ago during our last major economic Crisis… the 1930s' economic calamity. The gloves will come off and the selfishness and brutality will quickly rise to the surface.

There are very different dynamics to this Recession, Depression or Economic Compression… however you wish to describe it… compared to the 'Great Depression' of the 1930s.

This economic *Crisis* has different characteristics mostly because at no time in our history have we had so many people depending on government payments… to feed themselves and to simply exist. These payments are propping up and keeping the present false economy in play.

But make no mistake… we are in an economic Crisis.

Most American politicians and bureaucrats have termed these payments *'entitlements'*… which makes everyone who served their country or worked their career providing the tax base that powered this country for years sound like beggars and free loaders for relying on these payments. The term *entitlements* for those who served and worked in America is a misnomer and an insult. These aren't entitlements… but contractuals.

These are *'contractuals'* owed us by our government… by a *Contractual Agreement.* These are bilateral contracts, the first of which… the Old-Age, Survivors, and Disability Insurance Act or OASDI… commonly known Social Security… started in 1935.

By that agreement we paid our money to our government in 'good faith' relying on our government's promise to invest that money wisely for our later years and in turn pay it back then in 'good faith'. But they have long ago spent these funds and not enough is coming in to replace what was spent… somewhat similar to what happens when a Ponzi scheme fails.

The commitment made to the working people of this country is being defaulted upon. These *contractuals* cannot be repaid… and they never could have. Bernie Madoff went to jail for a similar scheme.

Medicare, Medicaid, Social Security and most other federal programs of like are broke. Most of these systems were never financially feasible in the first place. This bridge for this gap is our new 'healthcare mandate'.

The proper title of "Patient Protection and Affordable Care Act" or PPACA implies that this program is to the benefit of the American people... however, this program is a total deception by that title. In reality it is a *medical triage system* and *tax revenue program.*

So now comes the rationing of health and medical services. It will be a system of limited services, that will be curtailed if you're no longer a 'productive member' of society. If you don't work or pay taxes... you aren't a productive member of society and aren't worth keeping around. So you'll eventually be denied medical care under PPACA... and won't get health care unless you have the means to pay for it out of your own pocket.

Present annual payment hikes don't account for true cost of living increases and certainly will not in the future. These hikes are calculated by a purposefully illusionary inflation index designed by the Federal Government. One item left out of this index is energy... a base cost of virtually everything.

If the government had to increase federal pension and Social Security payments according to the true inflation index... which has been around 10 to 11 percent annually... the Federal Government would financially collapse within a few years.

Payments under the present system will still come and still increase annually... but this money buys increasingly less each year... and what Social Security, Federal Pensions, retiree income and Unemployment Insurance Payments will buy in the near future... will be much less and little or nothing if hyper inflation strikes. Those who receive these *contractual* payments will be angry when this happens.

But they won't be as angry and become as violent as another group. That will be those who receive *entitlements...* what they believe is their *'birthright payment'* regardless of having done little or nothing to fund the system that pays them.

These people will be the angriest. They will riot, burn, kill and take what they feel they deserve. Those getting these *entitlement* 'handouts' will be the most violent when government payments will not provide enough for them to live the lifestyle they're accustomed to.

The point is... this creates a huge, huge potential for civil unrest in America, Europe and most Industrialized Countries. When payments won't provide enough to live on because of inflation... coupled with this dangerously different mental attitude... it will culminate in disaster.

The fact that most people still have discretionary spending money, limited as it may be, is propping up the economy and keeping some of this hostility in check. But if the bond markets, pension funds and stock market lose their value... you will see hyper inflation, another real depression... *and widespread violence.*

The Authors believe current economic 'hard times' are not a normal economic cycle, will continue for a protracted period of time and that the economic *Crisis* will get much, much worse before it gets better.

Another book we suggest reading is *"Aftershock"* by Robert and David Wiedemer and Cindy Spitzer. These authors have been pretty accurate in their economic forecasts so far although we think they've miscalculated in their belief of little civil unrest from economic problems.

Civil unrest and violence will increase as the economic Crisis gets worse.

But violence will become extreme and widespread *if* a *Catastrophic Event* occurs during the midst of this economic *Crisis* that changes this *Crisis* into *A Failure of Civility.*

Most of us don't think that a *Catastrophic Event* and the resultant *Crisis* will be that bad. Most people also feel they can rely on the Federal Government and expect them to take care of everything.

The Authors pray to God that life never becomes what we describe here… we pray that we are wrong. For the conflict and the 'darkness' that the Authors have taken part of… to cast its cloud over American society is a fear that we wish never materializes. But because of that possibility… we prepare for the worst.

This new mentality in people and the government's gross inefficiency and incompetence only shows during a *Crisis*… like Hurricane Katrina. It was especially apparent where there was a shortage of *Critical Life Supplies and Services*… those areas experienced *A Failure of Civility.*

2-The anger in America

In addition to *"I deserve it!..."* there is an anger in persons seething just below the surface of our society over other issues. Witness the 'Occupy Movement'. There is a feeling of inequity, of being cheated and abused by corporations, businesses, government and society in general by many Americans.

This is Class Warfare in its purest form and is on the verge of spilling over into mass violence. The Occupy Movement is almost 'anarchist' in nature and this type of rebellion never leads to a better society… just to more draconian laws and repression.

On the racial front it is worse. The Authors champion of the modern day, Martin Luther King, did much to advance racial integration in the world. We have the utmost respect for the changes this man made in our society through non-violence and his sacrifice for the betterment of mankind.

What Martin Luther King did to advance racial integration is being undone by blacks, whites and others with the aid of our Federal and State Governments, the news media and some of King's former inner circle. The prejudices and inequities this man despised are again coming to the forefront of America with these enablers and protagonists.

Although King wasn't facing hungry, crazed mobs in a post apocalyptic world, he was pressing for societal change. King was a man of vision and strength who would be shocked at how his dream for integration has been twisted, especially by those of his own race.

The most frightening aspect of this growing racial divide is that most of our 'firemen'… the political and religious leaders of this country… are not trying to calm the flames of racial situations that flare up. They're not trying to resolve issues and create tranquility amongst Americans… they're fanning the flames of the fire.

The Los Angeles Riots

The 'fireman' is supposed to put out the fire with water, not throw gasoline on it. They're aided greatly in this by the sensational story seeking news media. We need another leader like Martin Luther King who saw simply *people*… not *color* and *differences*.

This same racial and ethnic friction is growing between Hispanics, Chinese, Vietnamese, Asian Indians… and we could go on and on. This is the opposite direction America should be going… especially with all the other challenging issues that confront this nation.

But people in America continue on… segregating along racial and ethnic lines by self labeling their group. In the Authors' view the terms African American, Irish American, Mexican American and such, detract from and create divisions in the American homogenous dream that past immigrants came here with and aspired to live in.

These terms and attitudes… whether you're white, black, brown or green… like Kermit the Frog… are preventing mainstream America from being homogenous and eventually harmonious. *Past immigrants* wanted to be part America… not have their *country* part of America. The fire is blazing underneath the 'Great Melting Pot' of America... but the divisions between Americans are not melting away… they're becoming more defined.

People need to step back, sit down, close their eyes, take a breath and think of *the great majority of people* of each race, gender, creed, religion and sexuality… who are *not* what the news media portray as representative of those minority groups and who *don't* want to impose their beliefs on and control the *majority*.

The majority of us don't want sides and don't take sides, aren't antagonistic on issues and just want to live our lives privately and get along with each other. We, for the most part do, despite this propaganda of hatred that is relentlessly flooding American's thought.

Of greater concern to the Authors... is not the anger and growing polarization of Americans concerning ideological, racial, religious, political and lifestyle groups... it's *the potential for violence between those groups.* Some of the above issues were the root cause of the Spanish Civil War and indeed the American Civil War.

Regional frictions over ideologies, social norms and lifestyles are becoming a potentially violent issue worse than anytime since the American Civil War. The 'Great Melting Pot' of America has become a boiling pot of rage. All we need is the catalyst of a *Catastrophic Event* to cause it to boil over.

But let's continue with another question...

Do you have faith in your government when you have an emergency?

Read just part of their record...

2-The failure of government emergency services and FEMA

Every State, most Counties, some Cities and the Federal Government have emergency and disaster services to aid in case of a *Catastrophic Event* and the resultant *Area Emergency*. Every State has emergency plans and an emergency agency to deal with an *Area Emergency* in their State. However, when the magnitude of the *Area Emergency* is too much for a State or locality to handle, the Federal Government usually gets involved.

FEMA is the primary Federal Emergency Response Agency, the first letters of their title making up their acronym. Outside of the American Armed Forces, FEMA is the only entity in the United States with enough resources to respond with *Critical Life Supplies and Services* to a major *Area Emergency* in the United States.

Although we're not picking on them, it is FEMA's job, not the American Armed Forces, and FEMA's responsibility to help resolve a major *Area Emergency*. But maybe someone should pick on them. *Here's only part of their record...*

Hurricane Hugo-1989 FEMA was criticized for its response to Hurricane Hugo, which hit South Carolina in September 1989.

Hurricane Andrew-1992 Hurricane Andrew struck the Florida and Louisiana coasts and devastated most of the region. FEMA was widely criticized for the agency's lethargic and inadequate response to Andrew. This famous statement just about summed up their response and was made by Kate Hale, The Emergency Management Director for Dade County, Florida... *"Where in the hell is the cavalry on this one?"* FEMA and the Federal

Government failed to shelter, feed and sustain the approximately 250,000 people left homeless in the affected areas within a reasonable time.

Hurricane Katrina in 2005-Many of the same issues that plagued FEMA during Hurricane Andrew in 1989 were also evident from their response to Hurricane Katrina in 2005.

If you don't know about the failure of your Federal Government to come to the aid of those affected by Hurricane Katrina, especially in New Orleans, you should get out more often.

You need to watch or read the news. It was *and still is* six years later, in many cases, a disaster.

The statement by a Congressional Commission that held hearings on FEMA reported that *"Many of the same issues that plagued the agency during Hurricane Andrew were also evident during the response to Hurricane Katrina in 2005."*

That statement should convince you that you cannot rely on FEMA or government emergency relief agencies by any acronym for help. *After having 25 years to correct their problems, countless reorganizations and even a Congressional Chain of Command revision, FEMA is still what they were back then... bogged down in paperwork, rules and regulations... and unreliable.*

FEMA has handled many *Area Emergencies* successfully and they're not entirely incompetent. However, with the *incredible* resources they have, they just don't seem to be able to handle major *Area Emergencies* without extensive delay and confusion.

The desperation of the Katrina aftermath

Don't get us wrong, your government... Federal, State or Local will show up in some form or another, but *when* and *with what* and *for how long* is the question.

FEMA is excellent when compared to the Emergency Services of most other countries. However, when hours and days become critical, count on FEMA and other government emergency services being unreliable, slow to react and in many cases unable to accomplish their mission because of their own maize of rules and red tape... confusing even to those in charge of the organization.

Some *Catastrophic Events* would cause massive numbers of people to die within days unless outside emergency agencies respond within 48 hours or less. If your vehicles were inoperative, water system did not run, electricity and natural gas weren't available, gasoline was gone or couldn't be pumped and your grocery and convenience store were empty of food immediately, who would you go to and how would you go for help?

Sound far fetched? Again, we hope nothing like this ever happens, but the Authors have been without *Critical Life Supplies and Services* for extended periods of time and we've experienced the 'Dark Side' of people that became apparent because of this.

The Authors believe that everyone has a dormant 'Dark Side' to one degree or another. How it manifests itself in relationship to other people is unknown until the societal constraints that *Normal Civility* imposes on that person are removed.

That 'Dark Side' may be harmless to others or it may be brutal, sadistic and deadly, behavior. These dormant behaviors of people will succeed as their dominant behavior if law and order disappear… and each and every one of you will have to deal with them.

Almost all *Catastrophic Events* listed in this book have happened before and in regards to most all of them… it is not ***if*** they will happen again… it is ***when*** they will happen again, their intensity and how long the resultant *Crisis* will last.

In the spirit of the famous statement President John F. Kennedy's made years ago… *"Ask not what your country can do for you... ask what you can do for your county".*

Assist local government when you can... but rely on yourself and your neighbors through a Neighborhood Protection Plan. Be part of the solution... not part of the problem. Help keep America a country of strength by maintaining Normal Civility in your area.

2-Have a *Weekend Dark Ages*

To demonstrate the effect on your mind of the necessities and luxuries we take for granted do the following… Have a *'Weekend Dark Ages'*. Take the food from your freezer to the neighbors… tell them your freezer's on the blink. Then shut off your computer, your cell phone, unplug your landline phones, turn off your natural gas, turn off your water… and throw the main electrical circuit breaker off on your house for 24 hours.

Live in your house for that time and you'll find that you've just started to enter the twilight zone of the *Crisis* period that would happen after some *Catastrophic Events.* You will find it a new 'quiet time' and almost unnerving… the silence will be deafening. You will begin… *just begin... to know why the reality the Authors perceive that will come about when being without are not far fetched.*

But you still won't be in the state of mind that some of the *Catastrophic Events* we list would create, so if you're brave enough and *if you're healthy enough* to take this further, do not eat food or drink water for this period. When these two days have passed you will begin to understand, but you still won't have a complete comprehension of what it is like without food for extended periods of time.

Both Authors have gone without food for lengthy periods and in addition were under severe physical exertion. Hunger creates a thought process that is difficult to put into words. The Authors best describe it through the words of Native American Indians. In times of extreme hunger, they felt as if they...

"Rose from their bodies and began to communicate with the spirit world."

Yet the Authors are leaving out the part of desperate people breaking down your door looking for your food, water and threatening your life, beating or killing you over these items or anything else of value to them. This will not be simulated by you.

Nor can the rape of your wife or daughters or killing of your sons or husband by the few still well fed, evil, cunning marauders and gangs taking and doing as they please. They will last the longest. We've often wondered... *will they inherit the earth?*

Do you plan to rely on police for protection? During the Hurricane Katrina *Catastrophic Event*, over 30% of the New Orleans Police Department gathered their families and left the city along with the fleeing citizens. The 'beast' in people quickly surfaced there without law and order.

To complicate the issue for the New Orleans Police Department, most fleeing officers took their patrol cars to get ahead of vehicles congesting the roads out of the city. This created a vehicle shortage that greatly hampered the remaining officers of the New Orleans Police Department in patrolling, responding to emergency situations and maintaining *Normal Civility.*

Dictionary Definition
Cooperation
(Noun) People working together to achieve results... people helping each other achieve a common goal.

Depending on the type of *Crisis*, if you do *Stand in Place*, you may have little or no assistance and protection from law enforcement. This is much more probable should the *Crisis* be of a national, continental or of worldwide scope when there is no assistance coming from outside your area because *all areas* are experiencing the extent of your *Crisis,* or worse.

Further, should a *Catastrophic Event* be limited to the North American Continent, foreign powers would most likely attempt to take control of America... under the guise of 'assisting' us. The Authors doubt that they will be as humane and just to us as we have been to those in places of the world that American forces have been. If this sounds corny or unrealistic to you… you're living in a cocoon.

We'll cover items you need for survival and how they should be stored later in *Chapter 12* but one we'll mention here is communications. To be effective, you must have some practical form of communication between positions of your *NPP* Watch Center, *NPP* leadership and Group Members and between Group Members.

Hand held *two-way radios with a microphone/single ear piece* are the most effective means. They're cheap and in every Walmart, Costco, Target, Radio Shack and available through purchase on the Internet. Don't count on Cellular Phones or land lines working during a *Crisis*.

It's critical you have these small cheap two-way radios and it's crucial that they're stored in a Faraday Cage. *Chapter 12* will explain the Faraday Cage and how to easily build one.

The *microphone/single ear piece* for two-way radios is essential to keep your communications from 'broadcasting' around your Group Member and revealing their positions. Do not use any ear microphone/head phone that blocks both ears. Part of a guard's job is to have at least one ear open to hear noises at their Guard Post.

That deep, dark valley… Mankind has spent the majority of life on this earth in a deep, dark valley… in some degree of the state of *A Failure of Civility*. In Mankind's recorded history we have lived only the last 400 or so years and for a small number of centuries earlier in somewhat of an ordered, 'civilized' existence.

Despite the ongoing wars and conflicts interspersed with periods of epidemics, we have for the most part during those periods, shrugged off the starvation, disease and brutality towards each other… at least in most of the world.

We have become *'Civilized'...* especially in America. But this 'Civilization' we have is fragile and dependent on an ever more complicated and ever more vulnerable infrastructure to sustain it.

The population of Planet Earth is roughly 7 billion people. The greatest number of people recorded history ever shows. The Authors feel that we have a better than average chance of a massive population correction.

If population outstrips agricultural production, caused directly or indirectly, by any *Catastrophic Event…* the majority of the world's people… especially those in the industrialized world… accustomed to eating sustainable amounts of food or in excess, will be on subsistence amounts or without.

A Failure of Civility will then be most probable. Any competent Las Vegas odds maker would say that simply by the fact it has not happened for 400 or so years, the odds are now more in favor of it happening. We are now closer to the edge of the cliff into that deep, dark valley than we have been for hundreds of years.

You hear the cynic say… *"Yeah... well everyone is hyped up now just like they were with the Year 2000... the world was supposed to go into the chaos of the 'Dark Ages' then... yet nothing happened!"*

That's true… but all the fear and hysteria around the proposed *Catastrophic Event* of Year 2000, also known as Y2K, had two components that made it prominent… *an actual known time of occurrence... and the specific event itself was identified.*

The fever pitch of people across the planet is as intense or more intense over a decade after that known event transpired without incident. The odd issue is that now the intensity of concern about a *Catastrophic Event* occurring seems as strong or stronger *but there is no justifiably identified Catastrophic Event recognized... nor has a time of occurrence been determined.*

The following issues have occurred in the last few years that we see as unusual…

- ***Posse Comitatus.*** The Posse Comitatus Act was created in 1878 to curb abuses of American troops against American citizens on American soil, mostly in the Southern States after the Civil War. The 'gloves are now off' as the following was signed into law…

  On December 31, 2011 virtually all restrictions *were removed* from law enforcement *using United States Military Personnel for* surveillance, *arrest and detention indefinitely* of American citizens on American soil. Is the U.S. Government getting ready for mass riots or civil unrest?

- ***Our Federal Government*** has ordered an increase in their reserves of Meals Ready to Eat (MREs) emergency food of *7000%* in the last two years. *7000%!* The U.S. Government has also recently purchased 1 *billion* dollars in dehydrated emergency foods to add to those MREs and who-knows-what-else they already have stockpiled. Why have such *huge* emergency food reserves?

- ***Our government has recently announced*** the order of 450 *million* rounds of .40 caliber *hollow point* ammunition and 175 *million* rounds of 5.56 x 45 mm (for M-4, M-16 type weapons). This ammunition is for law enforcement agencies, *not for our military services*. Hollow Point ammunition is banned for use by armies under the Geneva Convention. These are huge orders, if not the largest purchase of ammunition for Federal Law Enforcement agencies ever. Why?

- ***Many scientists and countries*** seem to be preparing for the worst. For example, the Svalbard Global Seed Vault in Norway is an international effort which purportedly contains seeds for almost *every variety of plant life in the world* in case of *Global Catastrophe* and a new level of intensity of collection of seed has been underway.

- ***Most Industrialized countries*** have built or greatly expanded existing underground survival facilities in the last 15 years. In some countries these are numerous, stocked with food and water… they're virtual underground cities that can house tens of thousands of people and provide for their needs for months, if not years. Some of these facilities are top secret and are not for military purposes.
- ***The United States Department of Homeland Security*** now has powers to prioritize government communications over privately owned telephone and Internet systems in emergencies by seizing control of all communication. A similar directive gives them power to seize and control 'all resources' in the country.
- *We could go on…*

You and your neighbors *must depend upon each other in a team effort* to protect yourselves, your area… and America. You need to have a *Neighborhood Protection Plan.*

Almost every government seems to be preparing beyond what is considered normal for disaster. Should you be concerned? We are… ***you should be.***

Chapter 3
Catastrophic Events

In this Chapter we describe…

- **3-So what's going to happen that you have to prepare for it?**
- **3-The *Chart of Catastrophic Events***
- **3-The Chart of *Catastrophic Event* characteristics (Horizontal Headings)**
- **3-Definitions**
- **3-The Progression of the stages after a *Catastrophic Event***
- **3-Story-"*America's Legacy from its Leaders*"**

Solar Flare and Coronal Mass Ejection

Well, there comes a time when you have to get down to the nitty gritty… a time when text book definitions that give you 'pain in the brain' are necessary… so most of this chapter is just that.

If this starts to give you a headache… read it and assimilate it for a few days… then read it again. It will begin to make sense to you… we think.

3-So what's going to happen that you have to prepare for it?

The Authors have heard talk for years that begs that question. We hear this talk amongst people who are 'Survivalists', 'Preppers' or simply people concerned that this or that catastrophe is going to happen.

In their writings and conversations they refer to TEOTWAWKI. This is not an American Indian word spoken by the Hopi Indians. It is the acronym for 'The End Of The World As We Know It'. The other common acronym is SHTF, which represents the term when 'The S#!t Hits The Fan'.

The first acronym… TEOTWAWKI… pertains to those whose belief is that *A Failure of Civility* will be long term or permanent such as caused by a 'Nuclear Winter' or an Electromagnetic Pulse event.

The second acronym… SHTF… refers to a general description of standing in front of a huge air circulation fan and someone throwing a shovel full of dung from a camel that's had diarrhea into the whirling blades… which is immediately flung all over you. Even though there is no specific disaster that can be attached to the latter… it gets the point across.

All these people have one particular admirable character trait… they want to be *Self Dependent* and *survive.* This is human nature at its zenith. Regardless, the tempo of concern amongst these people is increasing and the average American has begun to be uneasy about their future.

Each person has their particular concept of one or more scenarios of disaster that will happen. Most people fixate on a certain type of disaster. Each person has an issue or issues that they are concerned can disrupt their ability to feed themselves or their family or cause other severe life threatening problems.

The Authors have never seen a comprehensive list of *Catastrophic Events* or a list with the characteristics of each… so here's our take on them…

Dictionary Definition
Catastrophic Event
(Noun) An event causing great and usually sudden damage or suffering… A disaster.

What is a Catastrophic Event…? Different types of disasters and emergencies that we call *Catastrophic Events* are presented here. A *Catastrophic Event* is an event that will *interrupt your normal life and that of the majority of people* around you… and it *may* progress to cause extreme suffering and death.

A famous or respected person's death could interrupt your life and that of the majority of people around you. This event could affect a nation or the world if the person was someone the masses of people loved and admired enough. This type of *Catastrophic Event* may be a tragedy, but it would not likely *directly* cause a *Crisis* or a long term interruption of *Normal Civility*.

Our definition of a *Catastrophic Event* excludes the death of famous and admired people. We cannot see how the death of one person would cause a shortage of *Critical Life Supplies and Services*, particularly food or water. We don't foresee one mortal person's death as ever *directly* causing a *Long Term Crisis* or *A Failure of Civility*.

We're not trying to scare you…this is a graphics created Tsunami wave (It's not real). It may be a surfer's dream… but it would be a costal inhabitant's nightmare. Maybe it won't be as big as this depiction… but a Tsunami over 1700 feet high struck the Alaska coast in 1958.
It would have been proportionally about this high.
Fortunately, the area was mostly uninhabited.

The Authors judge some *Catastrophic Events* that people believe are looming as 'hysteria' and have no common sense basis… so we haven't listed them here. Included in that category are an Alien Invasion and Zombie Attacks… we leave those for the science fiction writer and TV programs.

Further, if you believe that 'Zombies' and 'walking dead cannibals' are going to be a reality… we'd rather have you quit reading here… and the Authors are praying you don't have any firearms.

Just because three identical pieces of one of the Author's Captain Crunch float to the top of the cereal bowl and align perfectly on one axis… or the other Author's office globe continues to flip over, regardless of his attempt to keep it in its correct position… doesn't lead us to believe that a *"planet alignment disaster"* is looming or an earth magnetic pole shift is about to *"turn us upside down."*

Some *Catastrophic Events* cannot be protected from. If there is a deadly bio-engineered virus that is virulent, extremely contagious and is widespread enough it could kill everyone in a very short period of time and there would be absolutely nothing you could do to stop it.

If the planet Mars changes its orbit and collides with Earth… there is little any of us can do… *but pray.*

The Authors think that other *Catastrophic Events* ***that you can prepare for*** are more of a realistic and probable threat in the Reader's lifetime than some of these remotely possible 'doomsday scenarios'. So we list what we consider the probable and realistic *Catastrophic Events.*

Here's what a Catastrophic Event is in a nutshell... A Catastrophic Event is an event that will interrupt your normal life and that of the majority of people around you... and it may progress to cause extreme suffering and death.

We have listed 22 *Catastrophic Events* in categories that we think are plausible. Some have *the potential to cause the shortage of one or both critical items of* ***Critical Life Supplies and Services… food and water***.

In other words... two items that if people were without for long enough periods of time... there could be great violence... a disregard for Mankind's laws... and many people would suffer and die.

We've simply concluded that the ***shortage*** of one or the other of these two items of *Critical Life Supplies and Services...* ***food*** *and* ***water*** will ***always cause some degree of A Failure of Civility***.

Most people who have attempted to make a list and chart of possible *Catastrophic Events* find that it is extremely difficult to do. Semantics and trying to get your head wrapped around all the variables of them comes into play.

For instance… one *Catastrophic Event* can cause others. Multiple *Catastrophic Events* can occur in the same area as the result of the first one and then spread in geographical size or even spread globally.

The events and characteristics contained in this chart are the Authors' best estimates, but we're not scientists. Since most all of this is conjecture from the scientific community anyway… it's a guess from us also… our evaluation, speculation and our estimates based on voluminous reading and factoring in life experience.

Really...!? What scientist can honestly say that the magnetic pole reversals of this planet will not disrupt this techno charged world we live in. Can they really say with certainty that the pole shifts they've discovered from geological evidence didn't affect even our primitive world?

With all due respect… the Authors don't think scientists have that ability... not when the causes of the *Great Extinctions* continue to change every time a university gets a new grant to study it.

Of all the *Catastrophic Events* we list… one of the most frightening is Electromagnetic Pulse or EMP as it's commonly referred to.

Former United States Congressman and Speaker of the House of Representatives Newt Gingrich made a statement just after the destructive storms that hit the Washington, D.C. area in July of 2012 something to the effect of…

"The Washington-Baltimore area electric power blackout is a mild taste of what an EMP (Electromagnetic Pulse) attack would do to America."

With this *Catastrophic Event*, much of the world… but especially the Industrialized World… will ***immediately*** plunge into a *New Dark Ages...* like the darkness that overcomes a room when you throw off the light switch.

We may not have judged everything properly. We may have missed one or two events. So *if your opinion... conflicts with our opinion...* join the crowd and stand in line… it will be a long line. We've done the best we could *in our opinion.*

If you're simply interested in criticizing us, like some of the 'experts' whose only 'credentials' are that they excel at criticism… go ahead… there'll be a line for that too… and we're sure that one will stretch around the block.

Most naturally occurring *Catastrophic Events* are by their very nature unpredictable. If you can get a time-table on when one of these *Catastrophic Events* will occur, please tell us. We'd like to know the… *what*… *when*… and *where*… a *Catastrophic Event* is going to happen if you have some insight that we've overlooked.

We'd like to know. That is… unless this information comes to you from concentrating on and 'tuning in' to the cosmos or consulting with the 'Great Apache Father'. Although we don't totally discount the spirit world and the metaphysical, we need more than… *"you know when and where a disaster is going to happen because 'you can feel it in your bones.'"*

A Catastrophic Event may not happen for decades, it may happen in the next second or the basis of it may have started two months ago. This is a pretty broad stoke of the brush, but let's just say that we believe that the odds are much more in favor of one or more of the more damaging *Catastrophic Events* happening in the Reader's lifetime… *than not.*

Extreme Drought and Crop Failure

We believe that earth is extremely overpopulated for the amount of many *Critical Life Supplies and Services* available, taking into account the continuing strife, wars and the economic systems that control distribution of *Critical Life Supplies and Services.*

Even without the strife and wars or the economic control system and even if there were zero population growth… we believe a catastrophe in some form or another will come about during the Reader's lifetime.

A massive population correction can simply occur if the population outstrips the ability of agriculture to feed that population. There is a scientific name for this which we will not bore you with.

This type of correction may be a number of decades from happening, or it may have started three years ago. We believe that great masses of people on this planet will die because simple logic tells us that there are flat-out too many people for this planet to support and our system of food supply is too specialized, concentrated, complex and fragile.

Between now and then we're sure that a number of *Catastrophic Events* will occur that will be resolved by man and we've tried to take that into account with our chart.

Never underestimate mankind for innovation when driven by desperation. Unfortunately, much of mankind's innovation of the past is related to ways of more efficiently killing each other off. But in a pinch, a solution will be found for some events that threaten mankind.

Take water for instance... There's literally an ocean of it. Should potable water start to become scarce we know that the scientific community will within a few short years have a solution that defies imagination... like... *"Why didn't we think of that before!?"* Transporting water may be another issue, but we feel that will be resolved quickly as well. Could this cause *A Failure of Civility*?

Yes, but we also believe this *Catastrophic Event* will be detected in time and is within the realm of mankind's resolution to prevent this from becoming *A Failure of Civility* that is long lasting or permanent.

However, we're also certain that eventually a *Catastrophic Event* will occur causing a *Long Term Crisis* or *A Failure of Civility* that will not be resolved and it will simply hasten a massive population correction. Many, many people will die... with little of the ceremony that *Normal Civility* affords them compared to death through war and massive population correction.

We could go on describing the difficulties in charting these *Catastrophic Events...* however, we did this because we've seen no list of them with the different *Crisis Characteristics* they would probably have. Experts could go into infinite detail on the characteristics of each event... and that would have to be left to people more intelligent than the two of us.

The difference in ***basic characteristics*** of each *Catastrophic Event* is important ***to determine what special survival items*** you will need in addition to the basic *Critical Life Supplies and Services* for a particular type of *Catastrophic Event.*

It is also important to be able to visualize what kind of world you will live in through the effect of the characteristics from each type of disaster.

3-The *Chart of Catastrophic Events*

Most of what we list here as Catastrophic Events have happened in Mankind's recorded history. The Catastrophic Events the Authors feel are most plausible…

A. Financial collapse of the United States and world economies-Depression, mass unemployment and hyperinflation.

B. Cyber hacking and viruses damaging the infrastructure control computers creating *Critical Life Supplies and Services* shortages or disruption.

C. Electromagnetic Pulse E1/E2/E3 – Nuclear Weapon generated-destroying computers and the electrical power grid.

D. Class warfare in American and European countries or Racial/Ethnic wars or Federal versus State disputes over laws and 'States Rights' autonomy causing civil conflict.

E. Solar Electromagnetic Pulse E3 – Extreme X-Class Solar Coronal Mass Ejection (CME) striking Earth destroying computers and the electrical power grid.

F. Worldwide famine from crop failures-Wide spread drought or Natural fungal/blight problems.

G. Massive ejection from Volcanoes and the resulting cold summer-Crop failures.

H. World wide shortage or long term loss of potable water.

I. Nuclear 'dirty bomb' explosion or biological terrorist attack or chemical terrorist attack.

J. Worldwide pandemic of disease.

K. Fuel shortage or union strikes disrupting trucking and railroad distribution of *Critical Life Supplies and Services*.

L. Earthquake.

M. Tornado.

N. Hurricane.

O. Prairie or Forest fire.

P. Asteroid strike causing a 'Nuclear Winter'.

Q. Magnetic pole shift causing long term disruption.

R. Nuclear detonations severe enough to cause a 'Nuclear Winter'.

S. Conventional World War Three.

T. Tsunami or costal damage from open water waves.

U. Pandemic of food borne illnesses.

V. Nuclear power plant meltdown and radiation leak.

Information for specialized items needed is listed in *Chapter 12* under *"Specialized Items needed for certain Catastrophic Events"*.

3-The Chart of *Catastrophic Event* characteristics (Horizontal Headings)

Characteristics of Catastrophic Events on the Chart of Catastrophic Events are intended to show the nature of each event by the following…

- Each plausible *Catastrophic Event*
- The Authors' opinion of the odds of the *Catastrophic Event*
- Probability of *A Failure of Civility*
- Likelihood of a *Long Term Crisis*
- Shortage or disruption in the Food Supply
- Shortage or disruption of Potable Water
- Geographical area most likely affected
- Probability of Global Expansion
- Electrical disruption
- Communications disruption
- Transportation disruption
- Medical Services and Supply disruption
- Civil Unrest and Violence in Area
- Probability of Martial Law in an Area

A Catastrophic Events list of characteristics on a fold out chart is at the front of this book.

We have ranked Catastrophic Events…

First… by *probability of occurrence* which is the Authors' opinion reflecting *Highly Possible*, *Possible*, or *Little Possibility* of happening.

Second… by the *probability* of *A Failure of Civility.*

Third… by the *Likelihood of a Long Term Crisis.*

Fourth… by *shortage* or *disruption* in the food supply.

Fifth… by *shortages* or *disruption* of potable water.

Sixth… by the *Geographical Area most likely affected* regarding size of area.

The remaining headings indicate other issues that the Authors believe will happen as the result of each *Catastrophic Event*. Food or water *shortages* will cause some degree of *A Failure of Civility.*

3-Definitions

Normal Civility…

The Authors define *Normal Civility* as the time when there is a functioning effort of law and order, where a judicial system is the civilized method of dispute resolution between people, when there is a functioning commerce, when there is a working government maintaining essential services and when people are not fighting over *Critical Life Supplies and Services* to sustain their and their family's daily existence.

By the term *Normal Civility*, the Authors describe the way Americans live day to day without killing or brutalizing each other for *Critical Life Supplies and Services,* particularly *food* and *water*. *Normal Civility* also embraces law enforcement and a judicial system through which disputes are resolved even though law enforcement and a judicial system are not absolutely necessary to sustain life. However, *A Failure of Civility* would result if people were not held accountable to law.

Critical Life Supplies and Services…

We group together supplies and services that make *Normal Civility* complete. The Authors define these *Critical Life Supplies and Services* as food, water, hygiene supplies and facilities, shelter, law enforcement and judicial, medical assistance and medicines necessary for people to sustain life and prevent the spread of disease.

Of the above items, *the mass of people cannot be without two of them for a very long period… food and water.* Without those two, suffering and death and *A Failure of Civility* will occur. Without medical services and medicines, many people kept alive today by artificial means would die. These people are the 'Terminal Living'.
However, medical and medicines are not critical to sustainment of life for the mass of people. Without hygiene and sanitation supplies, widespread disease and death would eventually occur. In certain climates and time of year, the lack of shelter would cause the death of many people.

Catastrophic Event…

A *Catastrophic Event* is an event that will *interrupt your normal life and that of the majority of people* around you… it *may* progress to cause extreme suffering and death.

Catastrophic Event continued…

Catastrophic Events can spread but may not affect the entire world. Such an example would be an American or Israeli strike on Iran's Nuclear Facilities. In retaliation, Iranian sponsored terrorist activity in the United States, Israel, Europe and other countries could drastically increase causing Collateral *Catastrophic Events* in the countries Iran views as an enemy.

The same parallel could exist from a myriad of other simmering conflicts worldwide such as… North Korea invading or attacking South Korea, Russia invading one of its former Satellite States, Mainline China invading Taiwan, etc...

The same would be true of economic *Catastrophic Events* spreading. These could be the result of financial failure of a country's economy. This economic *Catastrophic Event* in one country could cause an economic *Catastrophic Event* in another country by banking or commerce interrelationships and may spread to other countries by the 'Domino Effect'. These could be just as deadly as war.

One example would be the collapse of the European Economic Union causing civil unrest and those economic problems spreading to the United States and causing civil unrest here. Another example is a situation such as an earthquake disrupting sanitation and health services causing contagious disease epidemics in the affected area and then spreading to other countries.

Global *Catastrophic Events* could come from Mutual Protection Treaties and Alliances, bringing further involvement of countries into a conflict that were originally not involved and thus spreading that *Catastrophic Event* in other countries. A global *Catastrophic Event* has the potential to expand and encompass the entire globe. The First World War is a prime example of military alliances that spread a *Catastrophic Event* of an act of war from two countries to involve the entire world.

Area Emergency…

The Authors define an *Area Emergency* as the condition after which a *Catastrophic Event* has occurred, but *Critical Life Supplies and Services* are available to all people just as they were during *Normal Civility*. There may be damage to property, infrastructure damage, or commerce and everyday life may be temporarily disrupted.

Crisis…

The Authors define a *Crisis* as *Critical Life Supplies and Services* being either rationed or controlled but *are sufficient* for all people of the area affected or assistance from outside areas will prevent a *Long Term Crisis* until enabling the return to *Normal Civility*. This is a worse condition than an *Area Emergency* where all *Critical Life Supplies and Services* are available as they were during *Normal Civility* without disruption.

Long Term Crisis…

The Authors define a *Long Term Crisis* as when the duration of the *Crisis* has begun to exhaust the *Critical Life Supplies and Services*. What *Critical Life Supplies and Services* exist are being rationed but reduced in amount below normal demand.

There are _shortages_ *or an insufficient amount for some or all people* of the affected area before further *Critical Life Supplies and Services* can be obtained.

This is a worse condition than a *Crisis* where all *Critical Life Supplies and Services* are being either rationed or controlled but are sufficient for all people of the area affected.

A Failure of Civility…

The Authors define *A Failure of Civility* as the condition in which some or all *Critical Life Supplies and Services* are either insufficient or exhausted for the majority of people. **During** *A Failure of Civility* people will fight like animals for two of the most important of the *Critical Life Supplies and Services…* food and water.

A Failure of Civility would include the inability of authorities to maintain law and order, the lack of a judicial system, the mentality of the mob becoming the normal behavior of most persons and a total absence of compassion and caring for others. It would be survival by brutality and use of force and it would be everyone for themselves.

Normal societal constraints of the rights of others and the significance and sanctity of life would soon cease to exist. The Authors believe indiscriminate killing would abound. The Authors further define *A Failure of Civility* as the crudest, most barbarous and brutal deviation from *Normal Civility* that society can get. Life would be the desperation of hunger, starvation, disease, fear, filth, squalor and death. Cannibalism will appear.

A Failure of Civility would be a *New Dark Ages.*

<u>Disruption</u> *of Critical Life Supplies and Services…*
food or water.
A *disruption* is less severe than a *shortage* of the food or water Supply… it is an *intermittent* supply. A disruption *may or may not* cause *A Failure of Civility* that is intense and continuous depending on the duration of the disruption.

<u>Shortage</u> *of Critical Life Supplies and Services…*
food or water…
With a *shortage* of food or water supplies, there *will not be enough food or water to sustain the life of the majority of people* and *mass starvation will occur.* This *shortage* will cause *A Failure of Civility* that is intense, continuous and extremely violent in all areas affected by food or water *shortage.* There will be many groups that survive by brute force and cannibalism.

3-The Progression of the stages after a *Catastrophic Event*

The worsening condition after a disaster, from the *Area Emergency* progressing to the eventual exhaustion of *Critical Life Supplies and Services* and the final stage of *A Failure of Civility,* is as follows…

Catastrophic Event→Area Emergency→Crisis→Long Term Crisis→A Failure of Civility

A *Catastrophic Event* would lead to an *Area Emergency* which could then lead to a *Crisis* and ***could*** eventually lead to a *Long Term Crisis*. The next stage would be a total breakdown of society which would be *A Failure of Civility.*

Consequently, the duration of a *Crisis* will greatly affect whether a *Crisis* turns into a *Long Term Crisis* as the longer a *Crisis* goes the more chance there is of exhaustion of *Critical Life Supplies and Services* unless there is supply from outside the area affected.

A further possibility that a *Long Term Crisis will not* become *A Failure of Civility* may come about if the mass of the population are given enough food and water to sustain life until they become so physically weak that they are not able to brutalize each other and literally 'die in place'.

A *Long Term Crisis* will most likely lead to *A Failure of Civility*, unless there is outside assistance to supply enough *Critical Life Supplies and Services,* especially food and water, or enough are obtained locally to restore the affected area to a *Crisis* status, *Area Emergency* status or the condition of *Normal Civility.*

We're on the edge of that deep, dark valley again…America and most of the world's *Normal Civility* is becoming increasingly fragile. As we said before, Americans have moved further away from the *"Garden to Table"* existence of past generations than ever before in the history of this nation… and that fact alone is dangerous.

3-Story-"*America's Legacy from its Leaders*"

"May the soul of Ronald Anderson rest in peace …" were the last words of the funeral service from their priest Father Chavez. Dan pulled Linda close to him to comfort her as she wiped the tears from her eyes and said "I love you honey! And I loved your Dad very much". Still she couldn't stop crying and with that, Dan began to sob.

They walked from the grave *to the suburban with their parish priest as the funeral home placed the huge concrete slab over the grave. The slab would prevent grave robbers, the vile activity of ancient times but again resurrected, from digging through the soft soil and robbing her father of the few pieces of jewelry she had buried him with.*

Linda would have cried more tears, but life in America as it had been over the last few years had taken the rest of her tears from her. Inflation had destroyed just about everything and everyone. First it was her mother and now her father.

Her father had been a healthy man but the guilt of not being able to pay for a complicated operation to save his wife had destroyed this grand man. He died from severe complications of a simple infection, but really from a broken heart Linda knew. It was ironic, Linda thought, her father was a doctor by training.

The funeral service had been quick and cheap *and a small group of people had attended despite the fact that thousands of people knew and respected her father deeply. Most would not venture from their homes or workplace to attend because the fear of being robbed or killed.*

The cost of traveling anywhere but to work was out of the question… at least for those who still had a job. Many had emailed their condolences… those who still had computer service. That was over $2200 a month for those who could still afford it.

Few letters would come because the cost of a stamp was over $18 and rising daily. The new courier service of bicycle tough guys had brought the most letters of condolence to them. All local though. Ten to fifteen tough young men with some firearms and baseball bats had become the new means of communication. Their price was ammunition or food for the group. They wouldn't take American dollars.

The Catholic priest had given the service at the grave on condition that Linda and her husband Dan give him a ride to and from the parish. He, like most people, preferred food over money because the dollar's worth became less by the day. He would have performed the funeral service for nothing, but Dan and Linda provided him food for the day. The value of church donations had dwindled to almost nothing as the money became more worthless by the day and people fought to pay for essential items.

The cost of driving anywhere had suddenly become as major an issue as the cost of medical care. It was less than 15 miles one way to take their priest back to the parish, but at $65 plus per gallon of gas and rising weekly, this simple drive of 30 miles was costing Dan and Linda about $130.

This day was dreary and biting cold. *There was no snow yet but it was windy with strong gusts. A blizzard was coming off the Rocky Mountains, headed straight towards them.*

It was a fast trip of 15 minutes as there were virtually no cars on the road. Linda saw a whirlwind of paper, plastic and debris billowing up and seemingly pursuing them like some huge dirty threatening monster when she looked into the rear view mirror. Garbage was no longer picked up. Most people burned it in their backyards even though it was against the law.

Dan drove quickly going through red lights, stop signs and sped twice the posted rate with the suburban. He knew they were vulnerable if they slowed or stopped at all. Gangs would rob them if they were lucky, rob and kill them if they were not. Linda held the family shotgun visible for all to see as a warning and Dan had another shotgun behind his seat and carried two automatic pistols.

There were no police on the road. *Most departments were staffed in name only. No city had the money to pay for these essential services and most cops had quit their jobs to become the private armies and bodyguards of those who could afford to pay them. Their new employers were the grocery stores, banks, the wealthy and those businesses that dealt in large sums of cash, commodities or valuables.*

This day was years in the coming. Her father and others had warned of it for years. Pleas for a Balanced Budget and spending reductions went unheeded. The massive infusion of money into the financial systems of the Western World had thrown the financial system into total chaos and the debates on what to do went on for months, but frankly, there was nothing that could be done. America and Europe had painted themselves into a corner with no solution in sight.

They arrived *shortly at the Catholic Parish. It looked like a fortress with its windows barred and boarded up. Parishioners had been taking turns guarding their priests and church around the clock. As they pulled into the litter strewn parking lot, a middle aged man who looked as if he had all the warm clothes he owned on, walked quickly from behind a wall towards the vehicle.*

His weapon, a 12 gauge pheasant hunting shotgun, was at the ready. Seeing who it was, the man acknowledged them with an abrupt waive, then retreated back to his makeshift guard post. Dan knew that there was another man just like him standing guard on the other side of the church grounds.

Dan carried two small boxes full of food *into the parish as Linda, carrying their shotgun, and Father Chavez followed him.*

"Please... sit down." he beckoned for both to take a seat in front of the rectory desk.

"I will miss your father greatly. He was a dear friend of mine. I can remember him coming to me for confession and having a great sense of guilt that he couldn't stop the very situation he knew we would be in... what his children would live through. The troubles of this day. What we are going through now!" Father Chavez said, his voice trailing off with a tone of anger.

"Father, I brought enough food for the Monsignor too. Is there anything else I can get for you? You're like a beacon of sanity in the lunacy of this wilderness we all live in now. You're more important to people than you realize Father. No harm must come to you." Dan stood up and placed his hand under his coat as if to remove something.

"Stop Daniel! I know where you're going with this. I am a simple man of God and I trust in him to protect me. The men outside were not my or the Monsignor's idea. But I must also say that after the robberies and the beating of Monsignor Thomas, it gives us a sense of security... at least until things turn for the better."

With that, Dan pushed the extra automatic pistol back into his waist band.

"Well, I can see that this discussion is going to go the way the previous ones did, Father. But if there's anything else I can do, please contact me."

"I will, Daniel."

"Honey, we'd better get going." He said as Linda stood up.

Father Chavez walked to Linda's side *and said, "Linda if there's anything I can do for you, you must contact me."*

Linda stood up, eyes almost swollen shut and started crying again.

Father Chavez put his arm around her to comfort her as they walked to the rectory door.

Ronald Anderson had become obsessed with the economic situation when the inflationary cycle began two years ago. He'd warned everyone about it for decades. His passion was his children and his country and he would not bury his head like most of the rest of Americans had done.

America had passed the point of no return. The devastation he predicted would hurt everyone, including those who belittled him, was upon this country he loved so dearly like an oppressive cloud. He was at the age that he finally resigned himself to live the remainder of his life quietly and peacefully.

It was too late now to stop the financial destruction so Ronald Anderson became quiet. He wanted to live the last years with his wife, but now she was gone. He felt he had failed in life and much of what he lived for was gone.

***As Dan got in and closed the door** of the suburban, the front page of a two week old USA Today newspaper blew up against the windshield and the gusting wind held it perfectly in place for him to read as he glanced again at headlines that read "Chinese attack Taiwan!" Anger welled up in him towards the Chinese and their threat to dump all their remaining American Treasury Notes if we intervened militarily to stop their invasion of Taiwan.*

The Mainland Chinese had invaded Taiwan two weeks ago and were now in full control of the island. All Taiwanese Government leaders and the country's elite were being executed by the thousands in televised 'People's Mass Cleansings' as the Mainland Chinese Communists called them.

But, Dan was more furious with those in Washington who had permitted this to happen. America was allowing this through an undisclosed agreement that was forced through Congress overnight.

It was an undisclosed agreement because Congress had decided that the agreement was too sensitive to allow it to be made public to the American people, so it was classified top secret under provisions of the Patriot Act II.

***Those in the administration knew** that the American public would be up in arms over this 1600 page agreement, most of which hadn't been thoroughly read by anyone, so they deemed classified and that the American Public had "No need to know". Unknown to Americans and most of Washington, as an obscure provision of the same resolution, the American Government had agreed not to interfere and had given the green light to the Chinese for future invasions.*

Vietnam, Cambodia, Indonesia, Malaysia, the Philippine Islands, Laos and even the 300 year old Monarchy of Thailand were in their sights. China, secure as the new Financial and Industrial World Power, was beginning to build a new Imperialist Empire such as the world had not seen in the last two centuries.

The newspaper finally shifted and blew off Dan's windshield.

Dan knew that this first concession to the Chinese would be far from the last. They would ratchet up their expansion threats and soon their military threat would come directly to America. The Chinese were treating America like a bad child who's been irresponsible with money and needed a spanking, but they were treating their neighbors' worse.

Washington was so desperately in need of currency*, that they had accepted a small amount of gold and China's promise not to force a default on the huge amount of U.S. Treasury Bonds they held, in exchange for America turning a blind eye to Chinese expansion plans. Congress passed the resolution despite the threats of the Chiefs of Staff, but no one paid much heed to these high ranking American Officer's attempts at intimidation, they no longer had a functional military to threaten anyone with.*

Chinese troops were massing on the northern border of Vietnam and the Chinese Carrier Groups 'Beijing' and 'Mao Tsetung' were sailing into the Gulf of Tonkin and the South China Sea that afternoon headed towards the Vietnam coast.

The Undersecretary of Defense, *a former Marine Veteran of Vietnam, resigned. In making his public resignation statement he said... "We lost 58,000 soldiers and the Vietnamese had over 2,000,000 dead in Vietnam in the days of my youth. Since then America has helped Vietnam rebuild their country and the Vietnamese people have become a strong financial and military ally of ours. The hatred between us is gone and we have become one people."*

"I've just gotten off the phone with my former adversary, The Minister of Defense of the People's Republic of Vietnam. He is a hardened soldier, a worthy adversary who I have become personal friends with over the last years. This man, who has little emotion but much compassion for his country, begged me that we airlift troops there and send Navy Aircraft Carrier Groups into the South China Sea to help protect them."

"He ended the phone call with and emotional plea... his voice breaking. Not thinking of himself, but thinking of what we two have discussed many times when together... the American and Vietnamese blood wasted there years ago... his voice was breaking because of his fear for the future of his country."

"The failure to honor our new defense treaty with Vietnam is despicable. Therefore, I will resign my position as Undersecretary of Defense immediately. This American Administration should be ashamed of themselves."

As Dan pulled out onto the road home, *a bunch of American one thousand dollar bills blew across the hood of the suburban like confetti. Dan could clearly see the face of Franklin D. Roosevelt on one as it stopped momentarily and then slid reluctantly off his windshield as he sped away.*

Can't happen in America? We have unlimited spending now because the United States Dollar controls the banking of the world.

The 100 Trillion Zimbabwe Dollar Bill resulting from Hyper Inflation in 2008

An effort is underway by the *BRICS nations... Brazil, Russia, India, China and South Africa...* to trade between themselves with their own currencies not valued against the American dollar. They have begun to do this in May of 2012… for the first time in almost 100 years.

Our reckless spending cannot go on indefinitely and the U.S. Dollar will suffer when all nations agree to replace it with another currency. We're like the owner of the bank covering his wife's overdrafts…that works until we no longer own the bank.

The Victoria Falls Hotel
Jungle Junction
VAT# 10010273
Tel:(+263 13) 44203, 44751
Reservations@tvfh.zimsun.co.zw

59 Joylene

Tbl 16/1 Chk 5816 Gst 1
23Mar'08 19:46

2 Castle
@ Z$95,6 Z$191,270,000.00
1 Min Water Z$95,635,000.00
1 Dinner B Z$956,350,000.00

Food Z$956,350,000.00
Beverage Z$286,905,000.00
Z$1,243,255,000.00
Z$1,243,255,000.00

A $1.2 Billion Dollar Supper

Hyper Inflation can't happen in America you say? Get your history book out… read the current news… start writing down the cost of a few basic items each month you purchase them… we're headed into inflationary territory again.

Can't happen here? That's what was said in… the Weimar Republic in Germany of the 1930s… in Argentina in the 1990s… and in Zimbabwe in 2008. The leaders of those countries thought reckless spending could go on forever… until their countries collapsed.

Consider going to lunch as one of the Author's friends did in Zimbabwe. They took two large suitcases along with them...

Not because they were going to travel after supper, but because the supper that cost $70 in U.S. Dollars was paid for in Zimbabwe dollars.

The two suitcases were stuffed with Zimbabwe 100 *Trillion* Dollar Notes which they needed all of to pay for this simple night out.

If you'll notice the sales receipt here all those zeros mean something. $95,635,000 dollars for a mineral water!? The Zimbabwe Dollar at one time was almost equal in value to the United States Dollar.

If the above sales receipt appears humorous and like a grotesque joke to you... understand that the economy collapsed and with it *all savings and all retirement and pension accounts.*

Cholera struck the country, thousands dies of starvation and AIDS because of a government that had no money or will to stop this.

All retirees are left begging on the street. Picture the grotesqueness and humor of yourself as the person one Author's wife knows... a former financially comfortable but now 83 year old ex-British woman left a widow.

Her and her late husband's pensions and savings are worth zero now and she has lost her home.

Desperation

This woman bakes pies for one dollar and sells them on the street to try to scrape enough money together to eat and pay the rent on her dilapidated apartment.

Chapter 4
The Psychology and Reality of Desperation

In this Chapter we describe…

- **4-The *Survival Mentality***
- **4-Proactive response**
- **4-Psychological and physical effects of *A Failure of Civility***
- **4-Get use to Triage**
- **4-*Extended Family and Friends***
- **4-Where will *Extended Family and Friends* be if a *Catastrophic Event* occurs?**
- **4-Points of logic to consider with *Extended Family and Friends* and your *NPP***
- **4-Get your list of *Extended Family and Friends* filed with your *NPP* Leaders**
- **4-*Outsiders* and *Intruders***
- **4-You must find balance between logic and emotions**
- **4-You must keep your morale high**
- **4-Your Right to Defend**

4-The *Survival Mentality*

Dictionary Definition
Desperate
(Noun) Careless of danger, utterly reckless… Measures undertaken in desperation or as a last resort… Critical, very grave.

Are you mentally prepared to protect yourself? There is a sign, a warning sign that some homeowners have put up on walls that warns others that they will defend their home with a firearm. The sign is meant as a warning to burglars and *Intruders* that if they come into the homeowner's house they face being shot and killed.

The sign reads… *"No Trespassing! Violators will be shot… Survivors will be shot again."*

We use this sign to illustrate a point…

First… the question is *"Can you shoot another person in defense of your home, your family, yourself or the people involved in your NPP?"*

The answer comes from most people as a quick, simple *"Yes, I could!"* even though the thought is in their subconscious that it will be traumatic.

Second… the question is *"If you shoot a person and they don't immediately die, can you shoot them again and again until they stop moving?"*

Most people are more hesitant when answering this question. This is a traumatic thought. The thought of *'Shoot until you stop the threat'* is more difficult to comprehend… and the act itself much more difficult to carry out.

As crude as this sounds, the point we're trying to make to you is that this is the mindset that you *must have.* This is the mindset you will have to have if *A Failure of Civility* occurs and you want your family, the members of your *NPP* and yourself to live. You will have to be heartless towards your enemies. You will have to have a *Survival Mentality.*

This is a geometric representation of a '*Survival Square.'*

The Survival Square has four components represented as sides of the square…

- ***Equipment/Provisions for the task.*** Your food, water, weapons, medical supplies.
- ***Knowledge.*** Knowledge in the use of your equipment and supplies.
- ***Training.*** Actual physical training with your equipment combined with tactics and coordinated movement of Group Members.
- ***Survival Mindset.*** The determination and resolve to accomplish the mission.

Each side of this square is dependent on the others holding it in place. If one of these 'sides' is absent, then the square collapses… representing failure.

As the saying goes… *"Attitude is everything!"* We translate that term to describe the mindset of a ***Survival Mentality***.

Survival Mentality

Knowledge *Training*

Equipment/Provisions

The 'Survival Square'

No amount of food, ammunition, weapons, knowledge, tactical planning, defenses, training or number of *Group Members* will enable you to survive without each Group Member's *primary* defense… the ***Survival Mentality***.

If the time comes, your *Survival Mentality* will require you to take another's life… *you may have to kill in an instant.*

Notice that we didn't say you will have to kill 'without conscience'. Only mentally deranged people and those in fear of danger for their life or the life of others kill human beings purposely… and only the evilest of human beings enjoys killing.

We are by nature, averse to taking another's life. But to survive, you may have to do just that… take lives and do it viciously and repeatedly. Most animals kill only to survive. You will have to become more mindless than an animal and it will affect your conscience.

You will have to 'shoot to stop the threat' and continue to shoot until your adversaries stop and you stop the threat. You are not shooting just to stop the threat… *you shooting to stay alive.*

You will have to become mentally calloused and you will have little time to do it in. You will have to become *determined*, because the people assaulting you will be *more determined* than you… *they will be desperate. You will have to have the* ***Survival Mentality***.

Your adversaries, which for simplicity we will consider everyone not within your *Neighborhood Protection Plan* Protective Perimeter known as *Outsiders* and *Intruders*, will be trying to survive and they will be driven by something you may or may not be motivated by… they will be hungry and thirsty.

So to the best of your ability, prepare your mind now. There are techniques in the *Chapter 10* on surviving a gun battle that will make this daunting issue easier to deal with… at least at the point when you have to do it.

4-Proactive response

Law enforcement maintains a 'Force Continuum' by which they *react*. They generally have to see an *escalation of the threat* towards them *first* ***before*** they can *increase the amount of force they use.* This is why so many police officers get killed in the line of duty making simple arrests or traffic stops. They are in a *reactive mode, not a proactive mode.*

The time it takes the human mind to realize the threat of a person drawing a gun or coming at you with a knife alone is enough time in which you can be killed because you do not have enough time to react to that threat. This, plus the time it takes for an attacker to 'bleed out' before they can complete their attack on you are crucial seconds. You'll learn more about this later.

The Authors' rule… in a close quarter's situation, a potential hands on attack or a situation that absolutely is going to lead flat-out to a fight is… *"The person who makes the first move usually wins."* ***Respond proactively!***

As much as you may love your fellow man or the thought of the *'Marques of Queensberry Rules'* and fairness is an inherent characteristic in you, heed our rule… "*There is no fair fight.*" If your *NPP* is activated, be ready to make the first move when in a threat situation… once you make that decision, make your move without conscious thought. *Be proactive in your response!*

4-Psychological and physical effects of *A Failure of Civility*

These are psychological and physical effects that *A Failure of Civility* will have on you and your *NPP* Group Members. It will be much worse for those not organized properly in a

Neighborhood Protection Plan. If a *Long Term Crisis* leads to *A Failure of Civility* you must have the mindset to accept the following because *you will have to accept these to survive*. You must get use to your thought patterns changing and you will have to accept those changes.

If a Long Term Crisis leads to A Failure of Civility… get accustomed to…

- ***Having skin boils.*** You'll think God has stricken mankind with the Biblical curse of boils in addition to what you're already experiencing… the evil of what humanity has become during *A Failure of Civility*. Boils will appear on people because of changes in diet, poor nutrition and generally poor hygiene.
- ***Using a bucket for a toilet.*** Water will be more precious for drinking and preparing food than for flushing a toilet or washing hands.
- ***Having no toilet paper.*** After even a short time during a *Crisis*, this is one of the first items to run out. Try wiping your backside with your hands the next time you have a bowel movement and then washing your hands with a cup of water. Water may be too precious to use abundantly and if you don't have toilet paper you won't have paper towels. If you wipe your hands on your clothes, you know what you'll smell like.
- ***Going without sleep and sleep depravation.*** Few Americans know what true sleep depravation is. The mind wanders, the person is unable to concentrate or do the most elementary tasks and most people become irritable and disoriented.
- ***Being in a constant 'On Alert' state of mind... fear.*** You will have sleepless nights or very light sleeping habits that make you feel in a constant state of fatigue. You will find yourself moving zigzag instead of walking in a straight line from point A to point B. You will walk from one Cover position to another Cover position without realizing you're doing it.

  You will be looking at your surroundings not as a building or forest, but as to where a threat could be concealed. Every building you go into, you will first scan the building rooms for threats and then scan for exits to enable you to get out faster than you got in if problems arise.
- ***Suffering from Post Traumatic Stress Syndrome… or PTSD… as it's commonly referred to.*** Talk to anyone who has experienced extremely traumatic events or have been in a combat zone for a length of time and they'll tell you what this is like if you can get them to talk openly about this.

  But even if they do, you still won't comprehend PTSD. Ask them how long it took them to adjust to a normal thought pattern. Most people are never the same again. Your mind will become numb to life and normal situations you used to enjoy will become meaningless, monotonous and boring. You will find little pleasure in things you used to enjoy. Numb.

You may suffer from deep fits of depression. You will sit with your back to a wall inside buildings like the gunfighters did in the Old West. You will avoid groups of people. When you do associate in the presence of a group of people you will become very uncomfortable, edgy, nervous and irritable. Certain noises may startle you. You will smile little and not feel happiness and the joy of life like you did before a *Long Term Crisis* or *A Failure of Civility* started.

- ***Smelling of bodily filth.*** You will not be taking a shower or bath every day and may not bathe for weeks or months. Again, water will be too precious to use for taking a bath or shower. Cooking food with it and drinking it will be the priority. You and the people around you… will stink.
- ***Your clothes being dirty and maybe to the point of disintegration.*** You will be wearing the same underwear for days if not weeks. Again water will be too valuable to wash clothes with. Clothes deteriorate extremely fast when not washed. The dirt and scum in cloth acts like *sandpaper* and will give literal illumination to the term 'threadbare'. Clothes will literarily fall apart after a period of time.
- ***Women having hygiene problems in addition to their menstrual cycle.*** Lack of bathing water will cause yeast infections and other female related problems in addition to the aversion of a woman not being able to fully conceal her menstrual cycle. Research the number of deaths of women resulting from poor female hygiene hundreds of years ago…it will reveal that many women died premature deaths from uterus and vaginal infections.
- ***Cooking and heating with firewood or other outside means such as barbeque grills.*** This won't be your weekend barbeque with friends or neighbors. *Everything* you cook will have to be done outside whether in the heat of summer or the frigid temperatures of winter. Cook *everything* on your propane grill for one week to see how long the propane lasts. Then change to firewood. All your cooking utensils must be able to be used over an open flame… no plastic allowed.
- ***Women and men not shaving.*** This issue will be particularly more difficult for women. Imagine your wife with the same amount of body hair or more than you have on her legs, in armpits, etc. As distasteful and unromantic as it sounds, it will be your reality.

  Within months… every American male with facial hair will look like a Taliban warrior.
- ***Grandma having a baby.*** Birth control problems. Expect some Grandmas to be mothers of babies again. As archaic as it sounds, most people will be abstaining from sex. It won't be on most people's menu but there will be pregnancies and these pregnancies will be most difficult to deal with in the first years of *A Failure of Civility* if it's permanent.
- ***Minor medical problems becoming deadly.*** The state of despair you will be in will affect your immune system negatively. There will not be an 'injection from your doctor' for

coughs and fatigue. Minor cuts and scrapes will become deadly infections from an increase in common germs that we have over used antibiotics on for years.

Both of the Authors have walked with infected feet from blisters for tens of miles carrying heavy loads through rough terrain, one over 20 kilometers through mountainous Africa with no shoes, just two pairs of socks. The poor state of mind from the pain and concern of worsening infection plus poor nutrition makes the infection worse and can lead to Sepsis, or whole body infection, shock and death if not treated properly. Good thing the Authors were young and stupid when this happened… too stupid to know the true danger of our situation.

- ***Everyone is sick and the 'Terminal Living' will die.*** If a *Crisis* turns into *A Failure of Civility*, you will find people so stressed out and their immune systems so run down that eventually everyone will be sick at one time or another.

  Those people that are dependent on insulin, oxygen, beta blockers and other items that medically assist them in staying alive will die within days, weeks or months. These people are… for lack of a more pleasant sounding term… 'The Terminal Living'… amongst us.

- ***Little or no artificial visual or auditory stimuli as we have in abundance now.*** After some types of *Catastrophic Events*, especially an Electromagnetic Pulse *Catastrophic Event*, there will be no communications or external stimulus like TV, cell phones, internet or iphones.

  The silence will be deafening. Picture yourself in a 'Normal Rockwell Painting World' with your family huddled around any functioning radio straining for a shred of news. Rumors will abound and the term *"No news… is good news"* will have new meaning to you.

- ***Walking wherever you need to go.*** After some *Catastrophic Events*, there may be no transportation other than walking or bicycles. Don't drive to the corner market tonight, walk there and experience this difference. Bicycles will be worth their weight in gold as will be vehicles that operate and fuel.

- ***Living on top of each other.*** Envision your home with the number of people that you plan to have under your roof. Most people will literally be living on top of each other. Now add irritable people, no air conditioning, cooling or heat, the smell of unwashed bodies, and crying children to this. Maybe think of everyone hungry on top of these issues.

- ***No trust.*** Anyone, other than your family, and depending on how trusting and close knit you've managed to get the people in your *Neighborhood Protection Plan*, any people beyond your Protective Perimeters described as *Outsiders* will be looked at as a threat even if you previously intimately knew and trusted them.

- ***Going Cold Turkey.*** Everyone will quickly shed all the inconsequential things in life that consumed much of people's daily thought and being. *"Does my hair look okay?"* type thoughts and the mechanics of satisfying addictions. Those who have these vices won't have them long because they won't have anything to give them their 'fix'.

Smokers, drinkers, legal and illegal drug consumers will be forced to go 'Cold Turkey' and the desire to have just one puff, just a smell of liquor or one pill or injection of a drug will consume these people's minds day and night... until they're 'cured'.

Be mentally prepared to see the 'Dark Side' of friends and people you know and love if *A Failure of Civility* occurs. This will include people you are related to by blood or marriage.

- ***Psychoses will be appearing.*** A few Americans are on some type of drug for psychosis... panic, anxiety and delusionary behavior and take drugs daily for these issues. Some *Catastrophic Events* will disrupt the supply of these drugs and after about 30 days these problems will appear in these people.

Years ago the most dangerous of these people would have been 'committed' to mental hospitals and kept off the streets because of the danger to others from their severe aggressiveness and disorders. We no longer commit these people, but they rely on drugs to be amongst us without harming themselves or others.

An estimated 1 % of the American population have severe psychiatric problems and will be amongst us without their drugs to curtail their disorders. If there are 10,000 people in your town, 100 lunatics of varying degree will soon appear amongst them.

- ***Drastically increased suicide and death rate.*** Some people, accustomed to decades of comfortable living during *Normal Civility*, will either take their life or simply give up on life if *A Failure of Civility* occurs. The conscious and subconscious lack of will to survive will make a minor scratch deadly to these people as their immune systems will go into remission and will not fight an infection successfully.
- ***10 times as much drinking of alcohol... until it runs out.*** People who hadn't used alcohol or have used it moderately, will drink... lots. Marijuana use will become prolific. Marijuana will be grown everywhere.
- ***Everyone experiencing weight loss.*** America's problem with obesity will disappear very quickly even amongst those with sufficient food supplies.
- ***Cannibalism.*** People will cook, eat the flesh and muscle and drink the blood of *people* when there is nothing else available or as easy to catch like most elusive animals. Your muttering statement of concern... *"What are we going to eat today?"* might be answered with heads that turn to gaze at you... with the thought of you... as their mouths water.

Hunger will drive rational and compassionate people to begin to consume the recently dead and then to progress to killing and consuming the living... for sustenance. People who have a vomiting aversion to the thought of eating their own species will quickly join in with the crowd as it becomes an acceptable 'norm' in these deviant groups.

- ***Everyone will be 'finding' God.*** Last but not least… the sudden thrust of people into the jaws of brutality, fear, hopelessness and desperation will cause them to find God… and prayer.

If the above conditions sound bad... be assured... the reality will be worse.

One survival point must be over emphasized. We cannot emphasize enough the importance of ***hygiene and sanitation.***

Waterborne microbes and disease can kill more people than armies of attackers can ever kill. Water must be filtered through fine mesh cloth or coffee filters, treated with chlorine or purifying tablets and/or boiled before being used for cooking, washing food, drinking or bathing.

Human waste must be disposed of properly and the dead must be buried deeply immediately. This must be done away from living quarters, being careful that neither contaminates food or water supplies or sources. The sick must be quarantined to keep disease from spreading. You will learn more regarding some of these issues in *Chapter 12.*

4-Get use to Triage

Dictionary Definition
Triage *(UK English) or (US English))*
The process of determining the priority of patients' treatments based on the severity of their condition or age and usefulness to the NPP... The term comes from the French Verb Trier... meaning to separate, sift or select.

Medical Personnel will have to divide the wounded into three categories…

- ***Category 1…***Those who are likely to live with the little care they receive…
- ***Category 2…*** Those for whom immediate intensive care might save them…
- ***Category 3…*** Those who are likely to die, *regardless of what care they receive.*

Category 2 are tended to first… ***Category 1*** are tended to second… and ***Category 3*** are comforted the best as can be… *but they are left to die.*

Triage rations patient treatment on a scale of need when resources are insufficient for all to be treated immediately. If you have few medical resources, medical personnel or medicines you will have to employ a triage system if Group Members are wounded or injured.

At its most primitive, those responsible for tending to the wounded after an attack or entrusted with their care afterwards have to make the decision who lives and who dies.

This sounds heartless and *is* during *Normal Civility*. The Authors hope that neither you nor they *ever* have to make any decisions regarding people like this... because we're compassionate like you.

However, this would be the *reality* of *A Failure of Civility* if it is prolonged or permanent and formal medical services and medicines are limited or do not exist.

4-*Extended Family and Friends*

Who's coming to dinner? One of the most difficult decisions that you will have to make in your life will be who will be part of your *Neighborhood Protection Plan* when a *Crisis* begins and especially if it turns into *A Failure of Civility*.

We're not pointing to the Group Members of your *Neighborhood Protection Plan*... We're talking about your friends, family members and *their* family members.

Where do you draw the line? When do you say, *"We have only enough food, water and provisions for X number of people for X amount of time?"* How do you turn away friends and family?

Have you drawn up a list of friends and family members and talked to each about this? Have you calculated the amount of supplies needed for each of these additional people daily? ***It's too late when the Crisis is upon you to deal with this. Use the Caloric Calculator in the back of the book.***

Open air Cooking

Let's use this term for simplicity. *Extended Family and Friends* are family and friends of *Neighborhood Protection Plan* Group Members who will be allowed into the *NPP* after a *Catastrophic Event* occurs, subject to their being able to get to your *NPP*.

In the best interests of the group and to keep your sanity... sort out who will be in your *Neighborhood Protection Plan* as *Extended Family and Friends* ***before*** a *Crisis* occurs. Put it in writing and keep copies... on paper, not a computer.

Make copies of this list and give them to your *NPP* Leaders so there is an understanding *before* a *Crisis* takes place. If *Extended Family and Friends* can get to your neighborhood area then they are allowed in.

Like each of the Authors' families, some of our family store provisions with us, some cannot afford to do so and some think *"Everything will be just fine..."* so they won't participate.

In addition, each adult family member has a boyfriend, girlfriend, in-laws, children, close friends… and the list goes on. They will all want safety, security and food to eat.

It would be best if your family members distant from your *NPP* implement the recommendations of this book where they live. However, some families will want to congregate together until the *Crisis* passes if they can get to your *NPP*.

The American Family Dinner Table

The members of our families who do not believe or cannot afford to, do not contribute to our store of provisions. But, if you're human, you will still love them just as much and certainly will not be able to deny them admittance to you group.

Unfortunately at some point, like a submarine commander, you'll have to *'close the hatch'* and leave some people outside the submarine, or risk drowning all on board.

Sort out these issues *now* so, God forbid, you won't be forced to leave a loved one out on their own. This gets down to stockpiles of food, water and provisions.

The Authors hope that none of the *Catastrophic Events,* the resulting *Crisis* and certainly *A Failure of Civility* ever occur. But it's not a matter of *if*… it's a matter of *when* some major crippling *Catastrophic Events* will occur.

If it happens in our lifetimes, God help guide us and be merciful on us all as we each make these decisions.

Make your *Extended Family and Friends* list now as you'll have plenty of decisions to make regarding others begging for help that will plague you if a *Crisis* begins to turn into *A Failure of Civility*.

4-Where will *Extended Family and Friends* be if a *Catastrophic Event* occurs?

Most families are scattered geographically. In some instances they may be close by and in other circumstances they may be hundreds of miles away.

Travel will be difficult or impossible, depending on the effect of the *Catastrophic Event*, their preparedness and how long they wait before they make an intense effort to get to your *NPP*.

It may get down to... *"If they can't walk to your NPP... they may not get there!"*

It is critical that you educate your family members to the potential of *Catastrophic Events* and the potential aftermath and get them involved with your effort. They should make arrangements with you for their share of the food, water and other survival supplies if they plan to get to your *NPP*.

Don't get lulled into the thinking that *"We'll deal with it when it happens!"* or *"We have plenty for everyone... we'll share!"* This will not be the reality of it.

4-Points of logic to consider with *Extended Family and Friends* and your *NPP*

Determine the *Extended Family and Friends* by 'Beans, Bullets and Bandages' so to speak. In other words determine the number of people you will allow in your *NPP* from the outside by food, water and provisions.

Points of Logic to consider...

- ***Will the city they live in be on 'Lock Down'?*** Will your family or friends be in a city where they can't leave because of certain *Catastrophic Events?* Many towns and cities will be cordoned off by law enforcement and roads blockaded to prevent people from leaving.

  Further, are the towns or cities on the route they plan to travel to your *NPP* going to be locked down? This will prevent their travel through these towns if they're on their travel route.

- ***Will vehicles function and gas be available?*** Some *Catastrophic Events* will cause inoperable vehicles and burn out gas station pumps.

- ***Consult our Calorie Calculator*** in the back of this book for their portion of the food supply but also taking into consideration water and other needs and requirements.

- ***What are they bringing to the table?*** Do they have specialized training? Do they have supplies or equipment to compliment your existing supply?

- ***Do they have medical problems?*** Are they just another mouth to feed, will their medical problems consume time and resources and detract from your group's well being or will they be able to contribute to the overall *NPP*.

This is an *extremely* difficult decision to make, especially with family. Who wants to leave Grandfather behind? This is the reality you may be faced with… but very, very few would be able to cope with. This decision may have to be made at some point for the survival of the other family members.

- ***Do you trust them?*** Are they felons, criminals, drug users or generally unfit people to be a Group Member? Unless they're family or extremely close friends, they may turn on your group.

4-Get your list of *Extended Family and Friends* filed with your *NPP* Leaders

We suggest you guide yourself by logic, but in doing so always keeping in mind that there is little reason for humanity's survival if people don't allow their emotions and compassion for others to be involved with their decisions.

That being said, we can give you some points to consider along with the means to determine those decisions by logical thought. Along with this list of *Extended Family and Friends*, make notations of what they are bringing with them and what their specialty training or other advantages are to the *NPP.*

Keep a copy of your Extended Family and Friends List for yourself. Update it when necessary and give an updated list to your NPP Leaders, again keeping copies for yourself.

You have to incorporate what provisions and equipment *Extended Family and Friends* will be bringing with them into your provisions and equipment list and when they are expect to arrive at the *NPP*.

When they arrive, make certain the *NPP* Leaders are advised of where these people will be staying, what their specialized training, if any, is and how they can be utilized in the *NPP*.

The Authors will certainly not attempt nor will we give you ethical guidelines or be your moral compass on this issue. This is a personal issue that will be extremely difficult to deal with, just as the many issues you will deal with regarding your *NPP* during a *Crisis* or *A Failure of Civility* will be difficult.

We can only suggest you go to the 'Well of Your Subconscious' and consult your Higher Power in making your decisions.

4-*Outsiders* and *Intruders*

Outsiders and *Intruders* are your biggest danger during a *Long Term Crisis* or *A Failure of Civility*. ***You and your Group Members risk contagious diseases*** from these people if they *even get close to your NPP* along with the physical threat from them.

Outsiders. *An Outsider is* ***anyone*** *who is not an NPP Group Member or an Extended Family and Friends Member. Even though an Outsider may not be overtly violent or trying to attack your NPP...*

an Outsider must be considered your ***enemy****.*

During a Long Term Crisis or A Failure of Civility... most Outsiders will be short of or without food and water and will most probably become Intruders at some point. Intruders are those who are using or will definitely use violence to take what you have.

There is more on handling of *Outsiders* and *Intruders* in *Chapter 6, Area Tactical Protection for a* Low Rise Residential Neighborhood. Realize that once an *Outsider* or *Intruder* gets in or is allowed into the *NPP* group they will know your strengths and weaknesses.

Once an *Outsider* is inside your *NPP* and sees your defenses, has an idea of your supply situation and knows your numbers, they can be the biggest danger you will have to your *NPP* if they reveal this to other *Intruders* voluntarily or under coercion.

The Authors *strongly* recommend *never* allowing an *Outsider* or *Intruder* into your Protective Perimeter. In a worst case scenario you cannot feed them. Help *Outsiders* on their way, but make *certain* they leave your area.

Realize if you give them anything you have just told them you have food. *Make no mistake Ladies and Gentlemen, if you feed anyone outside your NPP Group Members... they will be back... most likely with armed and hungry people.*

Intruders. *This is your adversary and greatest danger. An Intruder is an Outsider turned to violence and is* ***anyone*** *who is not an NPP Group Member or an Extended Family and Friends Member. This is the person you have formed your NPP to protect against.*

We'll use this term to describe those, be they individuals or groups... that are committed to taking your Critical Life Supplies and Services violently.

Intruders *are definitely your enemy... an attacker... assailants.*

Understand that feeding any desperate person, no matter how heart wrenching it may be not to, will invite trouble. Just like the vagrant begging money on the corner. Once you give them money, each time they see you they will be more aggressive in targeting you... you give to them and soon they will expect it from you *and* they'll be angry when you *don't* give them money.

Know you will be dealing with the mother of all motivations... hunger.

Feeding Outsiders could open up the floodgate and bring the fury of ***hell*** *to the doorstep of your NPP. If this doesn't sound very compassionate... be assured that it will be your reality if you violate this recommendation.*

4-You must find balance between logic and emotions

We've given you some Logical guidelines. But the emotions towards family and friends and probably even strangers will push logical thought aside when you see most people in need.

You must, *for the survival of your group,* find a balance between logic and emotion in deciding who will be in your *NPP*. *Do not* bring strangers into your *NPP*. It will be the end of you *and* your *NPP*.

It won't be pretty folks. But, you can survive and you must survive! For your spouse, mate, family, children, friends, neighbors, people, America and mankind... you must survive to help us come back from the brink of destruction if there is A Failure of Civility.

4-You must keep your morale high

A primary issue that will become much more critical if a *Crisis* or *A Failure of Civility* becomes long and drawn out is *morale*. As we said before, the saying is... *"Attitude is everything!"* You can substitute the word 'Attitude' with *Morale* or insert the word 'Positive' in front of *Attitude*. You and each of your Group Members must maintain a *positive attitude* to maintain *morale*.

> *Napoleon said that in a fight... "The moral (morale) is to the physical as three to one."*
>
> *What did he mean by that and how does it apply to you, your Group Members and your NPP?*
>
> *The spiritual and mental attributes of tenacity, positive morale, team work, dedication, the will to fight and the <u>Survival Mentality</u> are far more important than the number of opponents you have or their equipment.*

The more drawn out a *Crisis* or *A Failure of Civility* becomes the more dangerous bad morale becomes if not addressed. Each Group Member must stay positive even with prolonged high stress, rationing or shortages of food and water or the death of members of the neighborhood that will occur.

Negative Group Members need to be taken aside and talked to by other Group Members. Find out why this person has a bad attitude. If something can be done to address this person's problem do so to the best of your ability. Your *Neighborhood Protection Plan* must be the epitome of cooperation and you need a teamwork effort to keep morale high and cohesion between Group Members.

There are many ways to deal with the morale issue... laughter, prayer, reading out loud to groups, games, skits and plays to take people's minds off of the terrible circumstances around them. As many ways as there are to deal with this issue... it must be dealt with *point blank.* Bad morale is like cancer... once it starts to spread there's no stopping it until it destroys the host... and that will be your *Neighborhood Protection Plan.*

4-Your Right to Defend

The hysteria over violence in America has created doubt and a dangerous mindset in people.

People have become hesitant and question whether they have the right to use force against violence in defense of themselves or their family. *Any animal species that loses the will or ability to fight to defend themselves... quickly becomes extinct or an endangered species.*

> *You have the right and the duty to defend yourself, your family members, your friends and your neighbors anytime against great bodily injury or deadly threat. That is your immediate duty whether law enforcement is available to respond or not during Normal Civility, a Crisis or A Failure of Civility.*

The animal kingdom sorts this out quickly as a law of nature. Maybe they have more common sense than we do. You cannot risk the *paralysis from fear* of not acting or being concerned with liability in defending yourself, your family members, your friends and your neighbors.

'Zero Tolerance' policies teach the young not to fight from early childhood. In a perfect world, that may sound rational... but in the reality of society with violent people... that attitude will get you killed or severely injured even in *Normal Civility.* If there is *A Failure of Civility,* you will simply not survive without fighting to defend yourself and others... killing others if necessary to protect and defend.

You have the right to use deadly force against a person or persons to stop the *threat of death or great bodily harm against yourself, your family members, your friends and your neighbors,* if *law enforcement is not present or able to intercede at the time that threat is being acted upon.*

Protecting yourself, your family and property... like all law, has become complicated in the United States...

We'll try to give you a proper overview, but whatever we write here ***must be verified by you*** with *an attorney licensed and versed in the laws of your State* regarding… *detainment of persons… "Stand your Ground" laws… "Castle Doctrine" laws…* and the *Use of Deadly Force* in defense of *person* and in defense of *property.*

When we describe 'property', we mean only that property that you have rights to by rental agreement, lease agreement, title promissory or title ownership or by some other form of right. We primarily refer to 'Real Property' that consists of land and structures. *Your land and house in your neighborhood is your property,* but *another's land and house in your neighborhood* ***are not*** *your property.*

Understand that generally ***most State laws will treat you differently*** if you use deadly force to defend yourself, your family or your property *while you are on your property* ***compared to*** if you use *deadly force* to defend yourself, your family or your property *while* ***not*** *on your property.*

Further, most State laws view the use of *deadly force* differently if you are defending *person* versus *property.*

Further yet, some States *require you to retreat from a threat until you can retreat no further before* you use *deadly force* against an attacker. Then to complicate the issue again, about one half of States have the *"Castle Doctrine"* which basically says that you do not have to retreat *on your property* before you use deadly force against an attacker.

Yet still another difference between State laws is that about one third of the States allow you to *"Stand your Ground"* in defending yourself from an attacker *where ever you are.* In these States, you do not have to be on your property nor do you have to retreat before you use deadly force to stop an attacker.

Keep the above in mind *when you are off your property* inside your *NPP*, *outside* your *NPP* or if you have to move from your *Primary NPP Location* to your *Secondary NPP Location.*

Each Group Member still has the right to defend themselves against the *threat of death* or *great bodily harm* even if they are not on their own property. You must have cause to do this… it can't be an imagined threat, but a real threat.

Arrest or detainment of people are other issues. Don't begin to think you are law enforcement unless you are legally deputized by your County Sheriff or another proper authority.

Most States allow 'citizen arrest' for 'trespassing' if 'trespass notices' are posted or you advise the violator of trespass in advance of a citizen's arrest. The law generally allows you to detain a person for a reasonable period until law enforcement authorities can arrive to verify the violation of law for which you detained them and then release them or re-arrest them.

A *few* State Laws allow the use of deadly force against a person or person engaged in the destruction or theft of property.

Unless an Outsider or Intruder is attempting to burn down a home or the property is Life Critical Supplies and Services and a Long Term Crisis or A Failure of Civility exists, the Authors are against the use of deadly force to prevent theft or damage of property. Most property and your injured pride are not justification to take life.

Use your heads folks! Don't be trigger happy! Do your best not to take human life, injure others or violate their rights because you simply 'think you have the right to do so.'

Consult an attorney licensed and versed in the laws of your State regarding detainment of persons and the Use of Deadly Force in defense of your person and in defense of your property.

Better yet… we suggest that you get the book… "Self-Defense Laws of All 50 States" *by Attorney* ***James 'Mitch' Vilos*** *and Evan Vilos. This is one of the most comprehensive books on 'Use of Deadly Force' that has ever been written. Go to their website www.firearmslaw.com or purchase this book at Amazon.com or GunLaws.com and read it.*

Attorney Vilos is one of the foremost authorities on the Use of Deadly Force in the Untied States. He reviews jury decisions regarding Use of Deadly Force all across America and posts updates on his website.

If *A Failure of Civility* occurs, conduct the activities of your *Neighborhood Protection Plan* with this thought in mind… ***When Normal Civility returns, will your actions make you liable and if so can you justify your actions?***

We suggest that the *Primary and Secondary NPP Leaders* and each Section Leader keep a '*NPP Diary*' of every action that they take daily. Include a summary of each day's events… everything of significance. Keep detailed records regarding issues of the use of force in this book and write and sign separate statement copies to distribute to leaders and those Group Members involved in the incident.

It is suggested that any action that ends in the detainment, injury or death of anyone or an alleged violation of their rights because of your action… that *signed witness statements* be taken, *all parties involved have copies signed by witnesses* and that *each person keeps these in a safe place. Remember to include* in your statements, the Who, What, When, Where and Why of the action.

Also keep records of reasoning as to why you activated your *NPP*, issues of supplies, sickness, area violence not involving your *NPP*, inability of police, fire department or medical emergency calls, lack of response, etc. This should be kept in one ledger type diary and each section countersigned and commented on by each *Primary and Secondary NPP Leaders* and each Section Leader. Do not keep this information on a computer.

Regardless, it is your *right and duty* to defend yourself, your family members, friends and neighbors. You cannot risk the *paralysis from fear* of the concern of acting too soon, not acting or being overly concerned with doing something wrong in defending yourself, your family members, your friends and your neighbors.

Chapter 5
How to Organize your *Neighborhood Protection Plan*

In this Chapter we describe…

- **5-Why Stand in Place?**
- **5-One neighbor has to get the ball rolling… the *Self Starter***
- **5-Determining your neighbor's cooperation**
- **5-Your First Meeting**
- **5-There must be a leader**
- **5-Verify the leader's experience**
- **5-Your Second Meeting**
- **5-Try to work through your current Neighborhood Watch**
- **5-'Political Correctness' in your police department and forming your *Neighborhood Protection Plan* without them**
- **5-*Primary and Secondary NPP Leaders* evaluation of the *Primary Neighborhood Protection Plan Location***
- **5-Your image to your neighborhood, the public and law enforcement**
- **5-*NPP* Group Member job duties and capabilities**
- **5- The *minimum* number of people needed for different types of *NPP* premises**
- **5-What size should your *NPP* be?**
- **5-Classifying your Group Members**
- **5-Worst case scenarios in forming a *NPP*, farms and ranches**
- **5-Story-*"Riot!"***
- **5-Practice to prove it works**
- **5-Building Function**
- **5-Choosing your *Secondary NPP Locations***
- **5-Know the capabilities of each Group Member**
- **5-Find out which Group Members have special training**
- **5-Differences between people, tolerance and acceptance**
- **5-How to deal with Non-Participants**
- **5-The Principles of Leadership you need to employ**
- **5-*Chain of Leadership Structure and Control* for a *Neighborhood Protection Plan***
- **5-Encourage leadership and talk between Junior Leaders**
- **5-Location of your *NPP* Watch Center**
- **5-Fire Fighting and Prevention in your *NPP***
- **5-Making the decision to activate your *NPP***
- **5-*You must not hesitate to activate your NPP Group Members.***

5-Why Stand in Place?

For the majority of Americans, the equipment, location, retreat and resources to leave a populated area for a remote, less populated area, is beyond the possibility of most individuals.

There are far more resources in your neighborhood *than you will have trying to re-establish yourself miles away* 'who-knows-where,' amongst people you may or may not know. With little expense per neighbor, your effective protection will be greater because of your resources and the *Strength through Numbers* that you and your neighbors will have where you *Stand in Place.*

There is more safety for you in the Strength through Numbers of your neighborhood cooperating for their common protection than trying to "Go Remote."

A *Neighborhood Protection Plan (NPP)* is the preparation by your household, in cooperation with your neighbors doing likewise, for protection and survival within your neighborhood. Such a plan will drastically increase your chances of surviving a *Crisis* or *A Failure of Civility.*

Neighborhood Protection Plans across the country can keep the total destruction of America from occurring after a worse case Catastrophic Event.

If trouble develops, you think... *"I'll just grab my shotgun and stand by the front of my house and I'll blow anyone away who tries to hurt my family or loot my house!"*

The Authors would place bets on your outcome in the long term. Or maybe you and a bunch of the neighbors can do the same... but over a period of time, you'll find your 'cooperative protection' will all fall apart.

When you understand the number of people it takes, the organization and preparation involved with defending even a small neighborhood, you'll understand why you need to read this book and why we present this method of setting up your *Neighborhood Protection Plan.*

Our method of choosing your leaders combines the process of Group Member vote and qualification by the proven knowledge and experience of your leaders.

You can form a NPP Council to decide the many problems that you will encounter before and after a Crisis, but the defense of your neighborhood must be left to the absolute judgment and direction of your elected Primary and Secondary NPP Leaders.

But all this takes someone... a concerned neighbor and an American... to get the ball rolling!

5-One neighbor has to get the ball rolling… the *Self Starter*

Dictionary Definition
Organize
(Verb) To put together into an orderly, functional, structured whole… To arrange systematically for harmonious or united action.

We'll go to this first because without it… nothing will happen. ***Someone in your neighborhood has to get the ball rolling.*** Not because they want to be the *NPP* Leader, but ***because they want their neighborhood to be safe, protected and secure.*** Put leadership aside for now and we'll come to it later at the appropriate step.

As we said previously, the Authors are here to assist you in forming a cooperative protection of your neighborhood. *But we need **you** to help us help you.*

In every neighborhood, there is always one person who is concerned about safety and security. This person is usually a 'Self Starter,' not afraid to go out and talk to the neighbors about something that's in everyone's beneficial interest.

If you're reading this book… you're most likely this person.

If you are this person, regardless of *your* military or law enforcement experience, *you must first evaluate your neighbor's interest* in forming a *Neighborhood Protection Plan.*

You have to ask yourself these preliminary questions first…

- ***What is your neighbor's Attitude?*** Is there a cooperative attitude amongst your neighbors to form an emergency defense of your neighborhood? Don't just guess at this or assume there isn't. You will be surprised by talking with each of your neighbors.

  We have become an 'Urban Garage-Door Society' where, for the most part, people drive home and close their garage door behind them, seeking solitude and have little contact with their neighbors. Your neighbors will most likely *'come out of their shell' and will be interested when this is proposed to them*

  Forming a *Neighborhood Protection Plan* may actually bring your neighbors closer together and form bonds between people who previously had little contact with each other. *All people need and want a sense of security!* The knowledge that they can have it *in their own hands* and that it is a *Strength through Numbers* is reassuring to everyone. You need to build relationships with your neighbors… this is just being good neighbors anyway you look at it.

  However, if you don't have an interest from your neighbors, look for another area to go to in time of disaster. Look for a nearby neighborhood in which you know someone that you can determine conclusively has an interest in this. Organize there and you may want to stock most of your food and provisions there.

- ***Are your neighbors trustworthy?*** Have the many of your neighbors had serious problems with the law? Do you have convicted felons or gang members as neighbors? What do you know about these people outside of rumor?

  We're not saying that people can't change or that all felons are untrustworthy, but if you have people you feel that you can't trust or neighbors such as gang members … a cooperative effort won't work. *In this case…* you need to look to another neighborhood!

  You will be disclosing some information on what you have for property to your *NPP Leaders.* Beware if your neighborhood is comprised of questionable people. You should also check your local Registry of Sexual Predators. You don't want a pedophile watching the neighborhood children.

5-Determining your Neighbor's Cooperation

You won't be able to have any type of calm, rational discussion with your neighbors after a *Crisis* occurs, it will be too difficult. An *NPP* cannot be organized in the midst of the chaos of a *Crisis*. The preparation and training must be done beforehand.

Let's assume that like most neighborhoods in America that your neighbors are interested and law abiding citizens. Let's assume you're the Self Starter…

These are the steps you will follow to form your Neighborhood Protection Plan that we will explain in detail in this chapter…

1. ***Get Started.*** One or two *Self Starters* need to get the ball rolling.
2. ***Get help!*** Get four or five neighbors together, explain what you're doing and get them to help you. *This is important!* You must have help… and more help. This small group now comprises the '*Moderators*'.
3. ***Moderators survey your neighbors.*** Divide up the neighborhood. Survey all the neighbors with the *NPP* Survey Questionnaire and Address Checklist.
4. ***Moderators hold your First Meeting.*** Have the First Meeting of neighbors to explain the purpose of the *Neighborhood Protection Plan* and select candidates for leaders.
5. ***Moderators verify.*** Verify candidates for leader's experience.
6. ***Hold your Second Meeting to elect leaders.*** Elect the *Primary* and *Secondary NPP Leaders* at your Second Meeting.
7. ***Leaders and Group Members approach.*** Leaders should approach your police department and attempt to work alongside your current Neighborhood Watch Program if there is one. Proceed with or without police department cooperation or approval.
8. ***Leaders classify.*** Classify the Group Members and select Section and Junior leaders.

9. ***Leaders Determine.*** Determine the size of the *NPP* and where Protective Perimeters, Guard Posts, the Entry/Exit Control Point, Kill Zones, Secondary Fighting Positions, etc. will be.
10. ***Leaders and Group Members inventory.*** Ask each Group Member to give an honest list of what they have for personal supplies and equipment. You'll notice this is not on the Group Member Information form. Revealing what you have for food, equipment and supplies is a sensitive issue with most people, especially firearms. Find out what each Group member will let the *NPP* use for *communal* equipment and supplies. Inform Group Members what each must have and get an assurance from each that they will start accumulating the required items. Compile a list of items on hand for Communal *NPP* equipment and supplies.
11. ***Leaders assign.*** Assign duties to each Group Member.
12. ***Leaders and Group Members write it down.*** Leaders need to make a written plan for the *NPP*. Get help from Group Members with this.
13. ***Leaders and Group Members purchase necessary items and start storing.*** Equipment and supplies need to be purchased for the *communal NPP* and each Group Member needs to start storing food, water and ammunition.
14. ***Leaders and Group Members train.*** Put your written plan to the test by training exercises. Firearms safety and basic marksmanship must be started first.
15. ***Leaders and Group Members keep in contact and be ready.*** Have a function monthly so all Group Members can keep in contact with each other. *Keep your NPP alive!*

Most of the above will be done by leaders and Group Members after the election of your leaders. Primary and Secondary NPP Leaders MUST have assistance from Group Members in completing the organizational tasks or it will be too overwhelming for the leaders. Remember that everyone has their normal life to live in addition to organizing your Neighborhood Protection Plan and training. Leaders must learn to delegate and assign tasks.

The *Self Starter* must first talk to a few of his neighbors to discuss a *Neighborhood Protection Plan.* Get these neighbors to help you. Chose a place and plan for the *First Meeting* of your *Neighborhood Protection Plan.* Have the date and time of the First Meeting planned before you talk to neighbors.

Get four or five of your neighbors to help you so you don't feel like the 'Lone Ranger'. Choose outgoing and respectable persons who are not afraid to approach your neighbors. If *you're* that *Self Starter* divide up your neighborhood into areas for each person helping you to survey. ***You and your neighbors*** must go door to door in the neighborhood and talk with each of your neighbors.

Write down names and addresses of your neighbors prior to talking with them on the ***NPP Survey Questionnaire and Address Checklist*** which is **at the back of this book.** Make copies of it for all persons helping you. Ask neighbors one simple question which will quickly reveal their position in cooperating with you to form a *Neighborhood Protection Plan.*

Ask no more and say little after they respond to this question…

"I live in this area and I'm your neighbor. We're having a neighborhood meeting about protecting our neighborhood against fire and protecting it by against criminals, rioters and looters in support of our Fire and Police Departments if an emergency or a disaster strikes and they are unable to respond."

"I'm not in charge of this, but I'm helping others organize.

We're going to vote to elect two experienced people to lead our group at our meeting and we'll answer all your questions there.

Would you be willing to help the rest of us and come to our meeting?"

If they answer *"No"*, check the box next to their name and address, thank them and walk right over to the next neighbor's door. If they object to the term "whatever means necessary" … you most likely don't want them as a Group Member.

For the majority who will answer *"Yes"*, check the box next to their name and address. Tell them about your *Neighborhood Protection Plan* meeting and invite them to come to it. Keep it 'short and sweet' and tell them their questions will be answered at this meeting.

Do not let the attitude of some of your neighbors defeat your efforts.

5-Your First Meeting

You, the *Self Starter* and the neighbors who helped you survey… we're going to call *Moderators*.

Keep politics, ideology, religion, 'who has the best firearm' talk and the consumption of alcohol or use of drugs out of the discussions during the meeting.

You'll have to explain that some questions can't be answered until later. All questions will be answered after you have elected your Primary and Secondary NPP Leaders and the neighborhood has been evaluated.

You will conduct or *moderate* the meetings. *Moderators* must be businesslike and not 'Political' or 'Little Dictators'. *Moderators* must take turns talking to give a sense of cooperation in organizing the neighborhood.

Make the following meeting sign with a black marker on tag board or cardboard and place it high enough for all to see. Tailor your statements to the audience you are addressing whether it be a Low Rise Residential Neighborhood or a High Rise Residential Building.

This meeting is ONLY for the discussion and the evaluation of our neighborhood for a Neighborhood Protection Plan. This Neighborhood Protection Plan is to protect OUR NEIGHBORHOOD area in times of Crisis, civil unrest and disaster. Our objective is to PROTECT OUR NEIGHBORHOOD against fire if the fire department is unable to respond.

Our objective is also to PROTECT OUR NEIGHBORHOOD from looters and criminals if law enforcement is unable to maintain order.

Meeting Sign

The ***Moderators*** must point at this sign if the discussion starts to get 'off track' to bring the discussion back to the sole purpose of the meeting.

Moderators have to be people that can keep order at the meetings, have the drive and persistence to continue to work on and believe in the concept of a *Neighborhood Protection Plan*. Do not get angry or spiteful with neighbors who mock your plan or are negative.

Moderators must keep order, but must also allow a free flow of communication. If your *NPP* organizing effort is to be effective, it must get past this First Meeting... the most difficult stage... the rest will be easy as long as you keep the momentum going.

The Moderators must explain to all neighbors at the First Meeting that the procedure will be...

- ***Handout and ask.*** The *Moderators* should follow the guidelines of this book and hand out copies to each person ***Our Neighborhood Protection Plan Statement of Purpose*** and the ***NPP Group Member Information Forms*** in the back of this book to everyone. Ask for a show of hands of who wants to protect their neighborhood. The majority are going to indicate *"Yes"*.

Work with your neighbors who are enthused about this... and you and those enthused neighbors must work with the neighbors who are not as enthused but do want to participate. Have participants write down their questions on the back of the ***Our***

Neighborhood Protection Plan Statement of Purpose page. Explain that each of them will receive a visit from one of the *Moderators* to answer those questions.

Ask each participant to fill out the ***NPP Group Member Information Form*** and tell them that each will receive a visit from a *Moderator* who will collect these forms.

- ***To find leaders.*** Find candidates for leaders who can verify their past law enforcement or military experience or other suitable leadership experience. Information on candidates for leaders will be gathered by the *Moderators* before the Second Meeting. Trust, but verify!
- ***To Elect.*** Elect those leaders at the Second Meeting.
- ***To Review.*** Those elected leaders and Group Members will review the neighborhood or building as feasible for a *NPP*. Explain that a renewable water source is the first concern for a long term *NPP*. If a renewable water source is not available nearby or a water bore hole or open well cannot be dug, discussion can still proceed to creating a *NPP*, realizing that the *NPP* will not be able to be sustained on a long term basis.

  It must be explained that there will be an evaluation of a Protective Perimeter that allows the neighborhood or building to control who can come into the area, making the neighborhood or building safe and secure and protecting from fire in time of emergency… in essence, making the neighborhood or building 'Your Fort' in times of riots, disaster or civil unrest.
- ***To assure.*** *Moderators* must assure all participants that the *Neighborhood Protection Plan (NPP)* will be lawful and all members are required to act within the law. Inform all participants that the families and relatives of any law enforcement officer, public safety officer, fireman, doctor, nurse and emergency worker or hospital personnel will be protected by the *NPP* Group Members and will be safe during an emergency, freeing those emergency services people to do their job without concern.

Schedule the Second Meeting before you adjourn your First Meeting and inform neighbors of the time and date of the Second Meeting before you adjourn.

There will be those at your First Meeting who attempt to scare everyone by saying *"We're all going to get sued!"... "This is illegal!"* or attempt to be a coy "Devil's Advocate" or 'Fear Monger.'

Simply state to them that if they are so against *organizing to protect everyone in the neighborhood* that they're free to leave the meeting so the others can carry on with the task. Tell them that everyone is here is working towards the goal of organizing protection for the neighborhood and ask them to leave if they continue to interfere with your meeting.

Between the First and Second Meetings of neighbors, the *Moderators* have to visit each participating neighbor (Group Member) and answer any questions they may have. The

Moderators also need to get a completed ***NPP Group Member Information Form*** for each Group Member when they visit them.

Ask each Group Member to give an honest list of what they have for personal supplies and equipment. You'll notice this is not on the Group Member Information form. For most people, revealing what they have for food, equipment and supplies is a sensitive issue, especially firearms. ***Don't press the issue!***

Expect and accept reluctance until trust and familiarization develops in your group.

As you go further along in the organization of your Neighborhood Protection Plan, Group Members will be more inclined to reveal this information. You must work on assumptions to begin with and assurances from each that they will acquire what is necessary for each person.

You'll find that simply starting your NPP will be a catalyst and encouragement for Group Members to start storing food reserves, firearms, ammunition and other required equipment and supplies.

Keep the momentum going… by getting other neighbors to help you!

Moderators will have to…

Brief individual neighbors. Those who indicated an interest but didn't or couldn't attend the First Meeting have to be briefed. *You will not ever be able to get all members to attend a meeting* so plan on having to brief some members individually at their homes.

Also, *understand that you will lose enthusiasm from some members and some may decide not to participate.* This is the normal natural behavior of people and group activity.

Gather Group Member Information for leadership candidates. Prior to the Second Meeting, the *Moderators* should go through all the ***NPP Group Member Information Forms*** and draw up a list of candidates for leaders. Go to each of these candidates to verify the below information. Ask them if they want to be leaders and get a commitment from each that if they assume the task that they will carry out their responsibilities to the best of their ability.

5-There must be a Leader

Whenever an organization is formed and especially one of the nature of a *Area Tactical Protection* plan there becomes the issue of who is in charge. Americans, being independent, generally do not like to take orders unless they fully believe in the purpose of an organization and its leadership.

This can be complicated by the fact that one of your neighbors will be telling you and others what to do in a time of *Crisis. You must put this aside or your NPP will never function correctly.*

You must organize your *Neighborhood Protection Plan* and your *Chain of Leadership* carefully to create an organization that each member can believe in and will abide by without questioning instructions and orders.

Each Group Member must feel a pride in the *NPP* and feel that their job is an important part of it, rather than feeling that they are just a cog in the machinery, when taking orders.

Leadership is vital to the effort of the *NPP* being successful. *One person* will be in charge of your *NPP* and must delegate responsibilities to form and control the *NPP*. Your *Neighborhood Protection Plan* will be only as strong as the weakest link, so each person must also carry out their job and do so to the best of their ability and without question. But *one person* must lead.

We provide the following procedure of qualifying leader candidates so you can hopefully find *this one person* capable to lead your *NPP*. This procedure is not bulletproof. Some people who haven't had either military or law enforcement training have a natural aptitude for calm and effective leadership.

We've found some car mechanics that should have been doctors and some doctors that shouldn't have been working on people or cars… so formal qualifications and degrees sometimes mean little.

You may want to look to a law enforcement type if you have no military experienced people. Business executives may be great with helping organize and could make great leaders, but for this discussion you must concentrate on people with military tactical and perimeter defense planning experience.

Even though this sounds discriminatory to those who haven't had military or law enforcement training, it's the procedure we recommend. Your elected leaders, if they're good, will immediately spot others with leadership and tactical capabilities.

Understand one issue about Leaders. Leaders are usually people who are dominant individuals. That being said, you do not want an 'Alpha Male or Female.' Yes, you must consider women as having leadership capabilities.

There are some women in military service that are better leaders than their male counterparts. But Alpha male or females usually make decisions without consultation, compassion or consideration for the group. *Avoid them.*

You need a person who is calm under pressure, knows their responsibilities and can make a decision preferably with consultation… but can make a critical decision by themselves and then sticks to their decision. You need someone with fairness and compassion who won't ask others to do what he or she would not do themselves.

5-Verify the Leader's Experience

Go by this documentation process to verify candidates…

- The DD 214 (Defense Department Military Discharge document) or a DD 214 with a DD 215 Amendment will prove military experience.
- Every law enforcement officer will have a POST (Police Officer's Standards Training) Certificate for their law enforcement training certification.

The group must choose their *Primary and Secondary NPP Leaders* by choosing with *proof of experience*, be that previous military service or law enforcement or both.

We recommend that *experience* be the criteria through which you first compile your pool of neighbors from which the neighborhood will ***elect*** the *Primary and Secondary NPP Leaders*. This experience should be verified by your group. Don't take the word of a person vouching for their own experience or another's.

Don't be shy, ask for this proof. Your group will be relying heavily on this person's expertise and experience.

Don't find out the hard way during a *Crisis* that this person is *"A Story"* from neighbors and friends circulated in a bar that put an unqualified person in charge of you. Both Authors have run into people that profess to have been Special Operations Soldiers who, *upon being asked pointed questions… proves that they were absolutely not.* This type of person would be a disaster in leadership.

A Marine… is a Marine… is a Marine… *wrong*. Understand that there is a 'support' side to every branch of service. Does a cook in the Marine Corps have combat and tactics training experience?

Maybe so… but probably not as much as a 0311 Marine Rifleman. A Marine Cook has gone through the same basic training as the Marine Rifleman but their advanced training and the experiences of their enlistment are much different.

Look for combat experience or tactical training schools on the DD214. You don't want a 'Remington Raider' (named after the typewriter that was on the desk that they sat at their entire military service time) leading you, but having some training in tactics is better than nothing.

Chances are that you will have multiple qualified leaders. However once you arrive at the decision of who will be your Leader, keep foremost the qualifications and experience of others. The person in charge of your group will probably put those qualified and experienced people in other leadership positions.

Verify these people and choose your leaders *but once you have chosen, rely on your Leader absolutely* in time of *Crisis*… lawlessness knows no governance by vote or rights… people pursuing a lawless path intent on harming those of your group will be brutal. This requires all in your group to be cohesive and follow your leaders and their orders to the 'T'.

A note to former military and law enforcement people... If you have been elected the *Primary NPP Leader* or *Secondary NPP Leader*, realize your *NPP's* success depends on your Group Members, most of whom have probably never had any military training… so don't expect them to act like Army Rangers.

> ***Group Members** are each and every person who is taking part in this plan within the Protective Perimeter area of your Neighborhood Protection Plan and Extended Family and Friends.*

Leaders must work with them and *train with them* to teach them the basics. Leaders must remember that they went through months of tactics training or POST training to learn what they know and that *they* got 'wrapped around the axel' more than once in the process.

These leaders are the people you must rely on to setup and train the rest of your group in firearms, tactics and determining this book's information and applying it to your *Neighborhood Protection Plan (NPP).*

5-Your Second Meeting

Elect your Primary and Secondary NPP Leaders. The *Primary NPP Leader*, working with the *Secondary NPP Leader* will choose all other positions of leadership and evaluate and assign duties and positions to all other Group Members.

> *Hold your Second Meeting and vote on your Primary and Secondary NPP Leaders.*
>
> *Elect your Primary and Secondary NPP Leaders and be certain that the Primary NPP Leader approves of the Secondary NPP Leader.*

At this point Mr., Mrs. or Miss *Self Starter*, and you *Moderators*… you have done your primary job and *we congratulate you*. You can assist the *Primary and Secondary NPP Leaders* in organizing your *Neighborhood Protection Plan.*

Help, but don't interfere with your Leader's duties or decisions. The sooner you start preparing... the sooner you'll be ready.

Moderators must stay in touch with your NPP Group Members with periodic phone calls, email announcements, visits and somewhat regular meetings. Do not hold too many meetings... people tire of them.

Have a periodic block party and get to know each other. Introduce your Extended Family and Friends to the Group Members. America is not a land cursed with the 'Tribal Mindset'... we have a melting pot of all different people of the world... a periodic get together is one thing that made us great!

Use the organization of your Neighborhood Protection Plan to get to know your neighbors, create harmony and a better neighborhood in which to live.

You have to organize your Neighborhood Protection Plan and Group Members in advance of a Crisis.

A *Crisis* on hand will be in itself overwhelming without trying to accomplish who will lead and what you will do. You probably will not even have the time to complete the basics of your *NPP* before there is trouble.

History is full of examples of societies and groups failing to succeed in self preservation because of procrastination and lack of preparedness.

5-Try to work through your current Neighborhood Watch

In metropolitan areas that currently have them in place... we propose your *Neighborhood Protection Plan* to work alongside your Neighborhood Watch Program if you have one in place.

Neighborhood Watch Programs cooperate closely with the police. A neighbor is usually appointed Neighborhood Watch Captain. This person liaisons directly with your police department and informs each neighbor of the program and procedures.

The fact is confirmed that police departments are unable to completely protect their citizens during *Normal Civility* as evidenced by the creation of the Neighborhood Watch Program. Police departments need the citizen's assistance or this program wouldn't exist.

The *Neighborhood Protection Plan* is simply an extension of the Neighborhood Watch Program *only when there are area disasters or civil unrest.*

Neighborhood Watch Programs have an established chain of command and a liaison police officer within the department. Neighborhood Watch Programs work well when your police department can respond in reasonable time during Normal Civility.

During disaster and civil unrest when police cannot respond in a reasonable time or respond at all, you need a different program. One that you control directly and that is specific to your area.

The Neighborhood Watch Captain may have no law enforcement or military experience but is just an enthusiastic volunteer.

In that case our hat is off to him or her for their dedication in helping to make your neighborhood safe.

That being said, you need someone who can institute the recommendations of this book. Someone with a military or law enforcement background.

It is critical that the leader of your *NPP* be verified for experience as we state in this book.

Neighborhood Watch Program advisory sign

The worst case scenario is that if the current Neighborhood Watch Captain is not qualified, that he or she works in conjunction with the *Neighborhood Protection Plan* qualified leaders that have been chosen by their neighbors.

The fact that thousands of Neighborhood Watch Programs have been successfully organized proves that organizing a *Neighborhood Protection Plan* can be done. Neighborhood Watch Programs are a valuable tool in deterring crime. These programs send a message to criminals that intrusion into your neighborhood will be reported by neighbors and police will be alerted.

During civil unrest, one person's home can be easily attacked and could end in the beating or death of the homeowners and the looting of their home. Success by lawless elements at one home is contagious and will quickly focus their attention to your home and others in the neighborhood.

If a neighborhood has several families visibly organized to collectively resist criminals, the strategic and tactical advantage for these lawless elements becomes enormously more complicated. Most times criminals take one look and go elsewhere. This alone will not be a deterrent if there is a *Long Term Crisis* or *A Failure of Civility* though.

5-'Political Correctness' in your police department and forming your *Neighborhood Protection Plan* without them

We must advise you that the difference between 'Officers on the Street' and the ones running law enforcement agencies are profoundly different. The longer officers are away from the daily operations and 'hands on' experience of working the streets, the more most of them become 'management' and insulated from the reality of what's happening in their city.

Many of these same law enforcement agency bureaucrats also become, for the most part, 'Politically Correct'. This makes them very biased towards any citizen group organizing to use threat, force or violence to protect themselves, regardless of the fact that their own police department cannot protect its citizens.

They will mention the 'liability' of the city or its police department endorsing your *NPP*. But it's more so the concealed macho attitude of *"We don't need you... we protect the citizens!"* even though they can't. These types consider your protection their domain *only and the liability issue is used as an excuse.*

The Authors point out that 'Political Correctness' is really 'Tyranny by Politeness'. However, once you confront a outwardly pleasant and courteous *Politically Correct* person, you will find they are the furthest from polite, respectful or courteous that a person can be. They are Doctor Jekyll and Mister Hyde personalities or in layman terms they're two faced like most politicians.

This *Political Correctness* can filter down even to sergeant ranks in patrol commands. Your Neighborhood Watch police department liaison may even be *Politically Correct*... so could your Neighborhood Watch Captain.

Crime is very high in metropolitan areas during even *Normal Civility* and law enforcement is unable to be where needed when needed to protect the citizenry. The street police officer will tell you that point blank and the Authors know this from their experience.

A further fact is that many of these law enforcement 'management people' *are against Gun Rights by the law abiding citizen simply intent on protecting themselves and their families.*

They may ***say*** that they respect lawful ownership of firearms and simply want them out of criminal's hands, ***but make no mistake***, they would just as soon have no firearms ownership or possession by *anyone*, save the ownership, possession and control of their officer's weapons entirely by their police department.

If they had their way, they'd leave John Q Citizen trying to protect Joan, the kids and his home in his birthday suit. Joe wouldn't even have a baseball bat... he'd just be standing there in the nick.

If you ask the patrolman in the street, he will 'off the record' inform you that he respects law abiding citizens for defending themselves... even with a firearm. It is both Authors' experience that the 'Officer on the Street' knows that they can't be everywhere a threat occurs and especially at the immediate time of the threat. They know that it is up to the citizen to protect themselves until law enforcement can get there to deal with the problem.

So… don't expect you police department's cooperation… expect their objection to your *Neighborhood Protection Plan.* If the police department liaison to your Neighborhood Watch Program or your Neighborhood Watch Captain disagrees with your *Neighborhood Protection Plan*, it is most likely the influence of 'Political Correctness' from them or people above them in the department.

If there is no Neighborhood Watch in your area or if your police department will not cooperate, by pass them and set up your *Neighborhood Protection Plan.* DO NOT let your police department of city officials talk you out of setting up your *Neighborhood Protection Plan.*

Form your *NPP with* or *without* your police department's backing. *Form your Neighborhood Protection Plan* ***without*** *the help of your Neighborhood Watch Program if your police department objects to your plan or refuses to cooperate.*

As long as you own firearms legally, handle weapons responsibly and within the law and do not 'Obstruct a Public Right of Way' or cause a disturbance during *Normal Civility* when practicing your *NPP* training exercises, you are acting within your rights… *and authorities can do absolutely nothing to stop you… they have to obey your rights.*

If a *Crisis* begins and your police department has problems maintaining order, activate your *NPP*. You will find in times of civil unrest that *they will want you to control your area* responsibly regardless of their attitude towards your *Neighborhood Protection Plan.*

Your County Sheriff also has to obey your legal rights. As far as local law enforcement goes, be aware that your ***County Sheriff is the ultimate*** *law enforcement power in your County and his authority is supreme even over Federal Government agencies.*

Some larger cities have centralized 'safe zones' for law enforcement, emergency services and public safety members' families. But you still may want to advise your County Sheriff of your *Neighborhood Protection Plan* and offer safe haven for the department members' families.

Offer to shelter law enforcement, emergency services, doctors and nurses' families, National Guard member families, firemen and public safety member's families to enable them to do their jobs without worrying about their family's safety.

We suggest that to do so you move their family into your Watch Center building or a nearby building. This will reassure every law enforcement officer, public safety officer, fireman, doctor, nurse and emergency worker and all hospital personnel that they can do their job for the community knowing that their families are safe, fed and protected against what they are dealing with in the community.

But first you must do a simple evaluation of your neighborhood…

5- *Primary and Secondary NPP Leaders* evaluation of the *Primary Neighborhood Protection Plan* Location

Your *Primary NPP Location* will be the neighborhood that you live in or the one which you organize. However, just because this is your neighborhood doesn't make it suitable without asking yourself some questions first. There are some *Critical Life Supplies and Services* and other issues that you have to evaluate before you determine if your neighborhood will be your *Primary Neighborhood Protection Plan Location.*

You must plan your *NPP* for a *Long Term Crisis.* The most important of the two items of *Critical Life Supplies and Services* are food and water. Water is difficult and complicated to transport and store. Your *NPP* requires a renewable water source nearby or a water bore hole or open well to be dug. *You cannot rely on community wells with pumps, municipal water supplies, rain water or snow for your supply.*

Questions the *Primary and Secondary NPP Leaders* must answer first before proceeding to use your neighborhood for your *Primary NPP Location*

- ***Is there a water source?*** *You have to evaluate this first.* Read our information on *water* in *Chapter 12* ***first*** to help you evaluate this issue. Water sounds like an inconsequential item until... you don't have it... have to transport it... and have to make it suitable for consumption or hygiene use.

  Without a water bore hole or open well inside your NNP or a water source close by you do not have a sustainable neighborhood for a *Long Term Neighborhood Protection Plan* and must look at another area. This is especially difficult in metropolitan areas. You need a lake, reservoir, river, stream or other *water source that you can depend on year 'round.*

  We warn you not to base the ***long term sustainability*** *of your NPP on rain water or snow being sufficient.*

  You cannot depend on rain water or snow to provide you with a sufficient amount of water in most areas. Rainfall can be infrequent and it takes an incredible amount of snow to make a gallon of water. Water is difficult and complicated to transport long distances and store. Any water source too far away will be impractical.

  The following exercise *is just one* of the many issues you will have to calculate and give thought to so your entire *Neighborhood Protection Plan* is practical, feasible, sustainable and *proactive.*

Start doing calculations and thinking over issues like this…

Even though this exercise relates to water… we suggest that every aspect of your NPP be put to the test of an exercise like this.

How do you determine how far away is too far away for water? Haul some water! Do a *water run*. You can't rely on vehicles operating. Have a Group Member transport water in containers for that distance because that's how you'll probably be hauling your water… on foot.

Use your *average* physically fit person, not the best fit. Keep in mind the *Triple One Water Rule…* that each Group Member equals ***One Person* that needs *One Gallon* of water for *One Day.***

This is the *minimum* amount of water each person needs daily without consideration for rehydrating foods, bathing, toilet hygiene, tending to medical needs, etc. You really need to count on *one and one half* to *two gallons* per person per day being your minimum requirement for comfort, but we'll use one gallon for this exercise.

Water weighs approximately 8 pounds per gallon… which means if a group member carries 5 one gallon containers in a backpack… that's 40 pounds of water per Group Member plus their weapon and ammunition. That amount of water will provide the minimum for 5 people for one day.

This means that 20% of your Group Members will be transporting water and another 20% of your Group Members will be along to provide armed protection if you are doing this properly.

Also keep in mind that if there's a blizzard, rainstorm, freezing cold or scorching hot day, you will still have to haul your water supply.

This also means that 40% of your Group Members will be consuming more calories of food to accomplish this absolutely necessary task. If you have plenty of food to go around this will not be an issue… but if you don't, it will.

Even basic movement when the human body is undernourished is overwhelming except for the most physically fit… but even those people will eventually have exhaustion problems.

Further, making anything routine in a combat environment is dangerous. Making guard changes at the same time, conducting Perimeter Patrols at the same time and on the same route or going in the same direction are dangerous… your enemy can predict your next movement because you have revealed it to him in advance… like your daily *water run*.

This is especially dangerous where you're outside and away from your *NPP* Protective Perimeter. Issues like transporting items such as water over the same route and doing it daily will certainly get your *NPP* attacked or your Group Members on *water run* ambushed by *Intruders*.

If your Group Members are uniformly and relatively physically fit they can make a round trip in less than two hours, assuming that the terrain is flat and unobstructed.

Your Group Members should be able to make two or more trips a day and with rationing of your supply can build and maintain a water reserve for your *NPP*… but you must start with a reserve.

During the time that your Group Members are outside and away from the NPP on the water run, your defenses may be weak and vulnerable.

Do you have enough remaining people to defend the NPP?

Anytime *you go outside your NPP for a task other than patrol or reconnaissance you must provide the people performing that task with a 'Guard Element' whose job is specifically to provide security for those going to fill cars with gasoline, forage for food, hunt for game, etc.*

So how far away from your NPP should your outside water source be?

The Authors answer is no more than ***one mile maximum****.*

The above exercise *is just one* of the many issues you will have to calculate and give thought to so your entire *Neighborhood Protection Plan* is practical, feasible, sustainable and *proactive.*

Continuing: Questions the *Primary and Secondary NPP Leaders* must answer first before proceeding to use your neighborhood for your *Primary NPP Location…*

- ***Heating and cooking.*** This is not such a huge issue with Low Rise Residential Areas, but it is with a High Rise Residential Building. Most Low Rise Residential Area *NPPs* in winter weather areas have wood as a fuel source in areas surrounding the *NPP* and most homes in these areas have basements. People can survive most sub zero weather with sleeping bags and blankets in basements and cooking can be done outside… but still within the *NPP* Protective Perimeter… not so in High Rise Buildings.
- ***Are your neighbors able to defend?*** *You must evaluate this.* Are the majority of your neighbors *Dependent Persons* who need medicines and medical supplies to sustain their

life or are invalid? The fitness level of your neighbors must be sufficient enough to fight with firearms and to train by the tactics in this book and fulfill the duties outlined here.

Each armed person who is involved as a Group Member must be able to walk the area of your neighborhood and man a Guard Post. We will outline the requirements of Guard Posts in *Chapter 6, Area Tactical Protection for a* Low Rise Residential Neighborhood.

- ***Do your neighbors have weapons?*** *You have to ask each this question.* Is there at least one pistol, one rifle or one shotgun per household, preferably per person? If they don't have, can't afford, or won't have firearms, you again must look for another neighborhood.
- ***Do neighbors have the financial capability?*** *You have to ask them.* Are they able to buy and store food, water, and the limited medical supplies and ammunition for each individual weapon and share in a small neighborhood cooperative protection fund for the communications and specialized equipment needed?
- ***Your home is your home… but?*** Is your neighborhood defensible? *You have to estimate this by the guidelines in this book.* You have to evaluate what kind of existing Protective Perimeter you have versus how much effort will have to be made in constructing defenses to make it defensible.

  Is your house bullet resistant or is it like a cardboard box? What are the houses constructed of… stucco, brick, wood…. what type of roof… can your roof or house be easily set on fire? Do you have block walls or fences around your home or no walls at all?

  Are there great distances between a small numbers of homes? Is there a multi story building or anything of height next to your neighborhood from which *Intruders* can shoot down into your neighborhood or observe your *NPP* strengths and weaknesses?

  Are there too many underground sewers, utility and water drainage corridors which *Intruders* can use to get into your *NPP* unseen from the outside? Are there too many to block off or monitor?
- ***Excess supplies and equipment.*** Do you have a location within or close by outside your *NPP* where you can hide or bury your excess supplies and equipment beforehand to retrieve at a later date if you have to make an *Emergency NPP Relocation.*

5-Your image to your neighborhood, the public and law enforcement

As one saying goes… *"First impressions are everything!"* In regards to your *Neighborhood Protection Plan* it means your image. How are people in the neighborhood, the public and law enforcement going to perceive you through your attitude, dress and activities?

How will law enforcement and the public react to you if you're running around with military weapons while dressed in combat multi-cam clothing during training exercises or if a simple *Area Emergency* has taken place? Use common sense and *'dress for the occasion.'*

As another saying by Mark Twain goes… *"Clothes make the man!"* How you're dressed is critical as to how you're perceived by others and how they will react to you… this includes law enforcement. If there has been a tornado and you have a simple *Area Emergency* but you've activated your entire *NPP* to an unrealistic level of *'High Alert'* and are dressed looking like your going into battle you're overreacting and not using common sense.

Dress for the level of the *Crisis* !! *Review our recommendations to dress according posted in the areas of 'Low Alert', 'Mid Alert' or 'High Alert'* status of your *NPP*. Use common sense!

One of the Authors, being a 'cop on the street' for years, knows that after a disaster or emergency the reaction of officers would be totally different in the following scenarios…

A. The police officers pull up to a barricade manned by Group Members dressed in combat fatigues sporting long guns and pistols. This first contact would probably not go well. Why? Your law enforcement is patrolling and most likely responding to calls and the emergency at hand… you don't have the justification to dress or take your *NPP* to that level. If the emergency is rioting and looting… this first contact may be different.

B. If these same officers pull into that same entrance of that same neighborhood and see two men in civilian clothes loitering near that entrance with shotguns leaning against the wall or loose clothing that they suspect conceal weapons they would probably look on this as citizen's protecting their neighborhood. They would probably ask for identification, question what you're doing… and drive on.

The Authors' reactions as members of the public would be similar in the above situations… how you're dressed and how respectful you are would definitely affect our first contact. We would not react well to a combat clothing clad 'Rambo type' ordering us around with a weapon. Be courteous to the guy coming in to visit his parents.

Law enforcement and the public will react accordingly to you based on four things…

- The clothing you're wearing.
- Displaying weapons.
- The attitude you have.
- The Protective Perimeter defensive devices you've erected.

You must remain polite to all and respectful of the rights of those in the neighborhood and *Outsiders always*. Until you get to the *'Mid Alert'* or *'High Alert'* level of a *Crisis* when most civilities will have been discarded and law enforcement is unable to assist you… act accordingly. *But even then* maintain a respect for the rights of others… *always.*

Rule of Thumb. *Your activity level and control of access to your NPP area* ***must go up…***

…as law enforcement's ability to respond to and maintain control of your area ***goes down.***

When training, be considerate of the neighborhoods surrounding your *NPP* and Non-Participant neighbors within your *NPP* area. Understand that the noise you make and the disturbances you create will not be as welcome to some as much as they are acceptable to Group Members.

5-*NPP* Group Member job duties and capabilities

The following are all Group Members but divided into different groups determined primarily by the criteria above.

The following is a description of NPP Job Duties, what capabilities each person must have and the categories the Primary and Secondary NPP Leaders must assign each NPP Group Member to…

- ***Primary NPP Leader.*** This is you. You have been chosen *Primary NPP Leader* by your proven military or law enforcement experience and leadership as outlined in this chapter. You have been elected by the Group Members. You are the person directing and organizing the *NPP* and conducting the operation of it when activated. You must have leadership and people skills and must not be a dictator. You can perform dual duty as an *Alpha* or *Bravo Guardians.*

- ***Secondary NPP Leader-***This is you also. You are the *Secondary NPP Leader* chosen by your proven military or law enforcement experience and leadership as outlined in this chapter. You have been elected by the Group Members and approved by the *Primary NPP Leader.*

  You assist the *Primary NPP Leader* in organizing and assist with the operation of your *NPP* when activated. You must have leadership and people skills, must not be a dictator and must be able to work smoothly and closely with the *Primary NPP Leader*. You can perform dual duty as an *Alpha* or *Bravo Guardians.*

- ***LOP Guardians-***High elevation Listening Observation Post (LOP) positions. Group Members who are very fit and healthy people with excellent eyesight, hearing, evaluation, communication and observation skills.

- ***Inside Marksmen-***High elevation Marksmen positions ***Inside*** the Protective Perimeter. Group Members who are very fit and healthy people with excellent eyesight, hearing, with excellent marksmanship and observation skills.

- ***Outflanker Marksmen***-High elevation Marksmen positions ***outside*** the Protective Perimeter. Group Members who are very fit and healthy people with excellent eyesight, hearing, with excellent marksmanship and observation skills.
- ***Alpha Guardians***-Group Members who are physically and mentally capable of manning Guard Posts, handling firearms, gardening, hunting and doing defense construction work. Generally very fit people who can lift considerable weight and do hard work.

  Alpha Guardians can fulfill the duties of *Patrol Guardians, Roving Guardians, Response Guardians, Runner Guardians* and *Reserve Guardians* as outlined in the next section.
- ***Bravo Guardians***-Group Members who are mentally capable of manning Guard Posts, handling firearms *but have some physical limitations.*
- ***Runner Guardians***-Group Members who are communications runners and deliver supplies to Guard Posts. Some of these can be teenagers.
- ***Reserve Guardians***-Off duty and replacement Group Members for those who get sick in the positions of *LOP Guardians, Inside Marksmen, Outflanker Marksmen* positions, *Alpha Guardians, Bravo Guardians* and any other duty position needing replacement.
- ***Caretaker/Watch Center Guardians***-Group Members who have numerous physical limitations and are not capable of walking the area of the *NPP* for long periods or manning a Guard Post, but are mentally capable and could work in a Watch Center capacity of communications or monitoring supplies.

  These Group Members can watch children, prepare meals and assist with limited medical care. These can be children under the age of 14 and older persons who are infirm but capable of doing limited duties respective of their age and capabilities.
- ***Dependent Persons***-Children under the age of 14, people with Alzheimer's disease and the mentally deficient. Persons who are on psychiatric medicines that would render them unable to function reliably if these medicines were not available. You're not going to know this because they're not going to tell you.

  This will become apparent to all if certain *Catastrophic Events* occur and their psychiatric medicines are exhausted. Other persons who are... for lack of a more pleasant description... Terminal Persons... those whose lives would end if medical supplies and medicines were suddenly unavailable.
- ***Fire Fighting Guardians***-This has to be all Group Members who are physically fit enough to fight any fires within your *NPP* or that threaten your *NPP* from the outside. Depending on the numbers of Group Members you have, in a worse case situation fire fighting may have to be left to the older, less physically fit people.

Your *NPP* should be set up so the *Primary NPP Leader* and *Secondary NPP Leader* are *only one person positions* even though each may have Junior Leaders. Depending on the size of your group you can have numerous people filling in the other positions, but you must have enough to accomplish the tasks for the Sections outlined in this chapter.

Primary and Secondary NPP Leaders can *and should* act in 'dual duty' in the positions of guard just as the Group Members do. This is how a good leader knows 'what's going on in the trenches… by getting into the trenches'. The following chart is based on the fact that *Primary and Secondary NPP Leaders* are performing 'dual duty'.

Guard Posts are stationary positions inside but around the Protective Perimeter of the *NPP* including the Entry/Exit Control Point which must have a minimum of two guards at all times.

Patrol Guardians do walking patrol checks around the ***outside*** of the Protective Perimeter unless your *NPP* is a High Rise Building. If you're in a pinch for Group Members, this can be the double duty of the *Roving Guardians.*

Roving Guardians conduct walking guard ***inside*** the Protective Perimeter and escort Group Members to their positions during changes in Guard Posts. If you're in a pinch for Group Members, this can be the double duty of the *Patrol Guardians.*

Response Guardians are the 'Rapid Response Team' to reinforce a perimeter during an attack. If you're in a pinch for Group Members, this can be another duty of the *Patrol* and *Roving Guardians.*

The Watch Center can be maintained by off duty Group Members who are *Alpha* or *Bravo Guardians* not on duty. If there is an attack, one Group Member must remain in the Watch Center to monitor two-way radios and direct the *Runner Guardians.*

Don't ignore the Korean Veteran who is wheel chair bound. Some military veterans with disabilities can be your best *Bravo Guardians* if given a duty such as manning a Guard Post. *Extended Family and Friends* that plan on being at your *NPP* may increase the number of *Alpha* and *Bravo Guardians,* but you can't include them as part of your evaluation plan because you don't know if they will be able to complete the trip to your *NPP.*

5- The *minimum* number of people needed for different types of *NPP* premises

The size of your NPP is determined mostly by…

- The number of inhabitants of your neighborhood who will be Group Members… and
- The size and characteristics of your Protective Perimeter regarding the number of Guard and other positions you need.

The larger your defended area becomes... the more your defensive issues multiply exponentially. You need the minimum number of Group Members we list in the chart below for the particular type of *NPP* premises you have. More Group Members are better.

Minimum number of Group Members required for different types of Neighborhood Protection Plan premises

Per Single Suburban, Ranch or Farm House NPP		
Guard Post	*One Guard Post inside house*	*3*
Outflanker Marksmen and LOP	*Outflanker Marksmen and LOP combined*	*3*
Watch Center	*All Alpha/Bravo Guardians run Watch Center*	
Response Guardians	*All Alpha/Bravo Guardians*	
Total number of Group Members required for Single House NPP		*6*

Per High Rise Building Single Floor NPP with Two Entrances		
Guard Posts	*For one floor with two entrances*	*6*
Roving Guardians on floor	*Patrolling living units and corridors*	*2*
Watch Center	*All Alpha/Bravo Guardians run Watch Center*	
Response Guardians	*All Alpha/Bravo Guardians*	
Caretaker Guardians	*Can also help run Watch Center*	*1*
Total number of Group Members - Single Floor NPP with two entrances		*9*

Per High Rise Building NPP		
Guard Posts	*One* Entry/Exit Control Point - *2 guards*	6
Outflanker Marksmen, LOP, Guard	*One position on adjoining building*	6
Marksmen Positions	*Two sides of the building*	4
LOP Guardians	*Two sides of the building*	4
Roving Guardians	*Patrolling building and basement*	*2*

Watch Center	*All Alpha/Bravo Guardians run Watch Center*	
Response Guardians	*All Alpha/Bravo Guardians*	
Caretaker Guardians	*Can also help run Watch Center*	2
Runner Guardians	*Must be the fittest*	2
Total number of Group Members required for High Rise Building NPP		*26*

Per Low Rise Neighborhood		
Guard Post	*One* Entry/Exit Control Point - *2 guards*	6
Guard Posts	*3 additional perimeter sides*	9
Outflanker Marksmen and LOP	*One combined position on house outside NPP*	4
Marksmen and LOP Position	*One combined position on house inside NPP*	4
Patrol/Roving Guardians	*Two 2 man teams inside and outside patrol*	4
Watch Center	*All Alpha/Bravo Guardians run Watch Center*	
Response Guardians	*All Alpha/Bravo Guardians*	
Caretaker Guardians	*Can also help run Watch Center*	2
Runner Guardians	*Must be the fittest*	2
Total number of Group Members required - Low Rise Residential NPP		*31*

The above is our recommendation for ***the minimum number of people*** *needed for different types of Neighborhood Protection Plan depending on the premise type. You will have to* ***use Group Members in multiple role capacities****.*

Many Group Members spread out over a huge area will not create a realistic *NPP*. The more Group Members you have who are *Alpha Guardians*, generally the more homes or living units you can feasibly defend, dependent on the area your *NPP* covers.

Defensive perimeters are tremendously weakened if they are stretched over ***too large an area to respond to*** *and/or* ***too sparsely manned…*** *this type of perimeter is not easily defensible.*

You've had your meetings, elected your *Primary and Secondary NPP Leaders* and your leaders have evaluated the neighborhood as an effective *Primary Neighborhood Protection Plan Location*... or it is not.

You must <u>*estimate*</u> *whether your NPP size will be sufficient until you get further into forming your plan.*

Let's assume you're intent on forming a Neighborhood Protection Plan where you are and proceed.

5-What size should your *NPP* be?

Your *NPP* is a 24 hour, 7 days a week entity. Think of it as that... just like milking cows every day... but it's *all day*... every day.

Of the above positions most of your Group Members will have to be *Alpha Guardians*... fit enough to fulfill the duties of *LOP Guardians, Outflanker Marksmen, Inside Marksmen* and *Patrol/Roving/Response Guardians.*

You can get by with *Bravo Guardians* in Protective Perimeter Guard Posts and the Watch Center.

For each Guard Post you need 3 people. These will be on 2 hour shifts, 24/7. *Chapter 6, Area Tactical Protection for a* Low Rise Residential Neighborhood will describe in detail what we recommend for guard schedules and is where we will explain why you need the number of Group Members we advise you to have.

In a neighborhood of homes with four sides to your *NPP* Protective Perimeter, you will need a minimum of 4 Guard Posts including the Entry/Exit Control Point. You may need more, dependent on the length and the characteristics of your *NPP* Protective Perimeter.

You must have Overlapping Fields of View and Interlocking Fields of Fire for your entire Protective Perimeter around your *NPP* from each Guard Post.

The physical size of your *NPP* should be no larger than it takes a person to walk quickly the longest distance inside your Protective Perimeter from one side to the other with ease. Without radios you must be able to hear voice communications or see hand signals.

During a *Crisis*, members may have to rush from one side to the opposite side to re-enforce a perimeter area and to move carrying equipment at the same time. This is why your *NPP* Watch Center should be centrally located and your *Response Guardians* stationed there... they theoretically have the same distance to move to any area of the Protective Perimeter to re-enforce that perimeter.

Other factors come into play in determining a feasible NPP size…

- The availability of **communication** from all Guard Posts to your Watch Center. If you don't have two-way radios, you will have to rely on voice communications, hand signals (daylight only) or runners. You cannot rely on cellular phones and land line phones working.
- The number of armed and **capable people** your *NPP* has to guard the length of your perimeter 24 hours a day, 7 days per week.
- The **physical size of the area** that you are defending. The physical length and width of your *NPP.*
- The **type of terrain** of your area.
- The **climate** and current weather of your area.
- The **type of Catastrophic Event** as to how it *has* and *will* affect your Group Members.
- The **physical and mental condition of your Group Members**… *NPP* Leaders must constantly evaluate this.

Make sure you utilize women to their best capability. Women can make excellent defensive Group Members and if armed and trained can be as capable a defender as a man.

If it's necessary, you may have to break your *NPP* into areas by block or street, each having their own subordinate leaders, *Chain of Leadership* and each having their own Watch Center Section, Communications/Intelligence Section and Supply Section functioning under the overall direction of the *Primary NPP Leader* for the common good of the entire area.

By having your *NPP* compartmentalized into smaller areas, if the entire area is too big, your *NPP* will be manageable, information will flow quickly between leaders or *NPP*s and movement of defenders within an *NPP* will be effective. If a *Crisis* develops or *A Failure of Civility* occurs and you find manpower shortages cause your Protective Perimeter to be vulnerable, *immediately* reconfigure it.

5-Classifying your Group Members

The *Primary and Secondary NPP Leaders* must review each Group Member's completed ***NPP Group Member Information Form.*** **You can make more copies of the form** from the back of this book if necessary.

To know how many ready, willing and able Group Members you have, the Primary and Secondary NPP Leaders need to classify the Group Members of the neighborhood by their personal estimate and from the information which will be on each Group Member's NPP Group Member Information Form…

- ***Leadership skills.*** This has been done for the first two positions by your election as *Primary and Secondary NPP Leaders*. The others are the Watch Center Third Leader, Communication/Intelligence Fourth Leader, Supply Fifth Leader, Medical Sixth Leader and Junior Leaders which will be chosen by the *Primary and Secondary NPP Leaders.*
- ***Firearms proficiency.*** You won't know proficiency accurately at this point but you can get an idea from talking to people. Most won't brag about something they know they will have to prove at the firing range if the *Moderators* advise them of this beforehand. However, the Authors' recommend that you take people individually or in pairs to the range to see what each knows. Keep the number small for safety. Question them about safety first and then observe their firing proficiency.
- ***Specialized Training.*** What military, law enforcement, firearms, medical, radio communications, electronics or electrical training, fire fighting and fire prevention, food storage and preparations, construction experience, nutrition and cooking expertise, gardening-fishing-hunting knowledge, vehicle repair knowledge or training, chemistry education or training does each Group Member have?
- ***Physical capabilities.*** This can almost be determined by sight but you must inquire of each person if they have physical problems of any kind and how severe they are.
- ***Mental capabilities and attitude.*** This is obvious with most people and will become more apparent as you interact and train. As the Bible says… "The meek will inherit the earth." However, that maybe in the afterlife and you don't want them taking you with them prematurely. You also do not want 'Rambo types' manning guard positions as both this type of person and the 'meek and faint of heart' will cause problems and grief for your *NPP*.
- ***Medical needs.*** You need to know who has life threatening issues if medical services or medicines are not available.
- ***Age.*** For people *too old or younger than 14 years of age*. The Authors have seen battle hardened children of 9 and 10… however we detest the use of children in conflict. You may want to set a higher age limit than what we recommend. If *A Failure of Civility* occurs and is protracted, you will eventually be using children based on their physical capabilities regardless of age.

5-Worst case scenarios in forming a *NPP*, farms and ranches

What do you do if…?

There are only a small number of neighbors for a large area to defend, you are in a small rural town or you are on a rural farm or ranch.

Understand that many of these small towns are not that far from large metropolitan areas and roving gangs, once they have looted everything in the city, will travel in search of necessities… they will eventually make their way out of the cities and will show up on the doorstep of these towns.

Answer… Consolidate as many people as you can get into the most defensible house or houses in one area or the most defensible farm or ranch building of in the best defensible area. A small town is just a *Neighborhood Protection Plan* expanded… hopefully with the encouragement and assistance of the city fathers and law enforcement.

A farm or ranch, even though remote, will sooner or later be attacked in force if *A Failure of Civility* occurs and especially if it becomes long term or permanent. Count on that.

Farmers and ranchers will need to band together in a common location, choosing the most defensible farm or ranch area to defend or move into their closest smaller town with an *NPP* program. You will need *Strength through Numbers*. Even the best trained Special Operations Soldier cannot defend as an individual.

If you decide to form a defense of your farm or ranch, this may require people to move into one or two homes or buildings that are the easiest to defend. Understand that you must have the *Strength through Numbers* to defend your house, farm or ranch… put the macho attitude aside… you cannot do it yourself.

If your NPP consists of one or two houses or buildings *it is critical that you employ as many Outflanker Marksmen as you can. Cover every possible approach area by which Intruders can attack your NPP house or building. Firing on attackers from 200 or 300 yards after they're near or at the front of a house and they can't determine where the fire is coming from is a powerful proactive tactical maneuver.*

Watch not to create Friendly Fire Incidents.

Friendly Fire Incidents *happen when the weapons fire of one or more Group Members kill or wound their own Group Members by accident.*

If your neighbors aren't interested in defending themselves and you still want to stay in your property, you can fortify your home and defend it. Consider this only if you have enough Group Members to adequately defend your home or homes. Find people that to the best of your knowledge and instinct you can trust.

The most defensible home or buildings can be simply a house, or houses, that are specifically heavily fortified and have the majority of your food, water, ammunition, and provisions. Preferably two houses or buildings constructed of brick or predominantly non-flammable materials should be heavily fortified that can give each other Supporting Fields of Fire.

5-Story-*"Riot!"*

"I was working swing shift and was still sleeping at 10:30 in the morning when the ringing of the bedside telephone took me out of my dreams. I was a police officer in a large metropolitan area."

"The frantic voice on the phone was my 'beloved' sergeant telling me... Get in here as soon as you can... all hell is breaking loose!"

"My normal shift didn't start until that afternoon but as my sergeant's ending statement was... "Until further notice, you're on 12 hour shifts! Get in here as soon as you can, Mark!"""

"I took a quick shower, shaved and sped to work. Upon arrival at my area station we were quickly briefed on what was transpiring. Riots, starting in another city had quickly spread to other cities, including ours."

***"Our city administration,** bowing to the 'political correctness' of semantics labeled this problem "Civil Disobedience". But to us, the street cops... we knew the truth... these were riots."*

"You would think that we'd have had the proper equipment for riots... but that wasn't our case. Once again, the people in charge who polish the seat of their chair with their pants had been so far removed for so long from real police work and 'the streets' that we had little equipment for riot control."

"Our department hadn't bought any mostly because no one in charge seemed to want to bring up the subject or riots...it was a sensitive topic that wouldn't help them with their career promotions."

***"Riot duty** to a police officer is unlike any other type of police work. We quickly found we had walked into the likes of a combat zone. During riots, like cockroaches... when the lights go out... the rioters come out. Only it was daylight outside and the rioters were out in force."*

"Our department was so swamped that we could only handle high priority calls... unless it was a life or death situation we just couldn't spare the officers to respond. Some areas of the city were much worse than others. Officers were pulled from the upscale areas to respond to the lower socio-economic neighborhoods... that's where it hit the hardest... and in the neighborhoods surrounding these areas."

"Many of the people involved in these riots were habitual criminals, troublemakers and hard core gang members who took the opportunity of police officers not being able to respond to settle old 'scores'. Shootings happened everywhere. We'd quickly load them into an ambulance and take them to the hospital or morgue... and we couldn't even process the crime scene."

"We didn't have enough shotguns, rifles, helmets and ammunition. Officers began to bring their own shotguns, rifles and ammunition from home despite the violation of

department policy in doing so. Thankfully, we had good radio communications... but without that we would have been sunk... totally ineffective."

***"I have never seen** such chaos and confusion in the upper police and city administration as I saw during these riots. The indecision was unbelievable. The decisions that were made by high ranking police officers were so bad that their decision was more than unbelievable."*

"These assessments and commands were given by those cowering in the command posts and totally detached from what was going on. They may have well as been on another planet. If it wouldn't have been for the cops in the streets, including a few sergeants and lieutenants, we would not have functioned at all as an effective deterrent."

"Case in point. We were given orders to block and stop a large mob of people. Block them from what!? They were simply loitering in the middle of an intersection. We piled into our eight patrol cars with multiple officers in each."

"Unfortunately the Captain in charge who was several miles away from the area of these loiterers ordered us down a road that landed us right into the middle of this fuming crowd. In the military's terms we had driven into a 'Kill Zone"."

"The bricks, blocks and anything else that could be thrown at us began to hit the cars in addition to them shooting holes through our police cars. I was in the second car and grabbed the radio microphone and yelled to the driver of the first car to "Punch it! Run them over if you have to... but get through that crowd!""

***"This was like most** of the incompetence of decision making during the riots. You can't command an action when removed from the reality of the situation. Few of the police administration went outside the command posts until the majority of rioting and looting was over... many of us suspected because they were in fear for their life."*

"One police administrator... himself fearful to go out on the street... relegated his ego to throwing his weight around threatening to fire people if they didn't hand out equipment he'd never purchased. We looked at each other wondering if he'd gone insane."

"Luckily one department member... who cared more for the officers on the front line than the administrators did... arranged to secure Kevlar helmets and flak jackets for us from the military. He also managed to get us an armored vehicle. He was one of the true unsung heroes of this riot who was never recognized for his efforts... most likely because his efforts would highlight and embarrass every department administrator's incompetence."

"The National Guard unit that had been called up by the Governor was confined to 'administration' duties by our department. The department hierarchy feared the liability of arming them and putting them out on the street would reflect on them if they used their weapons against the rioters. We were astounded at this decision as overwhelmed as we were with problems and manpower shortages of quelling and confining this outbreak of hostility."

"This was also the result of our police administrators confusion, lack of command authority and prevailing macho attitude of "Our department can handle this!" while not knowing the roof was about to fall in and these rioters were gaining strength and

organization to head downtown and to spread out across the city. The blank looks and lack of command decision from our department leadership did nothing to further the officer in the street's confidence."

"The adrenaline 'dump' was unbelievable and totally exhausting during this period. I collapsed in bed as soon as I got home and before I knew it the alarm clock was ringing and I was back on the 'front lines' witnessing the total lack of decency of people towards one another."

***"The number of beatings,** rapes, lootings, the amount of arson, the number of home invasions, murders and almost every other conceivable crime will never be known. Attempts were made to compile statistics and prosecute some people identified but very few were convicted. The 'City Fathers' and politicians wanted this smudge on the city "to just go away." As the saying goes... "People got away with murder!""*

"The mobs began by looting anything and everything. I found a line of shoes from the front door of one shoe store lootings that I responded to that looked like the proverbial 'cookie crumb trail' strung through the parking lot to where they'd jumped into their cars and sped off with their loot. What they couldn't carry off they burned. Businesses that had been around for decades were burned to the ground. The common picture of rioters carrying off TVs and electronics was a reality and everywhere. We didn't have time to pursue most of them."

"Then they spread out into the surrounding neighborhoods. Fire Fighters, who are usually respected by the public, were being shot at by the very neighbors of properties they were trying to save from fire. After the first day, firemen wouldn't go into many areas unless they were accompanied by police escorts. Even then they and the police officers were fired on by snipers."

***"Those shooters** who were not so concerned with us seeing them stood and fired at us, surrounded by and using the Cover of young children as shields, knowing we couldn't fire back for fear of hitting the children. When we tried to out flank these shooters, they simply crawled over walls and disappeared into the dark of night."*

"Most police officers are brave. Some aren't. This riot 'sorted out the men from the boys'. Some people just need to have a badge and gun to prove they're someone. The actions of those were disheartening. The remark was made by an officer at the onset of the riots that... "I didn't become a police office to get shot at!" He refused to go out 'on the line' or much outside our command post."

"Somewhere around twenty police officers threatened to resign if they had to go into riot areas. They should have been fired on the spot... they were a disgrace to the badge they wore... and to the oath they took. My partner and I had an officer assigned to us who we could always count on being flat on the floor in the back seat of our patrol car when the shooting started. Most are still with the department."

"If you were anything other than black in some neighborhoods you were in deep trouble. Police had to literally 'rescue' people from angry mobs who were threatening to beat, rape and kill them. One such family, of Asian Indian descent, who before this coexisted with

their neighbors, had to be loaded into a vehicle in a police convoy and taken out of the area through a hail of rocks, bricks and gunfire."

***"Roving gangs** of up to 300 people hit stores, breaking windows and grabbing everything they could. The stores were picked clean to the shelf fixtures... and in some stores they took the fixtures. Because of our department's inability to respond to calls, no one was really safe anywhere at anytime in this sprawling city of one million people."*

"One front line of police officers outnumbered more than 10 to 1 literally fought hand to hand combat with a mob of rioters trying to break through the cordon we'd imposed between them and the downtown city area. If these officers hadn't stood their ground, God only knows the extent of violence and destruction the city would have experienced."

"If you think your police department will protect you and you're safe from the next round of riots understand this... even though our department acquired equipment and training and did much to prepare for this type of problem after this riot, as time went by and the further removed we became from that last riot... the training diminished, trained and experienced officers retired and eventually the administration and department got into the same rut of complacency. Their attitude is the same as before... "Let the next guy worry about it... I'm retiring soon.""

"Since the last great riot, our city, as have most of the other cities throughout the country... done away with "The Projects" as these building complexes for the low income and 'impoverished' were referred to. The people from these Projects have now, by city and federal decree, been dispersed throughout the metropolitan areas by low income housing assistance programs. This means they're living in your neighborhood."

***"The theory** of the diffusion of these people from these Projects was to "Break up the gang mentality that fuels riots and looting and to help them 'assimilate' into society." In reality, they've just distributed the cancer of this mentality throughout the metropolitan areas. Our city went from 8 major gangs before this riot to well over 100 after this relocation program. The problem is now dispersed throughout our city ten years after this riot."*

"If you think the fire under the boiling pot of rage that blew the lid off that pot long ago has been extinguished, think again. The lid's on the pot but the fire is still burning and the pot is still boiling... until next time. It's still there... and it's more intense than it was before. We have a grotesquely larger problem and an attitude in our society of "I'll get what I want... even if I have to take it violently."

"They will be at your doorstep the next time... because they're your neighbors now."

This is not a fictional account like most of the stories in this book. Mark was a veteran police officer who lived in a city of over one million people that experienced riots for over a week.

What you read here is not what you'd read in the 'official records' of that city or police department… it is the truth of what happened during that riot… from a seasoned and senior police officer who battled these mobs of people 'toe to toe'.

5-Practice to prove it works

You must have a written plan to follow... but most importantly you have to physically practice it to prove your plan works.

The realism of your *Neighborhood Protection Plan* must absolutely be determined by holding *training exercises*. As the saying goes... *"The proof is in the pudding."* Make sure any fault in your plan is not because of actions of Group Members, but more in the design. When you have *training exercises,* be patient with your Group Members.

Law enforcement and military conduct training exercises continuously until the exercises become so ingrained in their minds that they become a reflex action.

You must know whether your written plan is practical and reasonable... you must find out what works and what doesn't work... doing a training exercise brings your plans written on paper to reality.

The purpose of training exercises is to make the movements and actions second nature in a stressful situation and to confirm the reality of a written plan.

Without actually blocking off your entry and exit points, simulate doing so while checking your protection plan and alternative plans. Check your communications equipment and skills in using this equipment.

We suggest you contact an NRA Certified Firearms Instructor and take your Group Members to an authorized shooting range to practice proficiency with firearms and weapons. Practice your movements, patrol formations, Cover and Fire Movements and anything else done with firearms *without ammunition being present.*

Can you maintain your *NPP* for *six months?* Remember the Psychological and Physical Effects that *A Failure of Civility* will have on your *NPP* Group Members as mentioned in the above chapter.

Count on less people being capable of defending your NPP the longer A Failure of Civility goes on. Sickness, fatigue and mental disorder will take its toll.

5-Building Function

Five interrelated aspects characterize all buildings... *function, size, height, materials*, and *construction methods*. The two additional aspects of *exterior openings* and *floor plans* determine the interior layout of a building.

The most important characteristic is the reason for the building... *its function.*

The four categories of building function are…

- ***Residential.*** Residential includes single-family and multi-family Low Rise or High Rise housing.
- ***Public and Civic.*** Public and civic includes church-type and government buildings, schools and gyms, airports, and stadiums.
- ***Commercial.*** Commercial includes hotels, restaurants, and retail stores.
- ***Mixed-Use.*** Mixed-use includes a combination of commercial and residential buildings.

Each of these building functions incorporates different building materials and designs. *The reason Building Function is important is that if you are forced to relocate to a Secondary NPP Location… the construction of some types of buildings gives you more protection from small arms fire than others. Choose accordingly.*

Generally, Public and Civic buildings give you the best protection against small arms fire. Many are built like the proverbial 'Brick S#!t House.' They're constructed of concrete, brick or stone.

See *Chapter 10, Firearms, Safety, Basics of Marksmanship and Surviving a Gun Battle* for the effect common small arms cartridges have on different types of building construction materials.

5-Choosing your *Secondary NPP Locations*

When you organize your Neighborhood Protection Plan you must select alternative locations that we call Secondary NPP Locations as part of your initial plan. Your *Secondary NPP Location* is an alternate *NPP* incase you are forced to abandon your *Primary NPP Location.* We will cover *Security in Motion* for both *Planned* and *Emergency NPP Relocation* in *Chapter 11.*

Again, we advise you that a sufficient and renewable water source is the crucial issue in determining the viability of your *Secondary NPP Location* being a long term sustainable *NPP.*

Refer back earlier in this chapter for *Questions the Primary and Secondary NPP Leaders must answer first* before proceeding to use a location for a *Neighborhood Protection Plan.*

Is there a water source? *You have to evaluate this first.* Read our information on *water* in *Chapter 12* ***first*** to help you evaluate this issue.

You need a water bore hole or open well inside your *NPP* or a reliable source of water outside but close to your *Secondary NPP Location* just the same as your *Primary NPP Location.* You need a lake, reservoir, river, stream or other renewable water source *that you* *can depend on year 'round and is **one mile or less from each of your Secondary NPP Locations.***

*We again warn you not to base the **long term sustainability** of your NPP on rain water or snow being sufficient.*

The *Secondary NPP Location* is not selecting just one alternative location. The Authors suggest that you designate *three* locations for your *Secondary NPP Location.* These locations should be at varying distances from your *Primary NPP Location*. One close… such as another nearby neighborhood that is defensible… one some distance such as 20 miles… and one a considerable distance away such as 100 miles.

The *choice* for a move to each of them has to be evaluated separately by up to date intelligence on each *Secondary NPP Location*, the current state of your manpower, transportation mode, supplies, and fuel if you are moving by vehicle. This means that some Group Members will have to travel to your *Secondary NPP Locations* and gather up to date information on each.

This move is referred to as a *Planned NPP Relocation* and will have to have the input from *all* Group Members when preparing for this relocation. Which *Secondary NPP Location* you move to will be determined by what is causing you to move and whether your choice of a *Secondary NPP Location* will have the same problem as you're having with your *Primary NPP Location.*

The procedure we recommend named a *Planned NPP Relocation* will be totally different from a situation in which your *Primary NPP Location* has been over run and you have escaped with the basics by an emergency escape route or another issue causes you to immediately move.

5-Know the capabilities of each Group Member

Evaluate *all* members of your group. Get to know each other as this is simply good neighborly relations as well as decisive to the group's function. Get to know the strengths and weaknesses of each member.

For example, not all people feel comfortable with firearms, weapons or the intent to use them against another human being, even in defense of themselves, family or the group. You must be able to select those with the 'Survival Mindset' for direct security purposes.

That mentality is in most males and some females whether or not they have military or law enforcement experience. These people should be the Alpha and Bravo Group Members that comprise your armed defense. That being said, we strongly recommend that *all* members of the group, even the younger members, know the basic concepts of safety and how to use and maintain weapons and reload magazines if applicable.

A 72 year old female or male member of your group who is not healthy enough for security can watch children, cook, be your communications coordinator and do other things that will free more physically able individuals for other more strenuous or demanding duties.

5-Find out which Group Members have special training

Find out from your members whether they have expertise in the following areas. Don't use solely computers for *NPP* data storage… use paper and pen or pencil. As the result of some *Catastrophic Events* your computer will be useless and you will not be able to retrieve the information. Keep paper hard copy files on your *NPP* printed from your computer or compiled by hand.

Have each Group Member check the following areas if they have expertise in them...

- Military training
- Law enforcement training
- Firearms training
- Medical training
- Radio communications, electronics or electrical training
- Fire Fighting and Prevention
- Food storage and preparations training
- Construction experience
- Nutrition and cooking expertise
- Gardening-fishing-hunting knowledge
- Vehicle repair knowledge
- Chemistry training or education

Ask each member to each complete the ***NPP Group Member Information Form.*** **You can make copies of the form** at the back of this book.

5-Differences between people, tolerance and acceptance

The world is too small for bigotry and prejudices. A former Special Operations Soldier probably said it best… *"As we fought for the ideals of freedom and for those on the left and right of us, we judged each other only by the most important of characteristics... nerve, courage and the willingness to stand in harms way for others... those abstract values that transcend the color of skin or the shape of eyes. Whatever our race, creed or ethnicity, at that time we were one."*

As another said… *"Everyone's equal in a fighting hole!"*

During a time of *Crisis*, you will need the help of *everyone* in your neighborhood. If they have the experience and training, you must accept taking orders from them… whatever the *color of their skin, their gender, their sexual persuasion, their religion, their customs, or the shape of their eyes.*

You will struggle as one if A Failure of Civility occurs.

If you can't think this way, don't bother forming a group.

The surviving people in the world… God forbid it comes to that… don't need to begin rebuilding on the prejudiced, redneck, religious fanaticism and dinosaur mentality of the past, even though our civilization may have taken a giant leap backwards in the interim.

5-How to deal with Non-Participants

Every neighborhood will have people who do not want to participate in formulating a *Neighborhood Protection Plan.* These are people who believe that all will be well and that they can rely on the government to take care of everything.

These are people that, for whatever reason be it naivety or a complacent attitude, believe that the *Neighborhood Protection Plan* or any other cooperative protection or security plan is not necessary and is over reaction to perceived threat.

Don't bother to argue with them about the failure of the government to come to citizen's aid in situations like Hurricane Katrina or the numerous other failures of timely assistance from Federal and State Government emergency services during times of *Crisis*.

Tolerate those people's opinions. Do not ostracize or anger them with your persistence that they must be part of the group. This is America and everyone has their right to their opinion.

If a *Catastrophic Event* does occur and leads to a *Long Term Crisis*, these people will quickly change their minds and want to become involved with the *NPP*.

Work around them until you can welcome them into the group. In a time of *Crisis*, you can't force these people to be part of your group, but conversely, they cannot compromise your *Area Tactical Protection*.

Each situation is different and you must adapt your planning to these people. You must have your plan designed around these people not being part of your group, but also have your plan designed to later include these people as part of your group.

5-The Principles of Leadership you need to employ

The following are Principles of Leadership and are 'Tried and True.' As you read through the following, keep in mind, *"Leadership is not a Dictatorship."* Be aware of the old saying that "Power Corrupts… and absolute power corrupts absolutely!" *…it's true.*

You were elected to lead, not to be the moral compass of others. Everyone is different and it's dangerous to try to read the inner motives of others. Delegate, but hold people accountable and don't give people too much responsibility too quickly. Ensure that the *Secondary NPP Leader* can take over your duties fully if the need arises.

Humility and perspective are absolutely essential to leadership. Step back and think about what you do. Try to look at what you are doing from the other Group Member's point of view. *Learn to delegate…* give some of your responsibilities to your *Secondary NPP Leader* and other capable Group Members… this is the secret of good leadership.

Principles of Leadership you need to employ…

1. ***Know yourself and always seek self improvement.*** Recognize your strengths and weaknesses. Like Clint Eastwood said in the movie *"Dirty Harry"… "A man's got to know his limitations!"* False confidence in strengths that you project but are not there will cause death or injury. Go to the well of your subconscious and be honest with yourself. Everyone has faults… remember that other's lives will depend on you and your strengths… and weaknesses. Consult with others that have strengths where you have weaknesses. Try to make improvements on your weaknesses. *You are their leader.*
2. ***Be technically and tactically proficient.*** Learn everything you can about your job and become an expert on these issues. *You are their leader.*
3. ***Seek responsibility and take responsibility for your actions.*** You're the boss so… *'The buck stops with you.' You are their leader.*
4. ***Make sound and timely decisions… but make a decision.*** Spend all available time to consult with others and consider alternatives. But when the time comes to make a decision… make it! ***Indecision is much, much worse than a poor decision***. *You are their leader.*
5. ***Set the example... "Follow me and do as I do."*** *The 'do as I say and not what I do'* attitude doesn't work. Don't ask them to do what you cannot or will not. *You are their leader.*
6. ***Know your people and look out for them.*** Eat *after* your people eat and eat what your people eat *after* they have been fed. Consider them as equals, not as just underlings. *You are their leader.*
7. ***Keep your people informed.*** If you keep them up to date they will trust you enough to not ask you… why? *You are their leader.*

8. ***Develop a sense of responsibility in your subordinates.*** Give out responsibility in accordance with ability and potential. Make them part of the group equation. *You are their leader.*

9. ***Ensure a task is understood, supervised and accomplished and the report of the task being accomplished is given back to leaders.*** Consider each team member's skill level and willingness to perform additional duties. Check on their performance from time to time but don't give the impression you don't trust them. Give encouragement. *You are their leader.*

10. ***Train all members of your NPP as a team.*** Make sure all members of the team know the importance of their job and how it affects the team as a whole. Again, Give encouragement. *You are their leader.*

11. ***Employ and deploy your team in accordance with their capabilities.*** Know each member's strengths and weaknesses and use them to the advantage of the *NPP*. *You are their leader.*

Learn to keep your head about you and don't take things personally. Do not, under any circumstance, advertise your insecurities to your Group Members. That goes for *sharing* problems with the wrong people.

Some issues might have to become unsaid to most… no matter how deeply this bothers you… not even said to your spouse or family. Get your facts straight before creating misunderstandings. This will help the rest of the group feel better about your leadership.

The further you get into a *Crisis* and the more society breaks down… the more structure your *Neighborhood Protection Plan* and Group Members need. Make a written plan… it will help you stay focused and not miss important items and issues.

When everyone is thirsty, hungry, exhausted and depressed… learn to cut people some slack. Keep morale high. Get those good at this to create some entertainment for the *NPP*. Always tell the truth.

One lie will undo your credibility and undermine you and you'll pay a terrible price for it… *your credibility and the trust of your NPP Group Members.*

5-*Chain of Leadership Structure and Control* for a *Neighborhood Protection Plan*

The following is a scaled down example of a proper command structure... You may add to it as your *NPP* requires, but the following should be the bare minimum.

Primary NPP Leader

- The *Primary NPP Leader* evaluates the group as a whole, sets up and conducts training.

- The *Primary NPP Leader* oversees the entire *NPP* and organizes and implements the *NPP*.
- The *Primary NPP Leader* delegates some of the *NPP* responsibilities to the *Secondary NPP Leader.*
- The *Primary NPP Leader* makes sure the *Chain of Leadership* is understood by all Group Members of the *NPP* so each Group Member knows who and what areas they're responsible for and in turn each Group Member will know who they're responsible to and what area that person is responsible for.
- The *Primary NPP Leader* will determine by Group Member's experience, physical capabilities and the wiliness to take the responsibility, as to who will be in charge of additional Sections (as follows below).
- The *Primary NPP Leader's* duties should be executed in conjunction with the *Secondary NPP Leader*. Bring him or her into your decision making. This is necessary if they need to assume your command temporarily or permanently at some point.

Secondary NPP Leader

- The *Secondary NPP Leader* assists the *NPP* Leader in his preparation and planning.
- The *Secondary NPP Leader* coordinates with all other parts of the *Chain of Leadership* Structure to communicate the instructions of the *Primary NPP Leader* for a smooth flow of information and accomplishment of duties.
- The *Secondary NPP Leader*, in a situation where the *NPP* needs to relocate and the *NPP* is split into different sections, the *Secondary NPP Leader* will take charge of one of the sections at the request of the *Primary NPP Leader*. Ensures that their Junior Leader can fully assume their job.

Watch Center Section and Third Section Leader

- Updates all additional roster information and any other Group Member information of the *NPP*. This includes updating Group Members on briefings. Always keeps the group updated on the latest information and is sure they understand any changes fully and completely.

  Remember, when a *Crisis* occurs and endures, people may start to lose their comprehension of instructions… so be patient with your Group Members. Tempers may grow short… but make sure instructions are understood.
- Updates all information on maps or sand tables of the *NPP*.
- These people or this person takes inventory of all items, through Supply (below), critical to overall success of the *NPP*. Medical, tools, ammo, food, water, etc.
- Coordinates all fire fighting efforts and alerts the entire *NPP* of a fire.

- Assigns the Guard Post schedules on the *NPP* Protective Perimeter and ensures they are manned. Scheduling should be done with the *Primary and Secondary NPP Leaders* and Medical Sixth Leader. Leaders need to intimately know their Group Members individual health and welfare situations.
- Ensures that their Junior Leader can fully assume their job.

Communications/Intelligence Section and Fourth Section Leader

- Monitors all radio traffic be it from police scanners, emergency broadcast systems or the group's two-way radios. This is a job perfect for the less physically capable. It is important that notes be made of radio transmissions from outside the *NPP*.
- Relays all information to the *Primary NPP Leader and* the Watch Center to be properly distributed to the group, *only* upon the *Primary or Secondary NPP Leaders* instructions.
- Ensures that their Junior Leader can fully assume their job.

Supply Section and Fifth Section Leader

- Helps in the preparation and distribution of food for the group and makes sure Guard Posts have food, water, coffee or any other items needed while they are on guard.
- Transports, processes and treats, handles and stores all Potable Water with assistance of Group Members.
- With help from the other Group Members, prepares a 'hidden cache' of the majority of the *NPP's* supplies from which supplies are drawn but can quickly be concealed and hidden in an emergency.
- Keeps updating the inventory of all food, water, ammunition and provisions as they are used. This information must be immediately passed on to the *Primary and Secondary NPP Leaders* and the Watch Center Section to provide them current information.
- Ensures the *Emergency NPP Relocation Bags* are prepared and ready.
- Ensures that their Junior Leader can fully assume their job.

Medical Section and Sixth Section Leader

- Oversees the nutritional needs of the *NPP* Group Members and works in conjunction with the Supply Section in allotting food by individual needs. Dispenses vitamins as available.
- Has a plan for disease prevention and quarantine of Group Members that contact any transmittable diseases.

- Tends to the medical needs of all Group Members including gunshot wounds. Institutes a Triage System if medicines and wound treatment supplies become in short supply.
- Makes certain all hygiene facilities are functioning and hygiene policies are being followed for human waste and trash.
- Oversees the burial of the dead. Ensures that the deceased are properly and deeply buried, at least four foot deep for human bodies and a minimum of two foot deep for human waste and trash so that neither can contaminate food supplies, water supplies and to prevent disease occurrence.

  Burial sites must be covered with stones to prevent animals digging up corpses.
- Ensures that their Junior Leader can fully assume their job.

Junior Leaders

- Junior Leaders are nothing more than individuals that have been selected by the Section Leaders for a responsibility. These people work under a *Primary* or *Secondary NPP Leader* or Section Leader to help with the tasks.

  For example… If the head of the Supply Section has to step down for whatever reason, his appointed Junior Leader will then step up to fill his position. The reasoning for this is that he will already know the job and what has to be done to continue with a smooth flow for operational integrity.
- Junior Leaders will communicate the commands of the Section Leader to all Group Members for a smooth flow of information.

5-Encourage leadership and talk between Junior Leaders

Junior Leaders don't always require direction from the *NPP Leaders* in a leadership situation. In some instances, like their position on the Protective Perimeter, a Junior Leader may have the clearest view of what is happening and they may be better suited than the *NPP Leaders* to develop a tactical solution.

This is the ***only*** *exception to independent Group Member action.*

This type of problem solving involving direct Junior Leader initiative is critical to leadership. This empowers Junior Leaders to take decisive action and teaches them the value of close cooperation in achieving the *NPP's* overall purpose.

All members of the *Chain of Leadership* are responsible for teaching their subordinates their job so that if anything happens to them the next person in the *Chain of Leadership* can step up and fill their shoes. Each Group Member in the *NPP* should be able to step up and take over the person's job above them, to ensure your *NPP* remains strong.

5-Location of your *NPP* Watch Center

The *NPP* Watch Center should be located in the center of your *NPP*. This obviously must be inside the *NPP* Protective Perimeter but not exposed to where *Intruders* can view it as 'The Community Center' and see everyone coming and going.

This is an example of a good Watch Center house…
Brick can withstand most sporadic small arms fire

In this pre planning phase of your *NPP* you should have a location selected to hide or bury your excess supplies to retrieve at a later date if you have to make a *Planned NPP Relocation* or an *Emergency NPP Relocation.*

Located close to each other should be...

- Watch Center Section
- Communications/Intelligence Section
- Supply Section
- Medical Section

The *Primary NPP Leader* should be located close to these sections when not at the perimeter or on guard to allow ease of communications. The other Sections will also benefit from being close to each other.

It is important that each Group Member knows that information in the *Chain of Leadership Structure and Control* flows from the top down… *and* from the bottom up. This mcans everyone talks to everyone.

5-Fire fighting and prevention in your *NPP*

The defense of your *NPP* must be *a total concept* and all areas of protection must be considered… and of great importance is the threat of fire. Fire spreading during *A Failure of Civility* is an extremely high danger and your *NPP* must be prepared to deal with fire just as you prepare for any hostile actions taken against you by *Intruders*.

During a Long Term Crisis or A Failure of Civility, fire will be a drastically greater threat to you, your family and your Neighborhood Protection Plan than during Normal Civility for two reasons…

One… during the *Area Emergency* after a *Catastrophic Event,* all emergency services including your fire department will be overwhelmed. If the *Area Emergency* progresses to *Long Term Crisis* or *A Failure of Civility*, your area fire department may be crippled in fighting fires because of a shortage of personnel, lack of functioning vehicles, lack of fuel for vehicles or absence of water to fight fires with… or your fire department may completely deteriorate as a functioning unit in the worst case scenario.

Two… after a *Catastrophic Event* that causes natural gas, electricity and water services to cease functioning and especially if the *Area Emergency* progresses to *Long Term Crisis* or *A Failure of Civility*... you will be relying on open fire more than ever to cook and keep warm.

Most of these heating or cooking fires will be in makeshift containers… and in places that a fire should have never been… and around flammables and other materials that simply catch on fire. Fireplaces… mostly wood burning and those more decorative than safely functional… that have seldom been used for that purpose before… will be used for heating and cooking.

Do not attempt to use your natural gas or decorative fireplace for cooking or heating by burning wood or anything else in them*…* you will burn your home to the ground by doing this. *All fires should be outside if possible.*

Most of you making and using fires will have little concept of the dangers of fires from cooking or heating or a fire's side effects such as *carbon monoxide poisoning or oxygen depletion in enclosed areas.*

In High Rise Buildings the fire hazard must be taken very seriously as your outside areas for this will be adjacent to or on the top of your building. This is much different than Low Rise Residential where you can step out the front door of your home and still be within the Protective Perimeter of your *NPP* to cook or heat for warmth. Do not use fire for heating inside your High Rise Building.

NPP and Fire Prevention ....any good *Neighborhood Protection Plan* will have to include a fire prevention program and this must be discussed with every Group Member... every man, woman and child.

Remember to utilize people in your *NPP* with fire fighting and prevention experience. Active or retired fire fighters in your *NPP* can be a great asset.

If you don't have anyone in your *NPP* with a background in fire fighting... a great source of reference and assistance is your local fire department.

A Bucket Brigade in action

While *Normal Civility* exists, get your local fire department representative to visit your neighborhood or building and advise you of alternative heating and cooking methods and safe places using fire under the assumption that *A Failure of Civility* has occurred *and there is no natural gas, electricity, propane or water supply available.*

Fire department personnel are great people to help you by the very nature that they are chosen to be fire fighters and will be happy to help with your assessment. Although they will probably view your request as slightly odd, they will help you with advice.

Your neighborhood layout and the type of materials your building or homes are constructed from will have a bearing on the extent of your preparation for fighting fires.

Homes constructed of brick or concrete compared to a very flammable wooden structure with wood or asphalt shingles should be taken into consideration when you're doing your initial survey. The most flammable materials should have your fire fighting equipment close to them.

Vegetation inside your *NPP*, your homes and vegetation that's bordering your Protective Perimeter which could spread fire into your *NPP,* need to be taken into consideration in your survey.

Fire Prevention Procedures should be instituted when your *NPP* is activated and fires restricted. This should be done to minimize the attention the light and smoke that multiple fires can draw to your *NPP*.

Water will probably be in short supply. Consider using water in a swimming pool or having large piles of sand placed in strategic areas with shovels and buckets to transport it to where needed.

Shovels along with the buckets can also be used to throw dirt or sand on a fire to extinguish it. Use the old bucket brigades method of handing pails down a line of people like was used in the last century to extinguish fires.

Fire Prevention Procedures should be…

- Fires are not to be used *except* in areas where there is a person watching them 24/7. Go to a communal fire system if this is viable to minimize the danger of unattended fires getting out of control.
- The *Primary NPP Leader* must approve a cooking or heating fire separate of the communal fires.
- If a fire is detected by any guard or Group Member your *NPP* must have some device to sound the fire alarm such as a wheel rim suspended from a tree limb and struck rapidly with a tire iron or a radio alert.
- In High Rise Buildings, cooking should be confined to a roof area that is fire proof. Any heating fires for warmth must be communal and should be on a balcony or fire escape away from anything flammable.

  Because of the lack of wood or combustibles for fires in metropolitan High Rise Building areas, after propane and charcoal have been exhausted, there will be little or no fuel for cooking unless you have prepared a supply for this.
- If there is a fire, your Guard Posts must remain in position and go on a *High Alert*. A fire can be a decoy set purposely to draw attention away from an enemy planning to attack.

We recommend *each person* have an 'ABC' fire extinguisher. These are done once they are used so we recommend that your *NPP* buy as many *hand pumped pressure water refillable back pack type fire extinguishers* as you can afford. These hold about five gallons of water but are only good for 'Class A' fires of wood or trash.

These *refillable back pack type fire extinguishers* should be filled and kept full. The water needs to be treated with a few drops of bleach periodically to keep molds and fungus from forming but it does not need to be changed often.

They are somewhat pricey… but cheaper than your shelter… and what cost can you put on human life?

Realizing that many of your Group Members will be needed to fight a fire… you must be hyper vigilant about security at the same time. Use of *NPP* Group Members like the grandmas and grandpas to form the core of fire fighting efforts is a possibility in a worse case scenario.

In addition to removal of all potential flammables for a fire on the outside of your structures… you must also consider the inside of the structures.

When making your defensive positions within a structure, remove anything from the surrounding areas which can easily catch fire from muzzle blast.

Remember the total concept of your *NPP* is *"Safety and Protection"* and fire prevention and fighting is a part of that. Your LOP, Marksmen positions, Guard Posts and *Roving Guardians* must be especially alert to fires as part of their guard duty and patrolling inside your *NPP*. *Every Group Member must be on fire watch at all times.*

5-Making the decision to activate your *NPP*

The decision to activate your *NPP* and Group Members must be determined by what stage your *Crisis* is in.

To determine if a Crisis is leading to a Long Term Crisis or leading to A Failure of Civility, your NPP Leaders and Group Members must observe and verify the following...

- Is your law enforcement unable to respond to citizen calls for help?
- Is law enforcement unable to maintain order?
- Have you attempted to contact law enforcement outside your local law enforcement's jurisdiction?
- Have local government services broken down… leaving your *NPP* as the only effective maintenance of law and order in your area?
- Has Martial Law or a State of Emergency been declared?

In past riots… some of these guidelines did not apply. Law enforcement phone centers still answered calls and there was a limited and delayed response by law enforcement to citizen requests for assistance.

However, eventually law enforcement became so inundated with calls for service that there weren't enough officers to handle them and even though people were assured 'officers are on their way,' …they never showed up.

In the past, the looting of larger commercial stores happened first but then the violence and looting turned quickly to surrounding neighborhoods and subdivisions. Eventually law enforcement was so overwhelmed that they could not respond to *any* neighborhood calls.

5-*You must not hesitate to activate your NPP Group Members.*

The *Primary NPP Leader* must be aware that if government services disintegrate completely, there will most likely soon be *A Failure of Civility*... leaving your *NPP* as the only effective maintenance of law and order in your area.

The longer the *Crisis* persists, the more desperate people will become and the more vigilant you must be at your *NPP* Protective Perimeter. The volatility of a *Crisis* can change it to *A Failure of Civility* in mere hours.

Don't hesitate to give your command to activate your *NPP* to ensure all Group Members can get home to the neighborhood from work or errands.

Regardless of whether you live in a Low Rise Residential Neighborhood or a High Rise Residential Building, read the next two chapters. There is information crucial to each *Area Tactical Protection* in both chapters.

Chapter 6
Area Tactical Protection for a Low Rise Residential Neighborhood

There will be some repetition in the following chapters of this book to emphasize important issues. Regardless of whether you live in a Low Rise Residential Neighborhood or a High Rise Residential Building, read *both Chapters 6 and 7.* ***There is information crucial to each Area Tactical Protection in both chapters.***

In this Chapter we describe…

- **6-Low Rise Residential Neighborhoods**
- **6-The All-Around Defense… the *Neighborhood Protection Plan***
- **6-Field of Fire**
- **6-Interlocking Fields of Fire**
- **6-The Force Multiplier Effect, Economy of Force and the Element of Surprise**
- **6-The Significance of High Ground**
- **6-Supporting Fields of Fire**
- **6-The difference between Cover and Concealment**
- **6-The Clock System of Referencing Direction**
- **6-*JDLR* or *"Just Don't Look Right"***
- **6-Have *NPP* area intelligence photos, satellite images and maps**
- **6-The *Third Dimension* of your *NPP* Protective Perimeter… usually forgotten**
- **6-Assessing your Neighborhood for a *NPP***
- **6-Where to Set Up your Neighborhood Protective Perimeters**
- **6-How to set up your *NPP* Protective Perimeter**
- **6-*Outside* features your *NPP* Protective Perimeter must have**
- **6-Inside features of your *NPP* Protective Perimeter**
- **6-How to prepare your neighborhood right now**
- **6-Things *not* to do**
- **6-Things *you must* do**
- **6-You're in a *Crisis… Low Alert* procedures to institute**
- **6-You're in a *Long Term Crisis… Mid Alert* procedures to institute**
- **6-High elevation *Listening Observation Posts (LOP)***
- **6-Marksmenship Posts**
- **6-Story-*"While I Slept"***
- **6-Guard requirements and procedures**
- **6-Perimeter checks**
- **6-Denying access to your *NPP* by physical barriers-Foot and vehicle traffic**
- **6-Denying access to your *NPP* by physical barriers-protective perimeter aids**
- **6-Denying access to your *NPP* by psychological barriers**
- **6-Tactics that will make your *NPP* a *Proactive Defense***
- **6-*A Failure of Civility* has occurred… *High Alert* preparations to institute**

- 6-DO NOT bring *Outsiders* into your *NPP*
- 6-Handling *Outsiders* and *Intruders*
- 6-Protecting a 2 or 3 story condominium or apartment complex
- 6-Link up with other *Neighborhood Protection Plans*
- 6-Summer and hot weather, winter and cold weather
- 6-Passive response will get you killed… you must be proactive
- 6-The use of camouflage in your *NPP*
- 6-Your *NPP* must have flexibility, alternative and 'What if' plans

6-Low Rise Residential Neighborhoods

> ***Low Rise Residential Neighborhood defined.*** A number of single family homes, apartments and condominium complexes of no more than two stories in height.

Low-rise residential areas are normally adjacent to streets and in close orderly block areas defined by streets. This can consist of row houses or single family dwellings with yards, gardens, trees, and fences. Street patterns are normally rectangular or curving.

This Chapter is directed towards Low Rise Residential Neighborhoods. Because another physical dimension, the dimension of 3 or more stories of height is added to the High Rise Building Protective Perimeter and the water source and winter heating issue with High Rise Buildings, the Authors have divided *Area Tactical Protection* into two separate chapters… *Chapter 6* is the *Area Tactical Protection* for a Low Rise Residential Neighborhood and *Chapter 7* which illustrates *Area Tactical Protection* for a High Rise Building.

6-The All-Around Defense… the *Neighborhood Protection Plan*

The *Neighborhood Protection Plan* defense must be an All-Around Defense.

That phrase says what it means… it is a defense *that surrounds the entire area that you designate as being within the Protective Perimeter* of your *Neighborhood Protection Plan.*

It's as simple as drawing a line on a map around all of the houses or all of the condominiums or all of the property or all apartments involved in your *Neighborhood Protection Plan.*

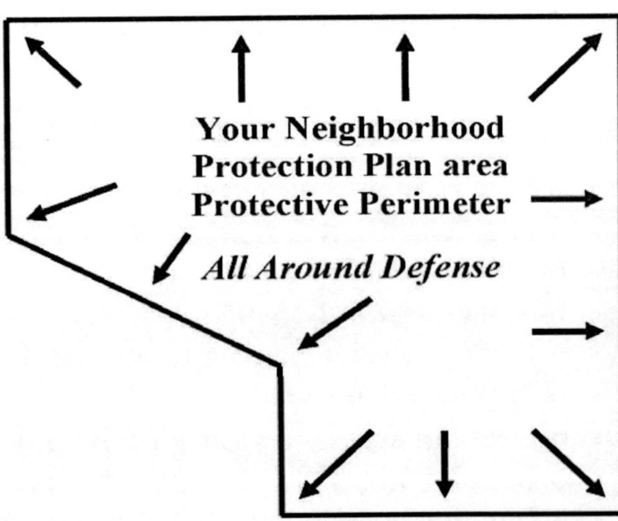

All-Around Defense of your NPP Area

This line, determined by fences, walls or

structures, defines your Protective Perimeter and you defend against all the area outside of this Protective Perimeter.

You must defend all-around your Protective Perimeter. You can't defend two or three sides… that's like defending the front and two sides of your home and leaving the back door unlocked and open.

6-Field of Fire

> ***Field of Fire.*** *The area outside the Protective Perimeter in front and to the left and right side of Guard Posts that the guard can fire on is called their Field of Fire. Each Guard Post's Field of Fire must overlap the Field of Fire of the position to their left and right. This is the concept of Interlocking Fields of Fire.*

Field of Fire. An enemy will observe, probe and find the weak points of your defense and then attack those weak points.

You must not have any undefended areas of your Protective Perimeter or any weak points.

This means each Guard Post must not only be able to view the area in front of their position on the Protective Perimeter, but each Guard Post must be able to fire *on the entire area in front of their position.*

That is their Field of Fire. That area of view and Field of Fire must overlap the one on each side of it.

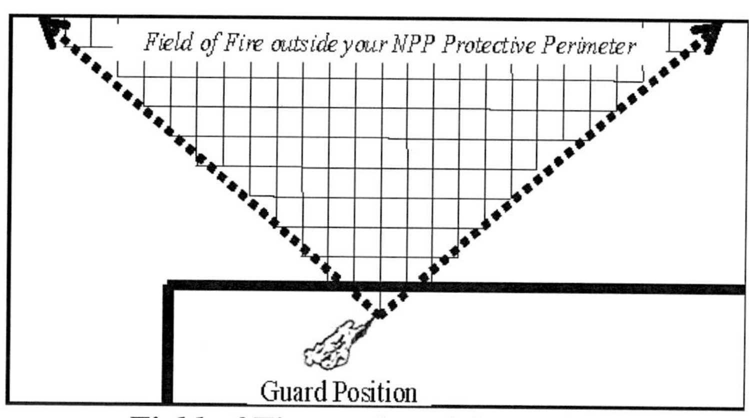

Field of Fire as viewed from above

6-Interlocking Fields of Fire

Interlocking Fields of Fire ensure that the entire Protective Perimeter can be covered by weapons fire from all Protective Perimeter Guard Posts and that Fields of Fire overlap each other as shown in the diagram.

This must be out to the furthest part of the Field of Fire from your Protective Perimeter as possible. This is simply to ensure your Protective Perimeter is covered by weapons fire in all areas around the outside of it.

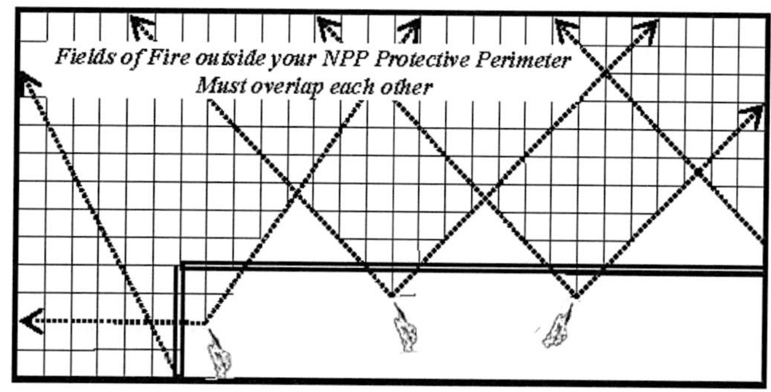

Interlocking Fields of Fire

6-The Force Multiplier Effect, Economy of Force and the Element of Surprise

If one Group Member can throw a gasoline fire bomb into the midst of ten attacking *Intruders* from your Protective Perimeter or your High Rise Building and turn them away, you are using multiple techniques of the Force Multiplier Effect.

If one Group Member as a *Marksman* can eliminate 5 *Intruders* with precise shooting from a roof of your Low Rise Neighborhood or balcony of your High Rise Building and turn an attack away, you are using techniques of the Force Multiplier Effect.

> ***The Force Multiplier Effect*** *is any tactic, equipment, technology or fortification that makes one of your Group Members equal more than one attacker. This includes the element of 'High Ground' or height with fortifications higher than the enemy and specialized weapons.*

A Protective Perimeter gives your *NPP* a Force Multiplier Effect and just as the term implies, each one of your Group Members becomes equal to a greater number of *Intruders* or attackers simply because your Group Members are in prepared stationary defense positions of Cover.

One Protective Perimeter Group Member becomes the equal of 2 *Intruders*, 4 *Intruders*, etc. depending on the sophistication of your defensive fortifications, your tactics and the proficiency of your Group Members.

> ***Economy of Force*** *simply means that your people are more efficient and it takes less of them to accomplish a task, including the defense of your NPP against superior numbers of Intruders.*

We consider the Element of Surprise a Force Multiplier Effect because of the devastating psychological impact it has on the enemy. Both Authors have employed the concepts of Irregular Warfare (aka Guerilla Warfare or Counter Insurgency) with much success.

Much of Irregular Warfare is based on the Indirect Approach and the Element of Surprise. We will cover the Element of Surprise in greater detail in *Chapter 9.*

6-The significance of High Ground

> ***High Ground*** *consists of terrain, buildings, structures, fortifications or anything that gives the advantage of height to one opponent on the battlefield against the other.*

The disadvantages to an attacker and the advantages to a defender of 'High Ground' are...

- The attacker has to exert himself because he is moving uphill to attack the defender in his prepared positions at the crest of High Ground. Conversely, if the defender attacks or counter attacks an enemy from High Ground the defenders, now the attackers, are moving downhill against their opponent and are not exerting themselves.
- If the approach to High Ground is prepared properly the defender can remove all objects that would give Cover to the attacker during his assault.
- The defender has total observation of the movements of the attacker.
- The defender can fire weapons down upon, roll and throw improvised weapons down upon the attacker.
- High Ground is a physical and psychological plus to the defender, a negative to the attacker.

If you can't occupy High Ground close to your *NPP*, you have to deny it to the enemy. The most plausible way to do that is with your Marksmen. They must be able to eliminate any attacker that attempts to use High Ground to their advantage and to your *NPP's* disadvantage.

Your Marksmen must be able to swiftly and surely direct deadly fire on any area of High Ground that your *NPP* does not occupy.

If you ever have to attack High Ground or are subjected to an attack from High Ground it will give renewed meaning to you of the saying *"It was like shooting fish in a barrel"*... that is... if you survive.

The Vauban Star Architectural Principle for Defensive Perimeter Fortifications was used as the ultimate in fixed defensive perimeter fortifications in its day. It was named after the military engineer for King Louis XVI of France, even though the original design was not his.

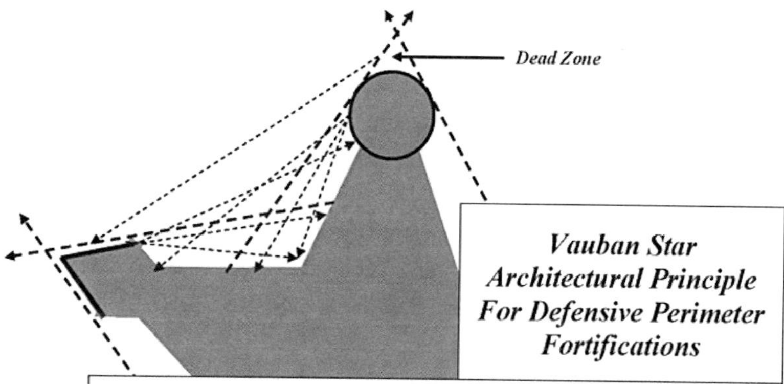

The Vauban Star defensive fortification created perimeter fighting walls in a geometric shape that left no 'dead zones'. The round wall tower at the top has a 'dead zone'. The pointed Vauban wall tower on the left is completely covered by defender Fields of Fire and the perimeter design provides Supporting Fields of Fire to almost every area of the perimeter between towers.

Keep these principles in mind and try to use them to some degree in designing your Neighborhood Protection Plan Protective Perimeter and Secondary Fighting Positions.

Crossfire by Supporting Fields of Fire devastate an enemy !!

Vauban Star Architecture Principle

We're showing you a diagram of this because it's such a graphic example of the principle of defensive perimeters that have Interlocking Fields of Fire and enables the use of Supporting Fields of Fire, which we'll cover next.

This design also enabled every portion of the Protective Perimeter to be covered by one or more Fields of Fire. These fortifications were built with numerous numbers of point configurations and some even in layer upon layer… like stair steps… of layered fall back fighting perimeters.

The points on the Vauban wall tower were a replacement for the round wall tower which had a 'dead zone' outside it. We show a round tower with 'dead zone' and a Vauban pointed tower that left no 'dead zone'.

We're showing you only two points of a five point pentagon Vauban fortification because we forgot what our high school geometry teachers taught us and we've found that it's too danged hard to draw the whole thing… and not make us look like kindergarteners.

Regardless of the number of points, all areas of this Protective Perimeter were geometrically configured to eliminate perimeter 'dead zones' and to have Interlocking Fields of Fire that created Supporting Fields of Fire. From an aerial view the entire fortification would look like a 'star'… hence the name.

All areas outside the Perimeter are subject to Fields of Fire and Interlocking Fields of Fire from the defenders and almost all areas are subject to Supporting Fields of Fire.

If you do not have a Protective Perimeter that gives strong divergent angles of Supporting Fields of Fire from the perimeter areas, investigate the possibility of a wall or structure outside your NPP that can be used as Cover for the 'B' component of Supporting Fields of Fire as shown in the 'L' Shaped Ambush diagram.

This 'B' component can be your Response Guardians.

Your *NPP* Protective Perimeter will not look anything like the Vauban Star. However, not all *NPP* Protective Perimeters will be circular or rectangular in shape. You may have part of your perimeter be an 'L' or 'Horse Shoe' shaped perimeter which will give you the advantages of Supporting Fields of Fire without going outside of your *NPP*.

If you are so fortunate as to have this type of perimeter around your *NPP* Protective Perimeter that allows you to have two or more firing positions *within* your perimeter at right angles to where an *Intruder* would be so unlucky to find themselves, you must use this. *This gives you a tremendous advantage over an attacker.*

You must create the illusion that these areas are *the route* an enemy must take to attack your Protective Perimeter.

Fatal Funnel. *This is a* ***narrow area*** *of obstacles* ***in front of*** *your Protective Perimeter or any area that either forces or deceives an enemy into moving through it so you can subject the enemy to an 'L' Shaped Ambush crossfire. After the enemy comes through this Fatal Funnel they will be in a Kill Zone.*

An 'L' Shaped Ambush is a crossfire from Supporting Fields of Fire. The Kill Zone area is not as easy for your enemy to get out of during the confusion and disorientation of them being hit by withering weapons fire from two diverse positions.

You must create a Fatal Funnel into Kill Zone or 'L' Shaped Ambush area by denying an *Intruder* access to all other areas with strong obstructions, Barbed Wire, etc., and purposefully create weaker defenses in the Fatal Funnel area you want your enemy to move through. In doing so, you must not alert the *Intruder* that the area they're moving into is a Kill Zone. We'll cover what a Kill Zone and an 'L' Shaped Ambush further on.

A doorway to a house that you are defending is a Fatal Funnel to your enemy if they come through it. A Fatal Funnel is created by building strong defenses in all areas *in front of your perimeter* except the area you want the enemy to attack by… there you have weaker defensive fortifications that you let your enemy 'discover' or make it easier for the enemy to remove.

This purposefully weakened defensive area must be set up skillfully and subtly to deceive the enemy into moving through it.

Human beings are like animals… they will take the path of least resistance. Think like them… they will walk through a valley rather than climb over the hills on both sides… which makes the valley a good ambush area and Kill Zone for you if you're in the hills on one or both sides of the valley.

Think like your *Intruder*… most unsophisticated opponents will take the physical and visual 'easy route' or 'The path of least resistance.' Use that to your *NPP*s advantage… but remember… *like animals they will sense a trap if your Fatal Funnel is not set up properly.*

The technique of using Supporting Fields of Fire to create a crossfire ambush creates a Kill Zone and is devastating to an *Intruder*. We'll cover Kill Zones in a bit.

6-Supporting Fields of Fire

Supporting Fields of Fire *are simply a 'stationary flanking movement' creating crossfire with weapons fire directed towards an enemy from two or more diverse angles. A Flanking Attack by movement or weapons fire is also known as an 'Enfilading' attack.*

For example, as in the diagram, the 'flanking' is done by fixed positions that subject an enemy to weapons fire at their front and from their sides at the same time.

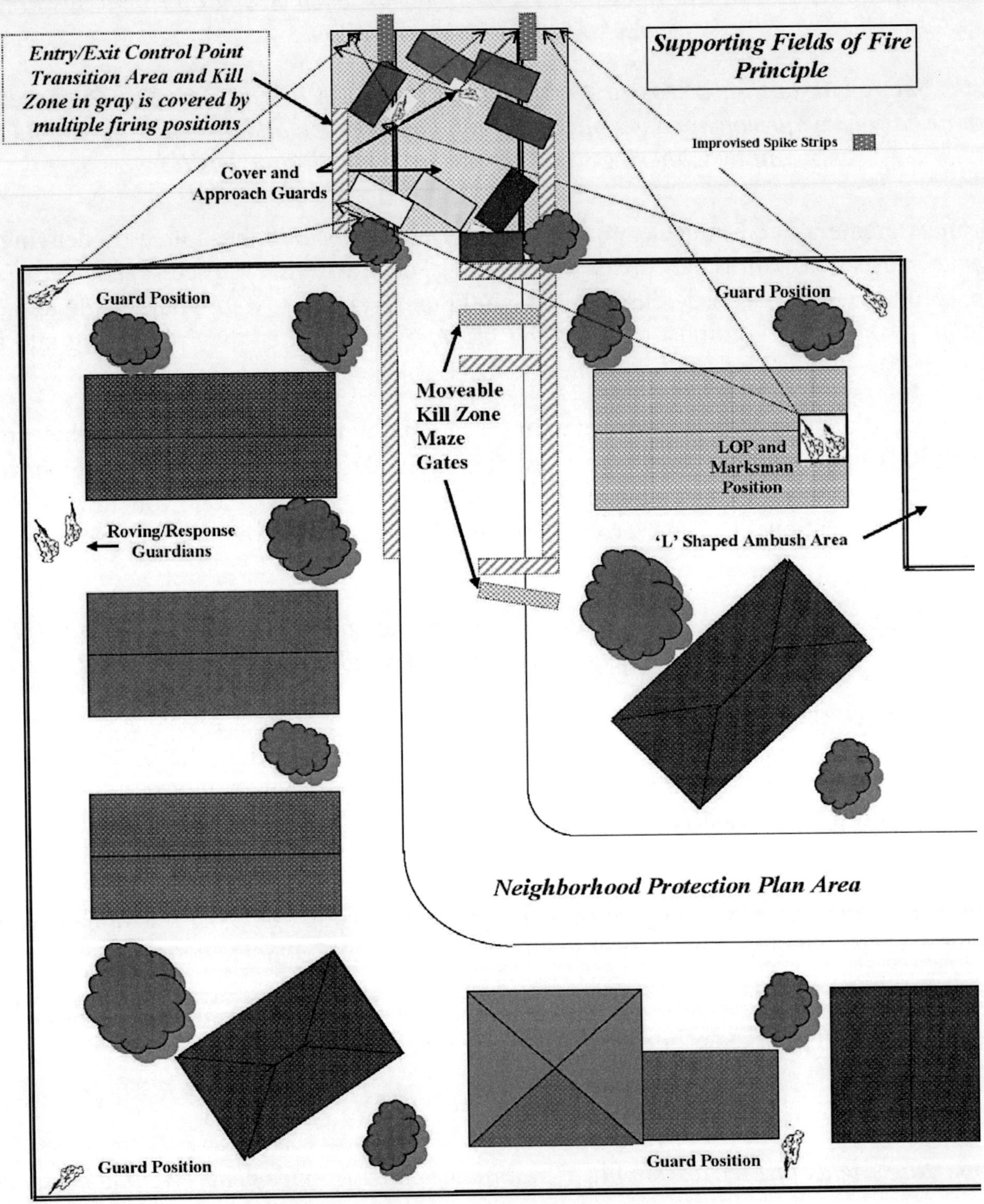

Supporting Fields of Fire Principle

Supporting Fields of Fire are different from Interlocking Fields of Fire because the purpose of Supporting Fields of Fire is not to ensure that an area is covered by weapons fire… it is purposely to subject that area to intense fire from different angles and multiple positions.

Again, you must be aware of the possibility of Friendly Fire Incidents and advise Group Members to avoid these.

6-The difference between Cover and Concealment

Cover. *You can hide behind a large rock... it gives you Cover... bullets won't go through the rock. You have Cover and Concealment behind a large rock...* ***this is good.***

Concealment. *You can hide behind a shrubbery... it gives you Concealment... the enemy can't see you but the enemy can shoot through the shrubbery and kill you if they think you're there...* ***this is not as good.***

You could stand behind bulletproof glass and you *may* have Cover but not Concealment, however the Authors are not big fans of 'bulletproof glass'… like the term 'bulletproof vest,' we think *it's an oxymoron.*

Contrary to the movies and popular thought, vehicles *do not* provide very effective Cover protection from small arms fire with the exception of the engine block, transmission and drive axles. Vehicles will give some protection against lighter loads of shotgun cartridges.

6-The Clock System of Referencing Direction

This is the only method we recommend for referencing direction by your *NPP*. The Clock System works by positioning an analog clock (the one with the big and small hands) horizontally… like laying it flat on a table. Unlike using the Clock System as relating to the direction your are traveling…

With your NPP… 12 o'clock will always be North.

Since the **12 o'clock position is *always the North direction***... consequently the ***6 o'clock position will then be South***, the ***3 o'clock position will be East,*** the ***9 o'clock position will be due West*** and any other direction can be estimated by the hour numbers on the clock, such as southwest being the '7 to 8 o'clock' position.

Guard Posts should be numbered as close to the numbers on the clock as possible.

A Guard Post would report like this… *"Guard 3... I see Outsider movement at 4 o'clock!"* which would mean that Guard Post 3, which is on the East Protective Perimeter, sees *Outsiders* from the *NPP*s 4 o'clock direction.

The approximate distance from the Guard Post can be added, however, many people are bad at estimating distances visually.

Now that you've got that straight... learn to read a topographical map and find your direction with a compass... forget GPS. People have begun to rely on their GPS positions without the proper understanding of a topographical map.

Plus, there are multiple map designator systems that can cause absolute confusion if trying to GPS coordinate with each other by different map setups. We have experienced this with the law enforcement personnel we have trained.

After some *Catastrophic Events* GPS will not function. Learn map reading and direction with a compass.

If you need to venture outside your *NPP* or conduct a *Planned or Emergency NPP Relocation* you'll need to know map reading with a compass.

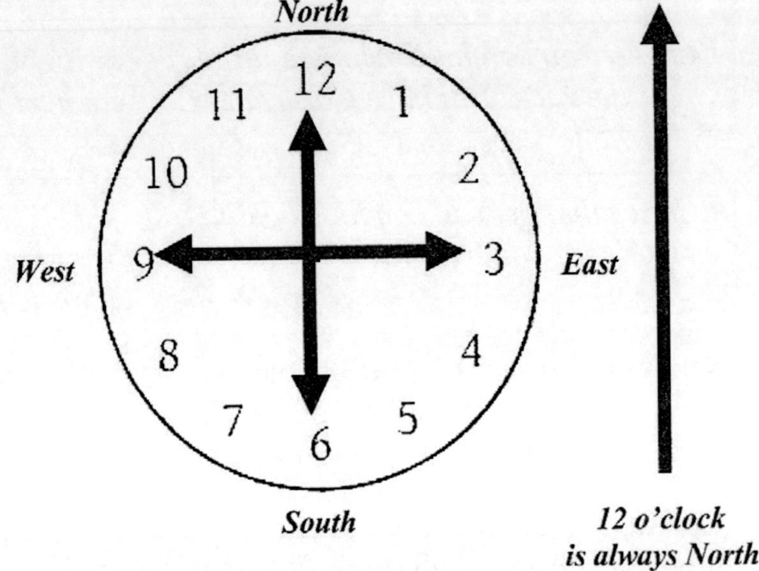

The Clock System of Referencing Direction

6-*JDLR* or *"Just Don't Look Right"*

A critical acronym to keep in mind during *A Failure of Civility* is *'JDLR'*. This acronym stands for the slang phrase "*Just Don't Look Right.*" We know that's poor English composition, but if something does not look right or looks out of place of the normal landscape... count on and assume something is wrong.

If people approaching your Protective Perimeter look nervous or jittery, go with your feeling of *Just Don't Look Right* and let others know about it. Attacks have been crushed before they could materialize simply by soldiers seeing something that *Just Don't Look Right* and alerting *all others* to it.

6-Have *NPP* area intelligence photos, satellite images and maps

You must have maps, photos and satellite images of your area. While computers and the internet function, print a series of satellite image maps of your *NPP* Protective Perimeter area *and the areas surrounding it.*

In addition to streets in proximity to your *NPP*, pay particular attention to structures, terrain features, drainage ditches, causeways, hiking and bicycle trails, canals that allow undetected *Intruder* movement towards your *NPP* and which can be used for emergency escape and movement.

The United States Bureau of Land Management or BLM, the United States Forest Service and other federal agencies have great topographical maps for a few dollars each. They may have these for your *Primary NPP Location* and for each of your *Secondary NPP Locations.* If not… get regular road maps… multiple copies.

These same terrain features can be used for your *NPP* emergency escape routes. You can use the 'Earth' feature of satellite photos to give you a three dimensional view of your surroundings, just like looking down from a height.

6-The *Third Dimension* of your *NPP* Protective Perimeter… usually forgotten

We cover this as a critical item of designing the *Area Tactical Protection* of your *Neighborhood Protection Plan* because this avenue of attack *and* defense *is overlooked by most people* in forming a Protective Perimeter.

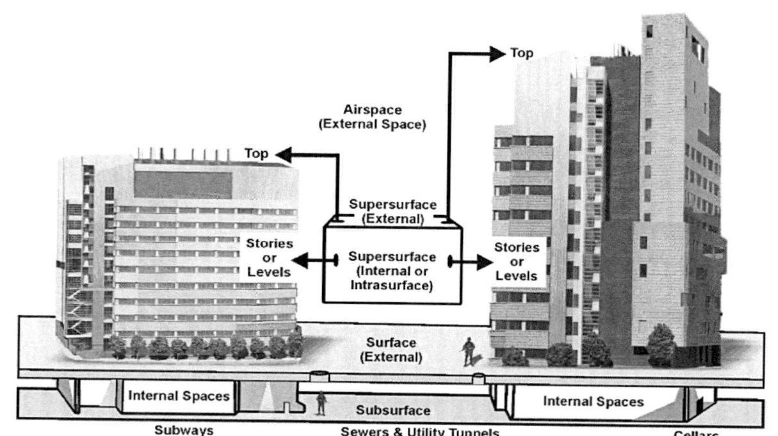

The underground world which exists in most city areas.

We're leaving out some factors of the *Third Dimension* of a Protective Perimeter because we don't think your adversary will have these capabilities. These parts of the *Third Dimension* are airborne troop drops, helicopter troop delivery capability, artillery and/or Air Support.

We don't think paratroopers or helicopter borne troops will descend on you, nor will *Intruders* have the capability of bombarding or strafing you with artillery and close Air Support. But have plans to deal with these anyway like Fall Back Fighting Positions and for a 'Just in Case'… holy snikees !!… What was that explosion !!??... situation. Use underground if it's big enough to house people and supplies.

Dictionary Definition
Tactics
(Noun) The military science that deals with securing objectives by strategy, especially the technique of deploying and directing troops… Maneuvers used against an enemy.

Your *NPP* Protective Perimeter must be determined by looking at *all three dimensions...* the dimensions of *width* and *length...* but also the dimension of *height/depth*.

Imagine standing in the middle of your *NPP* and doing this... looking *North*, along a North-South line to see your *First Dimension* of your *NPP*, that's the 12 through 6 o'clock position. Now you turn 90 degrees and look *West* along an East-West line to see the *Second Dimension* of your *NPP*, that's the 9 through 3 o'clock position... those two make the width and length of your *NPP*.

Now, still standing in the same place, look up 90 degrees into the sky along an imaginary line from deep in the ground coming out of the surface and continuing up to the sky... now you see the usually forgotten *Third Dimension.* Not just up... but down.

Many defense plans fail to take into account the *Third Dimension...*

What's under ground is commonly ignored when forming defenses... underground passages.

What's above ground is commonly ignored when forming defenses... above ground room to room movement in or movement on buildings.

Whole armies have been stopped dead in their tracks or defeated by enemy attacks utilizing underground and above ground concealed travel. One of the best examples is both the Russian and German use of underground sewers, utility corridors and room to room movement above ground to outflank and destroy units of their enemy in Stalingrad during that epic battle in World War II.

Underground Passages. *Underground passages are more of a* ***disadvantage to the defender*** *than the attacker.*

In large cities, underground, or subterranean passages include underground garages, walk-way passages, subway lines, utility tunnels, sewers, and storm drains. Most of these allow people movement through them.

Underground passages almost take the form of the mythological Trojan Horse... *they provide a way for the enemy to get inside your NPP* without being seen, heard or firing a shot... until they're standing right behind you like the Boogie Man.

Even in smaller towns, sewers and storm drains may permit defenders *and* attackers to move beneath the fighting to surface behind their enemy. Knowledge of the type and location of underground facilities and above ground building routes of movement is of critical value to both the attacker *and* the *NPP* defenders.

Underground routes and above ground building passage can provide the attacker the use of ground level attack, while simultaneously using above ground and underground avenues of attack. Your opponent can assault your *NPP* defenses from *inside* while attacking the *outside* by street level. You're then subjected to Flanking Fire… game over!

Depending upon the strength and depth of your *NPP* ground level defense, an attack along the underground or above ground avenue of approach can turn into the main attack. Even if the underground or above ground effort is not immediately successful, *it forces the NPP to fight on two or more levels* and to extend resources to more than just street-level defense. There is also the *Element of Surprise that can turn your NPP into chaos* from an underground attack.

However, given the confining, dark environment of these passages, they do offer some advantages when thoroughly evaluated and controlled by the NPP...

- A small number of Group Members in a prepared defensive position can defeat a numerically superior force in an underground passage by using it as a Kill Zone. Skipping Rounds is extremely lethal in this type of confined space with hard concrete walls.
- Underground passages can provide your *NPP* covered and concealed routes to move reinforcements within your *NPP* Protective Perimeter or to launch flanking attacks from behind an opponent's rear on the outside of your *NPP* Protective Perimeter.
- Depending on their size, underground passages can be used for communications, for the storage and movement of supplies, evacuation and treatment of wounded and as a safe haven for children. They can also be an emergency escape route.

Underground passages are more a disadvantage to the defender than the attacker...
so if you're not going to use them… control them. Barricade or guard them!

When we say ***controlled by the NPP*** we mean these passages either have to be *constantly guarded* or *solidly barricaded.* Manholes and access covers inside your *NPP* need to be welded in place and passage ways blocked off. Heavy items such as concrete slabs or large rocks can be placed over the manhole covers or a vehicle driven, parked and disabled with one wheel on the access or manhole cover.

Above Ground Concealed Movement. Even a building that has no doors connecting the rooms either above ground or in a basement can be used. Attackers *and* defenders can knock passage holes through most walls to allow concealed movement.

Another path for concealed movement for you *and* your opponent is the far side of roofs or balconies hidden from your *NPP* view or the enemy's view. Considering that your *NPP* Protective Perimeter should put buildings inside your *NPP*, rooftops are a great means of concealed movement for Group Members on the leeward side of the building.

Tunneling into your NPP. Be aware of an unusual and unlikely but a possible attack method... tunneling. Tunneling is digging an underground passage from outside your walls, under your Protective Perimeter to the inside of your *NPP*. If *Intruders* use explosives to blow a hole in your Protective Perimeter or if even one armed *Intruder* gets inside your *NPP* this can wreak holy hell on your defenders.

If your Guard Post sees movement of dirt in the Field of Fire or around your Protective Perimeter, don't discount tunneling into your *NPP*. Your Perimeter Patrol sweeps should be aware of any disturbed earth and this strategy being employed by your enemy, *especially from the inside of nearby buildings*. Check them.

You must consider *overhead power and communication lines* and *drainage exits in walls* of subdivisions as a possible means of entry to your neighborhood. *Intruders* can 'monkey crawl' any overhead wires leading into your *NPP* that are strong enough to hold their weight. Most wall drainage openings with reinforcing rod in them can be easily cut out with a bolt cutter or hacksaw.

It is difficult enough to fight off outside *Intruders*, but if you have to fight off *outside Intruders and Intruders inside* your *NPP* it will most likely cause your defeat, especially if *Intruders* get to your Watch Center and kill or capture your leadership.

6-Assessing your neighborhood for a *NPP*

Again, we advise you that a sufficient and renewable water source is the crucial issue in determining the viability of your *Primary* and *Secondary NPP Locations* being long term sustainable *NPPs*.

Refer back to *Chapter 5* for *Questions the Primary and Secondary NPP Leaders must answer first* before proceeding to use a neighborhood for a *Primary NPP Location* or choosing your *Secondary NPP Locations.*

Is there a water source? *You have to evaluate this first.* Read our information on *water* in *Chapter 12* ***first*** to help you evaluate this issue.

If you can't dig a water bore hole or open well inside your *NPP*... you need a reliable source of water nearby outside your *NPP*. Without a water source close by you do not have a sustainable neighborhood for a *Long Term Neighborhood Protection Plan* and must look at another area.

You need a lake, reservoir, river, stream or other water source *that you can depend on year 'round. You must have a water bore hole or open well inside your NPP or a water source* ***one mile or less from your NPP Location.***

We warn you not to base the ***long term sustainability*** *of your NPP on rain water or snow being sufficient for potable water.*

The Low Rise Residential Neighborhood provides the *NPP* unique advantages… mostly that you're fighting on 'your turf.' You know it, *Intruders* most likely don't. Further, urban areas are excellent for Economy of Force as defending in urban terrain typically requires fewer forces than on open ground.

If common areas are to be 'Landscape Fortified' you'll have to get your Home Owners Association involved with your plan. They, like much of the bureaucracy in the United States, will have members who are 'Politically Correct' also.

If your HOA thinks a *Neighborhood Protection Plan* will increase their liability and they object to protecting their neighborhood during a *Crisis*, as ridiculous as this sounds… bypass them and organize your street and neighbors.

The HOA can't stop you if you don't violate the HOA Rules and Regulations during *Normal Civility* and they certainly won't interfere if *A Failure of Civility* occurs. They'll suddenly have a keen interest in your ideas.

There will be two types of neighbors in your neighborhood regarding the formation of your Neighborhood Protection Plan...

- *NPP* Participants.
- *NPP* Non-Participants.

There may be two types of houses in your neighborhood regarding the formation of your Neighborhood Protection Plan...

- Border houses.
- Interior houses.

Non-Participant houses *may* be a problem if their house is on the border which is where your defensive perimeter will be.

Non-Participants will act one of two ways...

- Impartial.
- Hostile.

Your Protective Perimeter can be one house, a couple of houses, street by street or an entire subdivision. In *Chapter 5* we've given you guidelines on what size to make your *NPP*. This is primarily determined by the number of Group Members your *NPP* will have for the area they have to defend.

Take time to explain your *Neighborhood Protective Plan* to these Non-Participants. Most will simply let you form your plan with their house being involved even though they will not be participating.

Either way, you will have to work around these houses still making their house a part of your Protective Perimeter without intruding on their property or them. You may have to double your Guard Posts in this area for each side of Non-Participant's homes.

Non-Participants will quickly want to join if there is *A Failure of Civility* or if their security and safety becomes threatened. But until that time comes and since you're forming your *NPP* during peaceful times, you will have to work around them.

6-Where to set up your neighborhood Protective Perimeters

Maps and satellite images of your *NPP* area alone will not give you the most complete picture of your area because they lack the corresponding terrain elevation differences and the ability to visualize your area thoroughly from all perspectives in one place. You need a Sand Table.

Houses and property on the border of your *NPP* will define your Protective Perimeter. Your Protective Perimeter may be a wall, fence, street or imaginary line around the homes that are included in your *NPP*.

In addition to your Area Intelligence Photos, the best of all planning devices is the 'Sand Table' as used by military and law enforcement to give a three dimensional scale model perspective when planning tactics in an area.

Military use of a Sand Table

Images, maps and the Sand Table should be kept in the Watch Center building. A Sand Table incorporates the *Third Dimension* of terrain changes and the heights of area objects. It will give you the best visual reference to planning your Protective Perimeter.

Make your sand table model as realistic as possible… include bushes, homes, sheds, garages, walls, etc. Mold the contour of your neighborhood and the surrounding area with common sand.

After you form the sand it can be sprayed with lacquer to hold it in place. Use kids' model cars, cotton balls for bushes, small boxes for houses, cardboard strips for walls, etc. Put *everything* on it. This model will be of great help to those who do not understand maps.

The photo shows a large area military operations sand table. Your sand table can be a few feet square as long as it reflects the area inside and outside your *NPP*.

Remember one important advantage you'll have. If you formulate even a fairly good plan, it will probably be very effective against numerically superior *Intruders*. They don't know your area or the terrain. *You do*.

This is a *huge* tactical advantage in warfare. Many wars have been lost by overwhelmingly superior forces fighting inferior forces on unfamiliar ground and especially if that inferior force has pre planned defensive positions and tactical plans.

6-How to set up your *NPP* Protective Perimeter

If armed *Intruders* try to force their way in, you want to force or deceive those *Intruders* into attacking under unfavorable circumstances to them, and to defeat or destroy that attack. When 10 *Intruders* attack a two man Guard Post and suddenly 4 other *Response Guardians* quickly react to fire on them from another direction and defeat them… that is the result of a *Proactive Defense.*

While the *offense* may be the most essential type of operation in a conflict, *the defense is the strongest*. The strength for the *NPP* is the ability to have prepared positions before an attack and to make use of 'Economy of Force.' Economy of Force is the ability of fewer people to defend successfully against a greater number of attackers.

The military usually sets up 'layers' of defenses. An External Perimeter and an Inner Perimeter. Most terrain features, manpower and the close proximity of structures do not allow for an External Perimeter. Consequently the Authors exclude the External Perimeter for the purposes of this book and your *NPP*. We've condensed this into a Protective Perimeter with Fall Back Fighting positions within your Protective Perimeter.

You must know your neighborhood area. By know it, we mean walk your neighborhood with your Group Members. *"Know your area... walk your area."* Don't just look at, but examine every feature of your neighborhood.

Most importantly, walk the outside of your neighborhood to see your perimeter from an *Intruder's* view point and prospective. Your elected *NPP Leaders* must walk *all* of the neighborhood inside and especially the outside. We suggest that photographs of your Protective Perimeter be taken from various distances to know what an *Intruder* will be seeing.

Look at your *NPP* from the highest vantage point that an *Intruder* could use… because they *will* use this vantage point to look at your *NPP*. Look at second story window positions or elevated positions next to your Protective Perimeter as a position for an enemy… because they will use these too.

Look for high vantage points as well as the lower places of Cover and Concealment. Look for high vantage points such as the roofs of two story houses for observation points and positions to put the *LOP Guardian* positions, *Outflanker Marksmen* and *Inside Marksmen* positions.

A high vantage point that gives you a commanding view of your entire areas is critical for not only defense but for gathering intelligence of the surrounding area during a *Crisis*.

Check *all* underground and above ground passages. Curb side drains usually offer an area large enough to place a sentry with his weapon. Conceal these positions from *Outsiders* who might be checking out your area intent on attacking.

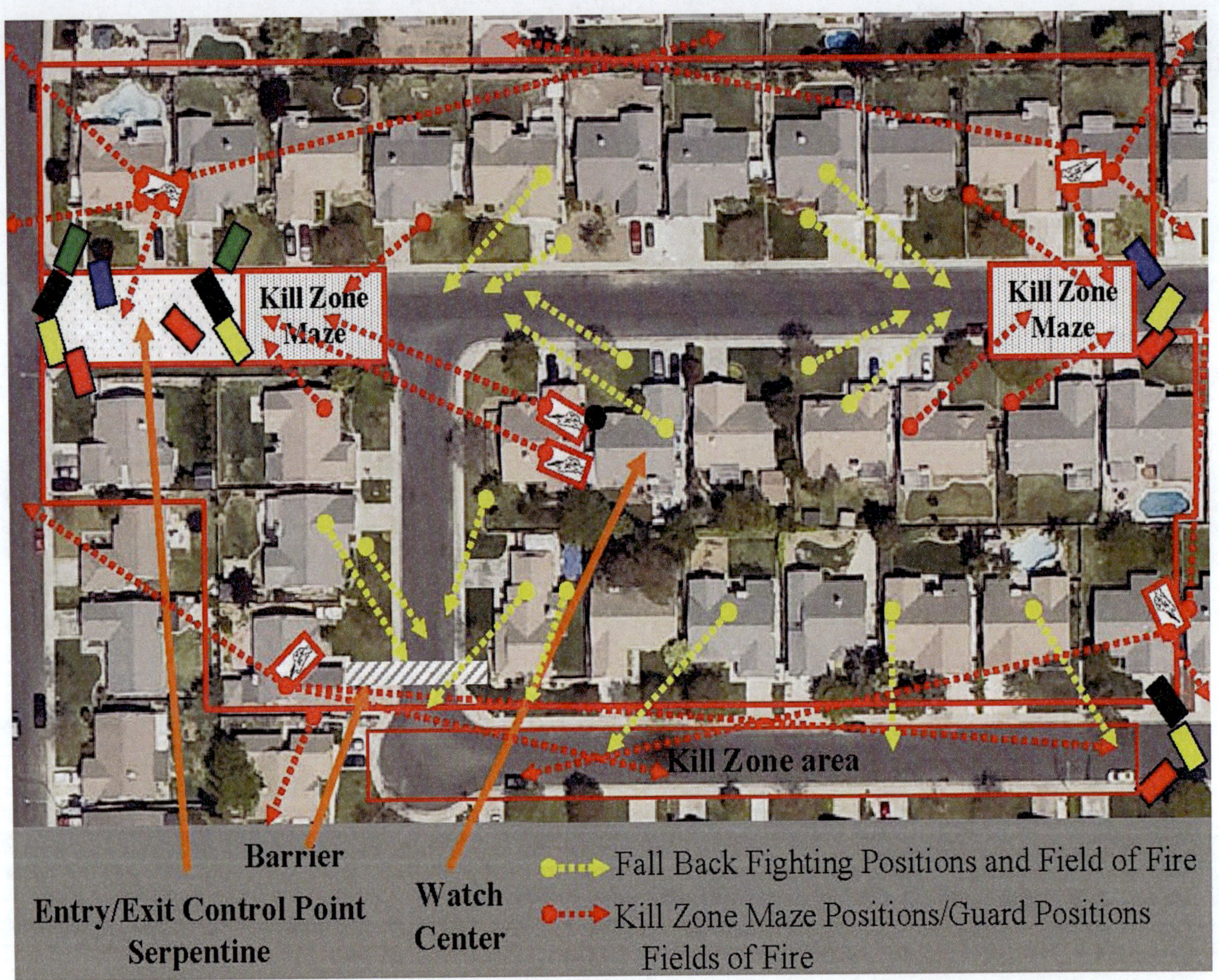

Neighborhood Protection Plan Protective Perimeter design example

Neighborhood Protection Plan Protective Perimeter example. In the *Neighborhood Protection Plan* sample photo you'll see an example of how to plan and set up your Protective Perimeter. This example will probably look 'busy' and confusing to you.

As with all diagrams and examples of tactics in this book, read on, learn the terminology and meaning of each. Then review this diagram and the others over again. The tactical applications will begin to make sense to you.

In this particular neighborhood *NPP*, notice there are 4 swimming pools within this Protective Perimeter. At an average of 15,000 gallons of water in each pool… that's about 60,000 gallons of potable water if it's treated.

By estimating that at 2.5 people per home and 29 homes… there are roughly 75 people in this *NPP*. The water in those swimming pools will provide over two and one half months of potable water for each person, considering some evaporation loss will take place before it's all consumed.

6-*Outside* features your *NPP* Protective Perimeter must have

The outside of your Protective Perimeter should have these features...

- ***Overlapping Fields of View*** from Guard Posts that see the entire Protective Perimeter.
- ***Clear Fields of Fire*** around the Protective Perimeter and as far out as possible. Remove anything that obstructs this and gives Cover or Concealment to the *Intruder*.
- ***Interlocking Fields of Fire*** that cover the entire Protective Perimeter.
- ***Supporting Fields of Fire*** that cover as many areas of the Protective Perimeter as you can.
- ***Field of Fire surfaces difficult to move on.*** Place rubble that is hard to walk or run on but gives no Cover. Install Punji trenches, Abatis' or downed trees or string Barbed Wire or Concertina Wire and alert devices around your perimeter. See *Chapter 8*.
- ***LOPs.*** Depending on your neighborhood layout, one or more high elevation Listening Observation Posts (LOPs) that can see the entire Protective Perimeter or the area of the adjoining Protective Perimeter and the most likely approaches to the perimeter.
- ***Marksmen Positions.*** Depending on your neighborhood layout, one or more high elevation Marksmen positions that can see the entire Protective Perimeter or most of the area adjoining the Protective Perimeter and the most likely approaches to the perimeter.
- ***Outflanker Marksmen Position.*** It is crucial that you have at least one *Outflanker Marksmen* position. That is Marksmen *outside* the Protective Perimeter that can aggressively and precisely fire on *Intruders* around the Protective Perimeter, especially the main approach and can accurately fire on *Intruders* who get inside your Protective Perimeter.
- ***Hold the High Ground.*** If you have High Ground adjoining your *NPP* and it is not part of your *NPP* Protective Perimeter, Marksmen must be able to fire on it to deny the enemy the use of it.
- ***Combined LOP* and *Marksmen positions.*** If you have enough qualified Group Members and radio communications we recommend one or more *combined* LOP and *Outflanker Marksmen* positions in high vantage points *outside* your *NPP*. These can be

extremely effective in alerting your *NPP* to threats and the *Outflanker Marksmen* positions can act as a counter-sniper to eliminate sniper threats to your *NPP*.

- ***Placement of Guard Posts*** that allow multiple positions to fire on the most likely approaches as Supporting Fields of Fire. Especially the street approaches to your neighborhood.
- ***Allows rapid response by foot.*** A small enough area to allow your *Response Guardians* and your *Guardian Runners* to move quickly from one side of the Protective Perimeter to the most distant side by the shortest route. They will have to do just that if you are attacked.
- ***Limit Stakes*** should define Fields of Fire for Guard Posts.
- ***Ambush areas.*** 'L' Shaped ambush areas as Kill Zones close to but outside of your Protective Perimeter that your *Response Guardians* and Guard Posts can use to ambush *Intruders* adjoining, but outside your Protective Perimeter.

Range Cards are simple stakes or landmarks set out to give a defensive position the distance to a point in their Field of Fire, such as 100 yards, 200 yards, etc.

They can also be used in the multiple roles as Limit Stakes to define the left and right limit for a defensive position's Field of Fire.

The Authors do not believe in Range Cards with the exception of their use for the Marksmen positions *inside* and *outside* the *NPP*.

Range Cards are beyond practical usage for most Low Rise Residential Protective Perimeters because of the inadequate distances between most properties and the limited training Group Members will have.

The Authors do, however, believe that Limit Stakes, defining the left and right limit of each Guard Post's Field of Fire should be used to give some fire control discipline to each Guard Post. Guards should not be shooting at *Intruders* outside of these Limit Stakes unless a Guard Post is in danger of being overwhelmed.

Further, the Authors are great believers in 'Barbed Wire' and especially 'Concertina Wire' also known as 'Razor Wire'. Barbed Wire and Concertina Wire are cheap, easy to use to restrict entry into areas with and gives an *Intruder* no Cover or Concealment.

You can get Barbed Wire at most building supply or farm supply stores. You will need heavy leather gloves to place Concertina Wire and Barbed Wire.

Barbed Wire or Concertina Wire are great obstacles to *Intruders* and can be used to define areas and create obstacles in each Guard Post's *Field of Fire*. Concertina Wire is made for this purpose and can be purchased for about $80 a roll through the internet for enough to cover 50 lineal feet.

Concertina Wire has the added advantage over Barbed Wire that it will stand on its own… you don't have to string it over anything to keep it up off the ground. 50 lineal feet is enough to cover one entry/exit area of most subdivision streets.

6-Inside features of your *NPP* Protective Perimeter

The area inside the Protective Perimeter of your Neighborhood Protection Plan should be configured like this...

- ***LOPs.*** Depending on your Protective Perimeter layout, one or more high elevation *LOPs* that can see the entire Protective Perimeter or most of the area of the adjoining Protective Perimeter and the most likely approaches to the Protective Perimeter.
- ***Marksmen Positions.*** Depending on your neighborhood layout, one or more high elevation Marksmen positions that can see the entire Protective Perimeter or most of the area of the adjoining Protective Perimeter and the most likely approaches to the Protective Perimeter.
- ***A Watch Center*** in a central structure inside your *NPP*. Watch Center buildings must be 'blacked out' at night during a *Crisis*. No white light must be visible from the outside. *Check the building from the outside at night to verify this.*
- ***A Kill Zone*** as part of your *NPP* Entry/Exit Control Point.
- ***Fall Back Fighting Positions*** or a Defense in Depth.
- ***One fortified house***, preferably your Watch Center location as a last stand or 'Alamo' fighting position.
- ***One or more emergency escape exits*** which we will cover in *Chapter 11*.

Beware that Supporting Fields of Fire between different *NPP* Group Members can create Friendly Fire Incidents of Group Members firing on their own Group Members. You'll have enough people shooting at you if you're attacked, without your own Group Members hitting other Group Members by accident. Plan your Guard Posts locations with Friendly Fire Incident prevention in mind.

Use the proper weapons on hand for different Guard Posts. Don't use a shotgun or pistol for long range. Use common sense!

So, you've got a lot of things going for you… let's move on.

6-How to prepare your neighborhood right now

Almost all of the following can be done for little expense for each neighbor or to the *NPP* if everyone chips in or if your HOA agrees to fund these.

One of the many preparations your neighborhood can make that serves the purpose of protecting residents even during *Normal Civility* we label 'Fortification Landscape'.

This is subtly changing or installing landscape to serve as part of your fortifications while at the same time improving the beauty of the neighborhood and homes.

Decorative rocks or decorative concrete fixtures. At the designated Entry/Exit Control Point short, decorative concrete walls can be poured in place or large decorative landscape rocks situated where you want designated Guard Posts.

These give tremendous Cover and Concealment. These can also be placed strategically throughout the neighborhood for Fall Back Fighting positions. If *A Failure of Civility* occurs, you can string strand Barbed Wire or Concertina Wire between or in front of them.

Landscape Fortification Bollards

Earthen berms can be installed in front of fences and walls and planted with ground cover. These prevent vehicles from ramming through fences.

LOP and Marksmen Cupolas. These can be constructed on one or more of your high vantage points in your neighborhood. If the time comes for their use, *these can be as simple as a piece of plywood over rafters in an attic to stand on, then cutting a hole at the peak of the roof...* to using existing windows on second story homes... or they can be as complex as building one in permanently to match the home with drop down windows.

Permanent LOP and Marksmen Cupola

These can be an unobtrusive and beautiful roof fixture that adds to value and enhances the look of the house. If you place sand bags on a roof behind painted wooden sides or a simple plywood box cut to fit the roof line and painted like a chimney... these are means to create good Marksmen positions and *Listening Observation Posts.*

Underground Passages. As we stated earlier... investigate them. Make preparations to either use or them or seal off underground passages. The Authors like the idea of using them if they're large enough and sealed off from the outside of the *NPP*.

Pre built Guard Posts. These also can be simple or as sophisticated as you design. They can be fortified and still blend in with landscape. Plant bushes, shrubs and flowers in them or build them as storage sheds next to your perimeter with the dual purpose of using them for Guard Posts. If the time comes when you need them, with little modification, they can be prepared. Make them as basic or refined as you see fit.

Thorn Bushes. Africans have used thorn bushes for millennia for barriers against people and predatory animals killing, stealing and stalking their livestock.

Thorn 'willow hatched' bushes as a barrier

Either planted around homes and villages or cut and piled high for permanent or temporary barriers they are nasty to try to get through as the Authors have personally experienced. These can be cut or burned down though.

Plant thorn bushes along the inside of your designated Protective Perimeter. If you don't have block walls or fences sufficient to keep people from climbing over them, these make great barriers that can constitute your perimeter by themselves.

Topping a wall with glass in masonry cement

These can be 'willow hatched' or trained by you while they're growing to cross over each other as in the photo. They give little Concealment and no Cover and they prevent people from getting into your *NPP* easily on foot. They are hardy and most take little water to survive and flourish.

Thorn bushes should also be planted to create 'walls' for potential Kill Zones that you designate within your *NPP*. Most thorn bushes grow to considerable heights, cling to walls and will improve the looks of the landscape scheme while providing virtually an impenetrable foot traffic obstacle for much of your Protective Perimeter and Kill Zones.

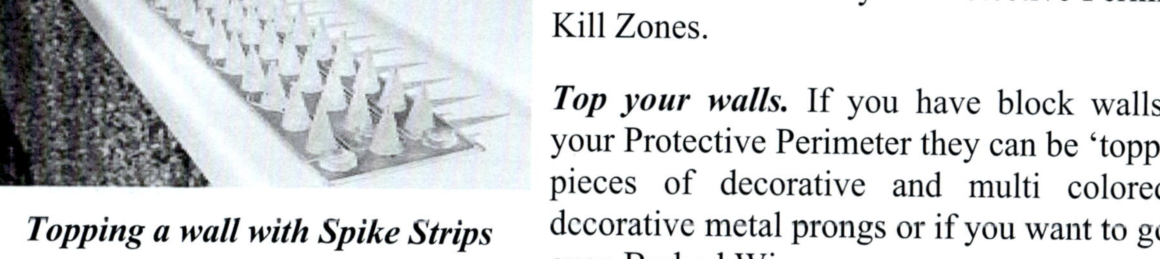

Topping a wall with Spike Strips

Top your walls. If you have block walls around your Protective Perimeter they can be 'topped' with pieces of decorative and multi colored glass, decorative metal prongs or if you want to go further even Barbed Wire.

These can be defeated by an enemy covering them with heavy clothes and crawling over them, but by themselves they keep people out and they slow *Intruders* down. Some local ordinances and some HOAs prohibit or restrict what you can put on your walls and what height your walls must be to install items like these.

Install metal door and window shutters. Roll down metal shutters are expensive, but make your home a virtual fortress when they're rolled down. Window bars are also expensive but the Authors feel they're more of a fire trap than protection.

In most Third World Countries, where 95 % of the people are 'Have Nots' and are constantly burglarizing the more well-to-do, some of the above are common deterrents they use that don't make a neighborhood look totally like a 'fortress.' Quite to the contrary... their developments usually look beautiful.

Roll up metal door and window shutters

You will see more and more 'Landscape Fortification' and overt fortification and security around subdivisions, buildings and homes in America as the social, political and economic situation worsens over the next years.

6-Things *not* to do

Don't allow independent action by Group Members. Independent action by Group Members without your *NPP Leader's* approval is dangerous to the entire *NPP*.

This point reflects on the importance of basic discipline. *NPP* Group Members have to rely on the knowledge and experience of the *NPP* Leaders and must follow orders explicitly. The *only* exception to this is Junior Leader's limited decision making.

Don't fire warning shots. If *A Failure of Civility* occurs *do not* use warning shots in an attempt to drive away *Intruders*. This simply draws attention to your *NPP* and wastes ammunition. Verbally warn but then *"Shoot to stop the Threat."*

Don't ignore any alarm... because the first rule of alarms is... that there is no such thing as a false alarm! You've heard the fable of *"The Man Who Cried Wolf."* Keep *JDLR* in mind if you have false alarms on any security issue.

Successful defeats have occurred by an enemy 'disarming' the alert mentality of a defensive position by repetitiously creating false alarms and then attacking with the Element of Surprise. *Treat every alarm as a threat and be alert when you investigate.*

Don't have light visible from outside. 'Black Out' not only your Watch Center area but all rooms with windows visible from outside your Protective Perimeter. Use green or red filters on flashlights if you must use light in these areas.

Do not open and close lighted room doors at night. During *A Failure of Civility* you will draw unnecessary attention from those that you do not want to spend an evening with if you do this. They won't be coming to play Pinochle with you.

6-Things *you must* do

Armbands. If you merge with another *NPP*, when *Extended Family and Friends* arrive or until everyone intimately knows every Group Member in the *NPP*, you must have some means of Group Members identifying each other in daylight, by night red or green filtered flashlight and in the heat of an action… identifying friend from foe.

We suggest armbands on *both* upper arms to identify friend from foe. Do not use anything that will make you a target… like white, light colored or fluorescent colors.

You must have something unique that is not easily copied by *Intruders*. Uniforms are cost prohibitive and many people may have similar or the same patterns or color if *A Failure of Civility* occurs.

This is something the seamstress types in your neighborhood can make for little cost. Mrs. Jones's curtains can be sacrificed for this in a pinch.

Passwords. Simple numerical passwords can be used at night and during the day for identification during darkness.

Example, set the *password number* at 12. If a Guard Post gives the *challenge* to an unknown person he calls out to that unknown person *"5"*. The unknown person must respond with *"7"*. The object being that the numbers given and received must add up to 12. Change the *password number* every 24 hours and keep voices down when challenging.

Carrying Weapons. Regardless of the stage after a *Catastrophic Event*, if the *NPP* is activated, everyone must carry their weapons *at all times wherever they go*.

Confine movement in the NPP during darkness. You do not want accidental shootings of Group Members at night. Keep children and anyone other than those on guard, inside or within a designated and restricted area.

You should have only your Roving Patrol moving outside the designated restricted areas within your building after dark.

Roving Patrols are *inside* the *NPP* Protective Perimeter Patrol *versus* Perimeter Patrols being an *outside* the *NPP* Protective Perimeter Patrol. Roving Patrols should also accompany guards to their positions during shift change at night.

You will not appreciate how nervous and 'trigger happy' people will become if *A Failure of Civility* occurs until it happens.

6-You're in a *Crisis*... *Low Alert* procedures to institute

The worse the *Crisis* gets the more elaborate your security measures and defensive preparation must become. Your *NPP* security and defenses should *match or exceed* the stage of the *Crisis*. Read our guidelines and then create your own.

You are in a Crisis situation in your area. Your NPP Protective Perimeter at this time should be on a 'Low Alert' footing and you need to institute the following...

- If you have radios, charge the batteries and setup your Watch Center base radio.
- Leaders should talk to all Group Members by phone if possible or visit each one. Brief them and advise them to be prepared to take their positions of duty.
- Put your Watch Center into effect and man it 24 hours a day monitoring radio stations and radio traffic then providing *NPP Leaders* with periodic briefings from police scanners and radio communications.
- Institute Fire Watch Procedures.
- Dress in casual civilian clothing without armbands. Do not overtly display weapons.
- Check area gas stations to see which are pumping gas and what lines are like. If vehicles operate, fuel all vehicles.
- Post a guard at each entrance to your *NPP*. Watch for anything unusual such as groups in vehicles. Be careful what you say to *Outsiders*... they may become *Intruders* attacking your *NPP* later.
- Check with other area *NPP*s and reliable sources to get or confirm information. Group Members may need to make trips to communicate with bicycles or on foot.
- Start the inside Roving Guards.
- Prepare alternative methods to keep insulin and temperature sensitive medicines cool.
- Watch for internal theft.
- Start enforcing light and sound discipline. Keep noise to a minimum and lights low or blacked out at night.
- Fill additional reserve fuel storage containers.
- Buy as much additional food as possible.

- Store as much water as possible.
- Buy as much additional ammunition and medicine as you can get.

Even though you have not set up your Entry/Exit Control Point, the guards at that entrance should talk to passersby's to get information on the area situation and communicate this to the Watch Center. Because rumors fill the air after disasters or disturbances, make sure all information is *confirmed* by more than one source before being shared with other Group Members. Watch for deceptive con artists and keep an ear tuned for rumor control.

6-You're in a *Long Term Crisis… Mid Alert* procedures to institute

The Crisis has deteriorated to a Long Term Crisis. Your NPP Protective Perimeter at this time should be on a 'Mid Alert' footing and you need to institute the following...

- Leaders should call all Group Members together. Brief them and post all Group Members to their positions.
- If you have radios, assign one radio to each *LOP Guardian,* one radio to each Marksman, one radio to each *Alpha or Bravo Guardian* at their Guard Post, one to the *Patrol Guardians* group, one radio to the *Roving Guardians* group, one radio to the *Response Guardian* group, one radio to each *Runner Guardian* and one radio for the *Caretaker Guardian. Reserve Guardians will be in the Watch Center and will use the radio of the position they have to relieve.*
- Heighten Fire Watch Procedures
- Increase light and sound discipline.
- Dress in casual civilian clothing *with* armbands. Dress in civilian clothing colors that match or are similar to the major color scheme of your environment. Do not overtly display weapons except at your Entry/Exit Control Point and within your *NPP.*
- Keep the Watch Center active 24 hours a day monitoring radio stations and radio traffic and providing *NPP Leaders* with periodic briefings and notifying them immediately of items importance heard on police scanners and radio communications.
- Start your Watch Center child care to free up Group Members for their duties.
- Man your Guard Posts with the exception of your *Outflanker Marksmen.*
- Increase inside Roving Guard activity and start the Patrol Guards on perimeter check.
- Blockade all entrances to your *NPP* with the exception of your Entry/Exit Control Point.
- Assign additional guards to your Entry/Exit Control Point area.
- Put the coffee pot on… make *lots* of it.

If this is a pandemic, the sick must be quarantined in a home or building away from others if they have infectious disease.

One Group Member is going to have to volunteer to be quarantined with them to tend to their needs wearing the proper eye, face masks, gloves and clothing to keep the pandemic from spreading to these caregivers. After leaving the quarantined area, the clothing they wore must be immediately washed with disinfectant or burned.

6-High elevation *Listening Observation Posts (LOP)*

Extreme care should be taken that this position remains concealed and no attention is brought to it. Read the items below under ***Other Guard Issues.***

This position, the LOP, is the 'Eyes and Ears' of the *NPP*. This position is probably the most important of your Protective Perimeter Guard Posts. This position, along with the Marksmen, *must* have a means of communications with your Watch Center.

If you combine your Marksmen with your *Listening Observation Posts* it allows them to engage any *definitely hostile* targets that threaten the *NPP* well in advance of the threat getting close to the *NPP*. The more combined *LOPs* and Marksmen positions you have… the more effective your Protective Perimeter will be.

This is you main Guard Post and should have view of all approach areas. Binoculars, spotting scopes, telescopes and rifle scopes must have Anti Reflection Protectors (see diagram) to prevent the enemy from seeing sun reflection from your binoculars and scopes.

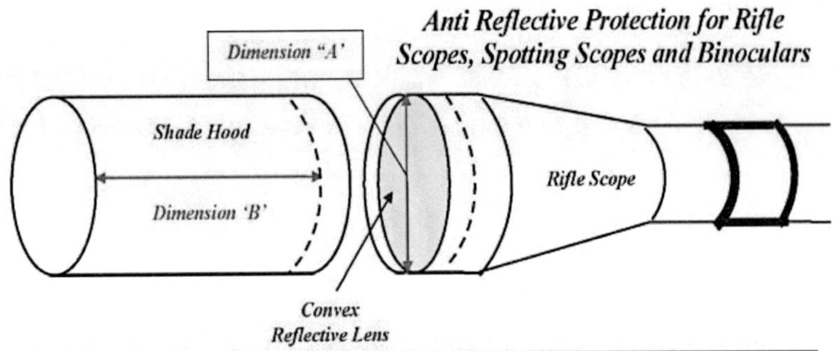

Anti Reflection Protectors for Binoculars and Rifle

6-Marksmenship Posts

These positions should be manned by your best Marksmen with long range telescope equipped rifles for observation and accurate shooting.

There should be at least one position *inside* the *NPP* and at least one position *outside* the *NPP* and between them they should be able to cover by fire most of the terrain *inside* your *NPP, around the* Protective Perimeter *and all the approaches*.

These positions, along with the LOP, *must* have a means of communications with Watch Center.

Outflanker Marksmen positions ***outside*** the *NPP* are more critical than *Inside Marksmen* positions ***inside*** the *NPP*.

The more *Outflanker Marksmen* positions you have… the more effective your Protective Perimeter will also be.

The Marksmen Position…

- Can be *inside* the *NPP* designated as *Inside Marksmen* or *outside* the *NPP* designated as *Outflanker Marksmen.*
- Covers avenues of approach, obstacles and areas not visible from Guard Posts.
- Obtains information by using the rifle scope like a binoculars.
- Can make preemptive strikes on *Intruders* on approaches to the *NPP*, around the Protective Perimeter and can fire on *Intruders* if they get inside the *NPP*.
- Can keep the enemy from regrouping or repositioning for an attack.
- Can assist with the flanking attacks made by your *NPP* Group Members.
- Can deter enemy infiltration attempts.
- Operates as an extension for your Perimeter Patrol checks.

6-Story-"While I Slept"

George Randall could hear his heart pounding in his chest in between his labored breathing… the rapid sound of "ka thump, ka thump, ka thump" filled his ears as he stopped and looked back to see if they were following him.

He was a lawyer by trade. Even thought he had never been in the military, he'd saved many a client's life that fate had placed in his hands. He'd brilliantly cut the legs out from most prosecutors in their criminal cases against his clients.

He was the man to go to in this city if you were the accused. Successful with his law practice beyond his wildest dreams, in this mundane task of protecting his neighborhood he had failed.

He crouched down in a ravine outside a burned out subdivision a couple of hundred yards down from his neighborhood… even though the black of night that was slowly turning to the twilight of dawn obscured most of it… he knew it was burnt down.

***The** fires had raged for over a day in this neighborhood a week ago. They had watched from the entrance of their NPP as mobs came and went from this subdivision beating and killing the homeowners, setting fire to and destroying the neighborhood. His Group Members had killed six of them as they made their way towards their NPP but it was too* *late for the people of this subdivision... the Intruders had gutted and destroyed their neighborhood.*

The drizzle of rain did nothing to stifle the stench, to the contrary it, seemed to make it worse... the pungent smell of burnt bodies and wood filled his nostrils.

That same hell had come to George's neighborhood so quickly fifteen minutes ago. He had hesitated at first when hearing all the yelling and gunfire... and then as he gathered his wits about him he ran from his Guard Post towards his NPP Entry/Exit Control Point. The guards there were gone.

***He turned** and ran towards the Watch Center just in time to see the muzzle blasts of the mob spewing weapons fire in through the open Watch Center door. He saw Samuel Baskin quickly step out and return fire with his shotgun, taking down two of the attackers before he was shot down. Intruders seemed to be swarming all over the place. He couldn't believe what he was watching.*

He'd fired at the Intruders after Baskin went down and knew he'd hit one or two of them. He was out of ammunition. Then every Intruder in the neighborhood seemed to be firing back at him. Four of them started firing and moving towards him. George ran towards his Guard Post.

"Did I fall asleep!?" he murmured as the seemingly odd thought floated through his mind as he frantically made it back to his Guard Post.

Usually posted in pairs at Guard Posts, his guard partner Pete was sick like most in their NPP, so this night he sat alone at his Guard Post. He faintly remembered the brief sound of jingling bells... he remembered thinking he'd seen a shadow move in the distance... then his mind went blank. His failure to remember anything after that plagued him for some moments.

"No... I couldn't have dozed off! I don't remember falling asleep!" he reassured himself.

***Then the thought stabbed at him... "**Those were our perimeter alert system bells!" he said aloud as a pang of guilt shot through him like a knife going into his heart.*

He quickly grabbed his ammunition bag and radio before climbing over the wall and running some distance from the Protective Perimeter.

He should have had his two-way radio headset on and his ammunition bag slung over his shoulder as he was instructed... he kicked himself again as he headed towards the ravine.

He tripped a bunch of alert bells running through the perimeter area and another pang of guilt stabbed at him reminding him of what he'd heard before the attack. His shoes were caked with mud and seemed almost impossible to move as he made his way to the ravine.

He put his headset on and stuffed the radio in his jacket pocket.

He blurted into his radio. "Post 9... anybody... come in!?" He almost yelled into his headset as he frantically called again, "Anybody out there, come in!"

"Keep your damned voice down!" came the angry but muffled reply back to him. It sounded like Jensen. He loathed this guy because of the 'U.S. Army Ranger' sticker on the back window of his pickup truck. George disliked the man because George thought he was a 'commoner'.

"Who is this?" *George frantically enquired as the light of now burning houses in George's subdivision lit the sky along with the rising sun.*

"Jensen, roving guard. Randall… you asshole… they came in through your section!"

"They couldn't have come through my section!" George responded emphatically.

"We saw them come through! If you didn't see them you were asleep, you prick!" Jensen screamed the subdued, piercing remark into his radio.

"I was awake… I know… " George's defensive but whining statement was cut off by Jensen.

"Shut up and get your ass over to the Entry/Exit Control Point. We're rallying everyone left to clear these bastards out of the neighborhood!"

A sense of urgency *started to dissipate the fear of death that had overwhelmed him… a fear for his wife and child. "I've got to get back there… Jennifer and George II are in there!"*

"God… please let my family be alright!" he cried to the powers for relief. He quickly made his way down the road to the Entry/Exit Control Point amidst the noise of gunfire, screaming and now raging fires in two of the homes of their neighborhood.

The sun was coming up as he approached the Entry/Exit Control Point.

"I'm coming up on the Control Point by road! Don't shoot!" he said nervously over the radio as he sighted the first of the group.

"Okay… everyone form a sweep line… move cover to cover. Make sure you're not firing at any of ours!" Jensen instructed everyone as he glared at George and pointed for him to get in line but saying nothing else.

"Tommy, we're sweeping the neighborhood starting from the Entry/Exit Control Point. Adjust your fire accordingly!" Jensen barked into his radio as the line began to cautiously move forward.

"Roger that!" came Tommy's cryptic answer.

The repetitious barking *fire, from their Marksman Tommy and his .308 rifle, could be heard in a steady rhythmic fashion "boom, boom, boom." George and the others knew with every report from his rifle an intruder would fall to the old Korean War sniper. George had watched this guy accurately hit targets one after another at the range that George could barely make out with the naked eye.*

The continuous and deadly fire from Tommy had killed many and demoralized most of the rest of the attackers. George saw the bodies of fallen friends and neighbors amongst the attackers as they swept through the area taking their neighborhood back.

"This is my fault!" he screamed to himself as he viewed body after body of the people he'd been responsible to protect. As calloused a man that George had become at his age, it affected him deeply seeing what he'd let happen.

But sheer trauma flooded George when Jennifer walked out of his home holding the lifeless body of their six year old son.

The sight tore George apart inside as a wailing animal sound bellowed from George and filled the air on this bright sunny morning.

6-Guard requirements and procedures

The danger of a sleeping guard. As a Special Operations Soldier stated his modified quote long ago…

"We sleep safe in our beds because rough men stand watch as our guardians in the night to visit violence on those who would do us harm. A soldier must seize every advantage to defeat his opponent. He must strike swiftly and strike hard... he who dares... wins. But under all circumstances those guardians must stand ready to protect the innocent and those too weak to defend themselves…"

> Go over the words again… *"We sleep safe in our beds because rough men stand watch as our guardians in the night to visit violence on those who would do us harm." A sleeping guard can get everyone killed!*
>
> *The weak... the strong! Your NPP safety depends on* **each** *person guarding these people and* **each** *understanding their commitment of...*
>
> ***…NOT ON MY WATCH!!!!!!!!!!!!!!!***

"But under all circumstances those guardians must stand ready to protect the innocent and those too weak to defend themselves…"

A sleeping guard can get everyone killed!

Don't ignore any alarm... because the first rule of alarms is… that there is no such thing as a false alarm! You've heard the fable of *"The Man Who Cried Wolf."* Keep *JDLR* in mind if you have false alarms on any security issue.

Successful defeats have occurred by an enemy 'disarming' the alert mentality of a defensive position by repetitiously creating false alarms and then going in for the kill with the Element of Surprise.

To set up an effective Protective Perimeter guard, you must have guards at intervals by which they have Overlapping Fields of View of the entire Protective Perimeter with no 'dead spots' that they can not see.

> *In the ideal scenario, manpower permitting, we recommend two guards per position to ensure alertness and to help each other stay awake. Two sets of eyes and ears are always better than one. At the bare minimum your roving guard should be at least 2 Group Members.*

Routine will get you killed. Routine procedures in a combat situation are dangerous. Making guard changes at the same time, conducting Perimeter Patrols at the same time or on the same route or going in the same direction are dangerous… your enemy can predict your next movement because through repetitiveness you have revealed it to him in advance.

This is especially dangerous where some of your Group Members are outside and away from your *NPP* Protective Perimeter. Vary your times, your formations, your procedures, the Group Members you use, the direction of your travel and the path you travel. In some situations it's *good to be late... or early*. In some situations it's good to *walk off the beaten path*.

Fire Watch. This is every guard's additional duty and every Group Member's responsibility… to watch for fires and alert the Watch Center if there is a fire.

Guard Shifts. *The average disciplined military guard* will be *alert* for only a maximum of 4 hours at one position. That guard's ability to see slight movement and effectively observe will deteriorate towards the end of that 4 hour shift. After 4 hours it's anyone's guess at what they will observe and at that point staying awake becomes the danger.

To understand the psychology of sentry duty as the military calls it, sit in a fixed position in the shadows for 4 hours in the dark of the night. Not because you want to… but *because you have to.* Your mind will start to play games on you…

"You feel relaxed... your eye lids are getting heavy... verrrry heavy." …like you hear the hypnotist say in the movies. You'll soon be asleep just like those people easily susceptible to hypnotism… no matter how hard you fight to stay awake.

But before you fall asleep, you'll see trees move that aren't moving… you'll imagine movement in the shadows… but there won't be real movement. Now put the heat of summer, rain, annoying mosquitoes, the cold of winter and snow, the full moon's light, a moonless night and a myriad of other conditions to your 4 hour stretch and you will know how difficult this critical job of guard duty is.

The Authors are adamant believers that the toughest, most disciplined and best intentioned person in this butt dull and tedious, but critical duty, is very susceptible to falling asleep.

We sometimes propped sharpened sticks against the underside of our throats while in a sitting position. If we started to doze off, the sharp stick poked us in the throat. When you're physically exhausted… guard duty is ten times as bad. Your Group Members may just be in that condition, plus they may be malnourished, hungry, thirsty and sick.

The Group Member should be on guard duty no more than 2 hours !!

Vary everything. Again… routine is the enemy of any defense. The Authors believe you should shake up guard duty constantly by varying the *time* a guard is at their position, vary the *position* the guard is at, vary the *time you change Guard Posts.* Change from Guard

Post 3 to Guard Post 9 and then from Guard Post 3 to Guard Post 6, etc. The key thought here is to *vary*… to make different each time period, position, time change. Complacency and routine will get you killed.

You must be certain guards *get some sleep in between shifts* and make sure *they are awake when they return back to duty* from sleeping. *If a guard finds themselves falling asleep they must put their pride aside and inform the Watch Center.*

Vary your guard change times. Change guards on the hour, then 45 minutes later, then 30 minutes later, then 55 minutes later, etc. *Change their positions but for no more than 2 hours total guard time per shift.* Let your guards know the length of these duty shifts, but change them frequently. The walk from one Guard Post to the next gets blood circulating and helps keep your Group Member guards awake.

When rotating Guard Posts, always do it in a clockwise manner, so everyone is on the same page, but do this so it's not noticeable from outside your *NPP*.

Guard Posts. The Authors believe in hidden Guard Posts. 'In the Shadows' is our belief. Gone are the days of guards marching back and forth around a perimeter with their rifle at the 'shoulder arms' position.

This was the procedure used to keep guards awake, walking back and forth around the Protective Perimeter with each guard meeting the one on their left and right at the beginning and end of their section of perimeter guard as the means of a full perimeter security check. However, this procedure prevented the guard's quiet observation of the approach and exposed the guard element to a stealthy attacker.

Some Guard Posts will always be exposed to some degree. You should use Cover and Concealment as much as possible in your Guard Posts yet without hindering their field of view of their area of the Protective Perimeter.

Most buildings provide numerous natural Concealment positions. In addition, thick masonry, stone, or brick walls offer excellent Cover protection from direct fire and can provide Concealment routes to and from Guard Posts.

However, to deter *Intruders* from walking off the street directly into your *NPP* Protective Perimeter or building entrance, at least one Guard Post should be an armed presence with a repeating weapon as a visual deterrent.

In any other Guard Post, if you can be in Cover or Concealment and still have a full field of view, be in Cover or Concealment.

Guard Communications. To be effective, you must have some form of communication between each Guard Post, *Patrol group*, Marksman and LOP position to your Watch

Center. Hand held store bought two-way radios are the most effective means. Don't count on cellular phones working during a *Crisis*.

The *microphone/single ear piece* for two-way radios is essential to keep your communications from 'broadcasting' around your Guard Posts and revealing them. Do not use any ear microphone/head phone that blocks both ears. Part of a guard's job is to have at least one ear unrestricted to hear noise.

The Pros and Cons of Two-way Radios. *Pros of these two-way radios...* they allow simultaneous communication throughout the *NPP*. Everyone can know what's going on at any time. *The Cons...* these are common citizen band wavelengths available to the public and anyone outside your *NPP* can monitor your transmissions if they have these radios and they work hard enough at it. You must assume that every conversation over these is being listened to by *Outsiders* or *Intruders*.

Midland Two Way Radios with Earpiece

These two-way radios have a great number of privacy codes in addition to the channels. Buy the 50 channel water resistant model two-way radios and learn to use the features to minimize the probability of your enemy listening to your radio chatter. *Be careful never to transmit anything such as names, number of individuals, time of watch rotations, locations, etc.*

Some people just love to hear themselves talk on the radio... keep your transmissions brief and to the point. Minimize your communications on these radios.

Number your Guard Posts by the Clock System of Referencing Direction and have a reference to them by number, never by Group Member name. This number should be posted in the Watch Center on your Protective Perimeter map and at each Guard Post.

To sound an alert, speak into your radio *"Number 4 alert!"* This indicates Guard Post 4 at 4 o'clock on the Protective Perimeter sees something that is possibly a danger. By this system, everyone will know where that is and the *Response Guardians* can respond to that perimeter area.

Number your Protective Perimeter map to match Guard Posts and have copies in clear plastic bags or laminated for the Watch Center and all guard, leadership and communications positions to literally have all persons on the same page when it comes to direction.

If in a High Rise Building you simply add the floor number. For example... *"Number 4, 6 alert!"* This will indicate to other guards and the Watch Center that Guard Post 4 on the 6th floor is aware of a danger or is requesting back up from the *Response* or *Roving Guardians*.

Roving guard. A roving guard is essentially a moving inside Protective Perimeter guard and able to respond to any request for assistance from any Guard Post. Furthermore, these roving guards can ensure fixed guards are awake and alert, temporarily relieve these guards if they need a bathroom break, bring food, hot coffee to them, etc.

Fire Watch. This is the *Roving Guardians* additional duty and every Group Member's responsibility… to watch for fires and alert the Watch Center if there is one.

Perimeter Patrol. *This is for Low Rise Residential and is not used in High Rise Building defenses.* A Perimeter Patrol is a moving *outside* Protective Perimeter guard whose duty it is to prevent an attack by the enemy using the Element of Surprise against you. These patrols should be intermittently done and their Patrol Formations periodically changed, their route or path changed and their direction of travel changed.

For example… they should travel on one Perimeter Patrol clockwise at 50 minutes past the hour, the next… counter-clockwise at 30 minutes past the hour, the following… counter-clock wise again at 15 minutes past the hour… then again clock wise at 40 minutes past the hour, etc. It's up to you to design you own varied procedures.

If there is an alert, all guards must remain at their posts. The threat must first be evaluated by the *Primary NPP Leader* after determining if the *LOP Guardian* or Marksmen can see any threat.

If the Perimeter Patrol is sent out to investigate they should leave from the opposite side of the Protective Perimeter that sounded the alert. They should then move far around to outflank or come up on the side or rear of any threat in their investigation while Marksmen covers their movement.

You must be aware that a common decoy tactic by an enemy is to make contact with one side of a Protective Perimeter and then fully attack the other side or another location. All Guard Posts should be on heightened alert if any alert is called out.

Keep your guard personnel busy. A key point to stress is do not let your guards get comfortable, warm and cozy. Anyone will fall asleep in that situation. *Guard duty is passive combat and requires discipline.* Guards must keep their blood flowing and be alert.

Limit your guard duty time periods. No more than 1 hour approximate per guard shift per post. Rotate the guards from one post clockwise to the next post each 1 hour or preferably by varied schedule.

The best case scenario is about 1 hour at one Guard Post then rotate that guard to the next Guard Post for another approximate 1 hour for a *total time of no more than 2 hours for guard duty per Group Member before they get off duty and get a chance to sleep.*

If you have enough guard personnel *2 hours* should be the limit of duty per Group Member per night or day. If not, then you may have to have guards do 2 hours on duty… sleep for 2 hours… and then 2 hours back on duty.

Other Guard Issues. Take these items into consideration with your Guard Posts...

- Guard Posts should be viewed from the outside to check their effectiveness… and Concealment and Cover.
- You may want to erect some form of shelter that doesn't stick out like a 'sore thumb' as visible from the outside as just that… a guard position.
- Use second story windows or roofs for perimeter Guard Posts when possible.
- Keep out of the light area of a window visible from afar. In doing so it narrows and restricts your field of observation and fire but entices an enemy to expose themselves if they don't see a guard presence.
- Coughing and sneezing will reveal Guard Posts. If you have a guard that's sick put him in an indoor position such as helping in the Watch Center until he gains his health back.
- Extreme cold also will reveal positions from exhaling breath vapor. Place scarves or masks over mouths to control this.
- Cigarette smoke, humming a tune, steam from a cup of hot coffee, farting, the reflection from eye glasses, rifle scopes and binoculars, movement and unnecessary noise will reveal your Guard Post.
- Sound travels much further at night as it does during the day and way further across open bodies of water at night. Remember being at the lake and hearing someone put their oars in a boat two miles across the lake. Keep quiet so you can hear your enemy make the noise.
- Establish covered or routes to and from Guard Posts that are concealed if possible.

Your NPP will not be worth the paper the plan is written on if you aren't effectively and aggressively guarding your NPP 24 hours a day, 7 days a week until Normal Civility is restored. Now go back and read the story "While I Slept" again.

6-Perimeter checks

The perimeter around your neighborhood must be checked frequently by at least two man Perimeter Patrols and again, should never be checked at routine times. Anyone observing your routines can use routine perimeter checks and guard change times as a way to penetrate your perimeter.

Intruders can and will plan their infiltration around any set schedule. Perimeter checks should be at random times and *especially just prior to sunrise and sunset.* History has shown that changing light periods are favorite times for attacks. Your *LOP Guardians* and Marksmen should be alert for any suspicious activity at *dawn* and *dusk.*

If there are dirt trails, paths, or vacant lots around the perimeter you can use a Border Patrol trick of dragging the area. This is a simple process of dragging old tires or weighted down fencing behind a vehicle or pulling this contraption with people.

This will turn the dirt so if any one walks on the freshly turned dirt it will leave a pattern that's quickly visible… whether it's foot prints or the attempt to brush them out.

Remember *JDLR… "Just Don't Look Right."* Always look for things that are different or out of place. The discoloration when a rock is disturbed will show darker color than the surrounding area. Foot prints, broken branches, disturbed surface area, grass glistening in the sun from foot patterns or anything that shows human presence or movement from other than *NPP* Group Members.

Perimeter Patrols should be discussed with leadership after each patrol. Any observations made by Perimeter Patrols should be discussed thoroughly. Remember *JDLR* and realize sometimes *little things* can be *big things*. Leaders should question *anything* patrol members have observed and investigate it further if it is warranted.

6-Denying access to your *NPP* by physical barriers-Foot and vehicle traffic

See Chapter 8 for a list of items you can use to deny and control access to your NPP.

You should institute the following measures only if A Failure of Civility has occurred and your police department, fire department and ambulance services are not able to respond to calls for assistance from citizens.

After you complete the following procedures, your police department, fire department and ambulance services will be restricted in their ability to quickly get into and out of your neighborhood.

You must provide for ambulance services and your fire department's access through your Entry/Exit Control Point *if they are still responding to fire calls or other emergencies.*

Your NPP at this time is going to be on a 'High Alert' footing.

During *Normal Civility* blocking off, obstructing or controlling the entrance and exit to your neighborhood's streets is considered *"Obstructing Public Passage"* or the violation of a similar type of ordinance by local authorities and is a misdemeanor in most areas.

However, during a time of *A Failure of Civility*, the Authors doubt that law enforcement will be writing you any tickets especially if you are helping maintain order in your neighborhood with a cooperative effort of the people of your neighborhood.

In most situations where there is a *Long Term Crisis* or *A Failure of Civility* and where vehicles are still drivable... ***Intruders coming to your NPP by vehicle are initially the most prominent threat to your NPP.***

To have an effective Protective Perimeter around your neighborhood you will have to have a plan to control foot and vehicle traffic by blocking off all ways in to your *NPP* and creating one Entry/Exit Control Point. A properly laid out Entry/Exit Control Point provides you just that... *control* over all entrances... and especially the main entrance to your *NPP*.

Common Barbed Wire

Initially, if *A Failure of Civility* has occurred, during each approach by *Outsiders*, you must have either your *Response Guardians* present during that approach, other Guard Posts that can fire on the Entry/Exit Control Point Kill Zone and Fatal Funnel or more than one guard at your Entry/Exit Control Point.

We recommend that your *Response Guardians* be there 24 hours a day during the first stages of *A Failure of Civility*.

There should be *only one* Entry/Exit Control Point**.** All other vehicle access streets and foot traffic access areas to your neighborhood will have to be blocked off with one row of vehicles in a V shaped pattern and preferably Improvised Spike Strips or Barbed Wire in front of these blockades. See *Chapter 8*.

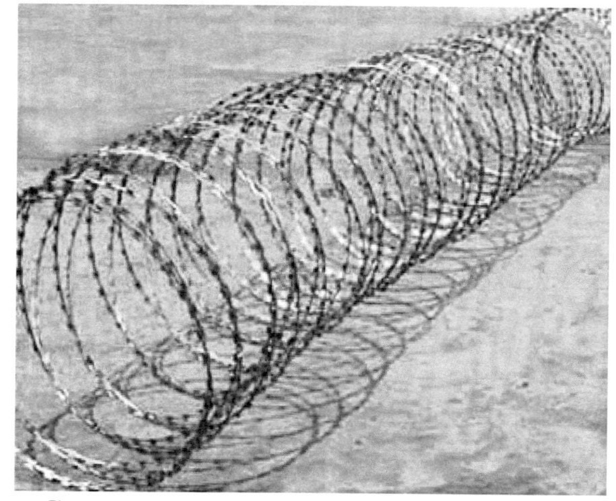

Concertina Wire or Razor Wire laid

These positions must also be guarded, but *only one* street entrance should be used to allow vehicles in and out. The one that is the Entry/Exit Control Point will be different than the others blocked off with vehicles and Improvised Spike Strips. See the Entry/Exit Control Point diagram.

The Entry/Exit Control Point ***Kill Zone.*** With one Entry/Exit Control Point you create a Fatal Funnel that turns into a Kill Zone where strategically positioned guards can eliminate or repulse an attack.

The Entry/Exit Control Point to your *NPP* should have a first and second checkpoint area spaced apart to keep vehicle and foot traffic away from your perimeter until you know it is not a threat. Your first checkpoint should be at the entrance of your *NPP but not inside your Protective Perimeter if your entrance allows this arrangement.*

The distance from your first control point to your second control point should be far enough to create a Serpentine path for vehicles and people to come and go slowly. This Serpentine area will slow down *Intruders* trying to rush into your neighborhood by vehicle or foot.

These areas before the first control point and between the first and second control points are your Entry/Exit Control Point Kill Zones. An additional Kill Zone Maze should be setup after your Entry/Exit Control Point.

Vehicles used in your Entry/Exit Control Point 'V' shaped formation should be *pointed outward towards traffic* coming towards the *NPP*. This helps prevent a ramming vehicle from pushing through your blocking vehicles and forcing their way through your Entry/Exit Control Point.

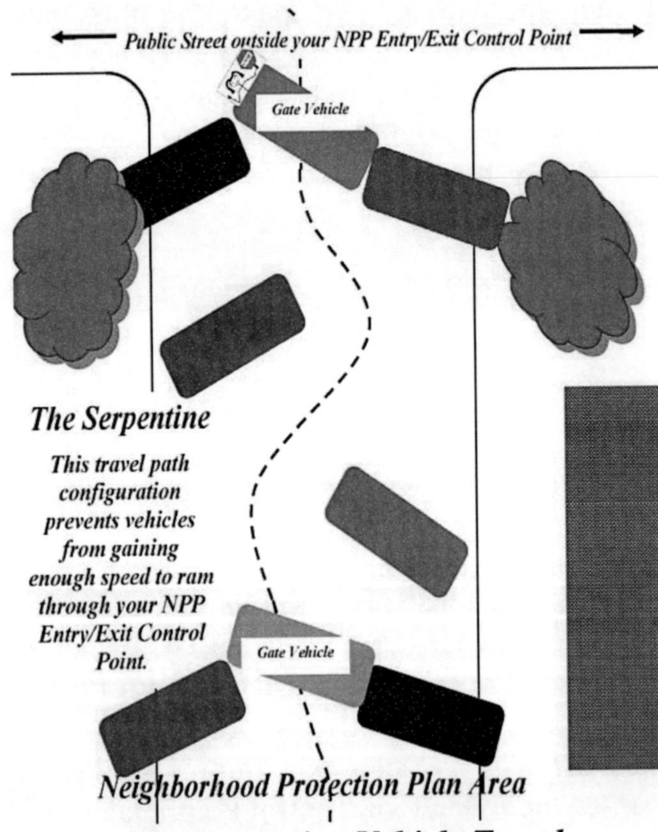

The Serpentine Vehicle Travel Configuration is the correct way to blockade your street entry using 'gate vehicles' and the Serpentine

Vehicles should be positioned to *contact each other* to make a more crash resistant mass and to prevent people from walking between them.

The Serpentine. Notice in the diagram that the *serpentine path a vehicle has to take to drive through* has turns created by other vehicles strategically placed between the first and second control points.

This is a 'Serpentine' path which prevents vehicles from gaining enough speed to crash through the last vehicle blockade of your Entry/Exit Control Point.

If a vehicle manages to crash through your first line of vehicles, they will not be able to crash through your second line of vehicles…

Abrams tanks and Armored Personnel Carriers excluded.

Improvised Spike Strips. These are an example of 'access deniability' and a way of forcing vehicles into a Fatal Funnel.

The Entry/Exit Control Point Fatal Funnel. The purpose of the Fatal Funnel is to create a single path outside your first vehicle barrier that foot traffic and vehicles have to follow to get to the first 'gate' vehicle of your *NPP* Entry/Exit Control Point. You may or may not have room enough for this arrangement at your entrance.

If a vehicle doesn't follow the path its tires will be flattened making it less maneuverable and slowing it down.

These also may force a threat to reveal itself by giving you the control over the movements of people or vehicles. If they have intentions otherwise, being restricted by access deniability barriers may force nervous threats to show their hand.

Take the keys out of blockade vehicles and let the air out of the tires on all but the 'gate' vehicle you're using on each 'V' blockade.

The gate vehicle is the vehicle you move back and forth to allow entry and exit. The keys for the gate vehicle should be removed and put in a place where everyone knows where they are. Keys from all other vehicles should be removed and kept in your Watch Center in case tires have to be re-inflated and the vehicles moved or used.

Except for the *gate* vehicle, the other vehicles used here should be neighborhood vehicles in the worst condition and not reliable for a *Planned* or *Emergency NPP Relocation.*

Watch for decoy approaches. During *A Failure of Civility*, ***All*** Protective Perimeter Guard Posts should be on *High Alert* when *any* foot traffic or vehicle approach is made to your *NPP* Entry/Exit Control Point in case this approach is a decoy to cover an attack somewhere else on the perimeter.

6-Denying access to your *NPP* by physical barriers-Protective perimeter aids

Blocking house windows and openings to deny access. Cover any outside house openings adjoining or that are a part of your Protective Perimeter with plywood, interior house doors, table tops, spiked window 2 x 4s, latticed Barbed Wire or anything else sufficient to keep *Intruders* out.

Table tops!? Mom's going to have a kitten! The worse *A Failure of Civility* gets… the less your furniture will mean to you… or Mom. Fasten these with screws or drive nails in at a sharp angle and board windows on the outside to prevent them being easily kicked in. *Drive nail heads all the way in so they can't be easily pulled out.*

Diving nails in at a sharp angle gives them much more holding power on what you've nailed. Second story windows and basement windows should also be covered.

Topping block walls, fences and open areas to hinder Intruders. Where local ordinances or HOA rules prohibit these in *Normal Civility*... put them up now. Premixed masonry in bags can be used to cement broken glass or metal prongs on top of a block wall. Barbed Wire can be strung and tied to existing fences and Barbed Wire or Concertina Wire should be strung across open areas.

Think of items you can put to use around you. If *A Failure of Civility* occurs there will be abandoned items everywhere. Use doors, concrete block and lumber from area buildings to help fortify your defenses.

Plastic flood sandbags are available in most building supply stores and can be filled with dirt or sand to help stop bullets. Placing rubble between boards is another way of constructing bullet resistant fortifications.

6-Denying access to your *NPP* by psychological barriers

Solar Powered Security Lights. These are relatively cheap if your *NPP* can install these. Solar Security Lights can be placed around your Protective Perimeter and either manually controlled or activated by motion detectors.

However, if you install these they can't be going on and off inadvertently without a real threat. If they do, they telegraph your position to potential *Intruders*. Security Lights must be in a 'dead area' of motion so they are not set off by accident or 'back light' your Guard Posts.

Canines… Man's best friend. Dogs are one of the best Protective Perimeter psychological and alert aids you can have. An alert dog can sense trouble before a human and if there is a *Crisis* dogs usually have a heightened sense for danger and will be ever more alert and perceptive.

Solar Powered Security Lights

Mrs. Pumpernickel's 5 star poodle may look nice, but that's not what you want for this mission… eat the Pumpernickel's dog. Get a proven security dog.

Get a large, calm and confident security type dog… a Doberman, German Shepherd type. Don't use Rottweiler's. The Roman Legions trained thousands of Rottweiler dogs prior to one epic battle… they loosed them towards their enemy prior to engaging mano un mano on the battlefield… only to find the Rottweiler dogs got confused half way to the enemy, turned around and came back to tear a few of the Roman Legionnaire's throats out before they killed them all.

Dogs can hear along a much broader spectrum of sound than a human can. Their sense of smell is so acute they can smell the adrenaline oozing from the skin of strangers. An aggressive dog is very intimidating to an *Outsider* whose intent is dangerous.

Remember the 'Terminator' movie where dogs were used at guard entrances to be on the lookout for 'People of Austrian descent who lift weights and have become naturalized American Citizens and elected the Governor of California.' If their sensory perception and discrimination is *that acute,* they can certainly verify your people at your Entry/Exit Control Point and sense some threats to you.

We suggest the most widespread use of dogs possible.

Use dogs at your Entry/Exit Control Point, with Guard Posts, with the *Patrol Guardians* on Perimeter Patrol and with the *Roving Guardians* on inside patrols. You did stock up on food for Rover… didn't you?

6-Tactics that will make your *NPP* a *proactive defense*

Outflanker Marksmen. High elevation Marksmen positions ***outside*** the Protective Perimeter that have Supporting Fields of Fire and Interlocking Fields of Fire with the *NPP* Guard Posts and the *Inside Marksmen* positions give an incredible advantage in defense.

These are Marksmen *outside* the Protective Perimeter that can aggressively and precisely fire on *Intruders* around the main approach, on Guard Post Fields of Fire around the Protective Perimeter and can accurately fire on *Intruders* who get inside your Protective Perimeter.

If your NPP consists of only one or two houses, is a Ranch House or Farm House, the Outflankers Field of Fire should include the most likely entry points of these houses, but should be at a sharp or 90 degree angle to those areas to prevent Friendly Fire Incidents.

Outflanker Marksman **Field of Fire coordinated with *Inside Marksman* Field of Fire.**

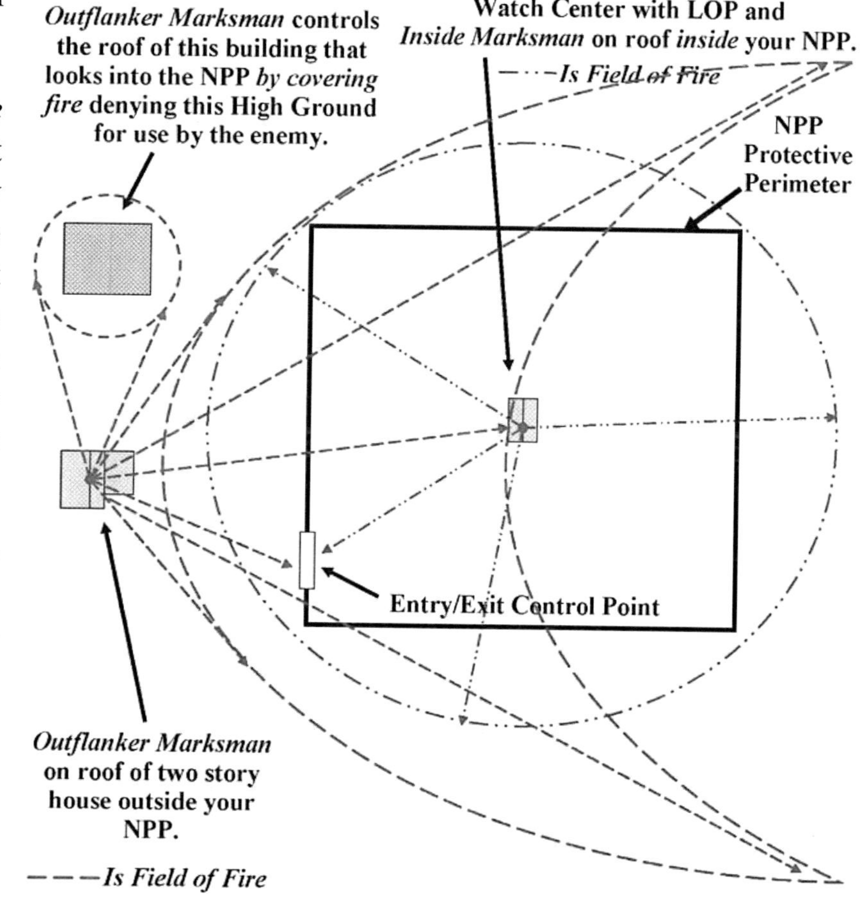

This position will give you a dramatic edge over Intruders!

> *Outflanker Marksmen are key tactical positions that in a worst case scenario should be employed more extensively if you are short of Group Members. The physical and psychological devastation that one or more of these positions can inflict on an enemy from 100, 200 or 300 yards cannot be understated.*

Understand that if an elephant corners a rat... the rat will fight desperately instead of fleeing. ***Always leave an escape route for Intruders unless they're in your Kill Zone Maze.***

'L' Shaped Ambushes. This ambush pattern subjects the opponent to withering Supporting Fields of Fire from two or more diverse directions and reduces the chance of Friendly Fire Incidents. This creates a crossfire as your enemy is in the Fields of Fire of both Component A and B.

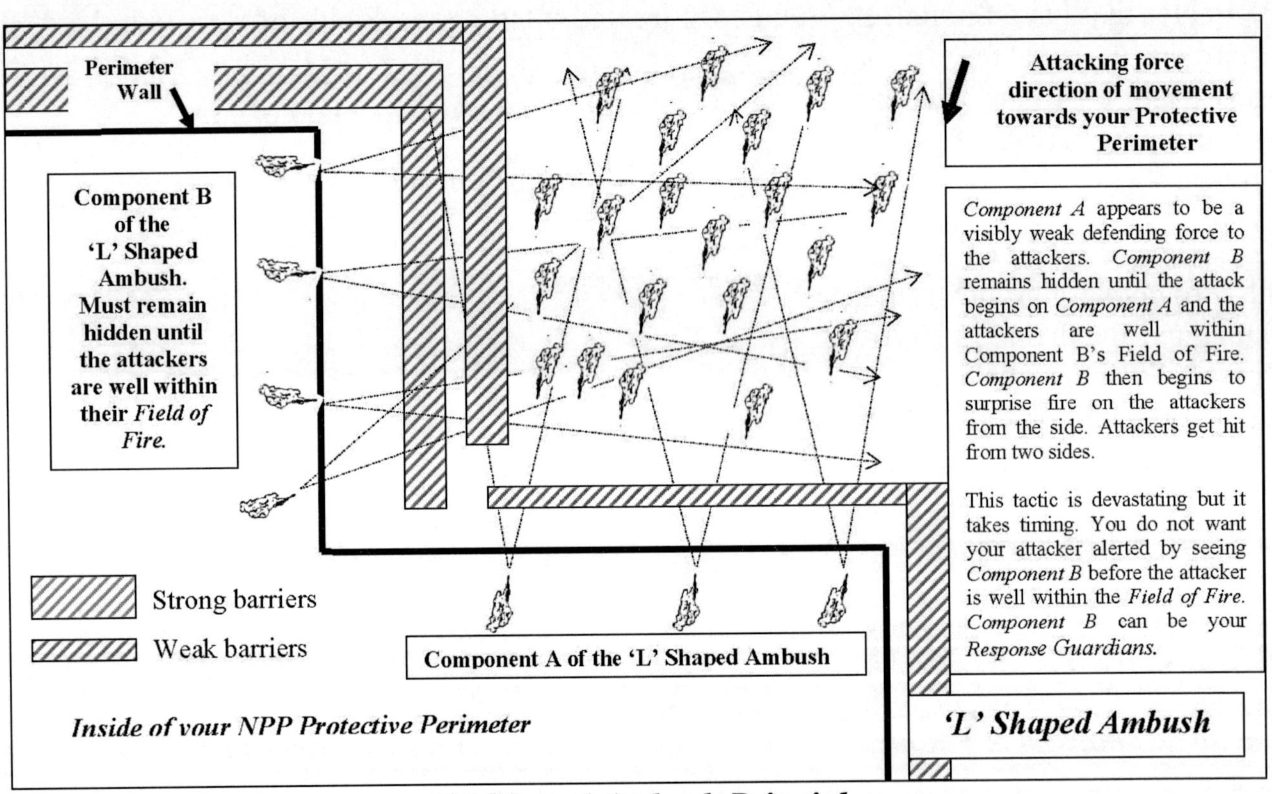

'L' Shaped Ambush Principle

The long part of the 'L' is the avenue of approach for the *Intruders* attacking your *NPP* and the short part of the 'L' is the surprise attack portion.

Your Component B will fire at the *Intruders only* after the attackers are well within their Fields of Fire. Component A should only sporadically fire until Component B fires to draw the attackers fully into everyone's Fields of Fire crossfire area.

> ***Suppression by Overwhelming Fire or 'Violence of Action'.*** *This is a heavy and continuous weapons fire used to limit the enemy's movement and to kill your enemy. Your purpose is to kill as many as you can but leave room for them to retreat and go elsewhere... if you're feeling charitable that day.*

An example of Suppression by Overwhelming Fire is if 10 defenders are engaging a larger group of 20 people and fire so heavily at that group that few of the attackers are able to return fire because they're taking Cover, dead or wounded.

In more recent times you've probably remember the term *"Shock and Awe"* from the opening strikes on Iraq in our War on Terror. This is in a sense... *"Killing a Fly with a Sledgehammer"... and taking the fight out of the Intruder so conclusively that they will never even think of coming back.*

Basically you overwhelm the enemy with so much firepower that you cause psychological defeat and instability to your opponent's attack plan *immediately*. Your *NPP* Group Members simply bloodies your *Intruder's* nose so bad they don't want to come back for seconds.

Kill Zones. A politically correct term for this is Engagement Area or EA to the military. However, we don't mince words in describing what this is for, because semantics aside... it is an area in which your can have a 'Turkey Shoot' and effectively kill your *Intruders* with little or no loss of *NPP* Group Members. *It is a killing zone.*

A Kill Zone restricts movement of your enemy and gives little Cover or Concealment to them while enabling you to pour withering fire into them. Your Entry/Exit Control Point should have Kill Zone areas and your *NPP* should have Kill Zone Mazes set up any place your think your perimeter can be breached or any area that makes a good Kill Zone Maze.

A Kill Zone Maze is the exception to keeping *Intruders* out of your perimeter and leaving a path for them to escape by. You let them into an area by leading them believe that they've overcome your defenses... but you have them in the area you want them to be in... then you eliminate them.

The tactic is to allow Intruders partially into your NPP... into the Kill Zone Maze.

This is particularly useful when you are outnumbered by *Intruders*. A Kill Zone Maze will give you a Force Multiplier Effect and will put *Intruders* at a *severe* disadvantage. It will give new meaning to the term *"Like shooting fish in a barrel."*

Creating and using a Kill Zone Maze must be done properly. A Kill Zone Maze inside your Protective Perimeter can defeat your entire *NPP* if you don't set it up properly. The point is to allow *Intruders* into this area like using a funnel, but *not allowing them in too far or giving the enemy the ability to get past your Kill Zone Maze.*

Kill Zone Maze barriers must be deceptive when viewed from the outside. The barriers cannot appear obvious to the *Intruders* nor can they give the *Intruder* any Cover. If *Intruders* decide that this area is a Kill Zone by looking at it, they'll simply avoid it and retreat to find another way to breach your perimeter.

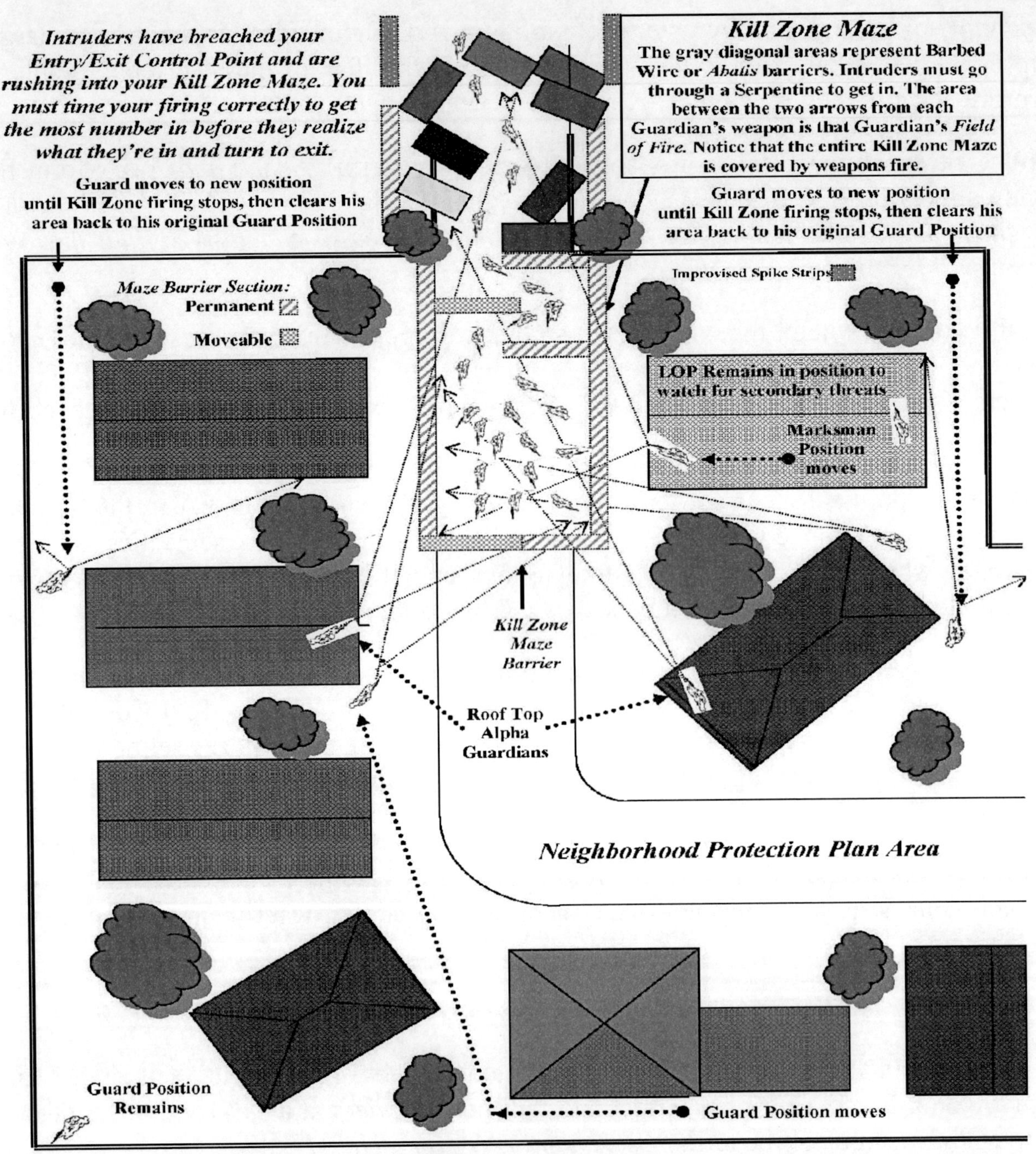

A Kill Zone Maze

The use of barriers of Barbed Wire, Concertina Wire, fencing and Abatis sharpened stakes pointed into your Kill Zone Maze area will force *Intruders* to stay in your Kill Zone Maze area… but to proceed only so far. You want them to come in, yet these barriers will contain them in the Kill Zone Maze area… but not allow them to have Cover or Concealment or advance any further.

Your Kill Zone must allow you a clear Field of Fire. This is difficult at the Entry/Exit Control Point to some degree because the vehicles you use to blockade your entrance give Concealment and some Cover.

Outside your Kill Zone Maze barriers but within your *NPP* Perimeter, you must have fighting positions for Group Members that are placed behind Cover and Concealment to protect Group Members from *Intruder* fire. Remember the difference between Cover and Concealment.

This Kill Zone Maze should be constructed of a combination of *moveable* sections of the Spanish Rider a.k.a. Knife Rest concept and *permanent* Concertina Wire, Barbed Wire or Abatis sharpened stakes. See *Chapter 8* for descriptions of these.

The sides of the maze should be permanent and the ends moveable so to allow vehicles in and out. A Serpentine section must be put in place to slow down and disorient *Intruders* and to prevent their rapid retreat.

When placing Group Members in fighting positions you must consider each Member's weapon and capabilities. Is the Group Member armed with a pistol, rifle or shotgun and are they rapid fire weapons? Is their weapon short range or long range effective? Do they have the *Survival Mentality* and are they proficient with their weapon? You must pick your Kill Zone Maze Group Members carefully.

You must plan against the dangers of Supporting Fields of Fire causing Friendly Fire Incidents when setting up any Kill Zone. You don't want to be shooting your own Group Members accidently.

The 'L' shaped ambush principle avoids this and must be applied to all Kill Zones Group Member positions. Also take the advantage of roof top firing positions. However, take care that these do not reveal the intention of the area you designate as a Kill Zone.

A Entry/Exit Control Point Kill Zone with a vehicle serpentine entrance that leads to a simple 'S' shaped serpentine walkway for your Kill Zone Maze will disorient and prevent the rapid retreat of *Intruders*, increasing your kill effectiveness. Remember, it's in the name. A Kill Zone is for just that, not wounding *Intruders*… but eliminating them.

When activating your Kill Zone make certain your LOP watches for secondary threats and that you leave enough Group Members on the perimeter to guard against other attacks on your perimeter while you are manning your Kill Zone.

Defense in depth or 'Fall Back Fighting Positions.' In addition to having one strong Protective Perimeter, Defense in Depth is layering of well placed covered and concealed

Fall Back Fighting positions. This principle has been explained like an onion… peel off one layer… and the onion is still there. These are nothing but a second line of defensive positions if your Protective Perimeter fails.

When *Intruders* peel back your primary line of defense… you're still there… at a second line of defense… your Fall Back Fighting Positions. This tactic causes the *Intruder* to lose momentum due to them running into progressive lines of defense each time they think they've broken through your Protective Perimeter. This is psychologically destructive to an attacker.

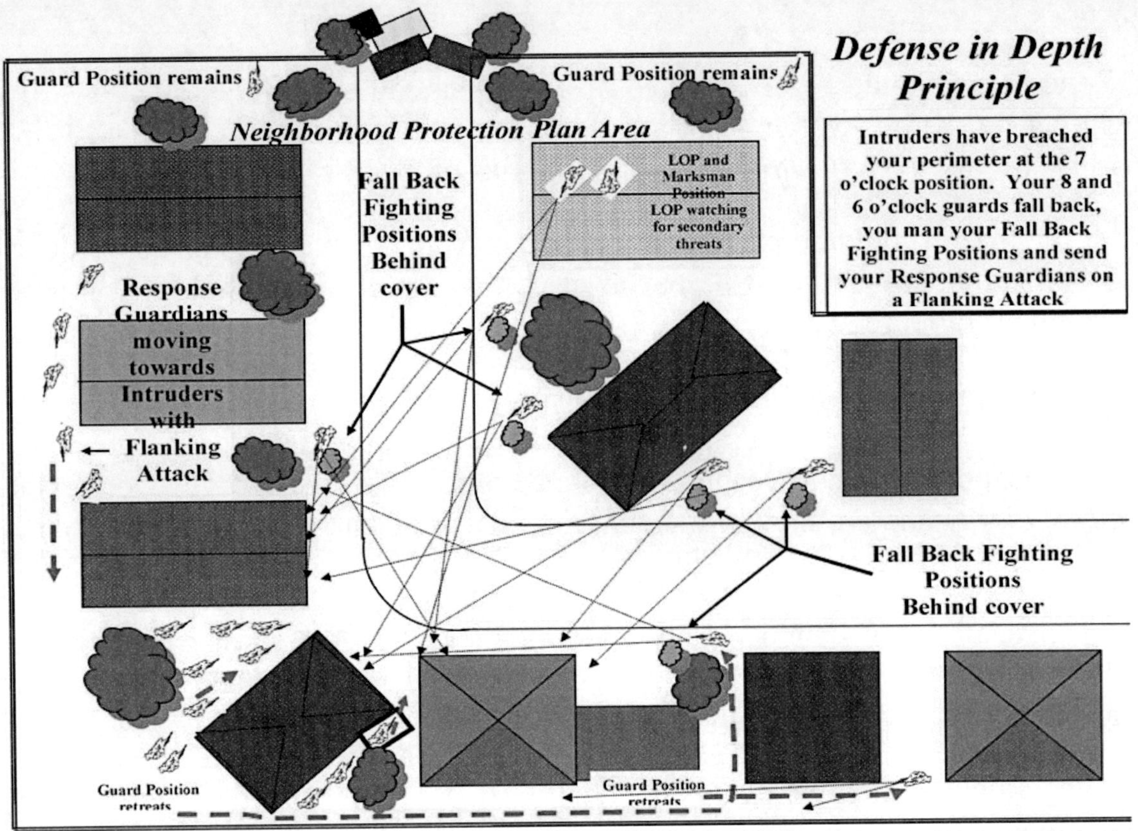

Defense in Depth Principle

Response Force. These are your *Response Guardians.* For the military or police this is a unit designed to respond in a very short time frame to emergencies. When used in reference to police forces such as SWAT teams, the time frame is mere minutes.

When used in reference to your *NPP* these are the *Response Guardians* of your *NPP*. These people need to be some of the most physically fit of your *Alpha Guardians* and they too need to respond in mere minutes.

Response Guardians are like the Little Dutch Boy. Their job is to rapidly respond to 'plug holes' in your Protective Perimeter defense by reinforcing a part of your Protective Perimeter that is under attack.

Response Guardians can also create L Shaped Ambushes of *Intruders* and be part of the Kill Zone.

For the Low Rise Residential *NPP* the *Response Guardians* along with the *Patrol/Roving Guardians, Inside Marksmen* and *Outflanker Marksmen* are the most *proactive* of your Group Members.

Fighting Hole viewed from above

Field of Fire Areas. All areas than can give Concealment to an *Intruder* must be removed if possible. You want a clear area and a level area if possible. You must have clear areas or Fields of Fire as barren of Cover and as far on all sides from your Protective Perimeter as you can make them.

This is not to say that this area should be fit to play a volley ball game on... quite the opposite. It should be strewn with alert and security devices, rubble, tree branches or anything else that alerts you to and makes movement across it difficult... but again doesn't give an enemy Cover or Concealment.

Sidewalk Man Hole

This obviously is difficult in most suburban areas with houses built close together, however it must be achieved to the point that you have a view and Field of Fire as wide and as far out as possible.

Man Holes, Fighting Holes, Spider Holes. To have a really viable *NPP* you must have prepared Fall Back Fighting Positions which Group Members can 'fall back' to if *Intruders* breach your perimeter.

You must position Fall Back Fighting Positions far enough from your Protective Perimeter. These can be Man Holes, Spider Holes or Group Member Fighting Holes.

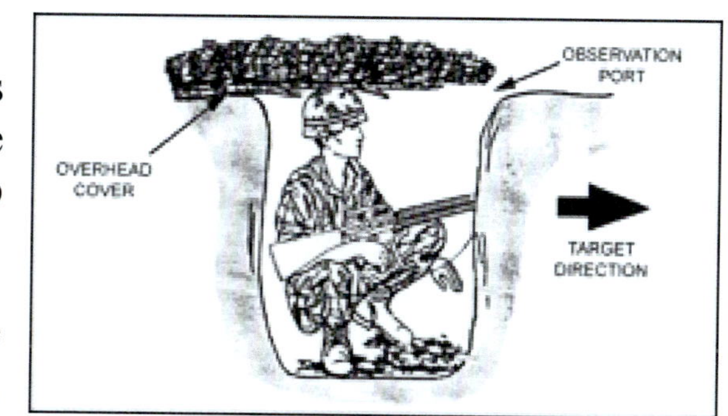

Spider Hole

These can consist of utility man holes... the round street cover type and sidewalk manholes, spider holes and fighting holes dug into the ground and sandbagged. In addition to these, you can heavily fortify a house that has the majority of your food, water, ammunition, and provisions.

Preferably two houses should be heavily fortified that can give each other Supporting Fields of Fire.

Remember… *be proactive.* If you have to retreat to your Fall Back Fighting Positions or fortified house… immediately send Group Members out the back door and move way around your attacker… then flank your attacker from the side... eliminate them! Do not hole up like a mouse or you'll die like one. *Be proactive… be bold! Flank, flank, flank… attack, attack, attack!*

Cover and Fire Movement. Cover and Fire Movement is the tactic of one or more Group Members firing at the enemy to force them to stay in Cover from which they'll not be able shoot back at your advancing group.

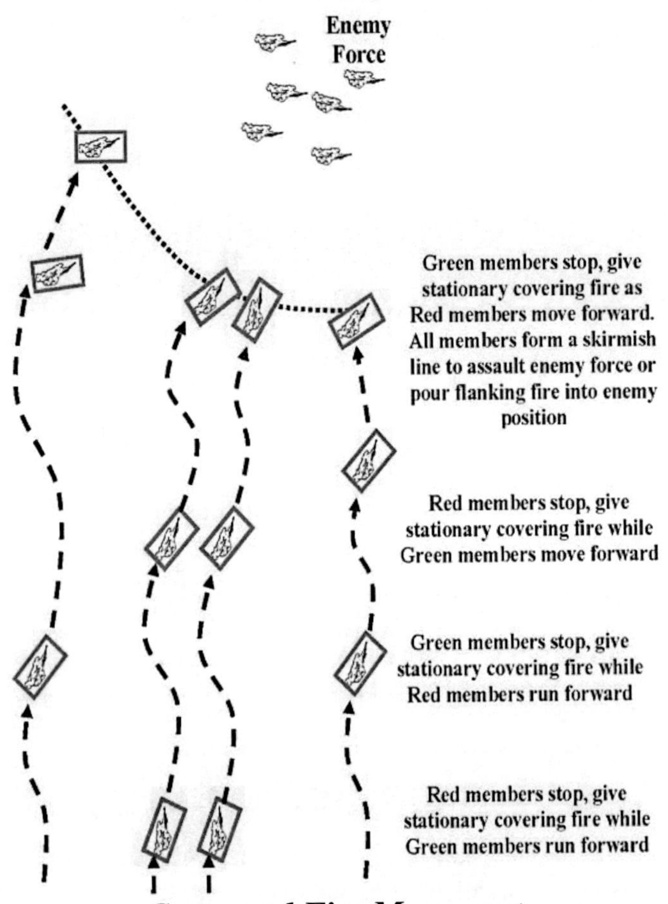

Cover and Fire Movement

At the same time, one or more Group Members move forwards or backwards to another position of Cover.

Then the roles of Covering Group Member and Firing Group Member are reversed until your objective is reached.

This has to be done with the *Firing* Group Members being a distance apart to the left and right of their line of movement so the *Moving* Group Member doesn't wander into the Field of Fire of the *Firing* Group Member.

If you are using this to flank your enemy… always protect your flank from the enemy flanking you.

This is a leapfrog method of movement to reduce the chance of the enemy killing Group Members during movement… by half the Group Members firing at the enemy… while the other half moves towards or away from the enemy. Be sure to move outside their firing Group Member's Fields of Fire. This tactic is used to retreat or to outflank the enemy.

Use the Skipping Rounds technique. Aim at the ground *slightly in front* of your target if it is on concrete or hard surfaces… about 6 to 12 inches.

On dirt, Skipping Rounds will create a shotgun effect thrusting debris into your attacker's eyes and face. Stinging and penetrating debris that can be lethal!

Hard surface *Skipping Rounds* will most likely cause lower extremity hits in standing targets or fatal hits on prone or crouching targets because the bullet fragments like a grenade.

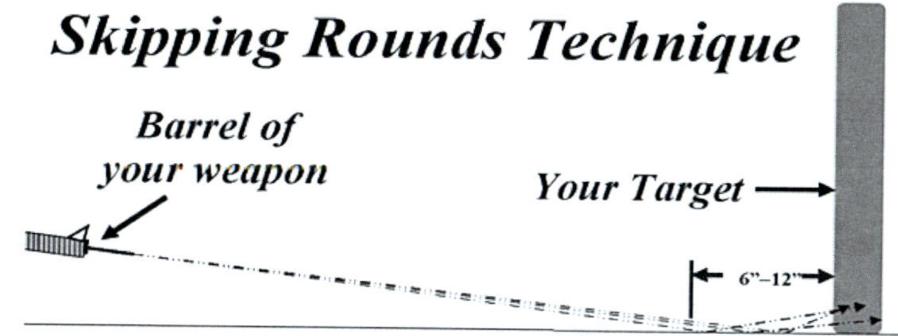

Skipping Rounds Technique

This technique is very effective when firing under a vehicle slightly in front of targets taking Cover behind them.

6-*A Failure of Civility* has occurred… *High Alert* preparations to institute

If a *Long Term Crisis* has gravitated to *A Failure of Civility* it's time to start preparing for the worst by finalizing your *NPP* Protective Perimeter defenses using the just mentioned techniques and recommendations.

If this time comes you must be ready to 'trash' your neighborhood to the degree necessary to provide adequate defense for your *Neighborhood Protection Plan.* Your neighborhood can be restored. Repairs can be made to just about everything but dead people.

Your NPP Protective Perimeter at this time is going to be on a 'High Alert' footing and you need to institute the following...

- Lock Down your *NPP* by setting up your Entry/Exit Control Point and the Entry/Exit Control Point Fatal Funnel and Kill Zone.
- Leaders should brief all Group Members at their positions, review their positions and advise them that *A Failure of Civility* has occurred.
- Keep the Watch Center active 24 hours a day monitoring radio stations and radio traffic and providing *NPP* Leadership with more frequent briefings and notifying them immediately of items importance heard on police scanners and radio communications.
- Heighten Fire Watch procedures.
- Dress for battle because that's what you're in… *A Failure of Civility.* Dress in casual civilian clothing *with* armbands or camouflage uniforms if you have them. Clothing colors must match or be similar to the major color scheme of your environment or camouflage painted. Display weapons prominently.

- Ready the fall back positions inside your *NPP*.
- Set up your inside Kill Zones.
- Post your *LOP Guardians.*
- Post your Marksmen *inside* and *outside* the *NPP*.
- Re-enforce your Protective Perimeter as much as possible.
- Block off all underground passage ways to your *NPP*.
- Board up the doors and windows of houses facing your Protective Perimeter.
- Cut down shrubbery, trees only if necessary, and remove any objects on your Protective Perimeter that will provide Cover and Concealment to an *Intruder*.
- Move any vehicles out of the *NPP*'s Fields of Fire.
- Gather children and *Dependent Persons* into central safe houses.
- String Barbed Wire or Concertina Wire where necessary.
- Increase the frequency of patrolling inside and outside your *NPP*.
- Prepare your *Emergency NPP Relocation* bags and equipment.
- Rehearse your *Emergency NPP Relocation* plan.

If this is a pandemic, the sick must be quarantined in a home or building away from others if they have infectious disease. One Group Member is going to have to volunteer to be quarantined with them to tend to their needs wearing the proper eye, face masks, gloves and clothing to keep the pandemic from spreading to these caregivers. The clothing they wear must be immediately washed with disinfectant or burned.

6-DO NOT bring *Outsiders* into your *NPP*

An *Outsider* or *Intruder* is ***anyone*** who is not an *NPP Group Member* or an *Extended Family and Friends Member*. You know an *Intruder* is your enemy but an *Outsider must also be considered your **enemy***.

Outsiders and *Intruders* are your biggest danger during a *Long Term Crisis* or *A Failure of Civility*.

If *A Failure of Civility* becomes long term ***you and your Group Members risk contagious diseases*** if these people *even get close to your NPP especially if the Catastrophic Event is a disease related disaster*.

As stated before, we strongly recommend not bringing any *Outsiders* or *Intruders* into your *NPP*. But you must have contingencies and may have to make an exception to this rule.

If you have to bring an Outsider or Intruder into your NPP...

- Never let more than one *Outsider* or *Intruder* inside your *NPP* at one time. From a distance, have them remove their clothes from above their waist. Have them turn around. Look at them from a distance for skin sores or mottling discoloration of the skin that may indicate they carry infectious disease.

- All Leaders and Group Members should wear gloves and masks. Only one Group Member should handle the person. This Group Member must wear gloves and a mask when searching this person. Don't touch your face or mouth after searching them. Search the individual thoroughly putting them in a prone or kneeling position, never standing, for your safety.

- Make certain they have no weapons on them. *Crotch, butt crack, breast search them, search under hats and in women's hair also.*

- Hand cuff or tie the person's hands behind their back, never in front of their body.

- Blindfold the individual, using a dark colored hood or material. Secure it so they cannot shake it off.

- Once they are restrained and blindfolded, disorient the person. This can be done by turning the person around several times, then taking them on a wild walking goose chase. If available, use head phones taped to their ears with loud music so they can't recognize voices or sounds to reveal people or locations. Be aware that noise and smells can reveal locations.

- If your *NPP Leaders* have to meet this person it must be from a distance. Remember disease. If you have to take their blindfold off do it in a closed, interior and as empty as possible room. Understand that if you reveal your Leaders faces, they may later use this recognition to target your *NPP Leaders.*

- If they must see your *NPP Leaders,* your Leaders should have their faces covered and only take off the blindfold in a dark area.

- When the subject leaves the area, *follow the same procedures of disorientation and blindfold.*

- Burn all Group Member masks and gloves and disinfect when you're finished.

6-Handling *Outsiders* and *Intruders*

As we stated before, you *never* want to bring an *Outsider* or *Intruder* into your Protective Perimeter except by following the above procedures.

If someone penetrates your perimeter and is captured, what should be your actions?

- Make certain they have no weapons on them. *Crotch, butt crack, breast search them, search under hats and in women's hair also.*
- Immediately restrain and blindfold them and follow the same procedures as above.
- Beware of disease.
- Keep them guarded away from the center of your *NPP* and be aware that just because they can't see anything, they can hear and smell. Keep them away from Group Members.

Your *NPP* must have in place guidelines of what to do with these people. Guarding them takes away from available manpower. Keeping them fed takes away from your food and water resources. You must treat this person as being sent as part of an *Intruder* group finding out about your *NPP* procedures.

The first question NPP Leaders should have...

- Is this person carrying disease?
- Is this person acting alone?
- Is there any evidence that this person was reconnoitering your area for an attack?
- How much has this person seen of our defenses and resources?

What we suggest to do with Outsiders and Intruders, depending of the level of the Crisis, is to...

- Have them picked up or drop them off at your local law enforcement agency.
- Drop them off in a remote location, after disorienting them warning them that they face dire consequences if they return to your *NPP* area.
- Depending on the level of the *Crisis* and the circumstances, let that be your guide. Your family, friends, neighbors and *NPP's* safety and security are at stake.
- Eat them.
- If you think we're serious about that, you're getting too involved with this book. Stop… stand up… stretch… go out for a short walk… return… read more.

6-Protecting a 2 or 3 story condominium or apartment complex

Even though Low Rise Residential Neighborhood covers only two story buildings, some apartment and condominium units will be two or more stories but do not fit all the parameters of *Area Tactical Protection* for a High Rise Residential Building.

We recommend the following for these buildings to make your Protective Perimeter secure...

- Use *Outflanker Marksmen* to protect your building.
- Board up the lower story windows and doors.
- Block off the main entrance door from the inside and make impassable the outside or inside access stairways.
- Gain entry and exit through one entrance door or by outside access stairway.
- Depending on the floor layout, provide room to room movement by knocking holes in the walls of adjoining rooms if *A Failure of Civility* occurs.
- If *A Failure of Civility* occurs and your unit doesn't have interior stairs for movement between floors, if possible use ladders and make a hole in the ceiling for Group Member vertical movement between floors.
- *Read Chapter 7 for additional information and ideas on how to better protect your buildings.*

We include them in Low Rise Residential *Area Tactical Protection* because the area of ground they cover will be so large compared to their height in stories.

6-Link up with other *Neighborhood Protection Plans*

As a *Crisis* evolves you may want to join other *NPPs* because of attrition of Group Members or the increasing sophistication of attacks by *Intruders*. Also, one *NPP* may have more people with medical expertise, another more tactical knowledge, etc. Share and exchange for the overall good of both *NPP*s.

We strongly urge your *NPP* to link up with adjoining *Neighborhood Protection Plans* whether this is joint control by each *Primary NPP Leader*, merging with the other *NPP* under one Primary Leader or just a Mutual Protection Agreement.

If your *NPP* shares a common perimeter, joint control or merging can eliminate part of each *NPP's* perimeter and can make the aggregate more powerful in defending themselves if done properly.

Leaders and *NPPs* can also pool their knowledge, training and resources which may help in making better decisions and a stronger defense.

At best, *depending* on how big the area of the two *NPPs* is, join your forces together. *This is dependent* upon how strong your confidence is in the other *NPP's* principles of organization, its ability to maintain its defense and their leadership being acceptable to your *NPP* Group Members and Leaders.

Basically, if you're 'on the same page,' make sure you cover the entire cumulative Protective Perimeter when doing this. Too big an area can be a communications and supply problem and will make it difficult for *Response Guardians* rushing to the aid of a besieged perimeter.

At worst, form a plan for Mutual Protection to help with each other's protection. A flanking attack by one *NPP* coming to the assistance of another *NPP* is usually a tactical maneuver that wins.

6-Summer and hot weather, winter and cold weather

Not many solutions can be given for issues of weather, especially if a *Long Term Crisis* turns into *A Failure of Civility.* Regardless of if electrical power, natural gas, sewer and water supplies are disrupted or permanently terminated… the weather… will be the weather… and you will have to cope with it.

Summer and hot weather. As uncomfortable and as extremely hot or as hot and humid as conditions are, you just simply have to sweat it out. A benefit of wet ground and light drizzly weather is that it will reveal foot prints to *Patrol* and *Roving Guardians.* Conversely, a hard rain will wash out foot prints.

Winter and cold weather. When you've stood or sat for hours at a Guard Post in freezing temperatures you gain new respect for 'cold weather.' Winter weather is the most dangerous and uncomfortable of the conditions for Guard Posts. You may want to shorten guard periods and rotate Guard Posts with Roving Patrol duties. Walking and moving helps keep guards warm.

> ***Dangerous weather conditions.*** *Blizzards and rainy weather in general are dangerous because they give defenders the impression that nothing will happen during bad weather. Some of the most decisive victories from attacks have been initiated during bad weather…*
>
> *such as the Normandy Invasion of 1944… 'D Day.'*

A benefit of light snow in winter weather is that it also will reveal foot prints. To the contrary, blizzards or winds will obliterate foot prints. The temptation is to have fires to keep guards warm… this will reveal Guard Posts. Heating rocks at a central location and putting them in blankets to take to Guard Posts is a much safer solution.

6-Passive response will get you killed… you must be proactive

Cover and Approach. The Entry/Exit Control Point of your *NPP* will be the most active place that approaches to your *NPP* will be made. The obstacles of the approach area must keep *Intruders* from getting too close to your entrance but on the other hand these must give them no Cover.

This area should be a 'Transition Area' outside your main Protective Perimeter entrance in which you can check out unknown persons and vehicles approaching your *NPP*. Do not let more than one person or vehicle in your Transition Area at a time.

This procedure is important for all Guard Posts to use but it will probably be used more at the Entry/Exit Control Point of your *NPP*. Any Guard Post must call for *Response Guardian* presence if an *Outsider* approaches them, but first must warn the *Outsider* to keep their distance. Don't let *Outsiders* closer than 50 feet of your Guard Post. Voice communication can be held from that distance.

Passive response to Outsiders approaching your NPP will get you killed. You must be proactive. By that we mean one guard with their weapon 'at the ready' walking out to approach the Outsider and that guard always close to Cover while the Marksmen inside and outside the NPP and one or more guards at the Entry/Exit Control Point are acting as backup for the approach guard and also scouring the area behind that Outsider looking for a secondary threat. In a threat situation be proactive… make the first move!

Watch the hands of an Intruder or Outsider… the hands are what will kill.

Guards must keep behind Cover as much as possible when approached and *Response Guardians* must do the same when they arrive at that Guard Post. Don't group up around a Guard Post and don't send all your *Response Guardians* when backup is requested from a Guard Post unless it is an attack. This can be a decoy for an attack on another side of your *NPP*. If one Guard Post is approached by an *Outsider*, *all* Guard Posts should be on *High Alert* for anything unusual in their area.

6-The use of camouflage in your *NPP*

To survive and win… the *NPP* should employ Cover and Concealment… but also use *camouflage* where necessary. This is also a science unto itself and we're going to cover only basics.

If your enemy can't see you… or can't see you clearly… you have less chance of being hit by their fire. We are most concerned with *camouflage* for stationary Guard Posts, *Outflanker Marksmen* and Patrols or Group Members that go outside the *NPP*.

Camouflage helps Group Members blend into the background and make it more difficult for an assailant to see you… and if they do it makes you a more difficult target to focus on. Urban camouflage was designed specifically for urban environments and helps give some degree of Concealment.

Camouflage clothing is expensive and if you don't have it at least avoid white and bright colors during summer months and black and bright colors during winter snow months.

Urban Camouflage Pattern

Wear colors that do not contrast you against your environment. Use simple white sheets worn as 'ponchos' to blend you in during snow months and give added warmth.

You can adapt somewhat to your surroundings by choosing clothing that is the base color of your environment and then painting it irregularly with other tones and colors.

This is 'poor man's camouflage' but it works and may save your life.

The theory abounds during *A Failure of Civility* to *"Look the part... play the part"* just like the destruction around you. The Authors disagree with this to some extent.

The Authors feel that if *A Failure of Civility* does occur that desperate people, like rats sniffing out food anywhere and everywhere, will find your *NPP* and attack you in an attempt to get what you have.

Camouflage to help blend into your surroundings

Obviously some of 'looking the look' may be necessary and *will occur naturally* with Group Members and your *NPP* without effort.

Your efforts to blend in with the disaster will be assisted by the degree of severity of the catastrophe… but the fact that you are eating… will not be able to be concealed from those who are starving.

To properly camouflage your Guard Posts you need to view and study your NPP area from the outside area and make Guard Posts look as much like the local terrain as you can. Tips to help you…

- Roof positions should blend in with house roof lines or chimneys. Roof positions can be a 'Roof Rat Hole' at the peak of a roof or the position disguised to look like a roof chimney or Heating/Cooling unit. 'Roof Rat Holes' will be unbearable during hot weather.
- *LOP Guardians* and Marksmen should wear a face mask or scarf over their nose and mouth in the cold of winter to minimize vapors from breath.
- Any reflective item must be concealed and all telescopic, spotting scopes and binoculars need to have an Anti Reflection Protection shade over the optics end. This must be a tube, longer from the surface of the optics to the end than the distance of the width of the optics, to prevent sun reflection revealing the position to *Outsiders* or *Intruders.*

See the diagram for rifle scope and binoculars Anti Reflection Protection in this chapter.

- Guards should stay in the shadows. Buildings in urban areas throw sharp shadows that can be used for Concealment. However, the position may have to be moved periodically as the shadows shift during the day. Positions inside buildings provide better Concealment. Observe and fire through windows at an angle as in the diagram below.
- Guards should avoid the area immediately around a window, doorway, or loophole that receives illumination from the sun. Group Members remain better concealed if they observe and when necessary fire weapons from the shadowed interior of a room.

  A lace curtain or piece of cheesecloth provides additional Concealment to Group Members in the interior of rooms if curtains are common to the area. These will conceal Group Members for observation but will bellow and catch fire if you shoot weapons close through them.
- Do have interior lights that 'back light' Guard Posts. Use red or green filters on flashlights to see in the dark, not white light.
- Continue to improve positions. Reinforce fighting positions with sandbags or other solid materials. Use sandbags to reinforce the wall below windows and adjacent to windows or doors to increase protection at these Guard Posts.
- Keep Guard Posts hidden by clearing away minimal debris for fields of fire. Look from the outside. Your Guard Posts, even without seeing the guard, should not be obvious Guard Posts.
- Choose firing ports in inconspicuous spots. Avoid single, neat, square, or rectangular firing ports. A lone hole or a regular shape is more easily identified by the enemy.

- Use dummy Guard Posts to distract the enemy and make him reveal his position by firing. Use deception in creating the illusion of a Guard Post with mannequins in semi Concealment just slightly visible. Move these periodically.
- Use the wet floor and areas in front of firing positions to keep dust from rising and exposing your position from the muzzle blast of your weapons.

The green squares superimposed on the photos of this building are good choices for firing ports. The red circles and ovals are not. The red circles representing the positions at the roof line would back light the shooter and make movement easy to spot.

U.S. Army studies show that regular shapes... squares rectangles, circles are quickly identifiable by most people as a probable firing positions... as are doorways and windows. Irregular shapes are not easily identifiable.

Choose Inconspicuous Firing Ports

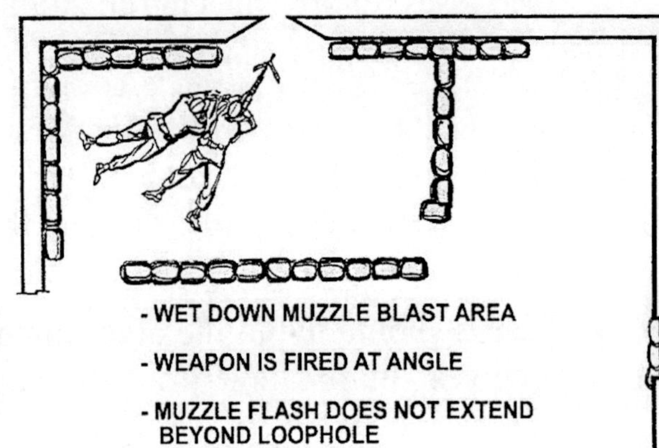

Correct Firing Position Concealment

When choosing firing ports, make sure you fire from well back of the opening so as not to reveal your muzzle flash. Wet the area down in front of your muzzle so dust from your muzzle blast does not reveal your position.

6-Your *NPP* must have flexibility, alternative and 'What if' plans

The *NPP* gains defensive strength through preparation of Defense in Depth, the use of *Response Guardians*, effective command and control and ***training***. Contingency planning also gives the *NPP* flexibility.

Contingency planning is simply training with your plan then acting as if it has failed and changing to an alternative plan. These are *"What if"* plans. Use your mind to envision anything and everything that can go wrong and create plans to deal with these situations and issues. Fortunately, most *Intruders* and roving bands will be poorly organized and unable to coordinate effective tactics against your *NPP* initially.

However, if A Failure of Civility is long-drawn-out and Intruders form gangs to attack those with food and water, guarantee yourself two things…

- *They will learn from their mistakes…*
- *Military hardware will fall into Intruder's hands and will threaten every NPP.*

Chapter 7
Area Tactical Protection for a High Rise Residential Building

There will be some repetition in this chapter and the previous chapter of this book to emphasize important issues. Regardless of whether you live in a Low Rise Residential Neighborhood or a High Rise Residential Building, read *both Chapters 6 and 7.* ***There is information crucial to each Area Tactical Protection in both Chapters.***

In this Chapter we describe…

- **7-The High Rise Residential Building**
- **7-Assessing your High Rise Building for a *NPP***
- **7-Get your HOA or Cooperative Board involved**
- **7-Bring the maintenance and security people and their families into your *NPP***
- **7-Story-*"Breakdown"***
- **7-The Clock System of Referencing Direction in a High Rise Building**
- **7-The *Third Dimension* of your *NPP* Protective Perimeter… usually forgotten**
- **7-Have *NPP* area intelligence satellite images, photos and maps**
- **7-Things *not* to do**
- **7-Things *you must* do**
- **7-Recommendations in securing your High Rise Building**
- **7-Immediately start storing water**
- **7-Where to set up your Protective Perimeters**
- **7-Outside features your building Protective Perimeter must have**
- **7-Inside features your building Protective Perimeter must have**
- **7-How to set up your Protective Perimeter**
- **7-How to prepare your building right now**
- **7-Building Assessment Exercise One**
- **7-You're in a *Crisis… Low Alert* procedures to institute**
- **7-You're in a *Long Term Crisis… Mid Alert* procedures to institute**
- **7- Perimeter checks-No outside Perimeter Patrol on a High Rise Building**
- **7-High elevation *Listening Observation Posts* and *Marksmen Positions***
- **7-Guard requirements and procedures**
- **7-*A Failure of Civility* has occurred… *High Alert* preparations to institute**
- **7-Denying access to your *NPP* by physical barriers-Foot and vehicle traffic**
- **7-Denying access to your *NPP* by physical barriers-Protective Perimeter aids**
- **7-Denying access to your *NPP* by psychological barriers**
- **7-Tactics that will make your *NPP* a *proactive defense***
- **7-DO NOT bring *Outsiders* or *Intruders* into your *NPP***
- **7-Link up with other *Neighborhood Protection Plans***
- **7-Passive response will get you killed-You must be proactive**
- **7-Building Assessment Exercise Two**

7-The High Rise Residential Building

This chapter is directed towards High Rise Residential Buildings. This type of residential building has the added dimension of 3 or more stories or levels of height and usually basements of one or more stories which need to be incorporated into the Protective Perimeter of an *NPP*.

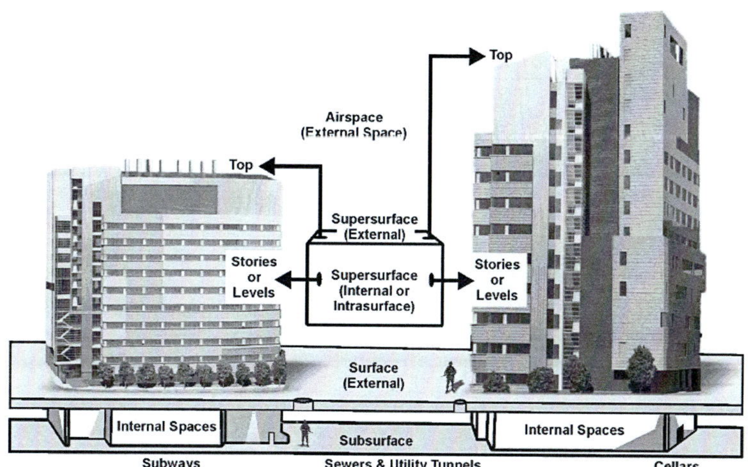

Typical High Rise Building Architecture

Because of this building's height, its form and the type of area they're in, this style of building requires a slightly different defense strategy. This type of Protective Perimeter will be *less proactive* than a Low Rise Neighborhood. It will be treated as a castle, because that is exactly what it is if it is fortified properly.

> ***High Rise Building Definition.*** *The Authors define a High Rise Building as apartments, cooperative ownership buildings and condominium complexes with three or more stories or levels of height. We're going to include commercial buildings in this category because their design and the principles of their Protective Perimeter defense are very similar.*

The element of height works to your advantage if your Protective Perimeter is fortified properly. This is the principle that made the medieval castle extremely defensible… high defensive walls with the defender far above the attacker on the ground.

Like the real estate saying *"Location… Location… Location…"* many survival experts think you're dead before you start to formulate a plan to defend yourself if your location is in a metropolitan High Rise Building or in the big city area period.

The Authors do not agree with this belief. We do believe that you would be better off in a suburban setting, but there are aspects of a High Rise Building that make it more defensible than a Low Rise Neighborhood… *if you can find a water and a heat source or underground area for winter survival.*

Because of these differences, the Authors have divided *Area Tactical Protection* into two separate chapters… the Low Rise Residential Neighborhood and the High Rise Residential Building.

These types of buildings are commonly found in our inner metropolitan cities. We'll refer to this type of building as a High Rise Building from this point on.

High Rise Buildings are typically of modern construction in larger cities and towns. For the purpose of this book, these consist mostly of multi story residential apartments. Some have separated external open area airspace in between the buildings. Some have connecting walkways between buildings either on the lower levels or underground. There are usually wide streets in rectangular patterns around these buildings.

The critical issue of water and a fuel source for heat for High Rise Buildings in sub-zero climates comes into play when deciding to form a long term *Neighborhood Protection Plan* for a High Rise Building… the same as the Low Rise Residential *NPP*. However, the location of most High Rise Buildings is generally in highly developed and populated city areas far from water and unlike Low Rise Residential areas has little in the way of combustibles for heating or cooking that can be scavenged in the area.

The Authors consider the protracted occupancy of a High Rise Building ***not feasible*** for a protracted *Long Term Crisis* or *A Failure of Civility* because of the water supply issue and a fuel source for cooking and staying warm in frigid winter areas.

Your building *NPP* may be able to sustain its occupants for a period of one month or more if water is responsibly rationed, if you have a roof reservoir of considerable capacity and if each inhabitant aggressively stores water… and if you can find a source for heat such as coal or large amounts of propane or fuel oil for the winter months and underground areas large enough for your Group Members to live in.

You need a minimum of 300 gallons of water per person *for a one month period of time.* For a longer period of time than that you need a reliable renewable water source.

Again, for your *Secondary NPP Locations* being long term sustainable *NPPs*, you need a *reliable renewable water source…* and in winter climate areas… *heating and cooking fuel and underground living areas.*

Refer back to *Chapter 5* for *Questions the Primary and Secondary NPP Leaders must answer first* before proceeding to use your building for a *Primary NPP Location* and in selecting *Secondary NPP Locations.*

Is there a water source? *You have to understand the logistics regarding water.* Read about *water* in *Chapter 12* ***first*** to help you evaluate this issue.

Putting a water bore hole in the basement of a High Rise Building is not impossible if you have the means to get through concrete and to ground soil. Some High Rise Buildings have such a problem with ground water seeping into their basements that they have to install sump pumps to pump this unwanted water out and into a drain. These will not give you enough capacity for survival in most buildings. You have to dig a bore hole or open well.

Otherwise, you need a lake, reservoir, river, stream or other water source *that you can depend on year round and that is* ***one mile or less from your NPP Location.***

We warn you not to base the long term sustainability *of your NPP on* ***rain water or snow*** *being sufficient for a water source.*

More than any of the *Critical Life Supplies and Services*, the amount of potable water stored will determine the length of time a High Rise Building *NPP* can be defended.

Underground living areas. The next item that has to do with *Critical Life Supplies and Services* for High Rise Buildings in frigid winter areas is *shelter*... primarily keeping warm in sub zero temperatures.

If your High Rise Building is in a winter weather area you will need to use these basement passages to keep from freezing in the winter months. Barricade and control basement and external passageways of a large enough area to accommodate all Group Members. Then secure access to and from these areas from your building *NPP*.

Underground passage ways, one or preferably two floors, below ground level have sustainable temperatures in frigid weather if fresh air circulation is controlled to prevent heat loss... but yet doe not cause oxygen depletion. The earth's temperature below ground is constant in most areas and is above freezing temperature 3 to 4 feet below ground level. This helps heat underground areas... ever so slightly... but it does.

7-Assessing your High Rise Building for a *NPP*

The High Rise Building provides the *NPP* unique advantages... mostly that you're fighting on 'your turf.' You know your building, *Intruders* and *Outsiders* most likely don't. Also, urban areas are excellent for Economy of Force, as defending a position in urban areas typically requires fewer forces than on open ground.

To proceed in organizing your High Rise Building with a *Neighborhood Protection Plan*, detailed maps and satellite images of your area and building are needed. You can print maps from internet mapping services and satellite images of your area then simply draw a characterization of your building's profile by hand if necessary.

Your Protective Perimeter will be determined by the number and location of Group Members that become involved in forming your *NPP*. Hopefully it will be your entire building. If not it will be some... if not the majority of people on your floor.

The first three floors are *critical for an effective NPP defense for your entire building. You cannot work around these Protective Perimeter Critical Units* if these people are hostile and refuse to cooperate with your plan. You will have to resort to your *NPP* encompassing contiguous floors. Preferably floors above floor 3.

There will be two types of neighbors in your building regarding the formation of your Neighborhood Protection Plan...

- *NPP* Participants.
- *NPP* Non-Participants.

There will be two types of units in your building regarding the formation of your Neighborhood Protection Plan for the entire building...

- Protective Perimeter Critical Units on the lower 3 levels.
- Non-critical units 4 levels and up.

Non-Participant units *are* a problem if their unit is one of the lower 3 level units on the exterior of the building, which is where your Protective Perimeter for the entire building *must* be.

Non-Participants will express one of two attitudes...

- Impartial.
- Hostile.

Take time to explain your *Neighborhood Protection Plan* to these Non-Participants. Many will simply let you form your plan with their unit being involved even though they will not be participating.

However, the issue of Intruders destroying your NPP by setting your Building on fire becomes a paramount concern if the entire three lower levels are not actively involved with your NPP Protective Perimeter.

Have a contingency plan to fortify the lower 3 floors anyway. Non-Participants will quickly want to join if there is *A Failure of Civility* or when their security and safety becomes threatened. Units with lower floor defensive positions will have to allow *NPP* armed members in their units if a *Long Term Crisis* or *A Failure of Civility* occurs.

At that time it will probably be too late to fortify the lower 3 floors as you would have if your HOA and Cooperative Board were involved with your planning from the start. You most likely won't have the proper materials on hand to fortify under these circumstances, however you can still set up Kill Zones, Guard Posts and fortify the lower three floors with improvised security methods.

If you can't get all three lower floors involved in your *NPP* and you can afford it, buy Concertina Wire or Barbed Wire as a stop gap defense during *A Failure of Civility.* These can be quickly installed in windows and in areas immediately outside entrances and windows around your Protective Perimeter.

Concertina Wire or Barbed Wire are not that expensive and can be purchased in rolls and stored easily in a basement area. It's not as good as boarding up windows by itself, but they make good deterrents. Concertina Wire or Barbed Wire has to be securely fastened in place to prevent it being pulled away with ropes.

You'll have to wait to see if that time comes during a *Crisis,* but since you're forming your *NPP* during the peaceful times of *Normal Civility*, you will have to work without the people in these lower three floors in the interim. When they do come around, have plenty of Concertina Wire available to string around the outside of your Protective Perimeter, to blockade their windows with and to form your Fatal Funnel and Kill Zone at your Entry/Exit Control Point and other areas.

7-Get your HOA or Cooperative Board involved

Although the above looks like we're getting 'The Cart in Front of the Horse' as the saying goes, it's necessary to understand the basis of the High Rise Building Protective Perimeter defense before approaching your HOA, Managing Agent and Cooperative Board.

To make your High Rise Building *Neighborhood Protection Plan* work for your *entire* building you will have to get your Homeowners Association or your Building Cooperative Board involved with your plan.

> ***Dictionary Definition***
> ***Protection***
> *(Noun) Protecting or being protected... A person or thing that protects.*

If common ground level areas of your High Rise Building are to be 'Landscape Fortified,' you'll have to have your Home Owners Association or Cooperative Board involved with your plan. 'Landscape Fortified' common areas can be done without presenting any hazard to people and they can enhance the beauty of your building.

Unfortunately, Homeowners Associations or Cooperative Boards, like the bureaucracy of most entities will be comprised of some members who are 'Politically Correct.' This is much more prevalent in major metropolitan areas.

There will be *two types* *of HOAs or Cooperative Boards* regarding the formation of your *Neighborhood Protection Plan. Those that* ***will be interested*** *in protecting the building and inhabitants... and those that* ***will not be interested****.*

Almost every HOA or Board seems to have one attorney as a member. These people are, for the most part... self important, egotistical and the proverbial 'stick in the mud.' They run scared of any issue for your building that they think will create the potential of a lawsuit… because that's what most of *them* do… sue people.

These 'Politically Correct' HOA and Cooperative Board members may be against using violence for any reason… even in defense of your person. Most detest firearms… they will be petrified and fearful of liability to their building resulting from the defense of the building and inhabitants and *will not* be in favor of an *NPP* for your building.

Considering the litigation hysteria in the United States over the right to defend, this may be a valid point with your HOA or Cooperative Board and their Insurance Underwriters.

However, considering the possibility of greater cost from the extensive damage and destruction of their High Rise Building during a *Crisis* that has the component of riots, looting and arson, the Authors would think that logic of their backing of an *NPP* would have more impact on them and their Insurance Underwriter.

You must assume that they will not be in favor of your *Neighborhood Protection Plan* for your High Rise Building. Let these people live in their dream world. If you don't violate their rules and regulations, they cannot stop you from organizing your floor members.

They would have a difficult time preventing you from having plans or an idea in your head… as long as you don't obstruct the building stairwells or physically implement any of what we propose in this book during *Normal Civility*.

Regardless, if the building Home Owners Association or Cooperative Board, Managing Agent and their Insurance Underwriter think a *Neighborhood Protection Plan* will increase their liability and they object to protecting their neighborhood during a *Crisis*, as ridiculous as that sounds, bypass them and organize your own floor.

Again, they can't stop you if you don't violate the HOA Rules and Regulations during *Normal Civility* and they certainly won't interfere if *A Failure of Civility* occurs. Just be aware… these will be the fools coming to you for food and water when there is none… and protection.

If they do attempt to stop you from organizing your floor… if they do interfere with your efforts… the Authors would hope that you suddenly have an epiphany and decide that it's time to move somewhere else that *will allow you to defend yourself, your family and your neighbors.*

Individual floors, ideally above floor three, can still band together by securing stairwells, elevators and any access ways to that floor. This makes an extremely effective Protective Perimeter if the floors are contiguous. Stairwells make natural Fatal Funnels and excellent Kill Zones for the defender, both coming up to your floor level and going down to your floor level.

If you can't get enough people on your floor to organize... the Authors hope you have the same epiphany. If you haven't, you'd better have devised plans to attempt to escape the city or move in with relative or friend of the same mindset as you if the time comes.

Passive reaction, burying your head in the sand or relying on the government will be the beginning of your road to misery and your probable demise if a severe enough Catastrophic Event occurs.

If there is *A Failure of Civility,* eventually individual floor *NPPs* will have to secure the entire building because of winter weather. You will not be able to keep from freezing to death in most High Rise Buildings in frigid winter weather. You need the basement area to keep warm in the winter and you'll have to have secure access from your floor *NPP* to the basement.

Do not move your NPP to the basement area... *it will not be defensible.* The basement area is for warmth and living for your Group Members but you must retain the height of your *NPP* Protective Perimeter to keep your advantage over attackers. You must secure the entire building.

To secure the building is to secure the first three floors, which in essence will be securing your entire building. If you can't secure the building with materials you will have to do it with a much weaker and less economic form of defense... sheer firepower.

Be advised that the fools in your building who were against your *Neighborhood Protection Plan* will now be coming for something to eat and drink. The Authors experience with this type of person is that they will not ask... they will demand and attempt to take these items by force.

The most acceptable weapon in cities with restrictive gun control laws is the hunting shotgun. The most effective weapon for defending a High Rise Building will also be the shotgun. The shotgun is one of the most effective weapons for close range defense, is a superb weapon for 'Close Quarters Battle' and is lethal up to 50 yards or more with 00 Buckshot.

That's half the length of a football field. Your High Rise Building *Neighborhood Protection Plan* should have a few long range rifles for Marksmen to make your *NPP* more effective, but shotguns will suffice.

One problem the High Rise Building Group Members will have in most metropolitan areas is firearms ownership. Most cities and States differ regarding their position on the Second Amendment and the right of citizens to possess firearms.

Firearms are the most effective means of defending yourself and your building and you can count on the criminals being armed in a *Long Term Crisis* situation or *A Failure of Civility*. Their firearms will literally 'come out of the woodwork.'

7-Bring the maintenance and security people and their families into your *NPP*

This is vital to the success of your *NPP* in a High Rise Building. If it is possible, bring your maintenance man and his family on into your *NPP*. If you have a private security firm controlling access to your building, you want to invite their employees who work in your building and their families to move into your building and be part of your *NPP* if a *Catastrophic Event* occurs.

If you believe that during a *Long Term Crisis* which begins to turn into *A Failure of Civility* that these people will stay on the job, think again. They will be with their families. No one knows your building better than these people… not even you, Mister and Misses resident.

This will be as good or better than the Christmas present you gave to them last year… or didn't if you were a cheap skate. Don't look at them as more mouths to feed… look at them as people to help you defend your building. You need these people!

7-Story-*"Breakdown"*

Day 26. *Today started out like all the others since our world changed abruptly. The radio stations that are still on the air say… "Order is slowly being restored in the city." That's beginning to sound monotonous. We've been hearing that for three weeks.*

I've got to write this down in my diary… it's too crazy and surreal to try to remember all this. I'm Nick Wilder. I was a stockbroker… that is up until the breakdown occurred. The turbulence and speed in which our city of 5 million turned into a war zone still haunts the few of us left in our building.

Most people, even those prepared for it, are still trying to get their head around the breakdown in services and the total lack of lawlessness that swarmed over our great city. Even with the National Guard called in to restore order… it was only a bandage on the hemorrhage of the life blood of decency that used to be the hallmark of this great city for decades.

I lived a very comfortable *and satisfying life before the breakdown. The luxury high rise building I lived in had all the amenities that we upscale metropolitan people could want. I, like most of my neighbors, worked in the finance industry or were professionals who brought home comfortable 6 digit incomes.*

None of us felt we had anything to worry about except another tax increase or a promotion. All of that seems like a distant dream now… the money is worthless, replaced by food, water, firearms and ammunition… an abstract but real currency. Items we took for granted and thought so little of now have great meaning and value to use. Simple items like plastic garbage bags and toilet paper. They're worth more than their weight in gold.

I should have paid more attention to what my friend Tony was saying... that trouble was coming. He brought it up the second time I met him after he moved onto our floor. Now that I think back... he wasn't just saying it back before all this started... he was preaching it!

Tony Stevens was one of the people in our building who seemed a bit 'out of place', so to speak. He didn't really fit in with the rest of us... not because of his outspoken manner... but because he was a police officer. Actually that description doesn't really do him service.

***Tony is a retired** and distinguished police officer turned highly paid crime consultant. He seems to have a Masters Degree in about everything. He was now a consultant to our city... a city desperate to find a way to curb a crime and murder rate that was putting us at the top of the list each year of the most lawless, crime ridden cities in the United States... one not to visit.*

Tourism, a big part of the financial picture in our city was slowing to a drizzle. Foreign and American visitors and tourists were afraid to come here. So like they say... "Follow the money." The city seemed to make that its principle concern... money... not the lawlessness that was becoming epidemic... a 'collateral issue' to them that would soon overwhelm everything else.

I liked Tony the first time I met him. He had an engaging air about him and the more I got to know him the more I knew he was someone I could trust. I quickly became very comfortable around him in a city where friendships took a long time to form... Tony is now not just my neighbor... he's my friend.

***He kept telling me** "Trouble was coming... big trouble! The street cop says it's getting lawless on their patrol beats!" I remember that as almost his coined statement. But, like everyone else I pushed it aside because of the overriding issues in my life at that time. My brokerage clients demanded every second of my time in a Bond Market atmosphere that had been getting more volatile by the day and more frightening by the second.*

After all, there was plenty of lawlessness on 'my street' too. The Financial District was rife with financial fraud schemes and insider trading scandals. It was a frequent occurrence that had been laid bare by the economic downturn. Lawlessness. I was seeing plenty of it... I thought.

All of us in this building were 'insulated' in a way from the growing violence in our city. Our lives consisted of 'from our building... to the financial district... and back.' Our shopping and dining out was mostly confined to the upscale business district surrounding our high rise building where almost all of the professionals in our building had their offices. We were living in a cocoon. Other than reading about the plight of our city in the newspapers and hearing about it on the news and from the people we worked with who lived outside of our little world... it didn't affect us... we were safe.

***"Nick, I want you to come to** the Co-Op Board Meeting next week at eight o'clock. It's a Thursday night," Tony said to me as he was leaving our building gym. "I'm going to present a security plan to them. I've got a number of people in the building who are coming* *with me… you'd give one more resident's respectability to us. I'm asking this as a favor, friend."*

The faint thought that Tony was becoming a 'pain in the ass' fluttered through my mind as I said, "Alright Tony, I think I'll be home by then."

"I'm counting on you then Nick."

Despite our protection by insulation from the problems of the city, I began to think it wasn't such a bad idea to do something about security and put a plan to the building Managing Agent and Co-Op board.

***I think back now.** It seems like a century ago that I attended that meeting and heard the astonished reaction and semi muted laughter Tony's proposal was met with as he laid it out to our Co-Op board.*

The typical remark from board members was that he was being an alarmist and that the police would handle any situation that arose. "Besides, we've got our own armed security people!" they all chimed in.

Their position was that putting a building security plan into effect was overreaction and that the police would handle any problems that our security people couldn't handle.

Our building Managing Agent Melinda added the 'coupe de gras' to the discussion when she said our building insurance policy would be cancelled because of the liability this security plan would create for the Cooperative.

Most of the smirks and much of the laughter came from our Cooperative Board President and powerful City Councilman Howard Green and a group of 'yes people' board members who favored anything he said.

***At that meeting** the board's attitude was evident by Green's statement… "Mr. Stevens. We want to thank you for your concern with everyone's welfare and safety here and presenting your plan to the board… but as you can see… we clearly aren't interested and don't have any more time to discuss this! Next item on the agenda, please?"*

After the meeting, Tony had 17 people from the 20 units on our floor approach him who wanted to know more about his proposal. They too sensed that there was trouble in the air and thought that what he had proposed to the board made sense.

There were those from other floors who felt the same way. Even though we weren't the majority in the building, we found that the majority of the residents of six floors of our thirty-five floor building wanted more information on preparing for problems. I volunteered to this group in the hallway outside the board room that we have a meeting in my unit. It was standing room only.

***Within a week** of that first meeting our intention to organize and implement a security plan got back to the Cooperative Board. The Managing Agent invited herself into our next meeting and informed our group by handing Tony a letter telling him to 'cease and desist' and stating to all of us… "I strongly advise each and everyone of you not to become involved in this endeavor as responsible residents of this building without the board's endorsement and approval… it's against our rules."*

"What specific rule or rules would that be, Melinda?" Came the quiet measured voice of the unimposing Bruno Haukstein, an attorney from the fourteenth floor who was with our

group and had help draft our building Co-Ops regulations. "You and the board members are invited to any of our meetings. Our meetings are open to all members of this building... including you, Melinda." Unable to cite any 'rule' that we were violating, Melinda stormed speechless out of our meeting.

Egos came into play then. *Howard Green tried to get the police department to shut our organizing down. As powerful as he was and as intensely as this influential Councilman pressured them, the Chief of Police gave him the answer... "Look Howard, I'd like to help you. But unless you can show us what they're doing is against the law... we can't cite them for a violation. Come on Howard... you can't stop them from organizing something like this! Councilman... I'm sorry... there's nothing I can do!"*

Our building security people refused to do anything to help us for fear of being fired. They had been warned by the board before we even mentioned our plans to them.

Tony's consulting contract with the city continued for another three years, but he was told it was going to be cancelled after that... due to the long arm of political influence... and Howard Green.

Maintenance man Carlos and his two helpers were also warned by the board. But the crime and violence in Carlos's neighborhood was so bad that some days he'd have to stay home with his family.

Quietly, on the promise *of no one revealing his involvement, Carlos showed us entry points to our building that we didn't know even existed. He also showed us the water shut off to each floor. He told us how we could control the water in the building and showed us every connecting passageway to the building in the basement from outside.*

Bruno Haukstein represented Mrs. Krauthammer who owned an apartment on the fourteenth floor. She'd been trying to sell her unit for two years. The apartment was now vacant with a minimum of furnishings as she, like many unit owners here now, preferred not to set foot in the city. She was now living by her children in a small Midwestern town.

She agreed that Carlos and his family could use her apartment as long as Bruno guaranteed to pay for any damages... on condition that the arrangement was kept quiet... and that Bruno take care of any problems with the Co-Op board if they found out. Carlos immediately moved his wife and children into the unit. His maintenance helpers moved in to other units within a week before the breakdown.

We decided that shotguns would be a good firearm for the type of defense we were going to have. We made several trips out of the State to buy shotguns and ammunition as permits were required in the city and the State sale always got back to the city police. We started storing food, mostly canned goods... and water.

We organized *our floor first. It took a while for the attitude "I'm not going to ration water!" to be overcome when they realized the gravity of the situation. Water... which each of us took for granted as the simple turn of a tap... would quickly become more valuable than gold.*

Day 7. *Local law enforcement and fire departments were stretched to their limits. The fire department was no longer going into some areas due to being shot at. They were forced to let homes and buildings burn to the ground. Standing on our rooftop, it was an* *eerie sight of columns of smoke... like funeral pyres... reaching up to the skies across the city. They were everywhere as far as the eye could see in all directions... we knew trouble had arrived... and it was for real.*

The sense of nervousness that had been felt by most of us was now quickly turning into a reality. There were attacks by blacks against whites, Hispanics against blacks and vice versa. Every racial and ethnic group was at each other's throats. Now it was the white people in the suburbs who were joining in with the beating and shooting of others.

***In decades past,** the whites had retreated into their homes, locked their doors and sat on the sidelines while racial issues that had boiled over into riots subsided... this time it was different. Their attitude towards intruders in their neighborhoods was... "Bring it On!" In the suburbs, whites were aggressively attacking anyone caught in their neighborhood who didn't live there. Since the police could not respond... they were imposing their own law.*

Councilman Green and the other Co-Op Board members still refused to consider any security plan for our building assuring the dwindling number of building residents who would listen that... "This will all blow over soon!"

At a standing room only emergency meeting of all building residents in the lobby, Councilman Green assured everyone that if there were problems... all he had to do was pick up the phone. He'd been assured by the Chief of Police that officers would be here in "Five minutes or less!"

***The day after** that meeting, Councilman Green 'disappeared'. To this day Councilman Green has not been seen. We were informed by Melinda that his family and he were escorted out of the building by heavily armed police. He and his family were then spirited away by police convoy to a 'secure location' for city officials. I told Tony they must need his 'visionary leadership' in other areas of the city.*

Only two of the Co-Op Board Members remained in the building. The rest of the board members and many residents with financial means quickly left the city. After these departures, we hastily made a list of everyone left in the building and an inventory of what we could use that was in the abandoned apartments. We have less than 200 residents left here and we began to secure the entire building.

***Day 15.** The violence has continued to escalate, even though the National Guard has been called in by the Governor and is patrolling the streets. Ours is not the only city in the state experiencing growing riots, looting and lawlessness. The National Guard is stretched far too thin. We are astounded at the stocks of food we had and how quickly residents went through them.*

John Fishburne has money and lots of it. He'd joined our group early on and paid for a lot of the food we stockpiled and containers for storing water. The character that had made him this fortune came to prominence during our catastrophe. Tony and I first thought he was crazy to suggest we 'buy' food and groceries from the local restaurant and stores. All of these small grocers and restaurants had locked their doors by now, their owners fearing to travel the city to work and their patrons fearing to leave their homes.

***Carlos used his locksmith tools** to open the locks of security bars and the alarm systems of these businesses. The alarm systems more because the noise from the alarm horns* *irritated us than our fear of anyone showing up. We went in a convoy with twenty or so Group Members and loaded anything edible or of use to us into our cars and hauled it back to our building. John Fishburne would then leave a check for more than the cost of the food and supplies along with his attorney's card.*

Of the eight building security people that our Co-Op Board had so much faith in, only two showed up for work this week. These two security guards no longer cared about the Co-Op board's threats of dismissal.

***They brought guns…** a number of rifles and pistols and lots of ammunition… the kind that former veteran military security type guys have… military type weapons, most of which were illegal in the city and State. These two guys came conditional that they could bring their families to live in our building. We quickly found accommodations for them.*

The two board members who remained in the building showed up at the Entry/Exit Control Point on our floor today asking if we had any food to spare. The smirks I recall on their faces just two months ago when Tony presented his plan to them have been replaced by a stoic and desperate look. They had a couple of 'tough guy types' with them who we suspected had weapons.

After our refusal to give them food, their politeness took a turn towards nasty. Their statement was that they'd come in and "F#&ing take what we want". Two 12 gauge shotguns pointed out the door of our floor in their direction quickly diffused the situation. As they turned to leave, we stopped them and threw out a couple of bags of food which they quickly gathered up then hurried off.*

***In fact 'take what we want'** was the prevailing attitude in most of the city. Across sprawling neighborhoods surrounding the metropolitan area, wholesale violence could occur just because you were in the wrong place at the right time… and now was the right time. Beatings, rapes and thefts were happening all over… that's if you were lucky… if you were unlucky you got shot. It's amazing in a city with some of the strictest gun regulations in the country… now many people were armed to the teeth… and most were criminals.*

Newscasts said two days ago that the National Guard is distributing military rations. We haven't seen any. Reports are that trainloads of food are coming from FEMA food reserves into the city. Despite the distribution of food to the point of saturating the city with boxes of rations, the violence continues. It seems that 'Pandora's Box' has been opened.

The feeling of freedom and the ability to do what you want to whomever you want still prevails in the city. The lawlessness seems to be more attractive to most than the previous order and regimentation that the people of this city had to adhere to. Law enforcement, even with the help of the National Guard can't get the lid back on the box..

***Day 20.** No one can really say what sparked this… the dismal economy and racial tensions that seemed to be encouraged by the very leaders who were supposed to try to calm them. But the total distrust in local, state and Federal Government simply fueled the fire.*

Regardless of the cause, Martial Law was declared by the President today and with it came the arrival of Federal Troops. Electricity and water were now sporadic due to maintenance workers staying home to protect their families. The Army was making attempts to get the electrical and water systems running again.

Mobs are appearing only blocks away despite the curfew and troops patrolling the streets. We took total control of our building today. Even though we had only makeshift security features, our two security guys gave all of us classes on how and when to use our firearms. These security guys, who before I think most of us looked down our noses at as being 'the common poor,' have a new 'rock star' image in our minds.

***Telescopes that had been used** primarily by the wealthy, upscale and bored of our building to pry into the world of neighboring high rise building residents were now put to use looking for danger on the streets surrounding our building. Two of them were taken by the security guys to the roof where they positioned themselves as our Marksmen with building residents as their observers.*

We made up for our poor defensive fortifications by posting more armed Group Members around the lower floors and entry points. We don't know how long we can commit this many people to Guard Posts 24 hours a day. At first, the roving gangs and looters steered clear of our building due to our heavily armed presence... but they're getting bolder now. Some even taking pot shots at our building. The security guys have shot three of them and the gangs seem to have put the word out on the streets to stay clear of our area for now.

***Those who had no interest** in our security plans are now coming to us asking how they can help. Food shortage is now becoming an issue with them and they are hungry of course.*

They tell us "We don't have anything to eat..." but then comes the concluding part of their statement... "but we have money."

To which John Fishburne replies... "So do I, but its not doing me much good now! You weren't interested back then and we aren't much interested in your problems now."

We'd give them a couple of loafs of bread and a few cans of soup and tell them... "Stay out of our way! Leave!"

We couldn't trust them then and we can't trust them now... but we can't let them starve either.

Life goes on... tomorrow will be day 27. The newscasts all say... "Order in the city is slowly being restored..."

...but don't go outside of the building.

7-The Clock System of Referencing Direction in a High Rise Building

Refer to the diagram regarding The Clock System of Referencing Direction in Chapter 6

This is the only method we recommend for referencing direction by your *NPP*. It is usually a two dimension direction system but with a twist for use in a High Rise Building. The Clock System works by positioning an analog clock (the one with the big and small hands) horizontally.

Since the **12 o'clock position is *always the North direction…*** consequently the ***6 o'clock position will then be South***, the ***3 o'clock position will be East,*** the ***9 o'clock position will be due West*** and any other direction can be estimated by the hour numbers on the clock, such as southwest being the '7 to 8 o'clock' position.

A Guard Post would report like this… *"Guard 3… I see Outsider movement at 4 o'clock!"* which would mean that Guard Post 3, which is on the East Protective Perimeter, sees *Outsiders* from the *NPP*s 4 o'clock direction.

The approximate distance from the Guard Post can be added, however, many people are bad at estimating distances visually.

In a High Rise Building a third element is added to the report to signify the floor level of the Guard Post so it would sound like this… "*Guard 3, floor 11… I see Outsider movement at 4 o'clock!"* which would mean that Guard Post 3 on the 11th floor sees people movement.

7-The *Third Dimension* of your *NPP* Protective Perimeter… usually forgotten

Look again at the diagram titled *'Typical High Rise Building Architecture'* at the beginning of *Chapter 7.* Notice the underground areas that your building will have. Most of these connect to other buildings or utilities areas outside your building. In most cities these go for miles and have many, many entrance and exit points.

This information is in the previous chapter. However, because of the danger of *Intruders* using these routes to breach your Protective Perimeter, we're covering it again. It is slightly modified for High Rise Buildings because of their uniqueness.

Underground passages are a serious issue for High Rise Buildings because almost all have numerous underground passages leading to and from the basements. This avenue of attack *and* defense *is either overlooked by most people* in forming a Protective Perimeter *or is not taken seriously enough.*

Your *NPP* Protective Perimeter must be determined by looking at *all three dimensions…* the dimensions of *width* and *length…* but also the *Third Dimension* of *height/depth.*

In large city High Rise Buildings… *underground features are numerous.* These features include underground garages, walking passages, subway lines, utility tunnels, sewers, and storm drains. Most allow people movement.

Many defense plans fail to take into account the *Third Dimension…*

What's *under ground* is commonly ignored by people… *underground passages.*

What's *above ground* is commonly ignored by people... *above ground room to room movement in or on buildings.*

Whole armies have been stopped dead in their tracks or defeated by enemy attacks utilizing underground and above ground concealed travel. One of the best examples is that both the Russians and Germans used underground sewers, utility corridors and room to room movement above ground to outflank and destroy their enemy in Stalingrad during that epic battle in World War II.

Underground Passages. Underground passages are more a ***disadvantage to the defender*** *than the attacker.*

Underground passages almost take the form of the mythological Trojan Horse… *they provide a way for the enemy to get inside your NPP* without being seen, heard or firing a shot… until they're standing right behind you… *like the Boogie Man.*

Knowledge of the type and location of underground facilities and above ground building routes of movement is of critical value to both the attacker *and* defender involving any *Area Tactical Protection.*

Underground routes and above ground building passage can provide the attacker the use of ground level attack, while simultaneously using above ground and underground avenues of attack. Your opponent can assault your *NPP* defenses from *inside* while attacking the *outside* by street level.

Depending upon the strength and depth of your *NPP* ground level defense, an attack along the underground or above the ground avenue of approach can turn into the main attack.

Even if the underground or above ground effort is not immediately successful, *it forces the NPP to fight on two or more levels* and to extend resources to more than just street level defense. There is also the Element of Surprise *that can turn your NPP into chaos* from an underground attack.

However, given the confining, dark environment of these passages, they do offer some advantages when thoroughly evaluated and controlled by the NPP...

- A small number of Group Members in a prepared defensive position can defeat a numerically superior force in an underground passage by using it as a Kill Zone. *Skipping Rounds* is an extremely lethal 360 degree attack in this type of confined space with hard concrete walls, floors and ceilings.
- Underground passages can provide your *NPP* covered and concealed routes to move reinforcements within your *NPP* Protective Perimeter or to launch flanking attacks from behind an opponent's rear on the outside of your *NPP* Protective Perimeter.

- Depending on their size, underground passages can be used for communications, for the storage and movement of supplies, evacuation and treatment of wounded and as a safe haven for Group Members and Dependents.
- Underground passages are necessary for living quarters for High Rise Building Group Members if your location is in a frigid winter climate area.
- Underground passages can provide your *NPP* covered and concealed emergency escape routes.

Underground passages are more a disadvantage to the defender than the attacker...
so if you're not going to use them... control them. Barricade or guard them!

When we say ***controlled by the NPP*** we mean these passages either have to be *constantly guarded or solidly barricaded, preferably both*. Floor manholes and access covers inside your *NPP* High Rise Building need to be welded or bolted in place or heavy items such as bags of sand placed over the manhole covers. Passage ways need to be blocked off with poured concrete, steel locking doors or sealed up with multiple layers of brick and block.

The threat from adjoining buildings. This may be an issue for your *NPP*. Holding the High Ground will work for you in your building when defending against ground level threats. However, if an *Intruder* has control of an adjoining building that is the same height as your *NPP* High Rise Building or higher, this can be a problem for you.

You may have to abandon one side of your *NPP* floors for living areas if this happens. You must still maintain the defense of that side of the building from the ground up to the third floor but move your Guard Posts inside the building. A path for concealed movement for you *and* your opponent is the far side of building balconies away from your *NPP* view or the enemy view respectively.

Attacking your Building through your basement. Be aware of an unusual and unlikely but a possible attack method... tunneling. In a High Rise Building this would probably be a more likely means of attack by knocking a hole through your building basement wall, rather than tunneling into your building. If a Guard Post hears noise or sees anything unusual in the basement areas of your *NPP* building, don't discount an attempt to break through the basement wall into your *NPP*.

Basement Guard. *Your Roving Guards should be aware of this tunneling strategy being employed by your enemy. We recommend a permanent guard on each basement level of your building and that this guard is a Roving Patrol.*

You must consider overhead power and communication lines, if applicable, as possible travel means to your building. *Intruders* can 'monkey crawl' any overhead wires leading to your building that are strong enough to hold their weight.

Again… it is difficult enough to fight off outside *Intruders*, but if you have to fight off *Intruders outside and Intruders inside your NPP it will most likely cause your defeat,* especially if *Intruders* gets to your Watch Center and kill or capture your leadership… *game over!*

7-Have *NPP* area intelligence satellite images, photos and maps

You must have maps and satellite images or aerial photos of your building and area. While computers and the internet function, print a series of satellite image maps of your *NPP* and the areas surrounding it.

In addition to streets and buildings in proximity to your *NPP*, pay particular attention to structures, terrain features, drainage ditches, causeways, hiking and bicycle trails, canals, subway and underground passage entrances *outside* your building and parking garages that could allow undetected movement towards your *NPP*. Physically visit to study them.

These same terrain features can be used for your *NPP* emergency escape routes. You can use the 'Earth' feature of satellite photos to give you a three dimensional view of some of your surroundings just like looking down from a height.

High Rise Building Area Satellite image

7-Things *not* to do

Don't allow independent action by Group Members. Independent action by Group Members without your *NPP* Leaders approval is dangerous to the entire *NPP*. This point reflects on the importance of basic discipline. *NPP* Group Members have to rely on the knowledge and experience of the *NPP Leaders* and must follow orders explicitly. Junior Leaders are the *only* exception to this.

Don't fire warning shots. If *A Failure of Civility* occurs *do not* use warning shots in an attempt to drive away *Intruders*. This simply draws attention to your *NPP* and wastes ammunition. Verbally warn but then 'Shoot to stop the threat.'

Don't ignore any alarm... because the first rule of alarms is… that there is no such thing as a false alarm! You've heard the fable of *"The man who cried wolf."* Keep *JDLR* in mind if you have false alarms on any security issue. Successful defeats have occurred by an enemy 'disarming' the alert mentality of a defensive position by repetitiously creating false alarms and then going in for the kill with the Element of Surprise. *Treat every alarm as a threat and be alert when you investigate.*

Don't have light visible from outside. Black out not only your Watch Center area but all unit rooms with windows and areas visible from outside your building. Use green or red filters on flashlights if you must use light in these areas. Do not open and close lighted room doors at night. During *A Failure of Civility* you will draw unnecessary attention from those that you do not want to spend an evening with if you do this. These people also will not be coming to play pinochle with you.

7-Things *you must* do

Armbands. If you merge with another *NPP*, when *Extended Family and Friends* arrive or until everyone intimately knows every Group Member in the *NPP*, you must have some means of Group Members identifying each other in daylight, by night red or green filtered flashlight and in the heat of an action… identifying friend from foe.

You must have something unique that is not easily copied by *Intruders*. Uniforms are expensive and many people may have similar or the same patterns or colors if *A Failure of Civility* occurs.

We suggest armbands on *both* upper arms to identify friend from foe. Do not use anything that will make you a target… like white, light colored or fluorescent colors. This is something the seamstress types in your building can make for little cost. Mrs. Jones's curtains can be sacrificed for this in a pinch.

Passwords. Simple numerical passwords can be used at night and during the day. Example, set the *password number* at 12. If a Guard Post gives the *challenge* to an unknown person he calls out to that unknown person *"5"*.

The unknown person must respond with *"7"*. The object being that the numbers given and received must add up to 12. Change the *password number* every 24 hours and keep voices down when challenging.

Carrying Weapons. Regardless of the stage after a *Catastrophic Event*, if the *NPP* is activated, everyone must carry their weapons *at all times wherever they go*.

Confine movement in your building during darkness. You do not want accidental shootings of Group Members at night. Keep children and anyone other than those on guard, inside or within a designated and restricted area of your building.

You should have only your Roving Patrol moving in the corridors and outside the designated restricted areas within your building after dark.

Roving Patrols should also accompany guards to their positions during shift change at night. You will not appreciate how nervous and 'trigger happy' people will become if *A Failure of Civility* occurs until it happens.

7-Recommendations in securing your High Rise Building

The following recommendations are made under the assumption that a *Long Term Crisis* or *A Failure of Civility* has occurred.

However, your High Rise Building has to be prepared and have the means to immediately fortify or institute these recommendations before a Catastrophic Event gets to those stages…

- ***Your present security system.*** Most High Rise Building security is intended for the random *Intruder* or burglar during *Normal Civility.* During a *Crisis* or *A Failure of Civility* this security system ***will not*** keep roving bands of *Intruders* or a mob out. Therefore, you will need to fortify and will need a Defense in Depth.

- ***Treat your High Rise Building as a castle and fortify it like one.*** If your High Rise Building has extensive glass front windows at the street level front, alley and side accesses… barriers must be installed over these areas. More so than just the street level, the first three floors need to have barriers installed. Many long extension ladders can reach to the third story of a building easily.

  If there are no grates or bars that cover these windows and doorways, they must be covered with plywood or some type of solid barrier. Your Homeowners Association or High Rise Building Cooperative Board should have metal window and door security systems installed on the lower floors that can be easily put in place.

  At the minimum they should have plywood barriers pre-built and stored for windows and doors with extra plywood sheets for reinforcement or replacement if needed. A solid barrier is best. Underground parking accesses that don't have barriers must also have provisions for barriers and they must be resistant to vehicles crashing through them.

  Steel doors not used for entry/exit that can't be welded shut, can be bolted shut. Get creative. This is where your maintenance man and your security people are necessary.

- ***The lower story window and door barriers*** are your first line of defense. You can't rely on these barriers alone. Like any Protective Perimeter, should they be breached, you must have a Defense in Depth. Again, a Defense in Depth is a defense of multiple layers or positions one behind the other to which you can retreat behind to stop *Intruders* gaining further access to your building. You must have Fall Back Fighting Positions behind the lower level windows and door barrier defense.

  When setting up your Fall Back Fighting Positions, have the area between the Fall Back Fighting Positions and the window and door barriers clear of any items that *Intruders* can use for Cover or Concealment. This creates the perfect Kill Zone.

The more fortified your building looks, the less chance that roving gangs will pick you for their target initially. Believe us… they will have plenty of other targets of opportunity… those who thought what's happening could *never* happen… have blind faith that the police and government will keep them safe, don't believe in firearms or using force to protect themselves against violence and didn't buy our book or institute our recommendations.

- ***Entry and Exit Points.*** You should have one Entry/Exit Control Point in your building. You should also have at least two other alternate escape exits, known only to the *NPP* members and used only in emergency as escape exits.

  Should your building be breached by *Intruders* and becomes indefensible or a fire gets out of control in your building, you will need to organize an orderly evacuation of the building to a prearranged gathering point preferably through these alternate escape exits.

  You must control the lower levels, securing the entrance and exit points to include above ground and underground walkways connecting your building with others, subterranean utilities corridors including sewer, electrical, communication, water and any other corridor where *Intruders* could enter your perimeter.

  These corridors when secured can be used to your advantage also, as concealed routes by which you can move from your building to other buildings without being seen and as winter living quarters.

- ***Outside fire escapes.*** Outside fire escapes must either be secured but preferably the lower parts dismantled for the first three stories. Get Emergency Fire Escape Ladders and have them in key locations in place of the fire escapes.
- ***Fire and Safety.*** Fire extinguishers should be positioned inside the building in hallways accessible to all residents to put out fires. Fire extinguishers should also be positioned inside the lower level of the building to extinguish fires to barriers.

  The positive aspects of a High Rise Building being easy to defend can quickly turn negative if fire breaks out. Fire will bring rapid and total devastation to your *NPP*. Fire drills should be held taking into consideration only emergency fire escape ladders and stairwells will be used to exit the building during fire drills or a real fire.

Emergency Fire Escape Ladder

- ***Elevators.*** Count on the elevators not working after some *Catastrophic Events* occur. There may be no electricity or the electronic controls may be destroyed. *Secure them by the method we describe further on in the book.*

- ***Water.*** Secure your rooftop cistern or water reservoir immediately. You will have to institute a water ration plan and each resident must adhere to it. If water is still pumping into your building's water reservoir, immediately have all residents fill all spare containers and bath tubs with water.

- ***Hygiene, sanitation and Safety.*** Sponge baths must replace baths and showers. Toilets cannot be used in the traditional manner. Urinating and defecating in plastic bags placed inside small waste baskets or a bucket or in a toilet as described in *Chapter 12* then securely tying them off afterwards will be necessary. All water traps must be plugged with rags to keep noxious gases from entering the building.

High Rise Building Roof Water Reservoir

- ***Heating and Cooking.*** You must assume that in a *Crisis* situation natural gas/propane will not be available for heating and cooking.

  Designated areas… with fire safety, carbon monoxide poisoning and oxygen depletion kept in mind… must be setup on each level for cooking such as barbeque grills out on balconies or the building roof top. Remember that smoke from fires will reveal the existence of people and will draw *Intruders*.

  Unless the Group Members of a High Rise Building have stored coal, fuel oil, kerosene or large amounts of propane gas, keeping warm in the winter will be a challenge.

7- Immediately start storing water

The critical issue is water… and this is something that can be stored in considerable quantities by each person for virtually no cost. Immediately secure any sources of extra water for your building such as roof top supply tanks and cisterns if a *Crisis* develops. Reference 'water' in *Chapter 12* first.

Group Members of an NPP should immediately start storing water ***upon the formation of an NPP***. Buy water storage barrels and a hand pump if you can afford it. These barrels come in sizes from 10 gallons up to 55 gallons.

A cheap alternative is to store water in 2 liter soda bottles… they must be thoroughly cleaned first before being filled with fresh water.

Emergency water storage barrels

Add *one drop* of *regular unscented* chlorine bleach for each gallon in the container to stabilize the water. Label these and mark the date on the label with a black marker. Rotate dumping, refilling and re-dating them to maintain a fresh as possible supply.

Do not consume this water except in emergency and then only if boiling it or running it through a water purifier that will remove the chlorine also. The more water Group Members store… the longer the High Rise Building *NPP* is sustainable.

Water is heavy! One gallon of water weighs 8 pounds. If you store 300 gallons of water you have 2400 pounds of weight… over one ton of water. This may be dangerous if you store water in 55 gallon containers or large amounts in one small area.

You must make certain your unit floor will support this weight and not collapse!

The containers must be spread out, preferably next to the exterior walls of your building, to prevent floor damage or failure of your floor. This is especially true of older buildings. Consult your building maintenance man or an engineer about this.

7-Where to set up your Protective Perimeters

The footprint of your building and from the basement and passages up to the roof or the floor that you organize will define your Protective Perimeter.

If you formulate even a fairly good plan, it will probably be very defensible against numerically superior *Intruders*. Many wars have been lost because the attacker didn't know the area they were fighting in as well as the defender. They don't know your area or the terrain… *you do*.

This is a *huge* tactical advantage in warfare. Many wars have been lost by overwhelmingly superior forces fighting inferior forces on unfamiliar ground and especially if that inferior force has pre planned defensive positions and tactical plans.

7-Outside features your building Protective Perimeter must have

The Outside of your Protective Perimeter should have these features...

- ***Overlapping Fields of View.*** Observation from Guard Posts that cover the entire Protective Perimeter.

- ***Outflanker Marksmen.*** High elevation Marksmen positions ***outside*** the Protective Perimeter that have Supporting Fields of Fire and Interlocking Fields of Fire with *NPP* Guard Post and the *Inside Marksmen* Fields of Fire.

  These are Marksmen ***outside*** the Protective Perimeter that can aggressively and precisely fire on *Intruders* around the Protective Perimeter and the main approach. *Outflanker Marksmen* will have to be in adjoining buildings or high vantage points.

  Outflanker Marksmen are key positions that in worst case scenarios should be focused on more if you are short of guard personnel. The physical and psychological devastation that one or more of these positions can inflict on an enemy from 100, 200 or 300 yards can not be overstated.

  Reference the diagram regarding Outflanker Marksmen in Chapter 6.

- ***Clear Fields of Fire*** around as much of the Protective Perimeter as possible and as far out as possible. Remove anything from around your building that obstructs this and gives Cover or Concealment to the *Intruder…* this includes vehicles.
- ***Surface difficult to move on.*** Place rubble that is hard to move on but gives no Cover around your building Protective Perimeter.
- ***Interlocking Fields of Fire*** that cover the entire Protective Perimeter.
- ***LOPs.*** Enough high elevation LOPs that can see the entire Protective Perimeter of your building and can watch the most likely approaches to the perimeter.
- ***Marksmen Positions.*** Enough high elevation Marksmen positions that can see the entire Protective Perimeter of your building and can watch the most likely approaches to the perimeter. You should have *Inside Marksmen* in your High Rise Building and *Outflanker Marksmen* in adjoining buildings or in high vantage points around your building covering your main approach and as much of your Protective Perimeter as possible. Marksmen must take into account the difference of trajectory when firing down from high positions.

  If you have enough qualified Group Members and radio communications we recommend one or more combined LOP and *Outflanker Marksmen* in high vantage points or adjoining buildings *outside* your *NPP*. These can be extremely effective in alerting your *NPP* to threats and the *Outflanker Marksmen* positions can act as a counter-sniper to eliminate sniper threats to your *NPP*.

- ***Placement of Guard Posts*** that allow multiple positions to fire on likely approaches with Supporting Fields of Fire. Especially the common and street approaches to your building.
- ***A Kill Zone*** outside your *Protective Perimeter, if your building entrance area will accommodate it.*

  Reference diagram regarding Kill Zones and Supporting Fields of Fire in Chapter 6.

- ***Ambush areas.*** If your building footprint allows one or more 'L' Shaped ambush areas close to your Protective Perimeter that your *Response Guardians* and Guard Posts can use to ambush *Intruders* close to but outside your Protective Perimeter.

Range Cards are simple stakes or landmarks set out to give a defensive position the distance to a point in their Field of Fire, such as 100 yards, 200 yards, etc. They can also be used in the multiple roles as Limit Stakes to define the left and right limit for a defensive position's Field of Fire.

The Authors do not believe in Range Cards with the exception of their use for Marksmen. Range Cards are beyond practical usage for most High Rise Building Protective Perimeters because of the limited distances between most buildings and the limited training Group Members will have.

The Authors do, however, believe that Limit Stakes, defining the left and right limit of each Guard Posts Field of Fire should be used to give some fire control discipline to each Guard Post. Guards should not be shooting at *Intruders* outside of these Limit Stakes unless a Guard Post is in danger of being overwhelmed.

Dictionary Definition
Tactical
(Adjective) Characterized by or showing cleverness and skill in tactics.

Outside your High Rise Building, considering that you won't be able to drive a wooden or metal stake into anything around you, use spray paint or features on adjoining buildings or streets in place of your Limit Stakes.

As the Authors stated before, we are great believers in 'Barbed Wire' and especially 'Concertina Wire' also known as 'razor wire,' are cheap, easy to restrict entry into areas with and gives an *Intruder* no Cover or Concealment.

Concertina Wire in its box

You can get Barbed Wire at most building supply or farm supply stores. You will need heavy leather gloves to place Concertina Wire and Barbed Wire.

Barbed Wire or Concertina Wire are great impediments against *Intruders* and can be used to define and create obstacles in each Guard Post's Field of Fire. Concertina Wire is made for this purpose and can be purchased for about $80 plus shipping per roll through the internet and that's enough to block off 50 lineal feet. 20 people chipping in equally would cost $5 each if freight is $20 for a box of Concertina Wire delivered.

Concertina Wire has the added advantage over Barbed Wire that it will stand on its own… you don't have to string it over anything to keep it up off the ground. 50 lineal feet is enough to create your Fatal Funnel at one entry/exit area of most buildings. It must be fastened in place though to keep *Intruders* from pulling it away.

7-Inside features your building Protective Perimeter must have

The area inside of your Protective Perimeter should have these features...

- ***LOPs.*** Enough high elevation LOPs that can see the entire Protective Perimeter of your building and can watch the most likely approaches to the perimeter.
- ***Marksmen Positions.*** Enough high elevation Marksmen that can see the entire Protective Perimeter of your building and can *Cover with Fire* the most likely approaches to the perimeter.
- ***Watch Center location.*** Set up your Watch Center in a center room of a unit inside your *NPP* on the fourth floor or higher. Watch Center units must be 'blacked out' at night during a *Crisis*. No white light must be visible from the outside. *Check the building from the outside at night to verify this.*
- ***A Kill Zone*** close to your *NPP* Entry/Exit. This Kill Zone will probably have to be in the lobby of your building.
- ***Fall Back Fighting Positions*** or a Defense in Depth.
- ***One fortified floor***, preferably your Watch Center location as a last stand or 'Alamo' fighting position.
- ***Escape areas.*** One or more emergency escape areas which is covered in *Chapter 11*.
- ***Guard Posts.*** Placement of Guard Posts that allow multiple positions to fire on likely approaches. Especially the common and street approaches to your building.
- ***Ambush areas.*** If your building footprint allows, 'L' Shaped ambush areas close to your Protective Perimeter that your *Response Guardians* and Guard Posts can use to ambush *Intruders* close to, but outside your Protective Perimeter.

Beware of Supporting Fields of Fire between Group Members so that these don't create Friendly Fire Incidents of Group Members firing on their own Group Members. You'll have enough people shooting at you if you're attacked, without your own Group Members hitting other Group Members by accident.

Plan your Guard Posts with Friendly Fire Incident prevention in mind.

Use the proper weapons on hand for different Guard Posts. Don't use a shotgun or pistol for long range. Use common sense!

So, you've got a lot of things going for you… let's move on.

7-How to set up your Protective Perimeter

Your building or the floor that you have organized as your *NPP* will be your Protective Perimeter. The purpose of the Protective Perimeter is to control who comes into your *NPP*… to keep *Outsiders* and *Intruders* on the outside of your *NPP*.

If armed *Intruders* try to force their way in, you want to force or deceive those *Intruders* into attacking under unfavorable circumstances to them, and to defeat or destroy that attack. When 10 *Intruders* attack a two man Guard Post and suddenly 4 other *Response Guardians* quickly react to fire on them from another direction and defeat them… that is the result of a *Proactive Defense.*

While the *offense* may be the most essential type of operation in a conflict, *the defense is the strongest*. The strength for the *NPP* is the ability to have prepared positions before an attack and to make use of 'economy of force.' Economy of Force is the ability of fewer people to defend successfully against a greater number of attackers.

Look at your *NPP* from the highest vantage point that an *Intruder* could use… because they *will* use this vantage point to look at your *NPP*. Look at elevated positions next to your building Protective Perimeter as a position for an enemy… because they will use these too. *You may have to occupy the roofs of buildings around you that tower over your building or interfere with your security.*

Look for high vantage points as well as the lower places of Cover and Concealment. Look for high vantage points for observation posts and positions *inside* and *outside* the *NPP* to put the *LOP Guardians* positions and Marksmen positions. High vantage points that give you a commanding view of your entire areas is critical for not only defense but for gathering current intelligence of the surrounding area.

Check *all* underground and above ground passages. What's underground is an issue that a High Rise Building *NPP* definitely has to evaluate thoroughly.

7-How to prepare your building right now

If your building has one, following the guidelines for your Neighborhood Watch Program on how to prepare your building against criminals will give you some guidance. Almost all of the following can be done for little expense for each neighbor or to the *NPP* if everyone chips in or by your HOA or Cooperative Board funding this.

One of the many preparations your building can make that serves the purpose of protecting residents even during *Normal Civility* we label 'Fortification Landscape.' This is subtly changing or installing any landscape adjoining your building to serve as part of your fortifications… while at the same time enhancing the beauty of your Building.

Decorative concrete wall fixtures. At the designated Entry/Exit Control Point short, decorative concrete walls can be poured in place where you want Guard Posts. These can also be incorporated as decorative flower planters at the front or as an internal part of the lobby desk away from the front door.

These give tremendous Cover and Concealment. These can also be placed strategically throughout the lower floors for Fall Back Fighting positions. If *A Failure of Civility* occurs, you can string strand Barbed Wire or Concertina Wire between them.

Decorative Sand Containers. You're not going to be able to walk out in the street and fill sandbags with sand, dirt or rock. We suggest buying or constructing flower planters large enough to hold sand for the number of sandbags you anticipate using. Get your construction or engineer types to calculate this.

Shrubbery and flower planters outside your building and inside your lobby and common hallway areas can be filled with sand and soil combinations that will sustain plants or simply sand if plants are artificial.

Underground Passages. As we stated earlier… investigate them. Make preparations to either use or them or seal off underground passages. The Authors like the idea of using them if they're large enough and in cold weather climates you will have to use them.

LOP and Marksmen Positions. These should be sandbagged positions on the upper floors or roof of your building with views of the approaches of all sides of your building.

Install metal door and window coverings. Roll down metal shutters are expensive, but make your building a virtual fortress when they're rolled down and locked in place. This is something an Insurance Underwriter should give a discount for. Window grates keep people out but *Intruders* can see through them, fire weapons through them and ignite fires inside your building even with these locked in place.

You will see more and more 'fortification' and security in America as the social, political and economic situation worsens in the coming years.

7-Building Assessment Exercise One

We aren't with you to review your building… but we'll *"Walk along beside you"* to give you procedures with this sample exercise by using photo commentary.

We'll warn you here that you should never share underground maps or building plans with anyone of adjoining buildings or outside your Group Members. Share only what's necessary for mutual security. Keep in mind compartmentalization for security and that you don't want to reveal too much information on your *NPP* Protective Perimeter to those outside your *NPP*.

You must know your building and the surrounding area. By know it, we mean Leaders must walk the building and the surrounding area with Group Members. *"Know your area... walk your area."* Don't just look at, but examine every feature of your building and the surrounding area.

Most importantly, walk the outside of your neighborhood to see your perimeter from an *Intruder* or attacker's view point and prospective. We suggest that photos of your Protective Perimeter be taken from various distances to know what an *Intruder* will be seeing.

Always have more than one person on your survey... get Group Members involved. Multiple heads are better than one when evaluating your building. One person may notice something that another doesn't.

Multiple High Rise Buildings side by side

In this photograph you see multiple High Rise Buildings which look as if they are connected as one continuous building. Generally, for fire code these buildings have a slight space between them or a fire resistant wall that extends two to three feet over the roof between buildings of the same height. There are usually no connecting corridors between buildings.

How do you defend them? Left and right directions below are relative to you looking at the photo, not being in or on the building.

You and your neighbors inhabit the red brick second building from the left. The building to the left of yours doesn't want anything to do with a *NPP*. The building to the right of yours has only the third floor as that building's *NPP*. How do you proceed?

Get with the maintenance man of your building or if you don't have one find the person who has the most knowledge of your building's construction and verify the following...

- Are the walls of your building next to the adjoining buildings fire proof and are they up to code to prevent the spread of fire started in adjacent buildings from spreading to yours. You can't depend on the fire department to show up or water for fire purposes being available.

  The threat of fire spreading to your building from others will make your building unsustainable for a *Neighborhood Protection Plan*. Expect lots and lots of fires in buildings if *A Failure of Civility* occurs.

- Find and plan on how to secure all points of entry to your building from the basement up to the roof.

- Study the roof area. Set up your LOP on the front and Guard Posts on all other sides of the roof to keep *Intruders* out. Sandbag the right side of the LOP if nothing else on the roof gives Cover from the castellated white building to the far right or place your *Outflanker Marksmen* on that building.

  Guard Posts can consist of one *Roving Guardian* but you need Cover positions to defend from. Your roof is an easy access point for anyone with a rope or ladder from the building to the left and *Intruders* can walk onto your roof from the building to your right. Use access denial items and methods to deter *Intruders* or to slow them down.

  See Chapter 8 for a list of items you can use to deny and control access to your NPP.

- The windows and store front door are easy entry points. They must be secured. Even with grates or bars add an additional layer of security by boarding them up from the inside. Have plywood pre cut and marked for each window along with all fasteners. Take a hint from hurricane area homeowners in preparedness. These people have everything prepared to secure windows and doors on their homes in a moment's notice.

- An *Intruder* with a ladder or rope can get to the first floor fire escapes in the front. Secure them by putting a Guard Post inside the window to the entry level and use access denial items and methods to deter *Intruders* or to slow them down.

  If *A Failure of Civility* occurs, get rid of at least your second story fire escapes. Pile them in front of your building to help deny access. Get emergency fire escape ladders and have them in proper locations.

- If *A Failure of Civility* occurs, get rid of the canopy on the front of your building and if necessary, the canopies of the buildings on each side of you. You need *clear* Fields of Fire and the canopy gives *Intruders* Concealment. *Only* if that tree offers any

Concealment or Cover for an *Intruder* cut it down. The Authors love trees… but you can plant a new tree later… or others may be planting you.

- You must board up the first three stories. The second and third story windows and roof may offer good defensive positions with gun ports in the window boarding. You can determine which windows to use by walking from window to window and evaluating the Fields of Fire from those windows.
- You must fight like holy hell to keep possession of your roof top or your *Intruder* will gain the advantage of High Ground over you. Imagine the building to the right of yours has been defeated and taken over by looters. They are attacking across the roof to seize your building through your roof top because it's the easiest route. This is where you radio your *Response Guardians* to come to the rescue.
- Your *Response Guardians* must practice getting to your roof top quickly and having prepared defensive positions there from which to hit the *Intruders* with Violence of Action. Again this is Suppression by Overwhelming Fire.

The other roof is not set up as a Kill Zone because your angles of fire are not diverse enough and attackers may have Cover… so leave room for them to retreat and go elsewhere. Secure the other building's roof top after you defeat them.

- If the defense of your roof fails, have a retreat plan from your roof and practice Cover and Fire Movement to vacate it. Have locks and chains stationed by the roof access door or the roof hatch.
- The *Intruder's* second route of access to your building will be by breaking through an adjoining wall from the defeated building next to yours. Have *Response Guardians* ready to move at a moment's notice from a centrally located position to fire on these *Intruders* with Violence of Action.

As soon as the slightest hole in your building wall is made by them… bloody their noses by firing as many weapons through that hole as possible. Force them to go down the street.

7-You're in a *Crisis… Low Alert* procedures to institute

The worse the *Crisis* gets the more elaborate your security measures and defensive fortifications must become. Your *NPP* security and defenses should *match or exceed* the stage of the *Crisis*. Read our guidelines and then create your own.

You are in a Crisis situation in your area. Your NPP Protective Perimeter at this time should be on a 'Low Alert' footing and you need to institute the following...

- If you have radios, charge the batteries and setup your Watch Center base radio.

- Leaders should talk to all Group Members by phone if possible or preferably visit each one. Brief them and advise them to be prepared to take their duty positions.
- Put your Watch Center into effect and man it 24 hours a day, monitoring radio stations and radio traffic providing *NPP Leaders* with periodic briefings from police scanners and radio communications.
- Institute Fire Watch Procedures.
- Dress in casual civilian clothing *without* armbands. Do not overtly display weapons.
- Start the *inside Roving Guards* on perimeter check. A High Rise Building *NPP* ***does not use*** an *outside* Perimeter Patrol.
- Post a guard at each walk-in entrance to your *NPP* and one at each vehicle entrance to your garage.
- If vehicles operate, fuel all vehicles and park them in your building parking garage or where you can watch them and get to them in an emergency.
- Fuel reserve storage containers.
- Buy as much additional food as possible.
- Store as much water as possible.
- Buy as much additional ammunition as you can get.
- Buy as much medicine as you can get.

7-You're in a *Long Term Crisis… Mid Alert* procedures to institute

The Crisis has deteriorated to a Long Term Crisis. Your NPP Protective Perimeter at this time should be on a 'Mid Alert' footing and you need to institute the following...

- Leaders should call all Group Members together. Brief them and post all Group Members to their positions.
- If you have radios, assign one radio to each *LOP Guardian,* one radio to each *Inside Marksman* and *Outflanker Marksman,* one radio to each *Alpha or Bravo Guardian* at their Guard Post, one radio to the *Roving Guardians* group, one radio to the *Response Guardian* group, one radio to each *Runner Guardian* and one radio for the *Caretaker Guardian. Reserve Guardians will be in the Watch Center and can use the radio of the position they have to relieve.*
- Keep the Watch Center active 24 hours a day monitoring radio stations and radio traffic and providing *NPP Leaders* with periodic briefings and notifying them immediately of items importance heard on police scanners and radio communications.

- Dress in casual civilian clothing *with* armbands. Dress in civilian clothing colors that match or are similar to the major color scheme of your environment. Do not overtly display weapons except at your Entry/Exit Control Point and inside your *NPP*.
- Man your Guard Posts.
- Increase *inside Roving Guard* activity on perimeter check. A High Rise Building *NPP* ***does not use*** an *outside* Perimeter Patrol.
- Blockade all entrances to your *NPP* with the exception of your Entry/Exit Control Point and your vehicle garage entrances. Garage entrances must continue to be guarded.
- Assign additional guards to your Entry/Exit Control Point.

If the *Catastrophic Event* is due to a pandemic, the sick must be quarantined in a building unit away from others to keep the infection from spreading. The characteristics of the pandemic must be determined and it dealt with accordingly… is it airborne, spread by bodily fluids or touch, etc. Act accordingly.

One Group Member is going to have to volunteer to be quarantined with them to tend to their needs wearing the proper eye, face masks and clothing to keep the pandemic from spreading to these caregivers. The clothing they wear must be immediately washed with disinfectant or burned.

7- Perimeter checks-No outside Perimeter Patrol on a High Rise Building

In the case of a High Rise Building, we do not recommend patrols outside the Protective Perimeter. The *Roving Guardians* will perform this perimeter check from the *inside* of your Building.

Your High Rise Building should be like a Medieval Castle and consider yourself 'Under Siege.' The only time you will be leaving your 'Castle' is for water runs and if necessity warrants it.

Intruders can and will plan their infiltration around any set schedule. Perimeter checks should be at random times and *especially just prior to sunrise and sunset.* History has shown that changing light periods are favorite times for attacks. Your *LOP Guardians* and Marksmen should be alert for any suspicious activity at *dawn* and *dusk.*

Remember JDLR… "Just Don't Look Right." Always look for things that are different or out of place. In your building and especially the basement areas… listen for noises… watch for dusty or wet footprints, broken glass, brick or concrete chips, disturbed surface dust… anything that shows human presence or movement from other than *NPP* members.

Inside Perimeter Patrols should be discussed with leadership after each patrol. Any observations made by Perimeter Patrols should be discussed thoroughly. Remember *JDLR* and realize sometimes *little things* can be *big things*. Leaders should question anything patrol members have observed.

7-High elevation *Listening Observation Posts* and *Marksmen Positions*

The LOP. This position, the *Listening Observation Post* or LOP, is the 'Eyes and Ears' of the *NPP*. This position is probably the most important of your Protective Perimeter Guard Posts. This position, along with Marksmen, *must* have a means of communications with your Watch Center.

The more *LOPs* you have the more effective your Protective Perimeter will be. In your High Rise Building you must have enough *LOPs* to observe the entire perimeter of your building.

This is your *main* Guard Post and should have view of especially the main approach areas to your building. Extreme care should be taken that this position remains concealed and no attention is brought to it.

Marksmen Positions. These should be manned by your best shooters with long range telescopic scope equipped rifles for observation and accurate long range shooting.

Binoculars, spotting scopes and rifle scopes must have Anti Reflection Protectors to prevent an enemy from seeing sun reflection from their lenses.

Roof top LOP and Marksman Position

There are two types of Marksmen Positions…

- *Inside Marksmen* **within** the *NPP* Protective Perimeter.
- *Outflanker Marksmen* ***outside*** the *NPP* Protective Perimeter.

Reference the Anti Reflection Protector diagram for binoculars and rifle scopes-Chapter 6

There should be at least one Marksman position *inside* the *NPP* and at least one Marksman position *outside* the *NPP*. Between them they should be able to cover by fire some of the area *around the building Protective Perimeter and especially the main approach.*

The Marksmen positions, along with the LOP, *must* have a means of communications with your Watch Center. The more Marksmen positions you have the more effective your Protective Perimeter will be. The more *Outflanker Marksmen* positions you have, the more efficient and lethal your building *NPP* Protective Perimeter will be.

The Authors recommend that you incorporate your *Outflanker Marksmen* positions with a *Listening Observation Post Guardian* as this allows them to work as a team when engaging hostile targets that threaten the *NPP* well in advance of the threat getting close to the *NPP*.

High Rise Building Outflanker Marksmen should be accompanied by two other Group Members. One to act in a dual role as a spotter for the *Outflanker Marksman* and also as a LOP.

The other must act as all around security for the group when they are moving to and from their position outside the *NPP* and providing rear security for them when they're in their position… in effect… 'watching their backs.'

Great care must be taken by the *Outflanker Marksmen* groups getting in and out of their position as quietly and as unseen by *Intruders* or *Outsiders* as possible. But, your *NPP* Entry/Exit Control Point guards must verify that the people who leave for this duty… are the people who return.

It would be possible for *Intruders* to kill these people and masquerade as them until they get into your *NPP* Protective Perimeter. Have a procedure of verifying them by having them 'stand off' a distance from your entry point. Then have them clearly show their faces and give them a *password number challenge* before allowing them into your *NPP*.

This might sound like an over reaction to security, but if *A Failure of Civility* occurs you will see things happen that you would normally never conceive of.

The Marksman Position…

- Covers avenues of approach, 'dead areas' and areas around obstacles not visible from Guard Posts.
- Obtains information by using the rifle scope like a pair of binoculars.
- Can make preemptive strikes on *Intruders*.
- Can keep the enemy from regrouping or repositioning for an attack.
- In some circumstances, can assist with protecting your *NPP* Group Members on water runs or within short distances from your building.
- Can deter enemy infiltration attempts.

Unless you have Thermal Imaging Telescopic Rifle Scopes, this is a daylight position and these shifts can be very long… like all the daylight hours. Each person can take turns observing in the other's position until the Marksman is needed.

7-Guard requirements and procedures

Review ***Guard Requirements and Procedures*** *thoroughly in Chapter 6. This is a critical part of your Neighborhood Protection Plan.*

7-*A Failure of Civility* has occurred… *High Alert* preparations to institute

If a *Long Term Crisis* has gravitated to *A Failure of Civility* it's time to start preparing for the worst by finalizing your *NPP* Protective Perimeter defenses.

Your NPP Protective Perimeter at this time is going to be on a 'High Alert' footing and you need to institute the following...

- Lock Down your *NPP* by setting up your Entry/Exit Control Point and the Entry/Exit Control Point Fatal Funnel and Kill Zone.
- Leaders should brief all Group Members at their positions and advise them that *A Failure of Civility* has occurred.
- Keep the Watch Center active 24 hours a day monitoring radio stations and radio traffic and providing *NPP Leaders* with more frequent briefings and notifying them immediately of items of importance heard on police scanners and radios.
- Heighten Fire Watch Procedures.
- Dress for battle because that's what you're in… *A Failure of Civility.* Dress in casual civilian clothing *with* armbands or camouflage uniforms if you have them. Clothing colors must match or be similar to the major color scheme of your environment or camouflage painted. Display weapons prominently.
- Ready your fall back positions inside your building.
- Set up your Kill Zones.
- Post your *LOP Guardians.*
- Post your *Inside Marksmen* and *Outflanker Marksmen* positions.
- Re-enforce your Protective Perimeter as much as possible.
- Board up the doors and windows of your building on your Protective Perimeter.
- If your elevator has openings on your Protective Perimeter, secure all elevator doors.
- Block off all underground entrances to your building.
- Cut down shrubbery, *trees only if necessary* and remove any objects on your Protective Perimeter that will provide Concealment to an *Intruder*.
- Move any vehicles out of the *NPP*'s Fields of Fire except those necessary.
- Gather children and *Dependent Persons* into a central safe unit.

- String Barbed Wire or Concertina Wire where necessary.
- Increase patrolling inside your *NPP*.
- Prepare your *Emergency NPP Relocation Bags*.
- Rehearse your *Emergency NPP Relocation* plan.

If this time comes you must be ready to 'trash' your High Rise Building to the degree necessary to provide adequate defense for your *Neighborhood Protection Plan*. Your building can be restored. Repairs can be made easily to just about anything but people with massive gunshot wounds.

If this is a pandemic, the sick must be quarantined in a home or building away from others if they have infectious disease. One Group Member is going to have to volunteer to be quarantined with them to tend to their needs wearing the proper eye, face masks, gloves and clothing to keep the pandemic spreading to others. The clothing they wear must be immediately washed with disinfectant or burned.

7-Denying access to your *NPP* by physical barriers-Foot and vehicle traffic

See *Chapter 8* for a list of items you can use to deny and control access to your *NPP*.

Your Protective Perimeter at this time is going to be on a 'High Alert' footing.

To have an effective Protective Perimeter of your building you will have to have a plan to control foot and if applicable, vehicle traffic, by blocking off all ways in to your *NPP* and creating one Entry/Exit Control Point. A properly laid out Entry/Exit Control Point provides you just that… *your control* over the main entrance to your *NPP* High Rise Building.

During each approach by *Outsiders*, you must have either your *Response Guardians* present during that approach, other Guard Posts that can fire on the Entry/Exit Control Point Kill Zone and Fatal Funnel or more than one guard at your Entry/Exit Control Point. With one Entry/Exit Control Point you create a Fatal Funnel that turns into a Kill Zone where properly positioned guards can eliminate or repulse an attack.

There should be *only one* Entry/Exit Control Point at this stage. All Group Member vehicles should be in your garage and it should be secured and locked. Depending on your circumstances and building layout, you may want to have Guard Posts in your garage. *If you don't post guards in your garage don't forget to have your Roving Patrol check it as part of their patrol.*

All other vehicle access and foot traffic access areas to your building will have to be blocked off. These positions must also be guarded, but *only one* pedestrian access entrance should be used to allow people in and out of your building.

The Entry/Exit Control Point Kill Zone. The Entry/Exit Control Point to your *NPP* should have a first and second checkpoint area spaced apart to keep foot traffic away from your perimeter until you know it is not a threat. Your first checkpoint should be at the entrance of your *NPP but not inside your building.*

The distance of your second control point should be from your first control point outside the *NPP* far enough to create a Serpentine path for people to come and go comfortably. This area will slow down *Intruders* trying to rush into your building. This area between the first and second control points is your Kill Zone.

If your building has a lower floor that is vulnerable to vehicles crashing through your Protective Perimeter, we suggest parking vehicles *the length of a vehicle away from and parallel* to these areas.

Even though this gives some Concealment and limited Cover to *Intruders*, we suggest also parking two or more vehicles close enough together to allow only a single person to walk into your Entry/Exit Control Point if you don't have other restrictive barriers.

Take the keys out of these vehicles and let the air out of the tires. Keys should be removed and kept in your Watch Center in case tires have to be re-inflated and the vehicles moved or used. The vehicles used here should be vehicles in the worst condition and not reliable for a *NPP Planned* or *Emergency NPP Relocation.*

The Serpentine. Notice in the diagram in *Chapter 6* on The Serpentine that the path a person has to take to walk through has turns created by obstacles strategically placed between the first and second control points. These obstacles should give as little Cover and little Concealment as possible. Concertina Wire and Barbed Wire are best for this serpentine path.

See Chapters 6 and 8 for methods and a list of items you can use to deny and control access to your NPP.

Improvised Spike Strips and Concertina Wire or Barbed Wire for a Fatal Funnel. These are an example of 'access deniability' and control and is a way of forcing people into the Fatal Funnel that is *in front* of your Entry/Exit Control Point.

The Fatal Funnel is in front of your Entry/Exit Control Point to control and guide people to your Entry/Exit Control Point and gives your entrance more fortification.

Fatal Funnels can also force threats to reveal themselves by giving you the control over their movements. If they have intentions otherwise… the Fatal Funnel may force them to show their hand.

Watch for decoy approaches. During *A Failure of Civility*, ***All*** Protective Perimeter Guard Posts should be on *High Alert* when *any* foot traffic approach is made to your *NPP* Entry/Exit Control Point or if vehicles appear near your building in other than normal circumstances. Be aware that an approach is sometimes a decoy to cover an attack somewhere else on the perimeter.

7-Denying access to your *NPP* by Physical Barriers-Protective Perimeter Aids

Your world is going to hell in a hand basket… install the following security devices *now*.

See Chapters 6 and 8 for a list of items and methods you can use to deny and control access to your NPP.

Blocking unit windows and openings to deny access. Cover all of the lower floor openings that are part of your Protective Perimeter with plywood, interior house doors, table tops or anything else sufficient to keep *Intruders* out. Reinforce with Barbed Wire if possible.

Fasten window coverings with screws or drive nails in at a sharp angle. Diving nails in at a sharp angle gives them much more holding power for what you've nailed. Second and third story windows and basement windows should also be covered.

Spiked window 'Porcupine' 2 by 4s. These are simply 2 by 4s with spikes driven through them to protrude like barbs towards the outside. Fasten them into your window frames like a lattice work.

Use Improvised Security Methods to block open areas to hinder Intruders. Where local ordinances or HOA rules prohibit these in *Normal Civility* put them up now.

Improvised Spike Strips and Barbed Wire can be laid and strung and tied in place. String Barbed Wire or Concertina Wire across open areas and *wire or fasten in place.*

Think of items you can put to use around you. After *A Failure of Civility* occurs there will be abandoned items everywhere. Use doors, concrete block and lumber from buildings to help fortify your defenses.

If you have put sandbag material in planters as part of your advance fortification process or if you have areas around your building that have dirt or gravel, fill your sandbags from these and stack them around Guard Posts to help stop bullets. Place rubble between boards to construct bullet resistant fortifications… think… imagine… do.

7-Denying access to your *NPP* by Psychological Barriers

Solar Powered Security Lights. These are relatively cheap if your building wants to install these. These can be placed around your Protective Perimeter and either manually controlled or activated by motion detectors. However, if you install these they can't be going on and off inadvertently without a real threat and at the same time telegraphing your position to potential *Intruders*.

Security lights must be in a 'dead area' so they are not set off by accident and 'back lighting' your Guard Posts making a silhouette of guards. If *A Failure of Civility* occurs, the streets of most metropolitan areas with be awash with blowing plastic bags, paper and trash which will set these off.

Bow wow! The Authors la la la love dogs! Dogs are one of the best Protective Perimeter psychological and alert aids you can have. An alert dog can sense trouble before a human and if there is a *Crisis* dogs usually have a heightened sense for danger and will be ever more alert and perceptive.

Mrs. Jaegerhiemer's wiener schnitzel dog will not work in this capacity. You need a good sized security type dog that's calm and confident. Dogs can hear along a much broader spectrum of sound than a human can. Their sense of smell is so acute they can smell the adrenaline oozing from the skin of strangers. An aggressive dog is very intimidating to an *Outsider* whose intent is dangerous. Dogs are like some people we respect… they will give their life for you.

Remember the 'Terminator' movie where dogs were used at guard entrances to be on the lookout for Arnold. If they can detect Arnold… they can verify your people and sense some threats to you… well, maybe not Arnold.

We suggest the most widespread use of dogs possible. Use dogs at your Entry/Exit Control Point, with Guard Posts and with the *Roving Guardians* on inside patrols. Tell us again that you have enough Purina Dog Chow for *man's best friend.*

7-Tactics that will make your *NPP* a *Proactive Defense*

See *Chapter 6* for a diagram of an L Shaped Ambush.

'L' Shaped Ambush formation. Since the High Rise Building is treated as a castle and you'll be staying inside the walls as much as possible, this formation for ambush will have limited use in a High Rise Building unless you have an area of your building that protrudes and overlooks ground level or an underground passage out of the building which you can use when this ambush formation is needed by which you can put flanking fire on your enemy.

This ambush pattern subjects the opponent to withering Supporting Fields of Fire from two different directions and lessens the chance of Friendly Fire Incidents. Your fire teams will fire at the *Intruders* from diverse angles as per the diagram.

See *Chapter 6 for a diagram of a Kill Zone.*

Kill Zones. A 'politically correct' Ivy League term for this is Engagement Area or EA to the military. Whatever semantics you use to describe what this is for won't lessen the fact of *what* this is for… it is an area in which your Group Members can have a 'Turkey Shoot' and effectively kill your *Intruders* with little or no loss of *NPP* Group Members. *It is a prearranged killing zone.*

This is different than your Entry/Exit Control Point Kill Zone because it will be *in front of* your building Entry/Exit Control Point. These can be set up in other areas of your Protective Perimeter also.

This technique will also have limited use in a High Rise Building unless you have areas of your building that overlook an area which you can use with this technique and attackers would want to attempt to breach your Protective Perimeter by attacking in this area. This is similar to an L Shaped Ambush formation with the exception that this will be setup specifically to draw in attackers but will not let them back out as easily. It's more like a trap.

Fortifications, usually Concertina Wire or Barbed Wire are placed so that a small section can be pulled away and *Intruders* can enter the Kill Zone. The *Intruder* thinks he has defeated part of your fortifications.

The *Intruder* is then forced to follow a simple maze to get to your Protective Perimeter. When you fire on them, they discover in the confusion and desperation that they can't find their way back out quite as easily.

This is the exception to keeping *Intruders* out of your perimeter. You let them into an area by letting them believe that they've overcome your defenses in the area you want them to be in to eliminate them.

This is particularly useful when you are outnumbered by *Intruders*. A Kill Zone will give you a Force Multiplier Effect and will put your *Intruders* at a *severe* disadvantage. It will bring new meaning to the term *"Like shooting fish in a barrel."* It will quickly instill a new respect in *Intruders* for your defenses and they will likely go elsewhere.

Creating and using a Kill Zone must be done properly. A Kill Zone can defeat your entire building Protective Perimeter if you don't set it up properly. The point is to allow *Intruders* into your area like using a funnel, but *not allowing them in too far or past your Kill Zone.*

The Kill Zone barriers must be deceptive when viewed from the outside. The barriers cannot appear obvious to the *Intruders* nor can they give the *Intruder* any Cover. If *Intruders* figure out your Kill Zone, they'll simply avoid it and retreat to find another way to breach your perimeter.

You can use Concertina Wire, Barbed Wire strung to over waist level, Spanish Rider or the Knife Rest, Abatis fortifications sharpened stakes pointed into your Kill Zone area or anything that allows the *Intruders* to come into your Kill Zone area, but only to proceed so far.

You want them to come in, yet these barriers will restrict them to the Kill Zone area not allowing them to have either Cover or Concealment or advance any further and hampering their way back out.

Your Kill Zone must allow you a clear Field of Fire. Above your Kill Zone and within your *NPP* Perimeter, you must have shooting positions that are placed behind Cover and Concealment. Group Members should have Cover that protects them from *Intruder's* fire. Remember the difference between Cover and Concealment.

When placing Group Members in shooting positions you must consider each Group Member's weapons capability. Is the Group Member armed with a pistol, rifle or shotgun and are they rapid fire weapons? Is their weapon short range or long range effective?

Even though your height above the Kill Zone will not create direct Friendly Fire Incidents to other Group Members, you must plan against the dangers of Friendly Fire Incident ricochets. You don't want to be killing your own Group Members.

The 'L' shaped ambush avoids most of this also but again beware of Friendly Fire Incident ricochets because of your elevation. When taking advantage of your elevated firing positions take care that these do not reveal the intention of your Kill Zone.

Remember, it's in the name. A Kill Zone is for just that, not wounding *Intruders*… eliminating them. When activating your Kill Zone make certain you leave enough Group Members on the perimeter to guard against attacks on your perimeter while you are manning your Kill Zone.

Response Force. These are your *Response Guardians.* For the military or police this is a unit designed to respond in a very short time frame to emergencies. When used in reference to police forces such as SWAT teams, the time frame is mere minutes.

When used in reference to your building these are the *Response Guardians* of your *NPP*. These people need to be some of the most physically fit of your *Alpha Guardians* and they too need to respond in mere minutes. The fact that they may have to climb stairs or descend means they really need to be the most fit of your Group Members.

They're like the Little Dutch Boy. Their job is to rapidly respond to plug holes in your Protective Perimeter, reinforce a part of your Protective Perimeter that is under attack, create L Shaped Ambushes of *Intruders* and be part of the Kill Zone. For a High Rise Building *NPP*, the *Response Guardians* along with the *Inside Marksmen* and *Outflanker Marksmen* are the most *proactive* of your Group Members.

See Chapter 6 for diagrams on Field of Fire areas, Defense in Depth and Skipping Rounds.

Field of Fire Areas. Anything that can give Cover or Concealment to an *Intruder* must be removed if possible. You must have clear and level Fields of Fire as barren of Cover and as far on all sides from your Protective Perimeter as you can make them. This obviously is impossible in most areas where High Rise Buildings are close together, however it must be achieved to the point that you have a view and Field of Fire as wide and as far out as possible.

Defense in depth, 'Fall Back Fighting Positions' or Secondary Fighting Positions. In addition to having one strong Protective Perimeter, Defense in Depth is layering of well placed covered and concealed Secondary Fighting Positions. This principle has been explained like an onion… peel off one layer… and the onion is still there. These are nothing but a second line of defensive positions if your Protective Perimeter fails.

When *Intruders* peel back your primary line of defense… you're still there… at a second line of defense… your Fall Back Fighting Positions. This tactic causes the *Intruder* to lose momentum due to them running into progressive lines of defense each time they think they've broken through your Protective Perimeter. This is psychologically destructive to an attacker.

Cover and Fire Movement. Cover and Fire Movement is the tactic of one or more Group Members firing at the enemy to force them into Cover from which they'll not be able use their weapons while one or more Group Members move forwards or backwards to another position of Cover. Then the roles of covering Group Member and firing Group Member are reversed.

This tactic may have to be used by your *Outflanker Marksmen* groups if they get ambushed outside your Protective Perimeter or if your Group Members lose control of a floor or the roof of your building.

This is a leapfrog method of movement to reduce the chance of the enemy killing you during movement. This tactic is used to retreat or to outflank the enemy. This has to be done with the covering and firing Group Members being a distance apart to the left and right of their line of movement so the moving Group Member doesn't wander into the Field of Fire of the covering Group Member.

Use the Skipping Rounds technique. If you are firing down on *Intruders* at a sharp angle… this technique will not be as effective the same as if you are on the same level as your *Intruder* or they are a distance from you. The Angle of Incidence of bullets striking a hard surface is much sharper and will change the Angle of Occurrence of their ricochet.

7-DO NOT bring *Outsiders* or *Intruders* into your *NPP*

Again… an *Outsider* or *Intruder* is ***anyone*** who is not an *NPP* Group Member or an *Extended Family and Friends* member. You know an *Intruder* is your enemy but an *Outsider must also be considered your **enemy***. *Outsiders* are your biggest danger during a *Long Term Crisis* or *A Failure of Civility*.

If *A Failure of Civility* becomes long term ***you and your Group Members risk contagious diseases*** if these people *even get close to your NPP especially if the Catastrophic Event is a disease related disaster*.

Read suggestions we give on bringing Outsiders and Intruders into your NPP in Chapter 6.

As stated before, we strongly recommend not bringing any *Outsiders* or *Intruders* into your *NPP*. But as with any plan, you must have contingencies and may have to make an exception to this rule.

7-Link up with other *Neighborhood Protection Plans*

As a *Crisis* evolves you may want to join other *NPP*s because of attrition of Group Members or the increasing sophistication of *Intruders*. Also, one *NPP* may have more people with medical expertise, another more tactical knowledge, etc. Share and exchange for the overall good of both *NPPs*. We strongly urge your *NPP* to link up with adjoining *Neighborhood Protection Plans* whether this is joint control by each *Primary NPP Leader*, merging with the other *NPP* under one *Primary NPP Leader* or just a mutual protection agreement.

At best, *depending* on how close the buildings are, join your forces together. *This is dependent* on how strong your confidence is in the other *NPP's* principles of organization, its ability to maintain its defense and their leadership being acceptable to your *NPP* Group Members and Leaders.

Basically, if you're 'on the same page,' make sure you can cover all Protective Perimeters when doing this. Buildings too far apart can be a communications and supply problem and will make it difficult for *Response Guardians* rushing to the aid of a besieged perimeter.

At worst, form a plan for Mutual Protection to help with each other's protection. A flanking attack by one *NPP* coming to the assistance of another *NPP* is usually a tactical maneuver that wins.

7-Passive Response will get you killed-You must be Proactive

Cover and Approach. Read about this issue in *Chapter 6* to keep your Entry/Exit Control Point guards from getting killed.

7-Building Assessment Exercise Two

In the next photograph, imagine you live in a single stand alone High Rise Building. ***Look at this photo as we're going to 'walk along side you' in assessing the obvious points of your Protective Perimeter that you need to be concerned with...***

- ***Get your maintenance man and his family*** to join your *NPP* and to move into your building during a *Crisis*, a *Long Term Crisis* or *A Failure of Civility*. If your building doesn't have one, find the person who has the most knowledge of your building to help you in your assessment. Always have more than one person on your survey. Two or more heads are better than one in evaluations like this.

- ***Upon the occurrence of a Long Term Crisis secure all water and ration it.*** If water is still available, sources of reserve water for your *NPP* are... water heaters, toilet tanks, a roof water reservoir if your building has one, filling bathtubs and all available containers.

- ***Look at the lower left corner of the building***, the doorway leading to the exterior stairway. This door needs to be permanently chained or fastened closed *from the inside.* This must be done from the inside in a fashion that can be quickly undone incase you decide this exit will be an escape route. You must have padlock keys or wrenches positioned next to the inside of the door to loosen bolts should you need to escape through this door.

- ***The windows on the lower level living units*** can be easily breached and have to be boarded up. Remember front, back... all sides. Board them up. Have plywood pre cut and marked for each window along with all fasteners. Take a hint from hurricane area homeowners in preparedness. They have everything ready to secure their house on a moment's notice.

- ***Flat lower level roof surfaces*** of the stairwell ground entry area can be used by *Intruders* to access your building if not properly secured. Windows three floors up from the stairwell ground entrance roofs must be boarded up. Conversely these can make great first line defensive positions if properly fortified with sandbags.

- ***Check the basement*** for any passage ways that a person could access your building by. Block them off in addition to posting a permanent guard in the basement.

- ***The porte-cochere drive through*** overhead cover at the entrance if not secured offers another route for *Intruders* to breach your building. If fortified it offers a low level platform for observation and defense.

A Stand Alone High Rise Building

- ***Look over second story windows*** and also the balconies of the second floor. Fastening plywood to the front of these balconies makes a smooth surface that is harder to climb. Not every one of these balconies and secured entry points can be guarded because you probably won't have the manpower, but having people in strategic locations as listening posts for multiple numbers of these entries can function as guarding them.

- ***Each end of this building has stairwells.*** Apply the simple devices we have shown in Low Rise Residential areas… most of these can be applied to your High Rise Building in some form or fashion. Items like Improvised Spike Strips on stairs, glued down break away marbles and the use of Concertina Wire or Barbed Wire can all be used to hinder *Intruders*. Review these items in *Chapter 8*.

- ***The Center column in this building*** houses the elevators and shaft. Secure the elevator doors *on each floor*. Use of an electric drill during a *Crisis* prior to a power outage to pre drill screw holes will allow you to quickly fasten these doors shut when the time comes. If you're into a *Crisis* drill small holes into the doors on each side of single, accordion or double elevator doors and the frame at the bottom and top.

Make the brackets and have them predrilled to the pattern of the holes you've drilled. If a *Long Term Crisis* occurs, screw a bracket of 18 gauge metal bent at a 90 degree angle into place to keep these doors securely closed. Use heavy screws.

- ***Secure the parking lot*** by blocking it off with your vehicles away from the building to deny access for other vehicles. Use other methods for access denial of foot traffic.

- ***Observe the roof.*** This is the perfect position for LOP and *Inside Marksmen* positions. Set up your observation posts and *Inside Marksmen* positions on both sides and they should be sandbagged for further protection.

Take the time to do an in-depth study of your area be it suburban or metropolitan. Consider all the things we have recommended and take these into consideration when doing your planning. We cannot stress enough, plan ahead and be ready in advance instead of waiting until the last minute… or you'll be splattered with s#!t' if The S#!t Hits The Fan!

Chapter 8
Alternative Weapons and Improvised Security Methods

In this Chapter we describe…

- **8-Close Quarters Unarmed Combat**
- **8-Alternative Weapons**
- **8-Improvised Security Methods**
- **8-You will need hand tools**
- **8-The best tool is…**

8-Close Quarters Unarmed Combat

Hand-to-Hand situation, also known as Close Quarters Unarmed Combat. We've provided two diagrams of nerve points and vital points of the body. They look more complicated than an electronic schematic and about as understandable as a Chinese road map. We had to memorize these points in addition to practicing endlessly with bare hands and with weapons striking these points until it is a simple reaction movement without thinking. You must do the same.

When in a Hand-to-Hand situation, also known as Close Quarters Unarmed Combat, don't start flailing away with your arms and fists like the school bully Mongo did during his 'windmill' attack on you.

In Hand-to-Hand Combat, the hands *and* feet are what will kill, not the eyes. Keep eye contact with your opponent's hands and feet, not his eyes while you're fighting. There is way too much to put into words here also but we'll give you some basics that you can remember.

Some simple techniques and body points to remember…

The Throat. In a life and death Hand-to-Hand fight the throat is the most vulnerable part of your male opponent's body. A strike to the front of the throat will crush the larynx or 'Adams Apple', shutting off air to your assailant's lungs… this will kill if a forceful enough blow. Strike with the hand held like a knife sideways, the closed fist straight on or the forearm or the upper arm sideways to the throat. We've seen some big guys go down with this method.

The Eyes. Stabbing in one eye causes both to water. Use your fingers, thumb or weapon. This movement will not kill, but it will cause most attackers to break off their attack on you and partially immobilize them, giving you time to strike vital points on them elsewhere.

The Clavicle. Don't use clubs swinging laterally. Swing down vertically on either side of the neck towards the front of your assailant. Once the clavicle is broken it disables most attacker's use of the arm on that side. Reach up and feel your clavicle. It's that pretty horizontal bone on each side of the neck that makes your wife look so beautiful in an evening gown.

The Top of the Foot. The foot bone structure supports hundreds of pounds from the bottom. However, it supports little weight from the top. Stomp on your assailant's foot just in front of the ankle. You'll break bones in the foot disabling most attackers.

The Knees. Get your assailant down on the ground. Strike the knees and ankles from the front or sides, not from the rear unless you're pulling them backwards at the same time.

Strike One Blow After Another. Like shooting or using a knife you have to repetitiously strike your opponent in Hand-to-Hand Combat. Strike one blow after another rapidly until you 'Stop the Threat.' Make rapid strikes to different vital points and nerve points of the body. Practice saying this while you practice combinations of body strikes... *"One, Two, Three, Four, Five, Six... he's down!"*

The Knife and other Sharp Weapons. Using a knife to kill is not just the action of stabbing... it is the action of stabbing and ripping... over and over again. Vital points are important. But again, like multiple shots are needed to kill and 'bleed out' an assailant... the more damage you do with stabbing and ripping the faster your opponent will bleed out and cease to be a threat. Stab... rip with your knife while it's in your attacker... stab again and rip again until your attacker goes down and out for the count.

You've heard the term 'cut throat.' This is one effective way to kill your opponent with anything sharp. Sever the jugular veins on one or both sides of the neck.

8-Alternative Weapons

Other than firearms, there are a few alternative weapons that are just as powerful if not more effective against *Intruders...* and some items which can be used for weapons in a pinch. Your *NPP* Group Members must learn the basics of these.

Fire. Fire... primarily in the form of Molotov Cocktails. Fire is a tremendous but much overlooked weapon. This crude but effective weapon in the form of the Molotov Cocktail was first used in the Spanish Civil War.

It was given its famous name by Finnish soldiers as an insult to the Soviet Foreign Minister of Russia who they fought in World War II. Molotov Cocktails are credited by the Russians with helping defeat the Nazis invaders during World War II.

Simply put, a Molotov Cocktail is a fire bomb in a narrow necked glass bottle such as a wine bottle or beer bottle. The bottle is filled with gasoline or other flammables. A rag, which is the igniter and is saturated with a flammable liquid, is stuck tightly in the open end of the bottle. The rag is lit on fire and the bottle is thrown against a hard surface that will break the bottle.

The contents of the bottle splash the area and burst into flames. Caution must be used that you don't start a fire in your own area or yourself. These containers should be stored separately outside away from buildings and not inside your *NPP* houses or structures.

Tampons work well as the igniter, but regardless of what you use, the igniter must be saturated just before you light and throw the bottle. Fire spreads and burns quickly… *don't ignite your hands, arms or your body!*

Spears. Spears are weapons that have been used for personal defense since the beginning of recorded time. This should be a defensive weapon, because once a spear is thrown, you no longer have it… and worse, it can be used against you. Tape a kitchen butcher knife to the end of a broom handle or a pole cut from a tree, an old wooden handle from a shovel… you get the idea.

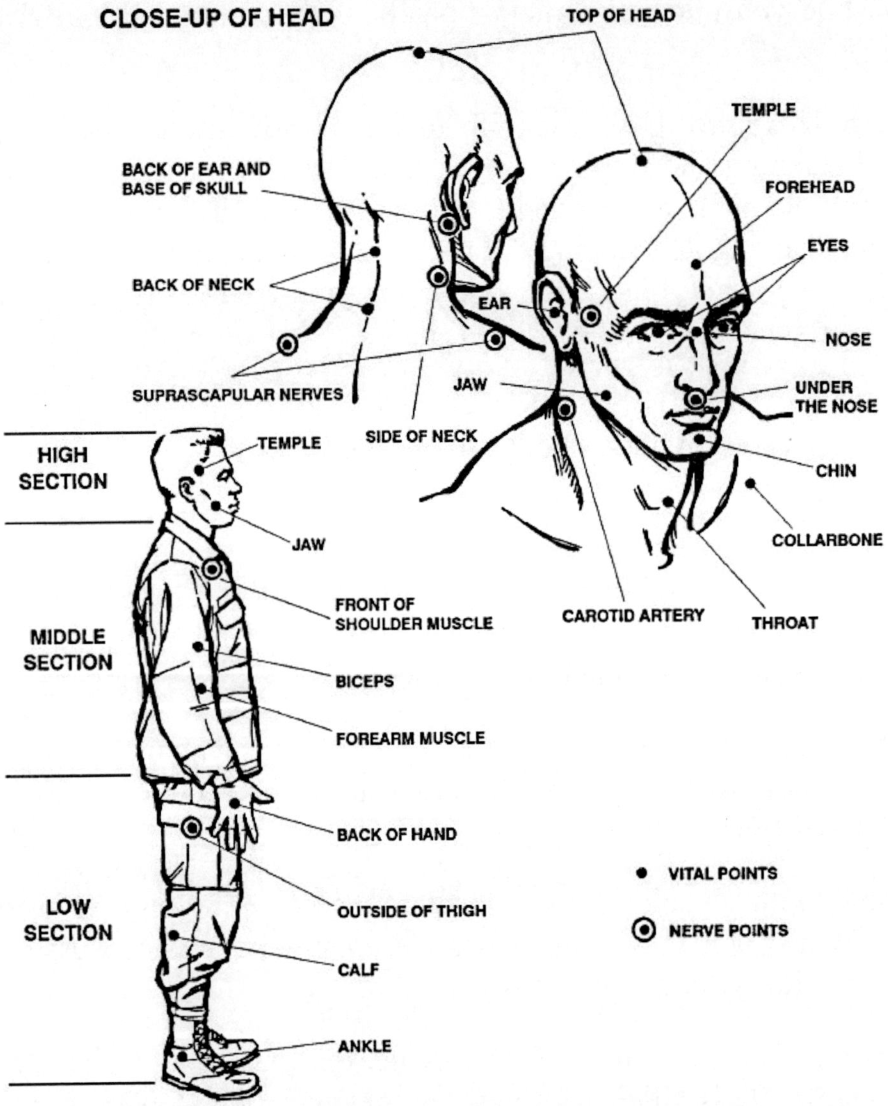

The length can vary depending on what you have to make it from and what you need for your situation. If you decide to use the spear as an offensive weapon, the common thrusting or throwing spears are approx 6 foot in length. The point of the pole is sharpened or a sharpened metal point is fastened to the end. Long bladed and short handled spears can be used like a sword close up and personal.

A pike, which is a form of spear, was used by the

Areas of the head and body to strike your assailant with Improvised Weapons

Greeks in their phalanx war formations. The difference in the spear and the pike is the length of the shaft.

The pike was long and could extend 15 feet in front of the soldier holding it, stopping attackers before the attacker could get close enough to use his sword or other close range weapons.

Crossbows, Long bows and Compound Bows and Arrows. Different from the crossbow… the long bow and compound bows take considerable strength and practice to become proficient with.

But these weapons have a place as they are *silent and deadly.* The Authors recommend that each *NPP* have at least one or more crossbows with plenty of shanks, also known as arrows. These are versatile weapons for hunting also.

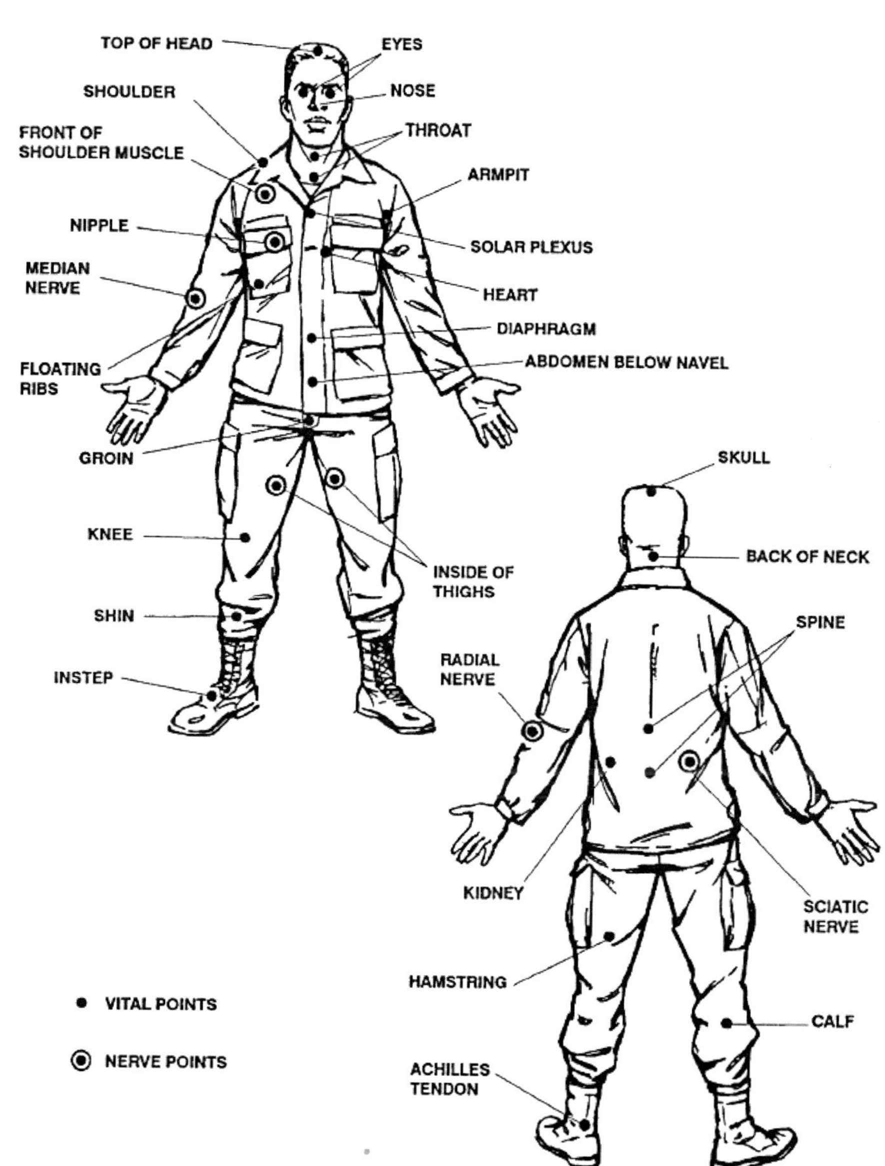

Areas of the body to strike your assailant with Improvised Weapons

Hand shanks. A common hand shank is a short hand weapon like a knife which your kitchen is full of. Shanks can be easily made by sharpening toothbrushes, wooden stakes, steel rods, etc.

This can be a very deadly weapon in close quarters attacks. Stick it in and rip it up or down while it's in your *Intruder*.

If your shank is plastic, stick in break it off inside your assailant's body.

Axes and Hammers. Everyone has a hammer in their household and some have axes. These have been weapons much longer through the ages than tools.

As gruesome as it sounds in using these to defend yourself… these, as well as many other implements used for war… were also used in everyday life.

Bludgeoning Weapons. The Dr. Seuss 'Rock in a Sock.' A sock with a rock or heavy item in the toe end that is used as swinging club. This is much more effective if used with the attitude 'The Grinch' had.

The Baseball Bat. A clubbing type of tool again. You may not bat .300, but the common baseball or softball bat can allow you to hit a home run… by saving your life… if you learn how to use it in a defensive situation.

Shovels. These can be sharpened and become very deadly as a weapon when used in a jabbing motion or swung like an axe. The small hand held shovels of World War I were used often in trenches for Hand-to-Hand Combat.

All Russian soldiers are taught to use their trench shovels as a killing weapon… they learn to throw theirs like a knife.

Sling Shots and Wrist Rockets. Wrist Rockets are metal 'formed' sling shots with a wrist rest and surgical tubing that is very tough and elastic.

You can propel a projectile at a tremendous rate of speed with these.

In addition to using these for hunting small game, these can be useful defensive weapons if you become proficient with them.

Look around your home and you'd be amazed the dual usage for many items in your home.

With your imagination you can develop a lot of ingenious devices as improvised weapons… but *you really don't want to bring these weapons to a gun fight,* unless this is all you have and then your attack had better be a flanking or rear attack and contain a big Element of Surprise so you can overtake your enemy and get their firearms.

8-Improvised Security Methods

Dictionary Definition
Improvised
(Verb) To have prepared or provided from available materials

Many items can be used to aid your *human* guard. You'll have plenty of time on your hands to make these if a *Crisis* occurs. Your *NPP* Group Members must learn the basics about these. Remember that these do not replace the human element and are only aids to you defense.

These can be defeated by an *Intruder* if they are a 'stand alone' defense. Protective Perimeters all need a human observing the area these security alert aids are in. Don't consider these items only for your first line of defense... you must incorporate some of these into your Defense in Depth, Kill Zones and L Shaped Ambush areas.

Use your imagination! These are just a few of the literally thousands of ways your can enhance your human guard. *Don't rely on any assisted guard devices being foolproof.* In a *Crisis* situation there will be abandoned homes... use the doors and lumber from those structures to help fortify your defenses.

Improvised spike strips for foot traffic. These can be cut to any size you need. Made from plywood, particle board or what we recommend... chip board which is exterior house sheathing. Chip board is more weather resistant and not as brittle as particle board and much cheaper than plywood.

Take a sheet of standard 4' by 8' sheet of ***one half inch*** chip board cut into two foot wide sections. This gives you two 2' by 8' or four 2' by 4' 'boards' which will cover 16 linear feet being 2 foot wide.

Use nails or screws 2 inches in length. Use ***Number 6 or number 8 Drywall or Deck Screws.*** They're sharper than nails, don't bend like nails and stay in the boards better than nails *if they're threaded to the head.*

Screws also stick in what steps or drives over them better than nails and as one Author's friend will testify to... they're very difficult to pull out after stepping on one that went through his combat boot. The screws or nails have to *protrude about 1 ½ inches* through the board. All screw or nail points obviously must be on one side. Space the nails 2 inches apart.

Improvised Spike Strips with screws

Use these as mobile or permanent defensive measures. If these are to be used as moveable strips, attach ropes to each end for guards to pull them in and out of place. An example would be their use in hallways. They can be installed in a hallway with hinges on one end and raised and tied up out of the walk way to allow passage. When you want to deny access to your hallway, lower them to the floor and screw or lock them in place.

If these are to be permanently installed, such as on the landings in a stairwell… cut them to size and use construction adhesive to glue them down.

Improvised spike strips with spike tubes for vehicle traffic. For vehicles… the next part is the most time consuming but it will flatten a vehicle tire *pronto*… even self sealing tires. Cut *7/32 inch or ¼ inch inside diameter* hollow steel or brass *tubing 1 ½ inch long* to fit over the existing screws as shown in the photo. *But, sharply angle one end so they can easily pierce a tire.*

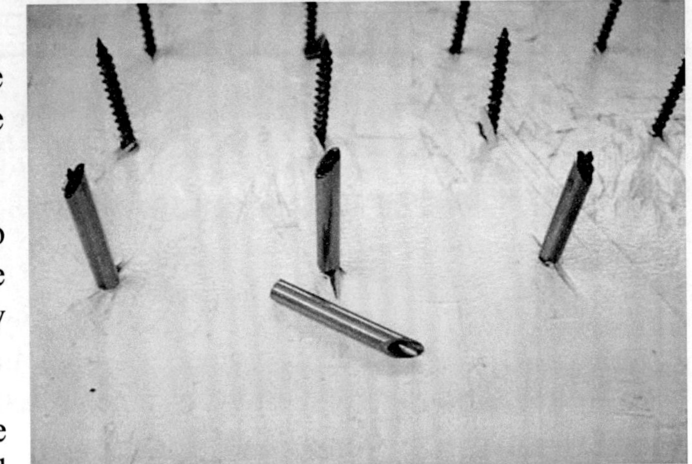

Improvised Spike Strips with Tire Spike Tubes

When a tire rolls over the spike strip the hollowed tube will stay in the tire and cause it to deflate extremely fast.

Even though most of us don't have money to burn... you can buy vehicle tire puncture systems from police and public safety supply stores and on the internet.

There are also solid and hollow tube *tetrahedron tire spikes* that are individual and thrown out in bunches… however you toss them… one spike sticks straight up.

What we show you in the photos is as good and as reliable as anything. The spike tubes will definitely flatten a tire fast… even a self sealing tire!

Improvised spike strips with spike tubes are one of the best ways to force vehicles into the Fatal Funnel at your Entry/Exit Control Point and to flatten their tires quickly if they decide otherwise.

Spiked window 'Porcupine' 2 by 4s. These are simply 2 by 4s with spikes driven through

Close Up

Lag Bolt fastening Spiked Window Porcupine

Spiked Window 'Porcupine' 2 by 4s

them to protrude like barbs on the outside. Fasten them into your window frames like a lattice work.

Nail the holy hell out of these and fasten them with long lag bolts counter-sunk into the wood framework around the windows and doors. A simple framework with barbed wire interwoven, tied and crisscrossed will also work.

Glue Marbles on the Stairways in dark areas. Good for Low Rise Residential Areas and High Rise Buildings. This sounds so simple it sounds stupid. But consider an *Intruder* trying to rush your position and having to run over marbles you have tacked in place with construction adhesive, super glue or Barge Cement… just enough to hold them in place until they're stepped on.

Put them every 3 inches in a diagonal pattern and the Authors guarantee your *Intruders* will be on the floor looking up at the ceiling. String treble fish hooks and line at eye level in these dark areas also.

Axle Grease on No Go Areas. Good for interior Low Rise Residential flat areas and High Rise Buildings. This can be purchased at an Auto Parts Store. Brush it on flat surfaces, stairwell steps and hand rails and your *Intruder's* butts will be on the floor muy pronto. Concentrated detergent can also be used for this but it dries out within a few days.

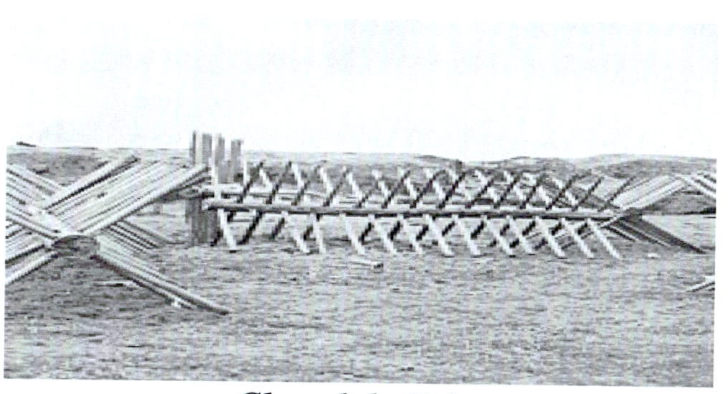

Cheval de Frise

Cheval de Frise and Spanish Rider, aka 'Knife Rest.' The Cheval de Frise… comes from the French Language term for *"Frisian Horse…"* owing to the fact that their opponents, the Frisians, had few horses and used these to stop French Cavalry charges against their positions.

They work great as an obstacle for humans also… they're virtually impossible to scale and give little Cover or Concealment.

Spanish Rider, aka 'Knife Rest' Barbed Wire Barricade

A similar barricade is the Spanish Rider also known as the Knife Rest. Where either of these names come from is a mystery to us. This is a wooden framework strung with Barbed Wire. It can be constructed of 2 x 4s or stout tree branches. This type of barricade can be prebuilt and stored in a back yard. They're light and when the time comes they can be easily put in place and moved around if need be.

Fish line and hooks as alert trip wire. Fishing line is cheap, three sided 'treble' fish hooks are inexpensive and tin cans are throwaway. Marry the three and you have one of the best Protective Perimeter alert items you can find if set up properly.

It is a no brainer to apply this to a Protective Perimeter. This method uses *non glare fish line* with *three barb fish hooks* on it strung between two points. Thin green floral wire from the Walmart flower crafts section works as great as 'Vietnam Era Trip Wire'... it can barely be seen.

The ends of the fish line are tied to tin cans as 'alarm cans' that make noise when the fish hook on the trip line catches into an *Intruder's* clothes or skin and pulls the alarm can down. Stones or marbles can be put in the alarm can to increase the amount of noise.

Set these up in zig zag rows from your Protective Perimeter on out. *The Intruder must not see the line, hooks or the alarm cans... and the better you camouflage and conceal the fish line, hooks and cans... the better this is as a Protective Perimeter alert device.*

Lay short runs of 50 foot or so of trip line per segment and place these haphazard outside your Protective Perimeter but covering all approach areas. You set the alarm cans in a place by each Guard Post out of view from your *Intruder*.

Animals may set these off Perimeter Alert Devices but remember there's no false what?... ***Don't ignore any alarm... because the first rule of alarms is that there is no such thing as a false alarm!***

The trip line with the fish hooks can be propped up with small sticks and covered with bits of grass or leaves or put in weeded areas or concealed below snow cover far enough off the ground to hook the *Intruder* while walking or crawling.

These can be set up in as sophisticated a system as you want to make it. They can reveal just about where the *Intruder* is that tripped the line.

Rattle and Roll. Buy small bells at a Dollar Store and paint them flat black or a color that fits into your area for camouflage. String the fish line with enough slack so it coils or is off the ground about six inches. Use *non glare fish line* and tie off the ends of each section of trip line.

The tie off object must move when it is pulled on. Something like heavy lead fishing weights work best. When the *Intruder* gets tangled in the trip line it acts like a bolo wrapping around their feet and ringing the bell. You can also use bells with the fish hooks as above.

After you install these alert systems you must look at it from your *Intruder's* view point. *If you can see it… they can also…* and they'll find a way around this or disarm it to attack.

Punji Pit. The 'Punji Pit' is a covert alert active defensive item… a booby trap. It not only alerts defenders… it injures attackers. If you look at the photo it shows a simple *Punji Pit* dug deep enough to bury pointed stakes pointed up towards the opening.

Punji Pit

The Punji Pit is concealed by covering it with branches, burlap or cardboard over supporting cross sticks and blending the cover material into the surrounding area by placing leaves, dirt or snow over it.

When an *Intruder* steps on the cover, it gives way and they'll impale their legs or body. Use these in an area of your Protective Perimeter where you create a Fatal Funnel directing your enemy into them.

These are nastier if you put human or animal feces on the points of the stakes. A wound from these gets severely infected and is usually fatal within a week. The late Special Forces legend and author Barry Sadler almost lost his leg this way.

The Abatis. An Abatis can be an effective obstacle if the stakes are long enough, spaced close enough together to prevent the enemy from crawling between them and buried deeply enough so they can't be pulled out.

The Abatis

The Authors love trees, but should you need to, you can cut trees down and point the trunk towards your Protective Perimeter… cut most lighter branches away and sharpen the remainder of the heavier branches that will then point towards your attackers.

The Abatis creates a 'fence' in parts of your Protective Perimeter. These are not covered as their presence is a menacing visual deterrent.

Wheel Drops. These are simply two foot by two foot holes dug down 18 inches with straight sides. Stager these in open areas where you want to stop most vehicles trying to get past your *NPP* Protective Perimeter if you don't have walls.

These are not big enough for an *Intruder* to use for Cover, but a wheel of a vehicle will drop right into them stopping most vehicles.

Rubble on Fields of Fire. *Never place any obstacle to hinder an Intruder that they can use for Cover.* Rubble, big enough and spaced closely enough in your Field of Fire, should be difficult to walk or run over.

Rat Trap Primer trip wire alert. It takes a little experimenting to adjust this device to function, but when you're done you'll definitely hear this when it goes off. Wear protective glasses when constructing and installing this and be careful. Exploding primers can throw off shrapnel enough to do physical damage. *Do not* try to set off a complete shell or cartridge with a device like this… this is for a *primer only.*

Rubble on your Fields of Fire

Use an old fashioned wooden rat trap with fish line as your trip wire. Don't use floral wire as the stiffness of it will make it difficult to set the trap. Bend the end of the square spring arm wire into a slight 'V' so it strikes in from the edge of the trap about 3/8".

Solder a wire 'tit' from 12 AWG solid copper electrical wire onto the apex of the 'V' of the spring arm so it strikes the wood of the rat trap. This is where you're going to drill your primer hole. Drill a ¼" hole in the rat trap exactly where that pointed 'tit' on the spring arm strikes. Spray paint the rat trap a color that blends into your environment. Tie the rat trap low on a tree or other immovable item at one end of your trip line area.

The rat trap must be set so it can't be seen and when the trip wire is tugged on it pulls the 'cheese spot lever' *down* to release the spring arm. Attach the trip wire to the 'cheese spot lever' on the rat trap.

String your trip wire loosely from the trap to ensure it is 6" to 8" off the ground and tie it off on the other end of your trip wire area. The trip wire does not have to be tight… rather it should be loose and coiled above the ground. You now have a trip wire… tied off on one end running across the area you want to detect movement on… to your rat trap.

Push a 12 gauge shotgun shell primer into the hole and put a piece of scotch tape over the primer to hold it in the hole. Carefully set the trip arm on the trap. When the *Intruder* walks into and pulls the trip wire the 'cheese spot lever' releases the spring arm… the spring arm snaps to the other side… the 'tit' on the spring arm hits the shotgun primer and walla… bang! You know something has tripped your alert system.

Remember… "There is no such thing as a fair fight… you fight to win!"

8-You will need hand tools

Make use of hand tools such as hand saws. Don't count on electricity being available. If you don't have hand tools… buy them. They're cheap and dependable. You need tools for both wood and metal use… a timber cutting cross saw, hammers, sledge hammers, hacksaws, metal shears, axes, shovels, light and heavy pry bars, etc… maybe a hand drill.

Your *NPP* should have an inventory list of hand tools that each Group Member has. A full check list of items needed is in *Chapter 12.* Always try to think of items you can put to use to help with your defense. There's millions of ways to build creative defenses and defense alert systems.

8-The best tool is…

Your mind and your vivid imagination! Look through your house and garage. Determine what you need and think of how to put it into use. ***Think, improvise and implement!***

Chapter 9
Offensive Tactics you may need for your *Neighborhood Protection Plan*

In this Chapter we describe…

- **9-Patrolling formations**
- **9-Hand and Arm Signals**
- **9-Room Clearing**
- **9-Basic Tactical Thought we think you must have**

We're not going to go into too much detail with Offensive Tactics because it would require months of study and practical physical training exercises in conjunction with weapons training exercises that we don't think will benefit you.

If you think otherwise, read and study on your own but keep foremost the thought of the KISS acronym for your *NPP*… Keep it Simple Stupid. Providing too much information to your *NPP* Group Members can be as dangerous as not providing enough.

> ***Dictionary Definition***
> ***Offensive***
> *(Noun) An attack or assault on an enemy.*

As we explained at the beginning of this book our concept of *Area Tactical Protection* is a *very aggressive* and *Proactive Defense.* Offensive tactics may also be needed to recapture part of your *NPP* area that an enemy occupies.

In time of *Crisis* you will find yourself and other Group Members forced to go ***outside*** of your *Neighborhood Protection Plan* area to defend your Protective Perimeter. We will show you the basics… you need to know these.

9-Patrolling formations

To go outside your *NPP* and come back in one piece, you will have to use Patrol Formations to minimize danger to your Group Members. These formations must be used when foraging for food or supplies, hunting, finding or transporting water, as part of your *Proactive Defense*... and in gathering intelligence or performing reconnaissance in an area.

The purpose of a Patrol Formation is to detect threats to the patrol before the enemy can act… to spread out Patrol Members so a minimum number are hit if the patrol is ambushed… and to give the patrol a quick defensive formation to repel attacks or to out flank the enemy.

There are three purposes for patrols… Reconnaissance, Combat and Man Tracking.

__Don't bunch up.__ A Key Point... When on patrol and terrain allows, do not bunch together unless in a 360 Degree Defensive position. Doing so makes you a concentrated target.

Patrol Members must keep distance between themselves when walking to avoid being a concentrated target.

If the situation and terrain allows... have the sun in your enemy's eyes when patrolling. *Never* move towards the enemy with the sun in your eyes if you can avoid it. The exception to this is if you're man tracking... then you must to have the spoor, or track of what you're pursuing, between you and the sun to properly follow it.

One of the Author's first combat actions was moving towards the enemy with the sun in his eyes... he remembers it *quite* well... but more so for the sound of enemy bullets cracking around his head as they tried to ventilate his skull.

The members of a patrol must remain in visual contact with one another and with the Patrol Leader. That means your head is always moving to scan, not only looking into areas where threats could be, but also turning to check your other Patrol Members and frequently looking back to the Patrol Leader for instructions.

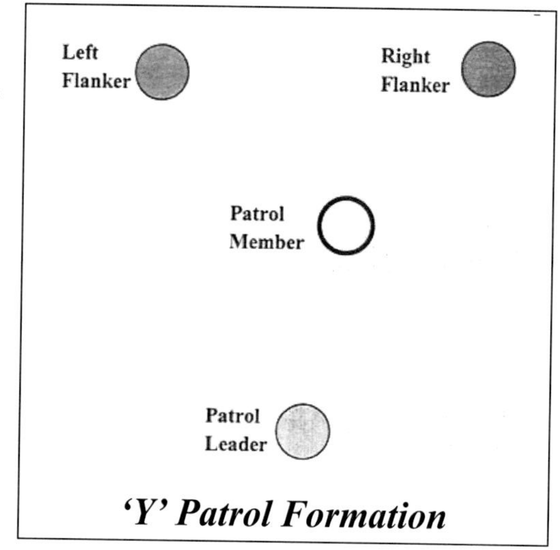

'Y' Patrol Formation

The position of Patrol Members should be... that the *Patrol Leader can see each Patrol Member and each Patrol Member can see the Patrol Leader at all times.* Patrol Members must frequently turn to look at the Patrol Leader for silent hand and arm signals.

The 'Y' Patrol Formation. In our time in the military the simplest and most versatile patrol formation taught us was the 'Y' Formation.

It consists of a minimum of four people. There is the Patrol Leader, a Patrol Member and the Left and Right Flankers. This formation can be quickly re-configured to cope with almost any tactical situation you may encounter on your Perimeter Patrol or when away from your *NPP*.

The 'Y' Formation gives overall security for each member as well as good observation of the area you're traveling through.

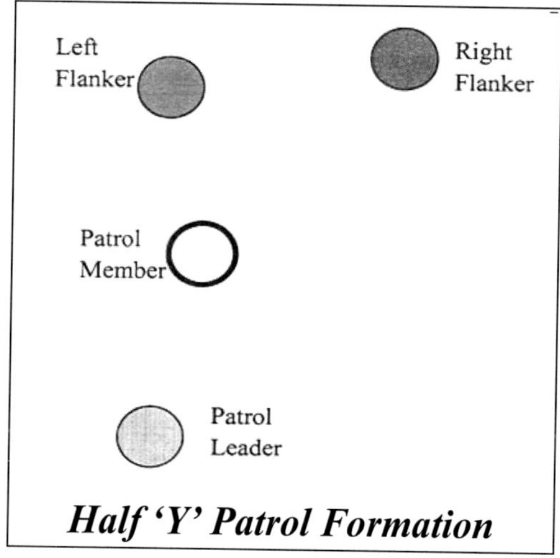

Half 'Y' Patrol Formation

The Half 'Y' Patrol Formation. This formation is used when the ground or vegetation are an obstacle to one of the Flankers or a threat to the group, such as walking through a ravine. Depending on the side the obstacle is on, that Flanker will switch to the opposite Flanker's side ahead of the Patrol Member and the Patrol Leader. This Flanker's primary area of responsibility is still the left or right side… depending on the flank he came from.

Left Flanker

Right Flanker

Patrol Member

Patrol Leader

Ranger File Formation

Ranger File Formation. This formation is used when there are obstructions on both sides and as such both Flankers have to move in to form slightly either side of a line with other the Patrol Member and Patrol Leader. The Flankers are in the first two positions of the file and are still responsible for their areas. Try not to group up. Even in a Ranger File along a narrow path of travel never walk directly behind the man in front of you and depending on the conditions, remain a minimum of 8 feet apart if the vegetation and the light conditions permit.

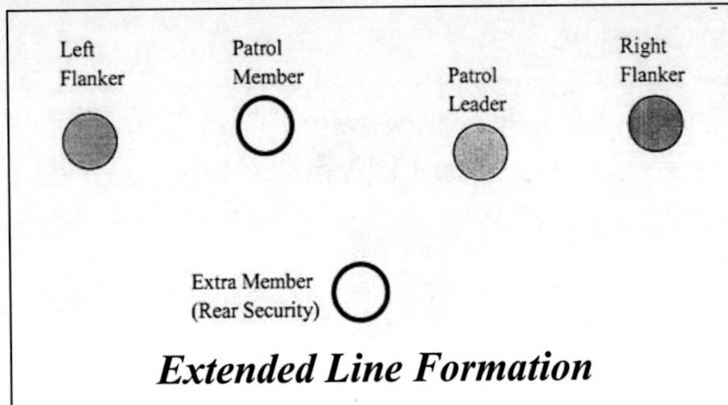

Extended Line Formation

The Extended Line Formation or Searching Formation. This formation is used when a large area has to be searched. All members are in a line abreast of each other. They maintain their distance but keep visual contact and move in a forward movement. This is also termed a 'Sweep Line' by some militaries.

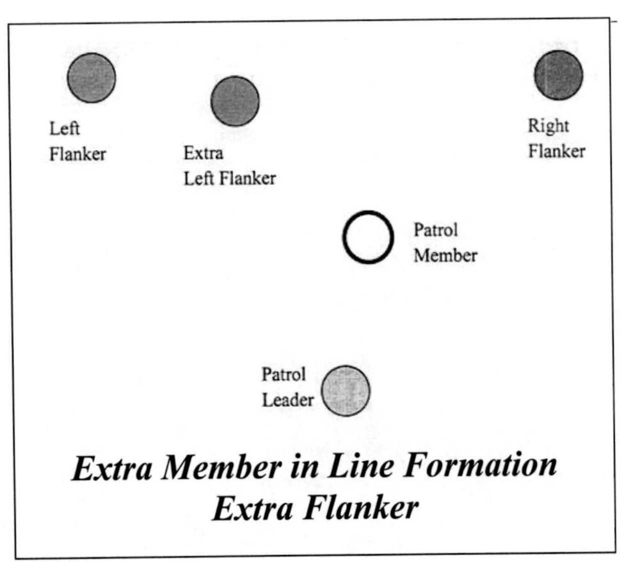

Extra Member in Line Formation Extra Flanker

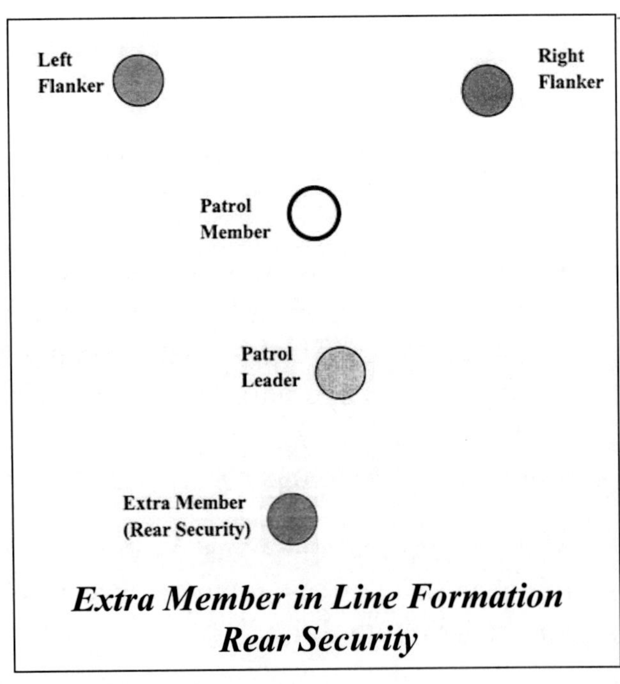

Extra Member in Line Formation Rear Security

Extra Member in Line Formation. If you have an extra Patrol Member you can use a fifth man as Rear Security or they can be placed out as an Extra Right or Left Flanker when in particularly tough terrain.

360 Degree Defensive Position. If you stop your patrol and the Patrol Leader signals everyone in for a discussion, immediately form a 360 Degree Defensive Position. This can be kneeling as in the photo or Patrol Members in the prone position and gives all around observation and security if you're on open ground.

360 Degree Defensive Position

9-Hand and Arm Signals

The use of hands and arms to communicate are a silent and efficient way for all team members to communicate with each other basic commands when *inside* and *outside* your *Neighborhood Protection Plan* area.

There is a list of *basic* hand signals that allows for group movement without talking and will not reveal your position to opposing forces. Conditions have to be light enough to see and the distance between team members again, requires them to be sufficiently apart for safety… but close enough for hand and arm signals to be seen and given.

Silent Arm and Hand Signals. Make sure your arms and hands are away from your body and give a pronounced and definite signal to your people…

- ***You.*** Simply point with extended arm at the person.
- ***Come here.*** Point to the individual with extended arm and then point to the ground.
- ***Move out.*** Arm extended above the head and then moved in the direction of travel.
- ***Go look.*** Point with extended hand to the person, then two fingers to your eyes for 'look' then point to the direction you want the person to investigate.
- ***All clear.*** Arm extended to the side of the body so all can see then thumb up.
- ***Go to Extended Line or Ranger File.*** Extend arm then bend at the elbow bringing hand up then down with your hand indicating what direction you want the line to form.
- ***Threat seen.*** Weapon up at shoulder height pointed in the direction of the threat.
- ***Gather around.*** Extend your arm straight up then move your hand around in a circle.
- **Go to Searching Formation… The Extended Line.** Both arms extended to your side to form a 'T'.

- **Go to The half Y Formation.** This is simply done by pointing to the Flanker and then pointing to the position which you want him to move to. Point to the Flanker that you want to move first. Get him in position. Then point to your other Flanker to have him mover further out.
- ***Go Further Out.*** Point to the individual then point in the direction you want him to move out towards.
- ***Freeze.*** The arm extended to the side with the forearm pointed up and the hand in a clenched fist.
- ***Stop.*** The arm extended to the side with the forearm pointed up and the palm open with fingers together.
- ***Go to one knee** or **get down.*** From the stop or freeze hand signal position, move the forearm down pointing to the ground.

You can add or subtract what you believe to be the best for your Group Members. Create others signals if you feel you need them. The hand signals should *be practiced and understood by **all** members* using them. You can use these at your stationary security positions as well.

9-Room Clearing

This may be necessary if you've lost control of a home, floor or room of your *NPP* and if you're checking out your *Secondary NPP Location* building. The military and police use these techniques which have numerous and complex forms.

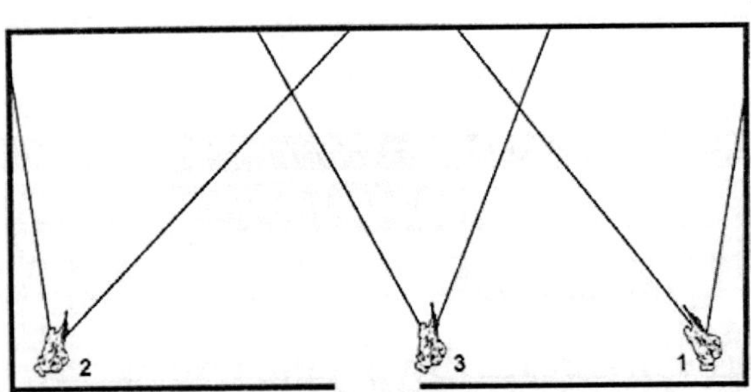

Room Clearing Three Man

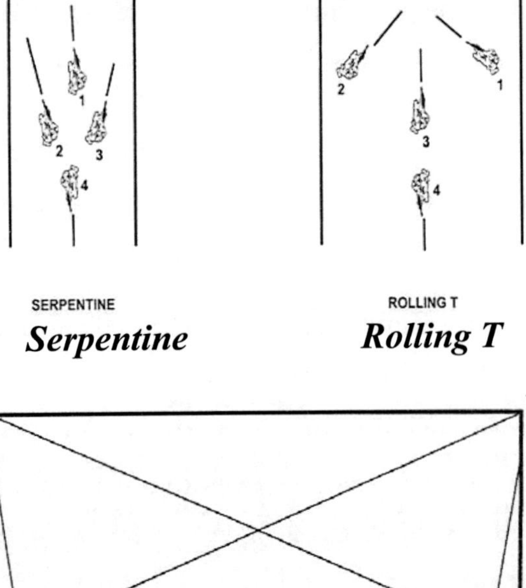

Serpentine ***Rolling T***

Room Clearing Two Man

If you're wondering what your Marine or Army son or neighbor did most of the time in Iraq or Afghanistan… this is it. *They did a lot of 'Room Clearing.'*

There are scores of variations of these formations… too many to list in this book. We're giving you just the basic formations for clearing hallways, clearing stairwells and rooms.

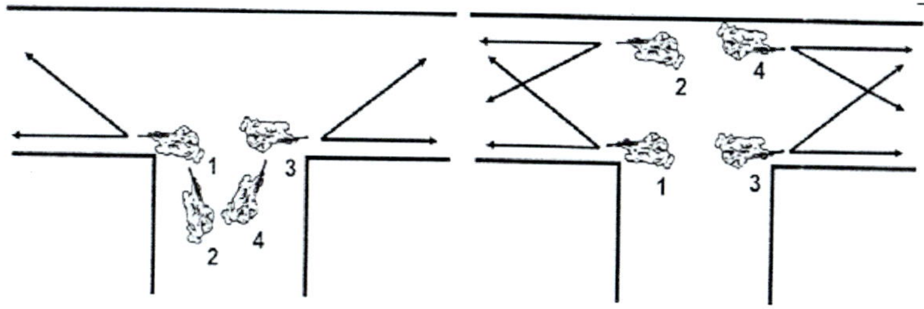

Hallway Clearing at the Intersection

You should have a minimum of four Group Members in two 'Room Clearing Teams'. You can do it with less if necessary. The pictures are pretty much self explanatory.

The important point is that all Group Members move together and give as much 360 degree coverage for the group to threat areas while moving as possible.

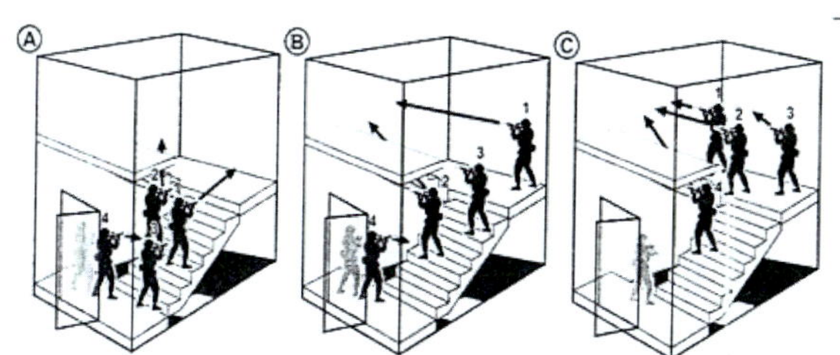

Room Clearing Starting up a Stairwell

Just because you've gone through an area and haven't seen a threat, doesn't mean you all have your weapons pointed in the direction you're traveling.

You must constantly provide rear security and all around security for the group.

Example room or building clearing verbal commands given in a loud voice…

Term	*Explanation*

"Clear"… Given by a Group Member to report their *area of observation* is clear.

"Up"… Given by a Group Member to report they are *ready to continue the search.*

"Room Clear"… Given by a Group Member to Team Members to report *the room is clear and secured.*

"Coming Out" or "Coming In"… Given by a Group Member to inform Team Members that they are about to exit a room or building or enter a room or building.

"Come Out" or "Come In"… Given by a Group Member to acknowledge that *it is safe to exit a room or building or enter a room or building.*

"Coming Up" or "Coming Down"… Given by a Group Member to inform other Team Members that they *are about to ascend or descend stairs.*

"Come Up" or "Come Down"… Given by a Group Member to acknowledge that *it is safe to ascend or descend stairs.*

"Short Room"… Given by a Group Member to inform other Team Members that *the room is small and others should not enter.*

"Man Down"… Given by a Group Member to inform other Team Members *that a Group Member is down and wounded or injured and cannot continue the search.*

"Go Long"… Given by a Group Member to direct another Group Member to take up security farther into the room or farther down a hallway.

"Gun Down"… Given by a Group Member to inform other Group Members that their gun has malfunctioned.

"Gun Up"… Given by a Group Member to inform other Group Members that their previously malfunctioning gun is operational again.

"Reloading"… Given by a Group Member to inform other Group Members that they are reloading their weapon. Follow with ***"Gun Up"*** when ready.

Weapon aiming is at the specific threat areas shown as you make your way into a room or up or down a stairwell. Group Members cover each other *being absolutely aware of other Group Member's positions so you don't shoot your own if you fire at a threat.*

Practice safe weapons handling when holding training exercises on Room Clearing. *During all training exercises, there should be no ammunition present.*

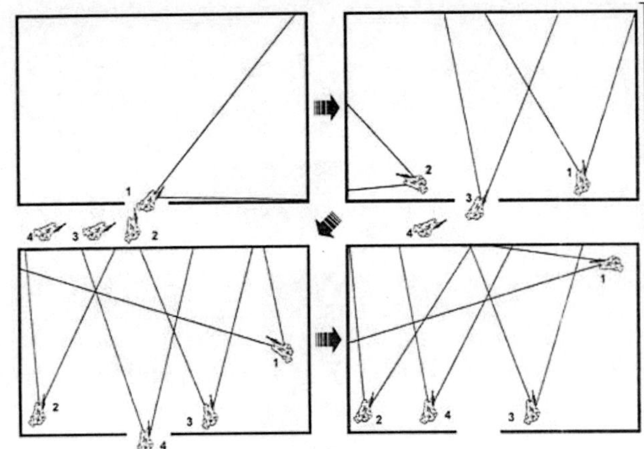

Room Clearing Opposing Wall Technique

Room Clearing at the Stairwell Landing

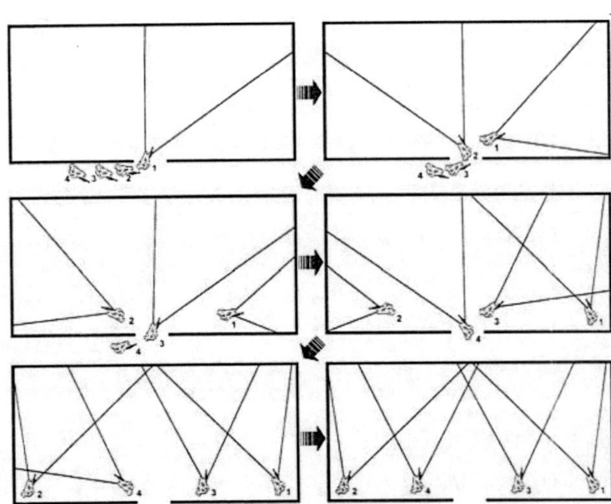

Room Clearing Strong Wall Technique

The lines projecting from the figures represent each Group Member's Field of Fire area of responsibility and direction of fire. Do not move your weapon out of your Field of Fire and do not move into another's Field of Fire until each room has been cleared.

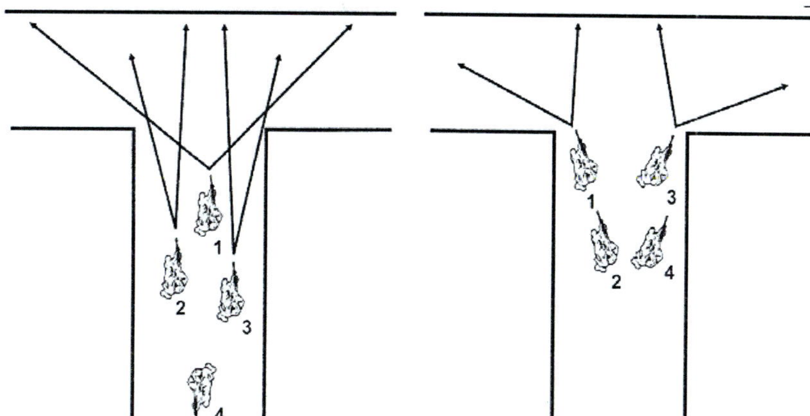

Hallway Clearing approaching an Intersection

We're hoping that your Protective Perimeter is made secure enough that you do not end up with *Intruders* inside your *NPP* area or building.

9-Basic Tactical Thought we think you must have

Indirect Approach Strategy. A belief both Authors have as a keystone to offensive tactics is the Indirect Approach Strategy. The Indirect Approach can take many forms, from contact with the enemy to no contact at all using passive tactics to defeat your enemy. Basically, our view of the Indirect Approach Strategy is *"Striking the enemy where they least expect it... when they least expect it... and how they least expect an attack."*

From first recorded use by ancient armies of the Indirect Approach Strategy during the Greek Wars to present day Irregular Warfare, this technique has defeated numerous and armies of far superior size, equipment and in strategic positions.

> ***Element of Surprise.*** *This is accomplished by striking* ***swiftly, boldly and ruthlessly*** *using one or a combination of the following... striking your enemy* ***when*** *they don't believe you will,* ***where*** *they don't believe you will and* ***how*** *they don't believe you're capable of attacking.*

Another facet of military tactical thought is explained something like this... *"The most audacious plan, executed with speed and sheer ruthlessness, will always succeed over the most carefully designed military plan."*

This doesn't mean you make a full frontal charge against a machine gun emplacement. Similar to the Indirect Approach Strategy, you strike the enemy *When, Where and How they least think you capable* with Violence of Action.

Use the Element of Surprise whenever possible. The Indirect Approach Strategy in military tactics usually gives you the Element of Surprise either partially or fully.

We consider the Element of Surprise a Force Multiplication Effect.

> ***Dictionary Definition***
> ***Flanked, Flanking, Flanks***
> *(Transitive Verb) To protect or guard the flank of... to menace or attack the flank of... to be placed or situated at the flank or side of... such as two stone lions flanked the entrance. Enfilading movement or an attack on your enemy.*

Flank, Flank, Flank! We cannot fully convey in words the tactical advantage that will benefit you from *Flanking* movements and weapons fire. This is also referred to as an 'Enfilading' attack. Attacking their side. *Flank your enemy... but always protect your flank from the enemy flanking you.*

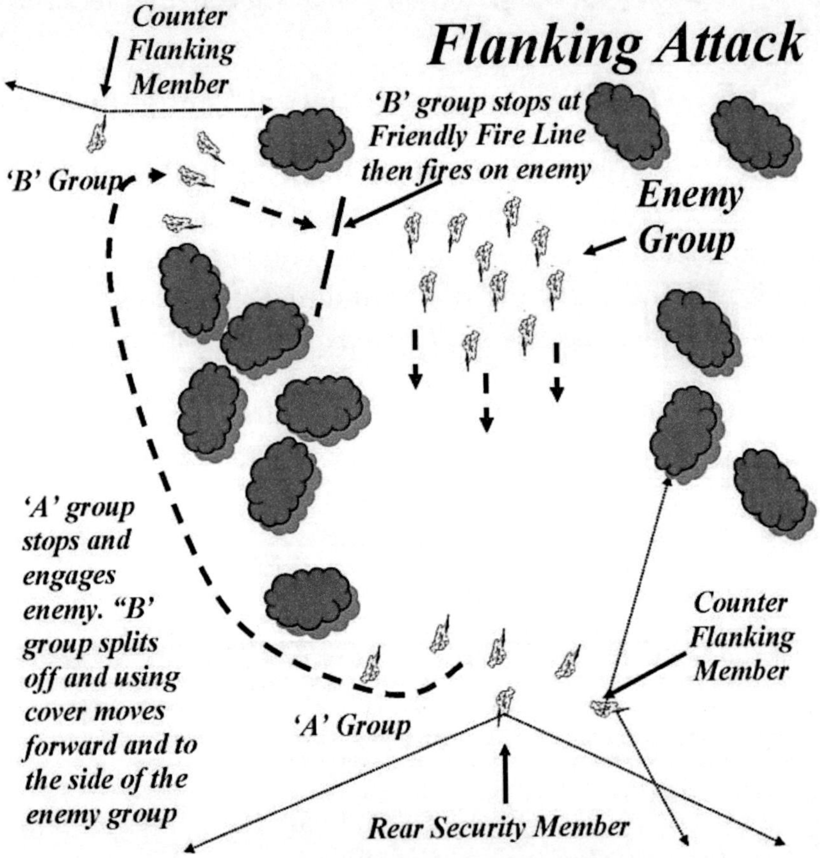

Flanking Attack Movement

One of the most incredible military tacticians for his day was the African Zulu Chief Shaka who developed the famous *'Buffalo Horns'* tactical formation. It is a dramatic example of not only flanking or enfilading movement, but how it was used to encircle and destroy the enemy.

The Buffalo Horns formation used simultaneous flanking movements on the left, right and rear of his enemy which, if successful, fully encircled the enemy force.

Shaka's military units were using short spears, which were not thrown but rather used in close quarters combat, so there was no danger of Friendly Fire Incidents as there would be with firearms. However, variations of this are used in modern military actions and Shaka's formation best illustrates how successful Flanking movements can be done.

Coordination and execution of this plan was by unit leaders who used hand signals and messengers. The scheme was elegant in its simplicity and well understood by his warriors.

By executing this movement, Shaka basically created his Kill Zone where he met the enemy on the battlefield.

The Buffalo Horns tactical formation was composed of four elements labeled like parts of a large horned buffalo's body seen from above looking forward as the animal looked. Imagine looking down at a buffalo and visualizing the buffalo's 'Chest' forward of its front legs, the 'Left Horn,' the 'Right Horn' and the buffalo's 'Loins' in front of the rear legs.

The main force, considered the *Chest* of his army, closed with the enemy and then stopped, holding the enemy in position with light attacks and stalling movements. The enemy, other tribes and even the far superior British Army usually hunkered down in battle formations waiting for the main frontal attack. *It would never come.*

The *Left* and *Right Horns* would then quickly move out from the left and right of the *Chest* and *Flank* the enemy, spreading around the sides to meet at the rear of the enemy without attacking until they had fully encircled the enemy. If an enemy was still stationary fighting off light frontal attacks at the *Chest* and did not *Counter Flank* the encircling *Left* and *Right Horns*, they were doomed.

As soon as the enemy was fully encircled by the *Chest*, the *Left Horn* and the *Right Horn,* Shaka's army would then close in from all sides and destroy the trapped force.

The *Loins* was a large reserve unit placed behind the *Chest* and ready to reinforce any weakened area of the encirclement if the enemy began to breakout of the encirclement… if not, they assisted the *Chest* and *Horns* in crushing the enemy.

What can we learn from Zulu Chief Shaka's tactics...?

Use Flanking attacks on your enemy. Because of firearms, encircling your enemy as Shaka's soldiers did in Close Quarters Combat is not an option. You will be shooting in the direction of your own Group Members. However, Flanking Attacks are devastating to an enemy if done as an 'L' Shaped attack… which subjects the enemy to weapons fire from two different angles… but prevents either you or your main group from firing on each other. *Flank, Flank, Flank! Attack, Attack, Attack!*

Use Outflanker Marksmen. We cannot overstate the benefit of *Outflanker Marksmen.* These high elevation Marksmen positions ***outside*** the Protective Perimeter have Supporting Fields of Fire and Interlocking Fields of Fire with *NPP* Guard Posts and the *Inside Marksmen.*

They are your present day *'Horns'* of an offensive and defensive action. They provide a flanking effect by weapons fire and can totally devastate your enemy… from all sides if you have enough of them in different positions and far enough apart to where their fire in the direction of another elevated *Outflanker Marksman* is not a threat.

This is a Marksman position *outside* the Protective Perimeter that can aggressively and precisely fire on *Intruders* around the main approach, any Protective Perimeter within their Field of Fire and can accurately fire on *Intruders* who get inside your Protective Perimeter in some instances.

Outflanker Marksmen are key positions that in worst case scenarios should be concentrated on more if you are short of guard personnel. The physical and psychological devastation that one or more of these positions can inflict on an enemy from 100, 200 or 300 yards from enfilading or flanking weapons fire can not be overstated.

If your *NPP* consists of only one or two houses, is a Ranch House or Farm House, the *Outflankers* Field of Fire should include the most likely entry points and approaches to these houses, but should be at a 90 degree angle to prevent Friendly Fire Incidents to those in your house. *Outflanker Marksmen* positions will give you a dramatic edge over *Intruders*.

If you do get out flanked by the enemy, use offensive Fire and Cover Maneuvers to retain the initiative and counter flank your enemy's flanking movements. Flank your enemy... but always protect your sides and rear from the enemy flanking you.

Avoid being isolated by the enemy outside of your *NPP*. Try to stay within your *Inside Marksmen* and *Outflanker Marksmen's* Fields of Fire when moving outside your *NPP* if possible.

Now let's get on with it... the occasion is here for 'trigger time' principles...

Chapter 10
Firearms, Safety, Basics of Marksmanship and Surviving a Gun Battle

In this Chapter we describe…

- **10-Firearms… You and your Group Members must know how to use them**
- **10-Children and you and firearm safety**
- **10-The National Rifle Association *Eddie Eagle Program***
- **10-The *Safety/Threat Evaluation Time Check***
- **10-Get competent training**
- **10-Story-*"Jennifer's world gets turned upside down…"***
- **10-Can you take another person's life?**
- **10-The 21 Foot Rule**
- **10-*The Human Hunter-Predator (HHP)*… don't be a sheep**
- **10-Look threatening to the *HHP***
- **10-'Tune in'… be alert and avoid the threat**
- **10-Handguns**
- **10-Carbines**
- **10-Rifles**
- **10-Shotguns**
- **10-The 4 primary firearms safety rules**
- **10-Marksmanship fundamentals**
- **10-Aim for 'Center Mass'**
- **10-If you're a lefty learn to shoot right handed**
- **10-The 'Walking Dead'**
- **10-Tips to Survive a Gun Battle**
- **10-Other firearms advice**
- **10-Concealment and Cover characteristics**

10-Firearms… You and your Group Members must know how to use them

Firearms are the most effective means of defending and protecting yourself and your *NPP*. You can count on the 'Bad Guys' being armed to the teeth during *Normal Civility* and more so during *A Failure of Civility.* Firearms will literally materialize in your environment… there will be many, many more in the hands of the criminals and lawless people than in law abiding people's hands.

Some people do not like firearms. No matter what attempt is made to gently and carefully introduce these people to firearms and training… nothing will change their attitude of fear and hatred which results from the unknown of firearms. These are people who must be assigned other duties in your *NPP*. They cannot be part of your Protective Perimeter defense force.

You must attempt to teach everyone in your *NPP* weapons safety and how to *use, maintain and load* the weapons available for your defense. Everyone must know how to use each and every weapon, including those of others in the *NPP*.

One area that your *NPP Leaders* will have to assist in educating the Group Members of your *NPP* on is firearms training. Training should be conducted for individuals to safely handle these weapons and to become proficient in them. Both Authors recommend that a National Rifle Association Certified Instructor be contacted by your *NPP Leaders* to give this training to small groups of the *NPP* at different times.

The *NPP Leaders* should be present during instruction or evaluation to assess each Group Member's firearms proficiency. Neither tactical training nor the defense of your *NPP* will be probable without firearms proficiency. If you are going to survive you must know how and when to use firearms.

Not all weapon types are the correct one for every person. A 12 gauge shotgun with 00 buckshot is fine for a larger frame person, but not for someone who is smaller in stature.

If possible... try to standardize your weapons and the caliber and type of ammunition they use. If there is A Failure of Civility in which you use firearms, the convenience of having the same cartridges and even the same magazines for that cartridge will become apparent.

The feasibility of standardization is beyond most people because of cost. We don't expect everyone to buy new weapons... however, simple procedures can be applied such as putting the same caliber weapons along one defensive area and noting what types of cartridges they use.

Your immediate reserve ammunition should be held at the Watch Center location to be delivered to Guard Posts by Runner Guardians. Ammunition should be divided and put in separate boxes marked 'Guard Posts 1,2,3', 'Guard Posts 9,10, 11', etc. going by the directional Clock System so everyone knows where the proper cartridges should be delivered in an emergency.

If in the heat of an attack on your *NPP,* if you yell to your *Runner Guardian* or radio *"Guard 5... Get me more ammunition!"* and they yell back *"What kind!"* you'll know what we mean by standardizing your weapons ammunition or dividing it up by Guard Post to keep your defense effective.

Not everyone has a vast fortune to spend on standardizing or buying new weapons, the ammunition they need and the added expense of buying magazines, holsters, belts and magazine pouches. This should not become the priority for your *NPP* and standardizing weapons can cause friction quickly within your group.

Standardization should be a consideration, but the priorities should be *organizing* your *NPP* and *training*. Use the *KISS rule... Keep It Simple Stupid.*

Another consideration is that of proficiency with both *primary* and *secondary weapons...* for example... *rifles and shotguns are primary weapons* and your secondary *weapon is your pistol* if you have both.

Rifles and shotguns are relatively easy to learn to shoot, but it takes an average of 40 hrs of training for the common person to *start* to become proficient with a pistol. Start on firearms training as soon as possible.

If you're buying new weapons... whether pistols, rifles or shotguns, you want to have firearms with a high capacity of ammunition that can be reloaded easily... preferably with high capacity magazines interchangeable with other's firearms. These high capacity magazine fed firearms are mostly military type weapons.

Again, having sufficient equipment, supplies and weapons is a priority, but *organizing* and *training* your group should be your most pressing priority. Far too many people who prepare for *A Failure of Civility* have plenty of Beans, Bullets and Bandages but don't have a plan to effectively use them if *A Failure of Civility* occurs.

Hold training exercises! You can host a *NPP* block party afterwards and your neighborhood Group Members will have some fun doing this. Everyone can tell stories at what a good shot they are.

Training exercises serve two purposes...

- ***First...*** to prove that your plan works on paper. If you have problems with your plan working properly make certain that your plan is realistic and the fault is the plan... not the Group Members failure to execute it properly.

  Plans usually look good on paper... but rarely work well in reality. Look at that 'unsinkable ship' the Titanic... looked *great* on paper, didn't it?

- ***Second...*** training exercises teach quick, knee jerk reaction by Group Members. It familiarizes all members and creates confidence and smooth operation of the plan. All the actors 'know their parts in the play.'

Your Group Members should have an informal debriefing by discussing the training exercise and getting feedback from everyone on how it can work better. This makes every Group Member feel like they're an important part of the *Neighborhood Protection Plan.* It also gives everyone something to look forward and is a way to help bond the Group Members together through socializing afterwards.

Make these training exercises and discussions constructive and fun… don't criticize Group Members in front of the whole group… constructive criticism should be given privately afterwards and if brought up to the group during a discussion, do so without naming people. Keep in mind… *"Praise in public... criticize in private!"*

Even with limited ammunition for real shooting experience, do *Dry Fire* exercises with your weapons. *Dry Fire* is pulling the trigger of your ***empty*** weapon to practice trigger control, sight picture and sight alignment.

The Authors have trained some pretty tough hombres and have many times heard macho guys going *"Bang... bang... bang!"* to simulate firing their weapons. They have an intense focus on the exercise… not concerned that they sound like kids at play.

Make certain there is *no ammunition* present and that weapons are not pointed at each other during training exercises. The *NPP Leaders* should personally check each weapon to ensure it's unloaded and the chamber is empty before beginning training. We suggest putting a white tie wrap through open firearms actions before starting. Regardless, *always follow firearms safety rules.*

As the story in Yugoslavia stated *"The first days of a catastrophe are the worst in terms of chaos and panic and* ***to be unarmed in chaos, panic and riots can mean your death."***

You may want to have a firearm on your person, or in your vehicle or workplace as you live your life in *Normal Civility* in case an emergency occurs and you're not in or near your neighborhood.

In this chapter we'll discuss basic firearms safety and use of handguns, rifles and shotguns for your *Neighborhood Defense Plan* during *A Failure of Civility.* Some of this will apply to the use of a firearm during *Normal Civility.*

10-Children and you and firearm safety

> ***Dictionary Definition***
> ***Safety***
> *(Noun) The condition of being safe... freedom from danger, risk, or injury.*

Firearm safety is one of the first issues we'll cover. Because children are precious to us and they are very vulnerability to danger from the self defense tools this chapter discusses, this must be explained first.

Of particular concern is where you store your firearms and especially your handgun when not carrying it. Most States and the Federal Government have laws against underage children (generally 18) having access to firearms. Some States, Counties and Cities require installation of a trigger lock or require locked storage of firearms anywhere children could have access to them.

Recently the United States Supreme Court ruled on Second Amendment Rights and stated basically that the rapid access of a firearm in self defense is a necessity and this essentially voids the use of trigger locks or locked storage by law. Despite that, children are a priority and must be taken into account regarding where and how you store your firearms.

Your Local or State Government or a civil attorney may still take you to task for not having a trigger lock on firearms if it results in the death or injury of a child by your negligence of safety. This may create criminal liability for you in addition to the trauma you will undergo from the loss or injury to a child.

Regardless of what the law says… *or the law doesn't say...* the safety of children is of paramount importance. They are precious… they are our future. No one wants the death or injury of a child from their firearm on their conscience if it can be prevented.

The ability of your children or visiting children getting hold of your firearms, whether you have educated them or not about not touching them is an evaluation you must very carefully make.

Trigger locks, unloading the firearms and storing ammunition separately, locking handgun boxes and storing your firearms in a safe are methods that ensure children will not be harmed by finding a firearm and causing an accidental discharge of it.

Do not attempt Child Safety by hiding your firearms anywhere a child can crawl, walk to, climb up to or dig around in. Put your firearms up and away… *way up and away...* don't just hide them!

> *Children can find the best hiding places you have and are especially curious of handguns. Put your handgun up out of reach of them!*
>
> *We mean **up** where they can't possibly climb to.*

For this *'up and away'* storage method of a firearm, we'll concentrate on the handgun. It should be unloaded with the magazine close by it or if your handgun is a revolver, a *'speed loader'* next to it. *Speed loaders* hold cartridges for easy mass insertion into your revolver's cylinder.

> *Remember... children can find anything...*
>
> *anywhere a child can crawl... walk or climb to...* ***they will find your firearm!***

The evaluation of the need for your firearm at home, in your vehicle, in your purse or at work must be thought out carefully. Lock your firearms in the trunk away from passenger access when you have kids in your vehicle or when leaving it in your vehicle.

If your vehicle is a suburban type of vehicle with no trunk, you need a locking gun case bolted to your vehicle's interior. We recommend handguns be locked in a storage box regardless of whether you store them in your vehicle interior or trunk.

10-The National Rifle Association *Eddie Eagle Program*

Studies have shown that programs such as the *National Rifle Association's Eddie Eagle Program* educate children of the 'curiosity' about guns and how to react responsibly when around a firearm or what to do when discovering one if adults are not around.

The Eddie Eagle Program teaches children…
If you see a gun… STOP!
Don't Touch…
Leave the Area…
Tell an Adult.

This education of children regarding firearms should take place early. But you must assume that other's children do not have that education. It is ultimately up to you to be the director of safety in your home, your vehicle and your workplace. The NRA website at www.NRAILA.Org has some of the best resources available to further educate yourself on firearms safety and firearms in general.

10-The *Safety/Threat Evaluation Time Check*

Obviously these very methods of securing your firearms safely… can also delay your use of it in time of need. We recommend you do a *Safety/Threat Evaluation Time Check.*

You must weigh and reach a balance with the following...

- What is your threat level or the probability of danger to you and your family, and
- The method you will use to secure your handgun, and
- The ability of children accessing your handgun by that method of storage.

We suggest you perform a practice rapid retrieval of your handgun by the safe storage method you use. This is a *Safety/Threat Evaluation Time Check.* Time yourself in seconds as to your response time to retrieve and load your handgun for an imagined threat. Imagine an assailant is threatening and chasing you in your home or other environment… can you have your handgun ready to defend yourself in that time?

While performing this *Safety/Threat Evaluation Time Check*, be careful if you go to the ultimate of the test by loading your revolver or chambering a cartridge in your automatic pistol, so as to not have an accidental discharge.

Training under time constraints simulates the real threat.

This *Safety/Threat Evaluation Time Check* should be done *many times* to simulate being under the pressure of a real threat. *Training under time constraints simulates the real threat.* God forbid, but if the real situation occurs, you'll be amazed how little fumbling you'll do.

10-Get competent training

We're providing some very basic information, but this doesn't take the place of practical training on the range from a competent firearms instructor. Preferably you will choose a National Rifle Association (NRA) Certified Instructor, trained in Firearm Safety, Home Firearms Safety and Personal Protection to instruct you with your firearm.

A Firearms Instructor who knows what he or she is doing will show little bravado or a macho attitude regarding using a firearm against another human being. If your instructor is testosterone or estrogen riddled, he or she should not be instructing and you should move on to someone more responsible who preaches restraint.

Just like the great Martial Artists, a good firearms instructor will teach *restraint above all else.* A good instructor will teach you that *the best fight is the one that you avoid!*

Training that emphasizes restraint… respect for others, humility, walking away from a potential fight and *Sanctity of Life* are issues that are paramount in your personal protection firearms instruction. You will be a far better person to remove yourself from a Deadly Threat situation, if possible, than to take another human's life. *Far better is the confrontation where all walk away.*

10-Story-*"Jennifer's world gets turned upside down…"*

"Oh, it's almost 2...00 AM again!" Jennifer Grant murmured to herself as the elevator slowed to the parking garage level adjoining the Atlanta Georgia Pharmcor office complex. The tiring thought of the 30 minute drive home ahead of her she'd made a couple of thousand times before racked her exhausted brain. Numbers were still sloshing around in her mind like the mental radio that plays the well worn tune in your head... you know, the song that you can't shut off, don't know where it came from and that won't go away.

"Ron is going to do his nut!" Jennifer thought. It was a frightening thought to her. She'd been married to him for eight years, but he still didn't understand her job. He would blow

up at her when she tippy-toed into the bedroom or lay cold and unemotionally by her in bed. But even in his sleep she could sense his growing anger towards her. She hoped he wouldn't confront her. She was too worn out to take it tonight.

Regardless, Ron would wake *tomorrow, shower, shave, dress in his patrolman's uniform and quietly leave without kissing her or saying goodbye. That's what had been happening lately and the thought was tormenting her again. It hurt her deeply. She began to wonder why she'd become an accountant.*

"Tell them to go screw themselves!" he'd told her yesterday morning. "This is the fourth night this week Jennifer that you've worked after midnight. You look like crap. Four and five hours sleep a night. You can't be doing any good for anyone working 18 hours a day!"

"Yeah, Ron! I'll tell Pharmcor to go screw themselves, just don't throw the Employment Opportunities section of the newspaper away!" she replied facetiously, "Pharmcor will be a great reference on my resume. I can put a note next to them saying, 'I'd rather you don't call this previous employer who fired me because their annual Stockholder's Financial Statement wasn't finished on time!' That would be great! I could look into working at the Speedy Mart down the road. They don't care about those kinds of things and that's about the only kind of job I'll be able to get as a CPA after that! Running a cash register!"

"Well at least then I'd maybe see you once and a while... unlike this. What are the words in that song... two ships passing in the night! I may as well be single, Jennifer. I'm going to be sitting by myself at dinner tonight. Friday night! The rest of our friends with their wives and me by myself!" Ron Grant snarled at her through lips of that chiseled face she loved so much. She couldn't bear to be at the breakfast table hearing the man she loved speak to her like that and she ran to the bedroom crying.

The elevator door opened, *breaking her thought and rush of hot humid Georgia air hit her face like she'd opened an oven door. It temporarily turned her thought away from her marital problems. A tall statuesque blonde, she strode out of the elevator into the dimly lit parking garage. The garage was almost empty of cars, with just the cleaning crew's and hers remaining.*

Even in the dim light, Jennifer was a striking woman. Like a Barbie Doll. Shapely, long legs, full breasts, long neck... just the thing that drew Ron's attention so many years ago. She still had that look and it was tearing her apart that her job was getting between her and her husband. Ron hadn't touched her all week.

But another man had been thinking about her every moment of his waking thought. Those long slender legs disappearing from the knees upward into the light gray skirt, created a lust of curiosity. She looked especially enticing tonight with her jacket draped over her left arm and her ample breasts enticing imagination from under her white sleeveless blouse. Her long blonde hair bounced with each step she took, projecting the impression of freshness and energy, revealing little of the exhaustion she felt.

***As tired as Jennifer Grant was**, she sensed something wrong soon after stepping out of the elevator. She'd walked some distance towards her car but felt it in the air. Then she saw a slight movement in the shadows just past her car. What Ron Grant had taught her and packed into her head... "Be alert... be aware of your surroundings... and avoid!" Jennifer was definitely alert now. Someone who shouldn't be there in the parking garage at 2 AM... was!*

Ron had often come home telling her how he'd sensed trouble as a cop and he was usually right. He and his partners had avoided trouble and even saved each other many times with what normal people considered this strange sense from fear. He'd told Jennifer we all have it. It's primal.

Ron had lectured her to practice being alert and aware of her surroundings and push everything out of her mind. Practice it, practice it, practice it! Practice until it turns on automatically like a knee jerk reaction. Especially when out in an area accessible by the public. We don't practice it because most of us are too preoccupied with other thoughts, he'd said.

***Along with the shooting** Ron and her did now and then on the weekend, she'd become as proficient in developing this sense from being alert as she had been with hitting the bull's-eye on the target. Jennifer had her car keys in her hand also, her finger on the alarm button just as Ron had told her to do as soon as the elevator door opened.*

Jennifer had hated guns. She had until she'd met Ron. Being a cop and teaching his wife personal safety had gone hand in hand. They fought and argued about this many times until she relented. Jennifer now loved to go out shooting at targets. It gave her a sense of safety, control over her environment and she had become addicted to making the holes in the paper silhouette target close together, or a 'tight group' which measures a shooter's control with their handgun.

Ron had taught her the basics of firing her Taurus .38 caliber revolver at close range. Three to seven yards. Since most shootouts, robberies and the like happen at that distance or less, that's how Ron had taught her to shoot... to hit the target at close range... to hit 'Center Mass.' Hit the area from the belly button up to the neck and between the armpits. Keep your eyes open and pull the trigger. Fire three or more times into the target until the threat had stopped.

She now slowed her walk and slipped her free hand into a compartment in her purse. She had the handgun securely in her hand as she looked out of the corners of her eyes. Jennifer was now butt wide awake... and scared. She estimated the distance back to the elevator door twice as far as the distance to her car. She also knew that the elevator door had closed and would have to be summoned... and she'd be just as alone and unprotected standing in front of the elevator as standing in the middle of this garage.

She decided the best option *was to continue onward to the relative safety of her car. Without being obvious while approaching her car, she looked at the space underneath and approached from the rear so she could see both sides. No one was there and there was nothing but the ominous black area of the shadow made by the concrete garage column to the right front of her car.*

Jennifer Grant's mind was on overdrive from adrenaline. Every sense in her body was screaming. Her eyes were dilated, her heart was beating wildly and her hands were cold and sweaty. As she walked along side her car and pushed the key button unlocking the driver door, she'd glanced into the back seat of her car to see that no one was hiding there. The lights of her car flickered as she pushed the unlock button.

The man who'd been thinking in-human thoughts about her all week... actually for months, moved at a speed that was almost in-human. He was very muscular blonde haired young man wearing a red tank top T-shirt and denim jeans. She could clearly see the blade of a knife protruding from his right hand. Before she knew it, he was out from behind the concrete column coming towards her.

She did not hesitate. She pushed her car alarm button, her hand still on the handgun in her purse. The blaring horn and flashing lights seemed to only make the man move faster around the front of her car. The shrill blast of the horn and this pleasant looking, almost handsome man moving towards her made her heart pound faster and filled her mind with confusion.

She looked into the man's eyes *as he moved around the front of her car. There was a wild determination in them and they were fixed on her! She moved back as he lunged towards her. Her hand still on her handgun, she fired through her purse once. He kept coming towards her as if she'd completely missed him.*

She quickly pulled out the handgun and desperately fired twice more. He slowed and staggered. In the flashing lights from her car, she could see bone fragments, bits of flesh and tissue that had fallen out of the back of his tank top T-Shirt into bloody clumps on the shiny floor. Her shots had gone right through him. The high powered bullets had cavitated through his chest, tearing and sucking parts of his spinal column and flesh out as the three bullets went in the front of his chest and exited through his back.

He staggered backwards slipping slightly in the blood and parts of his own body that littered the floor. She'd hit him, stopping him. He feebly walked backwards, turned and slumped against the waist high concrete wall of the garage in front of her car, then slid to a seated position.

His hands dropped to his sides and the knife clattered onto the floor as his hand opened. He sat there staring at her with a defeated, stunned, almost angry look on his face while he labored breathing. She'd hit him three times in the chest. Jennifer had not missed as she thought.

The red tank top turned crimson colored *as the distinct color of blood seeped out of the holes in his chest. She stood paralyzed pointing her handgun at him for what seemed like an eternity as he watched her.*

His breathing went from shallow to barely visible. The life still in him was holding him upright as he sat, but as that departed he slid sideways falling onto his side lifelessly onto the shiny garage floor.

Only the blaring of her car horn, shrill in the heavy night air, brought her to her senses and she fumbled to shut it off.

She wheeled around pointing her handgun in the direction of the sound of the footsteps running towards her. It was Jonesy, the night security man.

"Hey! Don't shoot! Security." he said as he stopped dead in his tracks raising his hands.

"Oh thank God! She yelled, "This man came after me with a knife! He was going to attack me. I shot him. I think he's dead!"

Jonesy walked to the man and knelt down feeling for a pulse on his neck.

"He's dead alright, Missus! Very dead! I'd better get the Police over here. Are you okay?"

"I'm still shaking, but I'm alright."

You sit down over here now, ya hear?" Jonesy said as he opened the front door of her car and gingerly helped her into the driver's seat.

Jonesy quickly checked the surrounding area *with his flashlight for other assailants while he called the Atlanta Police Department on his cellular phone, his only means of defense other than his Pepper Spray and nightstick.*

While he called the police, Jennifer Grant started crying. Not tears of fear, but tears of sorrow. Lying on his side, the man's eyes were still open. Even in death, his eyes were still fixed on her... staring at her. He was as handsome as her friend Jack Jenkins in accounting. She got sudden cold chills.

She looked at the flesh and blood on the garage floor that looked like the leftovers in a butcher shop, but that she knew were human. She suddenly felt like throwing up. She'd just killed another human being and she felt sick to her stomach.

As she stared out her car windshield at him dead on the floor, the flash of an image of him in a suit came into her mind. She felt sick. Even though she'd watched him with her very own eyes, she couldn't picture him doing what he'd just done. He was going to attack her with that knife!?

Anger overwhelmed her for a moment. *Anger towards this dead man for forcing her to shoot him... anger at herself for working to an hour that helped create this situation... anger over having that handgun in her purse...anger towards her boss for this deadline she had to make. Anger!*

Then suddenly she felt so alone. She wanted Ron here. She needed to have him hold her. She felt so empty. She wept and wept, torrents of tears flowing down her cheeks on to her white cotton blouse... leaving a light gray path where they'd soaked in.

She had killed another living, breathing person! Pangs of guilt stabbed at her mind and pierced her soul.

She felt like any goodness in her was invisibly flowing out of her like the blood still flowing out of her attacker and pooling on the garage floor...Jennifer stared at the dead man... and he stared back at her... she'd never forget that stare...

10-Can you take another person's life?

Using a firearm for lawful self defense is a tremendous responsibility. Unlike the story above, the Authors hope that you will never find it necessary to use your firearm in self defense.

> *In the profound words of one State Firearms Licensing Director, "If you do choose to arm yourself with a handgun you should also be armed with the most indispensable weapon of all... knowledge.* ***Only you can provide the wisdom, restraint and good judgment that the Law demands of those who possess the ability to take another human life."***

The use of a firearm in self defense during *Normal Civility* will subject you to laws that will only protect you if you have acted within your legal right. The fact remains that you may have to use your firearm... and you may have to take another's life. If you aren't mentally capable of doing that... don't carry a firearm.

The controversy in the use of lethal and non-lethal force rages on. Technology has advanced sufficiently to provide *some* reliability in using non-lethal force items such as Taser type devices in certain self defense situations.

Explore alternative self defense methods other than firearms also. But in this book, the use of firearms for Justifiable Deadly Force in lawful self defense is the only means the Authors recommend for defending yourself and your *NPP*.

10-The 21 Foot Rule

Other than a firearm as a threat, the next most common *deadly threat* comes from a knife, straight razor, carpet knife, stabbing instruments or a box cutter tool. The 21 Foot Rule is a rule that law enforcement will use to determine their Use of Deadly Force when confronted by someone with a knife, straight razor, carpet knife, box cutter tool or anything else that stabs or cuts.

If an assailant with a knife gets within 21 feet of a law enforcement officer, the officer has justification to shoot to stop the threat... and they will shoot!

If an officer has his weapon holstered and an assailant armed with a knife is closing in on the officer from 21 feet or closer, the officer will be stabbed or cut before he can draw his weapon, fire into the assailant... *and stop the threat.*

Most composition Kevlar type bullet proof vests worn by law enforcement officers can be stabbed through with a knife.

Only special vests afford cutting or stabbing protection, such as those worn by Prison and Correction Officers.

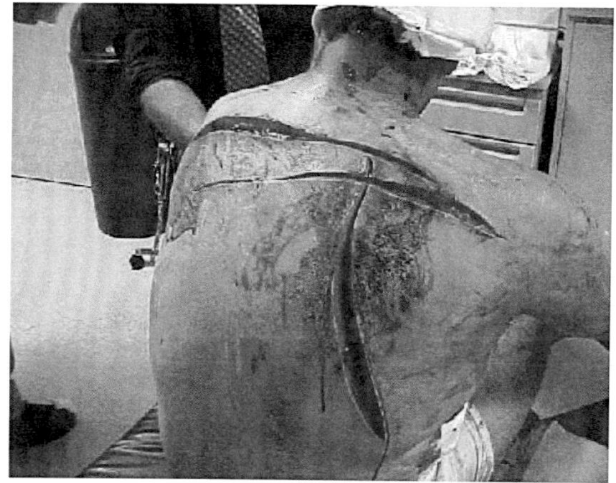

Result of a law enforcement officer cut by an assailant before the assailant could be stopped.

Law enforcement officers have The 21 Foot Rule beaten into their heads from the first day of their training... and it's no wonder.

Both Authors have watched training videos for law enforcement regarding an assailant with a knife and the damage he can do before he can be stopped when the attacker is within 21 feet of the officer.

There is really no practical defense for the average person against a knife attack other than the use of Deadly Force with your firearm to stop it.

Law enforcement officers will not hesitate to shoot to kill if the person is within 21 feet of them and won't drop the knife on their command.

10-*The Human Hunter-Predator (HHP)*... don't be a sheep

Both Authors have listened to presentations by veteran police homicide detectives that have thoroughly impressed us.

These presentations put into words a simple truth of the interaction between *victims as human prey* and what we have labeled the *Human Hunter-Predator,* or *HHP* for short… *criminals*. These homicide detectives' presentations sounded something like this…

The Human Hunter-Predator or HHP

"Humans are no different than the wildlife in Africa. A human criminal intent on attacking another human will stalk his human prey like a lion stalks a zebra herd. The criminal, maybe not even being very intelligent or high on drugs, will take his time and is shrewd and cunning."

"The criminal, like the lion senses the zebra herd, will sense the weak ones of the human herd. He will watch the way they walk, how observant they are to danger, their age, their apparent strength, try to find one that's wandered from the herd and measure their position from the Cover he needs to move close in to surprise and overcome that human prey."

"The lion will slowly position himself for this attack. It will be a total surprise to the zebra. The attack will be quick and it will be deadly. So will the attack on the human."

The cunning and shrewdness of the *Human Hunter-Predator* is astounding. This *Human Hunter-Predator* mindset is in every criminal… it's in every mugger, thief, purse snatcher, rapist and killer… and it will be common place amongst desperate people if *A Failure of Civility* takes place! If you project any weakness… you will be the *HHP's* prey!

The *Human Hunter-Predator* will usually go after only easy prey. This is not only important for you to understand during *Normal Civility*, but is important to understand if *A Failure of Civility* occurs. *The prey will be you*... if you let yourself look vulnerable. That's also your *NPP*… if it looks vulnerable… it will definitely be attacked.

10-Look threatening to the *HHP*

A key factor in the prevention of an attack on you is ***visual deterrence…***
having something visual with you that is threatening or you acting in a threatening manner towards a potential assailant.

Visual deterrence is projecting an image of strength or the ability to inflict injury or death on an attacker. It should be something that can be seen from a distance. That image will cause the *Human Hunter-Predator* to realize that he or she may have more to lose than gain if they attack. They are frightened off… by *visual deterrence.*

During Normal Civility, two types of deterrents to use when walking are…

- Carrying a police baton, a golf club or walking stick, and
- Walking a dog that is big enough to make you look like someone not to tangle with.

The *HHP* must think he will have his hands full if he comes after you because you can counter-attack. He will go elsewhere.

Make yourself a combative looking target! Cause the *HHP* to go elsewhere. Walk softly and carry a Big Stick! Or walk a Big Dog!

The theory abounds that during *A Failure of Civility* you have to *"Look the part... play the part"* just like the destruction around you. The Authors disagree with this to some extent.

The Authors feel that if *A Failure of Civility* does occur that desperate people without food, like rats sniffing for something to eat anywhere and everywhere, will find your *NPP* and attack you in an attempt to get what you have.

Obviously some of 'looking the part' may be necessary and will occur naturally with people and your *NPP* without effort. Your efforts to blend in with the disaster will be assisted by the type and the degree of severity of the *Catastrophic Event* and its effect on Group Members.

However, the Authors believe that part of a *Proactive Defense* is to *project an overwhelming presence of strength... especially in the beginning stages of A Failure of Civility.* That includes strong fortifications, armed presence and frequent armed patrols.

At some point after *A Failure of Civility* not even this will deter desperate people. By that time however two things will happen. There will be *fewer* threats... but there will be *greater* threats.

There will be less people because of starvation, lack of medicines, disease and murder. The remainder though, will be better armed and will have learned tactics because of their mistakes.

At that time you will have to find a balance between 'Looking the part' and projecting strength.

10-'Tune in'... be alert and avoid the threat

You can almost never go wrong being *alert* and to then *avoid* the threat. The most important aspect of personal security is to *be alert* and *be aware* in your surroundings. If you sense a threat to your security... or something *'Just Don't Look Right'*... is 'out of place'... or 'odd'... treat it as a threat and *avoid* that threat. Communicate that to others.

*If you are always **alert** and always **avoid**, you should always be able to evade the threat.*

The problem with most of us during *Normal Civility,* is when we are out of a secure environment... such as leaving work and walking to our car... our thoughts are on everything but our surroundings… we are not 'tuned in' to our surroundings. That's the most probable time that ***trouble will strike… when you're moving between the secure places…of being around people, at work, in your vehicle and in your home.***

If *A Failure of Civility* occurs you will live like a combat soldier. When you're a combat soldier in a war zone, you're on some level or other of a *constant alert* state of mind for trouble. We civilian folks, not in a war zone, think we're secure so we let down our guard against danger.

'Tune In' to your surroundings when you're traveling between the secure areas of a store, your car, your home and work. Practice this. You'll be amazed at what the primal sensory instincts will reveal to you. You may even become aware of a *Human Hunter-Predator* stalking you. During *A Failure of Civility*, be ready to *shoot to stop the threat.*

10-Handguns

Don't go spending money on new firearms unless you don't have reliable ones. Rather… buy ammunition, equipment and food. But… if you're considering buying firearms… here's our advice on what you should get…

A handgun is a short range weapon accurate to about 15 yards with most people's proficiency. The Authors consider a handgun a *secondary weapon*… in our words… *"If you know you're going to get into a gunfight, bring your pistol along… but shoot with your rifle or shotgun first!"*

Handguns are primarily one of two types…

A revolver, which has a revolving cylinder that holds multiple cartridges.

An automatic pistol, which has a detachable magazine that holds multiple cartridges.

The statement was made about Samuel Colt's invention of the six shot rapid firing revolver in the 1800s… *"God made man… and Samuel Colt made them equal."* As profound as this statement sounds… the Authors doubt that Samuel Colt had ever been subjected to intense automatic weapons fire.

A handgun is also referred to as a 'pistol.' If a handgun is properly fitted for size and to the comfort of a person and that person is taught well marksmanship, the handgun's mechanics, safe operation and safe carry practices… it is the most popular and one of the best suited defense tools to counter Deadly Threats to you from another human… and multiple human threats *at close range.*

We've seen far too many people ill-fitted to their handgun. Like shoes, a handgun must fit your hand, be comfortable and must be chosen for the purpose. Look at a handgun like you're getting a pair of shoes. It must fit and feel comfortable.

Glock Model 19 9MM Pistol

Ruger SP101 Revolver

The selection of a handgun is an issue that you must go over with your NRA Certified Instructor and the people at a reputable gun store. The *key word* in this selection is *comfort.* You must be *physically* and *mentally* comfortable with your handgun.

Your handgun must fit your hand. People have different size hands. You must have a handgun that *feels comfortable in your hand.* If the handgun doesn't fit your hand it will drastically affect your accuracy for the worse. You must be able to take the safety off the handgun with one hand easily and reload with ease.

Your handgun must fit your mind. Your handgun must also be mentally comfortable. By that, we mean that you must feel at ease that you know how to reload it, fire it and know how it functions by reflex… and blindfolded. You must be *intimate* with the operation of your handgun and it should almost feel like an extension of your hand… *like your handgun is a part of you.*

The Authors strongly recommend the Glock semi-automatic pistol in either 9mm or .40 Caliber S&W. The Glock handgun series have excellent reliability and state-of-the-art safety systems built into them. The time proven Glock for automatics and Smith & Wesson or Ruger revolvers are reliable, safe and great personal defense handguns.

Your handgun must be fired by you before purchasing it. We strongly suggest you fire your handgun or a type as close to it as possible, before purchasing it. There are gun stores with ranges that will let you fire the particular handgun you are purchasing.

Purchase what you *feel* comfortable with *after* firing it, not what someone else thinks is good for you. Gun Store owners sometimes have more interest in your money then your welfare. Go to other gun stores over a few days to try different pistols and *do not buy your handgun on the first visit or get pressured into buying it. Just say nothing and walk out if you feel pressure from a salesperson.*

This is where a National Rifle Association Certified Firearms Instructor comes in. Deal with an instructor that has no association with a gun store so they're a non-interested third party and realize no gain from what you buy. This will help insure that they have your interests in mind.

All self defense handguns worth carrying have a powerful cartridge and have some 'kick.'

Your handgun must fit your purpose. Handgun and rifles fire cartridges that are also commonly referred to as 'bullets,' 'rounds' and 'shells.' For shotguns the cartridge is termed a 'shell'. Cartridges consist of the projectile (bullet)... the cartridge case... an explosive powder charge... and a primer powder igniter... all assembled into one.

The diameter of the bullet is referred to as caliber and can be expressed in 'millimeters' for metric size... or fractions of an inch through the term 'caliber.' The bigger the millimeter or caliber usually means a more powerful cartridge. If you are target shooting for pleasure, a .22 caliber is acceptable and the ammunition is cheap. But a small caliber weapon should not be your choice for a self defense handgun or rifle.

Self defense carry requires, in our opinion, a minimum of a .38 caliber for a revolver or a 9mm for an automatic. What is termed 'stopping power' or 'shock effect' comes into play here. You want as much stopping power from your handgun as is comfortable for you to fire without tremendous 'kick.' The stopping power generally comes from larger calibers and is exponentially increased by using 'hollow point' expand on impact bullets.

Your handgun must be comfortable to carry. Carrying a handgun all day will soon make you realize the necessity of the proper holster for comfort. A semi-automatic pistol or a revolver should always be carried in a holster that encloses the trigger whether in a purse... in a holster worn on the belt... or by other means... to prevent accidental discharge.

For your *Neighborhood Protection Plan* the Authors recommend that you have a military style duty belt, belt holster and magazine pouches if your pistol is a magazine fed automatic... or 'speed loaders' if your pistol is a revolver.

This duty belt should be adjustable to allow you to make it several sizes larger to fit over bundled winter clothing. We suggest that you have 5 magazines for each pistol and carry the 4 spare magazines or speed loaders on your duty belt in pouches made for those individual magazines and speed loaders.

These accessories are very inexpensive if they're military surplus and can be purchased through the internet or at most military surplus stores and gun stores.

So again, fire the weapon you intend to arm yourself with *before* buying it and don't get pressured into a sale. Firearms are like vehicles in the short run… you'll take a loss if you buy something you don't like and try to immediately sell it for the cash to buy what you want. We again, recommend semi-automatic handguns should be of the Glock type in 9mm or .40 calibers.

You should have a *minimum* of 500 rounds of ammunition for each pistol *after* you learn to use the pistol by live firing it… 1000 rounds or more if you can afford it.

10-Carbines

Both Authors recommend the semi-automatic carbine as your first choice for an intermediate weapon. An intermediate weapon is a firearm in between a pistol and a rifle or shotgun. Carbines are a short barreled rifle that fires a pistol cartridge or similar. Their effective killing range is good to about 100 yards, depending on the caliber and other factors with the average person's capabilities.

Carbines are a *primary weapon*. Semi-automatic carbines typically fire one projectile at a time out the barrel each time the trigger is pulled.

We're not going to get into the detail of cartridges and calibers and what-not. It's too complicated and unnecessary and is a science unto itself. The Authors suggest you read and discover, talk to people who know weapons and then experiment and test before buying.

One Author has trained literally hundreds of people in handgun use. He has had a great deal of success with students learning to accurately shoot pistol caliber carbines. Firearms such as the KelTec Sub 2000, Hi Point Carbine and the Berretta Carbine are this type of weapon.

Kel Tec Sub 2000 Carbine

An additional advantage of the KelTec Carbine is that it uses the same magazine as some popular handguns. Different KelTec Carbines are fitted to take different pistol magazines and this can standardize your ammunition and reloading method.

The Glock, Sig and Berretta pistol magazines fit the KelTec Carbine and have the same basic procedures to load, sight, fire and control as the pistol… but the longer barrel and stock of the carbine seems to help students become proficient shooters sooner.

The Glock pistol is also used by a majority of our law enforcement and most of our private military companies and is a very dependable weapon. We suggest the Glock pistol with a KelTec Carbine of the same caliber where the magazines are interchangeable between both.

Like shoes, a carbine must also fit you and be comfortable to shoot. Again, look at a carbine like you're buying a pair of shoes. It must fit your body and your mind.

Get a sling for this rifle. A sling is a simple leather, nylon or canvas type 'strap' that attaches to your carbine or long rifle at each end to allow you to carry the weight of it on your full body with the sling behind your neck and across your shoulders. This also helps keep your weapon from being taken away from you by an assailant.

Rifles and shotguns should only be carried slung on your strong hand shoulder *when you are not on duty or at a Guard Post.* In these positions your carbine or long gun should be at the 'Ready' position at all times.

Webbing and Magazine Pouches

The ready position allows you to snap your carbine or long gun up to your shoulder and fire it immediately. Get a sling that goes around your back and over the opposite shoulder of your strong hand. This will allow you to carry your weapon in the 'ready position.'

You must have at least 10 spare magazines and magazine pouches enough for all your spare magazines and have at least 500 rounds of ammunition *minimum... after* you've learned how to shoot this weapon... 1000 rounds or more if you can afford it.

Like food... ammunition should be kept in a cool, dry place.

10-Rifles

Rifles are a *primary weapon*. For the discussion here, rifles have an effective lethality range to about 300 yards and more, depending on the caliber and with the average person's capabilities. *You should have at least one telescopic rifle and a Marksman who can consistently and accurately hit a target at 300 yards* as part of your *NPP*.

Rifles are also measured by millimeter and caliber and fire a bullet from a cartridge either by single shot or semi-automatic. Single shot rifles require a separate hand action to eject and chamber a new cartridge before the firearm can be shot again.

Semi-automatic rifles typically fire one projectile at a time each time the trigger is pulled. Semi-automatic is different from police and military fully automatic rifles where you pull the trigger and the rifle continues to fire until you take your finger off the trigger or the magazine runs out of ammunition.

People the world over seem to have a fascination with what we can't have… and this is true of fully automatic weapons also. They're illegal to possess unless you have a special federal license for fully automatic weapons.

You don't need fully automatic weapons. They cause the unsophisticated shooter to simply waste ammunition. Both Authors can hit their target, usually with one shot… we want you to learn to do this too.

For your *NPP* we recommend one or more rifles of military caliber such as the 7.62 x 51 mm NATO round, the 7.62 x 39 mm Russian 'AK' round or the 5.56 x 45 mm 'M-4, M-16 and AR-15' round for your rifles.

These are needed by your Marksmen and some of your other *NPP* Group Members for long distance shooting of up to 300 yards or further.

Rifles for your *NPP* must be considered primarily for self defense. However, you should also have .22 caliber rifles if *A Failure of Civility* becomes prolonged and you have to hunt game for food.

.22 caliber rifles make less noise, the ammunition is much cheaper than larger calibers and it's capable and more suitable for killing most small game. Purchase 500 rounds of .22 Long Rifle ammunition for each of your *NPP* .22 caliber rifles. Again, much more if you can afford it. How much? Lots and lots of it.

AR-15 5.56 X 45MM Type Rifle

You can fashion a 'silencer' or 'noise suppressor' that's good for a few shots for .22 caliber rifles. *These are illegal* but if there's *A Failure of Civility* we don't know who would be around to arrest you for using one of these. If there is… we're sure if you feed them… they'll just go away.

If you stuff a one liter soda bottle loosely with plastic grocery bags, stick the end of the rifle muzzle a few inches into the soda bottle opening, tape the bottle to the end of the muzzle of this rifle… this will virtually suppress all the noise of this rifle firing when hunting… to prevent *Outsiders* and *Intruders* from discovering you by the sound of your weapon.

This is not our invention, not rocket science and we're not revealing any great secrets. Information on 'suppression' and 'silencing' firearms noise is all over the Internet and in hundreds of books.

These are legal in some European countries… *but beware that in the United States there are serious penalties and or jail time if you make one of these... so don't.* This information is for the time when circumstances permit it and you need it… and we hope that time never comes.

Many weapons of the larger calibers are military type weapons available for purchase, ownership and possession in *most* States.

AK-47 7.62 X 39MM Type Rifle

Even though these civilian versions are not fully automatic, these are illegal to own in some States.

Forget owning one of these if you live in California, Illinois or New York and a few other States. *You must check with your police department to see if you are allowed to possess these.*

Most civilian versions of these military type rifles have a detachable magazine. For those of you who can legally possess these, which is the majority of Americans, we recommend a minimum of 10 magazines per rifle and 500 rounds or cartridges of ammunition per rifle *minimum after* you learn how to fire this weapon… 1000 rounds or more if you can afford it. More yet, if you can afford that.

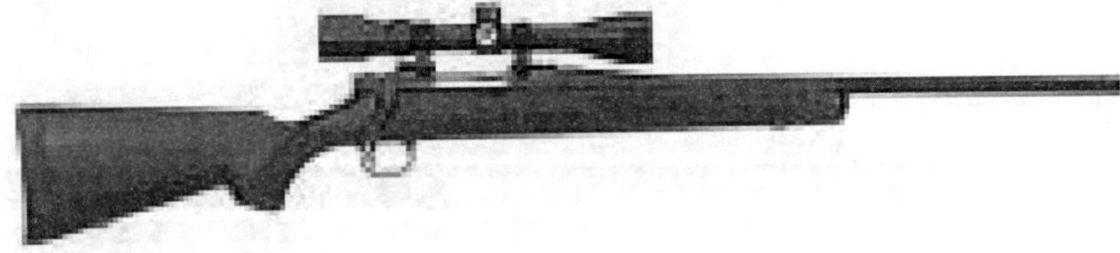

7.62 X 51MM Bolt Action Type Rifle with scope

The Authors also recommend that you purchase slings for your rifles and military style 'webbing' to hold your magazines or bandoliers for your non-magazine fed rifles.

***Webbing* is a military term** to describe a nylon or canvas-type-material harness to which you can affix magazine pouches, compass cases, pouches for first aid kits, pouches for Emergency Food rations, etc. when moving away from your base camp or on guard duty.

This webbing and the belts and bandoliers must fit comfortably over heavy winter clothing.

These items can be purchased through the internet, military surplus stores or gun stores. You can buy sophisticated, highly engineered webbing systems for hundreds of dollars… or military surplus for a few dollars.

Buy the military surplus webbing and with the money you save… buy more food… or what? Come on… think! Yes, that's correct… ammunition! Now you're getting the drift of it!

Like a pair of shoes fit the feet, the length of a rifle stock must also fit you and be comfortable to shoot. Smaller framed individuals will have a shorter rifle stock. Look at a rifle also like you're getting a pair of shoes.

10-Shotguns

Shotguns are an intermediate range weapon and are lethal to about 50 yards with the proper shotgun shell load and most people's shooting proficiency. For the purposes of this book, a shotgun is a *primary weapon.*

The most acceptable weapon in cities with restrictive gun control laws is the hunting shotgun. The versatility of the shotgun is that it can be changed from a hunting weapon to a self defense weapon just by changing the shotgun shell 'load'… or not. A normal hunting load will kill also, but it has to be at close range unless you're lucky.

The shotgun is also one of the most effective weapons for close range defense and is a superb weapon for 'Close Quarters Battle.' The shotgun is also the most effective short range defense firearm for those proficient and not so proficient with firearms… and almost every American family has one.

Shotguns typically fire multiple BBs, pellets or buckshot at one time out of the barrel. They can however, fire one projectile called a 'slug,' which is a heavy lead bullet. Shotguns are not measured by *caliber*, rather by *gauge.*

We're not going to go into how the 'gauge system' came about… we get a headache from it and we don't want you to get one.

Winchester 1300 Model 12 Gauge Shotgun

The Authors will confine their writing here to the most popular of the gauges, the 12 gauge shotgun.

The probability of hitting your target with a shotgun 'buckshot load' doubles at 50 yards over a rifle because of multiple pellets being fired at one time from a shotgun.

The 'load' of shotgun shells can be changed from a hunting load of small pellets to '00' also spoken as 'double aught,' which is 8 buckshot pellets of about .32 caliber diameter. Further, you can obtain *non-lethal* loads of a rubber and other wad types that generally will not kill, but will deter the most determined attacker.

Shotguns come in semi-automatic and pump action versions. We recommend the pump action as specific loads of shells are needed to reliably operate the action of semi-automatic shotguns.

The Authors recommend however, that if *A Failure of Civility* occurs that you *shoot to stop the threat... not to deter it.* The use of this non-lethal round may save you from killing the person that will eventually come back with more *Intruders.* This will attract more problems than it deters.

For your use of the shotgun with your *NPP* you need an over the shoulder bag or a bandolier for shotgun shells. Have at least 500 shotgun shells *minimum* of various loads, mostly '00' buckshot, *after* you have learned to fire this weapon accurately.

Again, like a pair of shoes fit the feet, the length of a shotgun stock must also fit you and be comfortable to shoot.

Smaller framed individuals need a shorter shotgun stock or they will have difficulty holding the shotgun and operating the pump mechanism on that type of shotgun. Look at a shotgun also like you're getting a pair of shoes… it must fit you.

10-The 4 primary firearms safety rules

Memorize these and abide by these four rules when you're training with firearms…

- Consider all firearms loaded until you ***do a physical and visual inspection of the chamber… stick your finger in it and look into the chamber.*** Keep the barrel pointed down at the ground or pointed in a safe direction while doing so.
- ***Keep your finger off the trigger…*** outside the trigger guard until you're ready to shoot.
- ***Never point your firearm muzzle at anything you don't plan on destroying.***
- Always ***be aware of your target and what's in the background… behind and beyond*** your target.

The Authors are astounded at how many times they have found their firearms were loaded when they didn't think they were. One of the Authors shot a hole through the end of his boot just missing all of the little 'piggies.' Maybe it was Mike… maybe it was Jack… we'll never say.

We cannot emphasize this enough… ***always do a physical and visual inspection of the chamber of your weapon to ensure it's unloaded!***

Before cleaning your firearm, again make absolutely certain that your weapon is unloaded. *Rather look a fool by checking it multiple times… than be a fool… who's had an accidental discharge.*

The gun's action should be open during the cleaning process and there should be *no ammunition present in the cleaning area.*

10-Marksmanship fundamentals

Marksmanship fundamentals are the foundation of all shooting. As the distance between you and your target increases… the fundamentals of marksmanship become even more important.

As with tactics, every shooting instructor has their variations and ideas about Marksmanship Fundamentals…

…here are a few examples of ours.

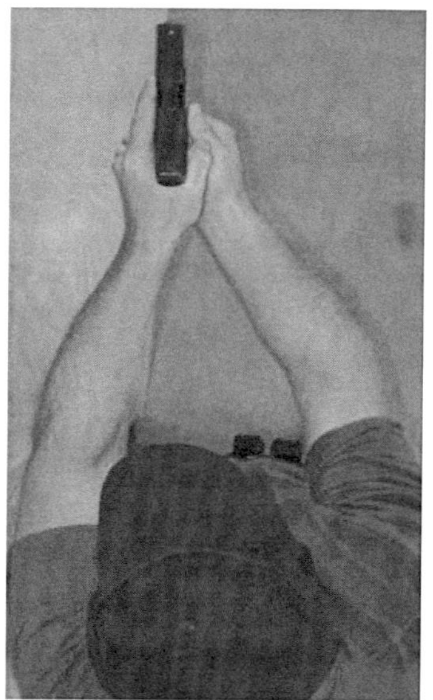

Incorrect

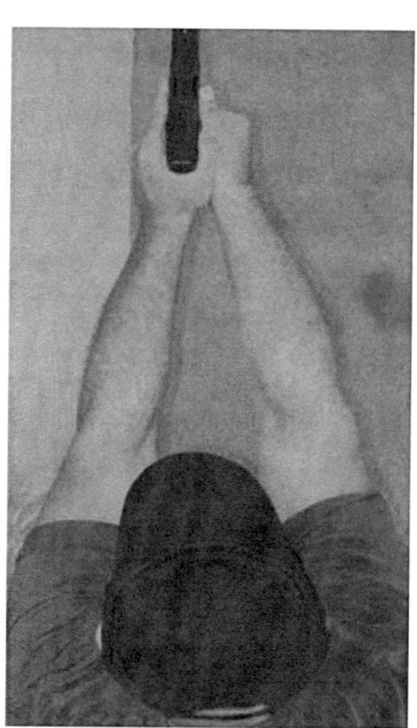

Correct

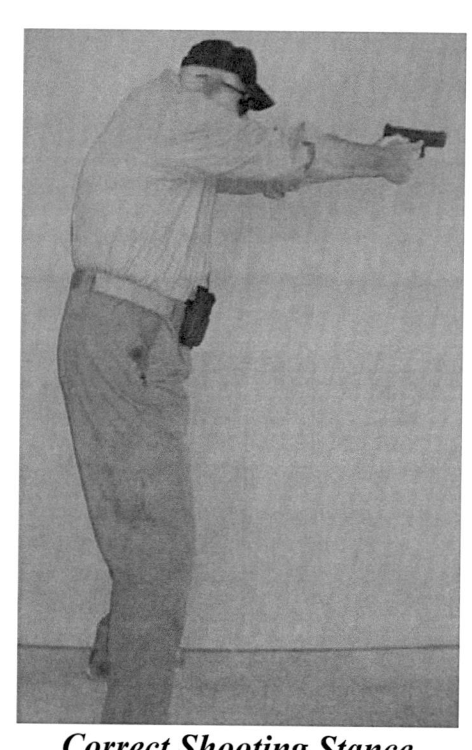

Correct Shooting Stance

Marksmanship Fundamentals are basically the same for almost every type of firearm. We're going to concentrate on the handgun regarding these Marksmanship Fundamentals. If you master these fundamentals for a handgun you will master the fundamentals for a rifle or shotgun…

Shooting Stance. This is the foundation of shooting a firearm. Without the proper stance your marksmanship with any weapon will not ever be good or consistent.

However, that being said, remember not to freeze in a shooting stance if around Cover. Put Cover between you and your enemy when available… *always.*

If you're in a great stance during a gun battle you're not using Cover or you're not moving to avoid being a stationary target.

Learn to shoot accurately on the move and from behind various types of Cover. Learn to do the 'salsa dance' with your handgun. But to start with you must learn to shoot from the proper shooting stance.

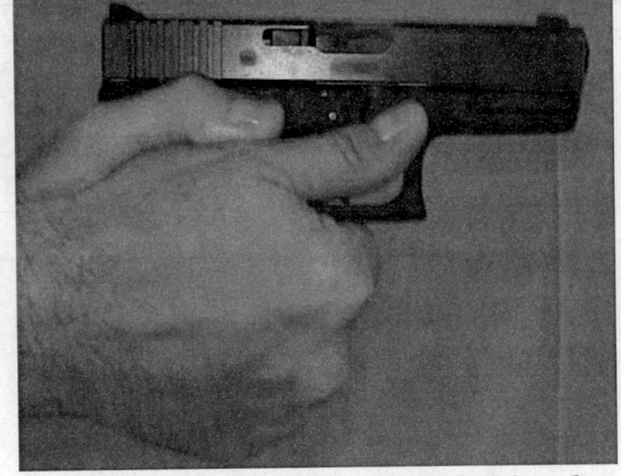
Correct Grip on a Glock Pistol

1. Your Stance…

A. You must make your body a solid and stable shooting platform.

B. You can use an Isosceles, Weaver, or modified Weaver stance. Your NRA Certified Instructor will demonstrate and teach you these.

C. You can be standing, kneeling, or prone

D. You must practice a close quarters draw and stance.

2. Your grip on your handgun…

Correct Sight Alignment

A. Is *established in the holster.*

B. Must be *high on the back strap of your pistol.*

C. When the pistol has been drawn and is pointed towards your target, *two hands must be gripping the pistol.*

Correct Sight Picture

D. Your thumbs must be locked down.

E. You must have a firm but strong grip on your pistol.

F. You must have your finger resting on the trigger midway between the tip and the first joint of your trigger finger.

3. Your Sight alignment…

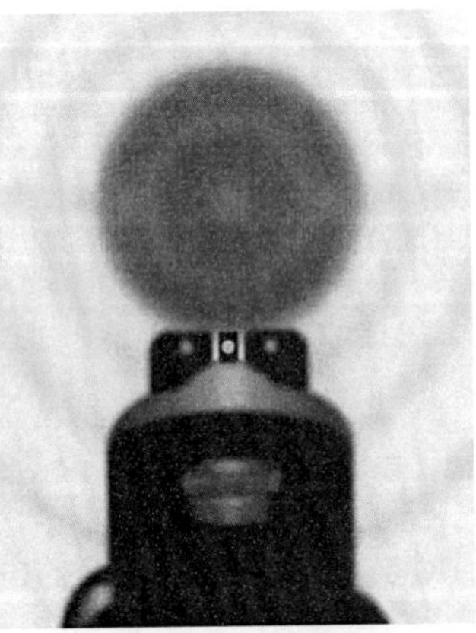
Clear front sight

A. Is the relationship between the front and rear sights.

B. Needs a straight line across the top of the post and notch.

C. Needs equal space (light) on both sides of the post when the front post sight is properly in the rear notch sight.

D. The front sight must be properly centered in the rear sight.

4. Your Sight picture…

A. Is the placement of sight alignment on the target.

B. Your front sight post is in focus… the rear sight notch is blurred… and the target is blurred.

C. Your front sight should look clear… not blurred.

5. Your Point of Aim…

A. Is at the *Center Mass* of your target.

B. Is through the master eye or dominant eye.

6. You must focus on the front sight and maintain that focus…

A. Keeping both eyes open will increase peripheral vision.

7. Your 'Arc of Movement' or wobble area…

A. Must be recognized and accepted by you.

8. Your trigger control…

A. Is the smooth and steady squeeze without disturbing your sight picture.

B. Your finger contact with the trigger should be between the tip and first joint when putting pressure on the trigger.

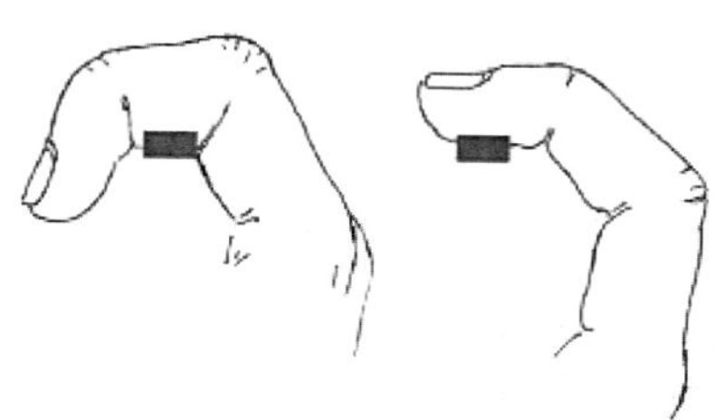

Wrong ***Correct***
Trigger Finger placement

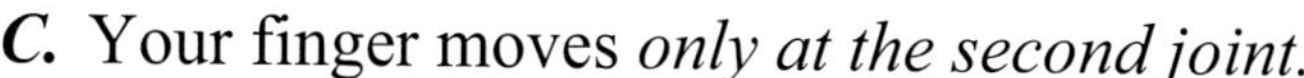

C. Your finger moves *only at the second joint.*

D. Your finger maintains contact with the trigger between shoots.

E. The ideal trigger control will result in a surprise shot.

9. Your 'follow through' is that…

A. All the above fundamentals are maintained even after the round has left the muzzle.

B. You reset the hammer sear by releasing the trigger… you re-acquire sight alignment… and re-acquire the target.

10. Your breathing should be…

A. A normal natural respiratory pause. Don't hold your breath for an extended period… rather learn to pull your trigger during a normal pause in breathing.

After learning the basics of firearms safety, firearms familiarization, basic marksmanship principles and live firing ***from an NRA Certified Instructor***, you are ready to move to the next phase of training.

Tactical training… such as shooting on the move… the use of Cover and Concealment… Cover and Fire Movement, etc..

One important thing to remember when shooting is that "Distance is Time."

That's a statement to reflect that as fast as a bullet moves through the air... the further the distance from your firearm muzzle to your target... the more that additional faction of a second allows your target to be in a different position than your sight picture presented when you pulled the trigger.

If possible attend a Close Quarters Combat Shooting course, or CQCS. There are a number of excellent courses across the country. Many are staffed by instructors with recent *urban warfare* combat experience in Iraq and Afghanistan.

There are also some excellent schools on Tactical Training.

These courses teach combat fundamentals, flanking and anti-ambush techniques of an offensive nature that will help you establish a *Proactive Defense* for your *Neighborhood Protection Plan.*

10-Aim for 'Center Mass'

Center Mass is the area of human anatomy that contains the most vital organs. The chest area from the waist up to the beginning of the neck and in between the arm pits. If you are intent on stopping a human attacker, this area is the recommended target area.

Center Mass on the silhouette pictured is the white and light red chest area. The corresponding lethal areas to hit on the head are also white and light red.

If you point your firearm, be mentally prepared to use it... and to use it to hit Center Mass... *to fire until you stop the threat.* You have to be mentally prepared with that process to take another human's life... to kill.

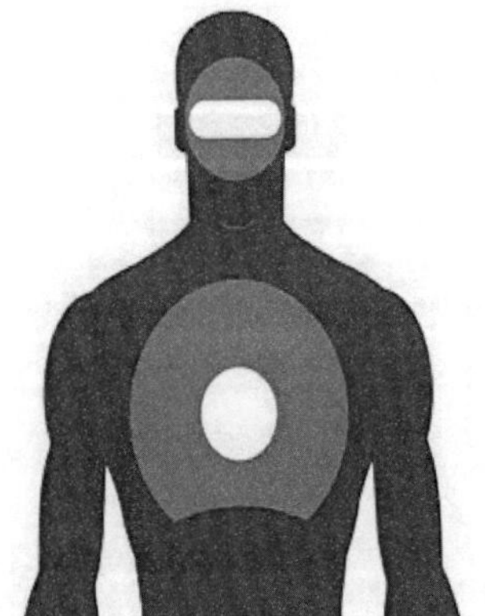

Center Mass

If you cannot do that, do not carry a firearm or it may be taken away by your assailant and used on you.

Always aim for Center Mass. If *A Failure of Civility* occurs, some *Intruders* will eventually acquire body armor... mostly bullet resistant vests.

If *Intruders* are wearing bullet resistant vests, aim for the following areas... the upper and lower legs, the groin area, arms and the head. If they're wearing body armor... use Molotov Cocktails and set them on fire. Shoot them afterwards to be humane.

If you are intent on shooting to wound, don't carry a firearm. A deadly threat is just that… a deadly threat. There are no 'niceties' when you have to use Deadly Force against such a threat.

Wounding. You increase the chance of that threat being successful against you if you wound your assailant.

If you try to wound your assailant, you will probably miss hitting altogether and like wounded animals… a wounded assailant will be more dangerous than one you've not hit at all.

A wounded assailant will become just that… like an animal… *an assailant that just keeps coming after you.* A further danger is that you may kill innocent people behind your assailant if your bullet misses or goes through a flesh only part of your assailant. Shoot to stop the threat.

10-If you're a lefty learn to shoot right handed

Learn to shoot with both eyes open! If you're going to learn to shoot properly, learn to shoot with your right hand and train your right eye to be dominant. Learn to shoot with your *strong hand* and your *weak hand.*

God wasn't fair when he made us, but most of us are right handed and so most firearms are designed that way. Adapt to this *even if you're left handed!*

You *do* need to know how to shoot with *both left and right hands* regardless of your strong hand. This will be the case if you're wounded or incapacitated in some manner and forced to use your firearm with your left hand if you're right handed. Also learn how to *safely* reload with your *strong hand* and your *weak hand... and one hand…* you may have to do that.

10-The 'Walking Dead'

Unless a single shot is to the smallest incapacitating target of the human anatomy… the brain, your assailant will not be stopped 'Dead in Their Tracks.'

Actually, the Authors have seen enemy combatants continue to shoot for hours that have had half their skulls blown off from head shots.

So there are parts of the brain that if hit will positively shut down an assailant's body in a split second that we teach in our Tactical Courses and that snipers learn… but we're not going to go into that because it's too advanced for the average person.

However, the common misconception exists with people that one shot to the Center of Mass is enough to kill an assailant. This is true in some cases, but an attacker can remain alive for seconds, minutes, even hours and days during which time they can still function to kill you or others… *so "Fire until you stop the threat!"*

One shot will not stop your assailant…

The assailant may be dead, but they haven't bled out. After an assailant is shot even multiple times, exclusive of a direct head shot to specific areas, they have about 15 seconds of blood circulating in their body.

During this 15 second period this 'dead' attacker's mind and body can still function to inflict death or great bodily harm on you or others.

Aim for Center Mass and fire 2 to 3 times or until the threat is stopped.

It's like shooting holes in a large container full of water, the bigger the holes and the more holes you shoot in it, the faster the water runs out and the faster it is empty… when it's empty it's 'dead' and *the threat is stopped.*

The more holes you put in the attacker's body the faster that assailant's body will *bleed out* thus depriving the attacker's brain of oxygen… which stops the attacker's brain from functioning… which stops the attacker's body from functioning… and which prevents that body from further attacking you.

Two or three shots are necessary to the Center of Mass to create a quicker *bleed out* that will reduce the remaining time that the assailant has to inflict harm on you.

We're not encouraging you to empty your weapon into each *Intruder*, but understand that to effectively and quickly kill you must fire at least two to three shots into an assailant.

10-Tips to Survive a Gun Battle

There are procedures and techniques you can use and little things that if kept in mind they can greatly increase your chances of survival during a gun battle. The Authors suggest that you write these down onto cards and while your practicing with your firearm memorize them and during your training exercises be aware of each of these items in different circumstances.

Dictionary Definition
Combat
(Noun) Fighting, especially armed battle... Any struggle or conflict.

- ***Imagine the Survival Mentality… learn to get into a Survival Mentality.*** Learn to get into a *Survival Mentality* … that of *determination and resolve.* You need to practice getting into a *Survival Mentality* when training with your firearm.

  You'll need to have this *Survival Mentality* to continue a gun battle if you're wounded… and it will keep you alive if you're not wounded.

  Pretend you're wounded in your strong arm… imagine this while reloading your weapon with one hand then your weak hand and shooting with your weak hand… *having the feeling of determination and resolve…* knowing that if you give up… you die! Practice firing your weapon at targets with a *Survival Mentality.*

  Remember the *Survival Mentality… "I will survive to go home to my family! I will not stop regardless of injury or circumstances and I will continue the fight... I will continue the fight!"*

- ***Keep on the Move.*** Moving targets are much more difficult to hit than a stationary one. *Do not be predictable!* In a gun battle keep moving unless you're in good Cover. Have your opponent guessing at what you're doing and where you are. You should learn to reload on the move… *never stay still during a gun battle unless you're in Cover.*

- ***Stay Small.*** Always try to make yourself the smallest possible target. If going over an obstacle, high ground or a ridge, to low ground… don't do it standing up. You're making yourself a target for your enemy. Go over *low* then *quickly* move into Cover.

- ***Down and scan, always 'Check your Six.'*** Once you engage an enemy with your primary or secondary weapon and the shooting has stopped and that attacker is no longer a threat to you… ***always*** consider there is more than the one threat you have seen. At this point you should ***immediately move to the left or right and lower your silhouette to a crouch…*** *never stay in the same position.*

  Keep your weapon to your shoulder shooting position but slightly lower the front about six inches from eye level. Then scan *left to right... right to left* checking any Cover or Concealment areas where any additional threat may be. Then 'Check your Six'… this means *check the area directly behind you* which is your '6 o'clock' position.

  You must learn to do this drill so that it comes naturally to you. Don't just go through the motions… *look !!* Look for things that *JDLR... "Just Don't Look Right."* Practice this drill by having someone stand behind you in your '6 o'clock position' and hold something that you're unfamiliar with but that you must properly identify after 'Checking your Six.'

  Learn to make what Special Operations Soldiers call the 'Penetration Scan' into Concealment such as foliage. Practice this by placing items back beyond the face of

Concealment… six inches in… twelve inches in… eighteen inches in… until you can spot these items during your normal side to side scan.

- ***Your weapon muzzle goes where your eyes go.*** Train to move your weapon where you move your eyes. In the split second from the time you see the enemy threat to you until you bring your weapon around to point to where your eyes have spotted the threat, align your sights and fire… is the split second that will get you killed. This fraction of a second can mean the difference between you living and dying.

- ***The Authors do not believe in laser sights.*** Learn to bring your weapon onto the target with a good sight picture and pull the trigger in one smooth movement instead of following your weapon laser dot and trying to align that on the target. That split second of trying to position your laser dot on the target versus aligning your sights can get you killed.

  However, if you can afford good optical sighting units for long guns such as Aimpoint or EOTech hologram sight optics these are more than worth the money. These can greatly improve your quick reaction shooting and accuracy.

Gosh… isn't this exciting!

- ***Learn to Speed Reload and Tactical Reload.*** When in a gun battle, there are two types of reloading. This discussion pertains to magazine fed weapons.

  A ***Speed Reload*** is when your weapon runs out of ammunition and you quickly replace the magazine after dropping the empty one out of your weapon. The magazine is changed to get you and your weapon back into the fight. Learn to do this while running. *Drop your magazine and leave it… it's empty… you can pick it up later.*

  A Tactical Reload is when your magazine is not empty but you place a fresh magazine into your weapon to ensure you don't run out of ammunition while you're firing and moving from one position to another or giving cover fire for another. You place the removed magazine in your pocket. It still has useful rounds in it. Consolidate the rounds of these magazines into full magazine loads during lulls in fighting while in Cover.

- ***Tactical reload before moving from one Cover position to another.*** When under fire, before moving to a new position ***always*** perform a *Tactical Reload,* which is a changing your magazine during a gun battle while in Cover. After the reload then travel serpentine or in an erratic movement to your next Cover position.

- ***Learn Cover and Fire Movements.*** Cover and Fire Movement is a maneuver to out flank an opponent or tactically retreat and is a common military tactic. See *Chapter 6* for an explanation of Cover and Fire Movement. Have every *Alpha Guardian* train in these tactics. Again… practice is the key to your success.

- ***Move from Cover or Concealment.*** If you're moving between Cover or Concealment and an open area, if possible, move from Cover or Concealment outwards towards a clear unobstructed area. Never move from clear areas to Concealment or Cover when patrolling.

- ***Take a knee periodically or if you stop.*** Again… you must always be conscious of how big a target you make to the enemy. Minimize yourself to the enemy. Take a knee behind Concealment, Cover or at worst in the open when patrolling and stopping and do it periodically when your group is on the move if your Patrol Leader approves it. Use the shadows for Concealment.

- ***Use Cover and Concealment.*** Always patrol, search and make your movements, if possible, from Cover or Concealment to Cover or Concealment. Choose Cover that is the most resistant to small arms fire.

- ***Don't be squinting from the sun.*** During a gun battle try to position yourself to move towards enemy positions with the sun to your back or to your left or right… *and in your enemy's eyes* on a combat or reconnaissance patrol unless you're tracking spoor. Spoor is evidence of movement of people or animals you're following… like footprints or broken or crushed blades of grass.

  If the sun is in your eyes… the sun is also illuminating you as a target and gives an enemy in the shadows the added camouflage of shade.

- ***Search down from the High Ground.*** Always search from High Ground to Low Ground if possible and if the terrain allows.

- ***Move wide around possible enemy Cover and Concealment.*** If the terrain allows, always move wide around and come up from the side on potential enemy positions of Cover and Concealment. *Sometimes you can see from the side what you cannot see from a frontal approach position.* Remember… flank… flank… flank! *Flank your enemy… and always protect your flank against the enemy flanking you.*

- ***Learn to hit targets that are on the Move.*** You must learn to hit targets on the move… this means leading the target. This is sighting your weapon slightly ahead of the target to hit the target when it's at the point that your bullet will meet it. You have to lead more the faster the target is moving across your front and the further away the target is from you.

- ***Learn to shoot at moving targets while you're moving.*** Practice keeping your knees bent and moving from heel to toe to heel to toe while moving and firing your weapon. This gives you a more stable shooting platform. Your weapon should be stable, not moving up and down or side to side. Your upper body should be like the turret of a tank if you turn to fire a different direction than what you're walking. Hips fixed and upper torso turning with your weapon stable towards the target.

A simple way to practice shooting on the move is placing a target stand in a common kid's wagon. Attach a long rope to it and from *behind* Cover pull the wagon with the target across the firing line or fix a pulley off to the side and pull your rope through that from behind the shooter.

If a person is pulling the rope in front of the line of the shooter they must be in protective Cover from the shooter and protective Cover from bullet ricochets that might come laterally from the target area. *This is a very simple and effective way to learn how to hit moving targets but it takes a practice to master this...*

... and Johnny is probably going to get a new Red Rider wagon for Christmas.

- ***Practice Firing at Targets behind Cover.*** Practice firing at targets that are behind Cover. You can count on approximately 85% of opponents being right handed and will appear to *your* left side of Cover when they come out to shoot at you because they're right handed. During lulls when they're in Cover behind these positions, aim to where you think they will be on *your* left side of their Cover and be ready for them to poke their snout out on that side.

- ***Learn to use Drake Shooting Techniques***. 'Drake Shooting' is basically 'Flushing Out by Weapon Fire' tactics. If it *JDLR* and the circumstances permit... fire into the Cover or Concealment area. You do not have to see enemy movement to use this technique. We used this technique to flush out terrorists we were pursuing but had temporarily lost sight of.

Use the Skipping Rounds technique when you Drake Shoot by firing six to twelve inches just to the front of the target you're firing at. Practice this at a firing range.

Set up a cardboard target *and fire six to twelve inches into the gravel in front of it... your bullet and debris strike will look like a shotgun hit the target.*

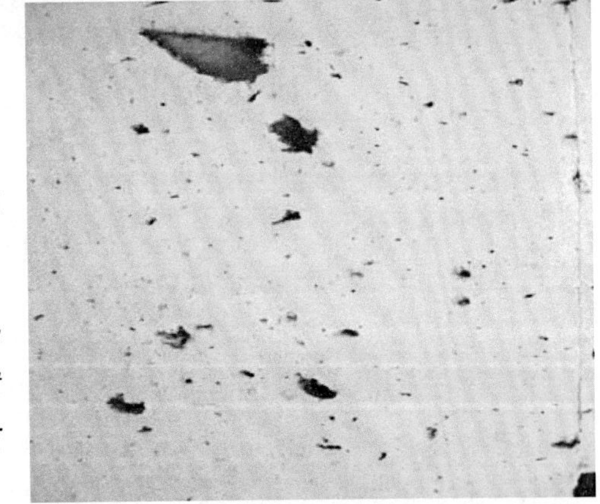

Effect of Skipping Rounds from one bullet...
Notice bullet keyhole effect

The photo shows the effect on a cardboard target from one Skipping Rounds bullet. This bullet caused impacts on about a one foot square area. This turns your rifle into a shotgun.

Drake shooting is very effective as most enemy tend to want to make a run for it as they think they've actually been seen... when they haven't. Be ready to shoot at a target on the move immediately after Drake Shooting into Cover and Concealment areas. In the real world make certain it's not your own Group Members.

- ***Don't Silhouette yourself.*** A silhouette is an outline that appears dark against a light background. This principle applies when moving towards the enemy over a hill or obstacle… into a darker area from a lighted area… or walking through a doorway into a dark room.

  A Silhouetted Person

  You are the outline that appears against the light background. The lighter background will silhouette you and make you the perfect target. If you have to move through a lighter to darker area … *go in or over low and do it quickly.*

  Standing in a doorway is commonly called standing in the Fatal Funnel. Criminals and your enemies will know of this. They'll know that you'll come through the door so they plan on shooting you when you come in that way. *Don't be predictable…* use a window or some other entry point as an alternative. Be an 'Indian in the Shadows' until you know what's going on around you.

  If going over a hill or obstacle don't do it standing up. You're making yourself into the perfect target for the enemy. Get on your belly and move over to the other side and into Cover *quickly.*

  Remember anytime you have light at your back going into a less lighted or dark area or over a hill or obstacle you are making a clear target of yourself… a great target! Like that black silhouette target you shot holes through at the range.

- ***Never shoot over a vehicle.*** Use the front or rear bumper areas to shoot from behind a vehicle… otherwise you may as well stand in the open. That's how little protection a vehicle gives you… actually it's worse because a bullet will create more danger to you passing through most parts of a vehicle as it fragments like a shotgun.

  The best vehicle Cover is the engine block or the axles for stopping rounds, but a vehicle is poor Cover. When shooting at an enemy behind a vehicle, remember to use the *Skipping Rounds* technique.

- ***Learn Long Distance Shooting.*** Long distance shooting is important to your *NPP.* You might want consider practicing out to 300 or more yards with a large caliber rifle. Learn to hit a target with a pistol out to 50 and 75 yards range.

- ***Shooting Down and Shooting Up.*** Learn to shoot uphill or downhill. The trajectory of your bullet will be different than if you are firing at a target on the same level as you are. Learn to adjust your sight picture for both various angles of uphill and down hill combined with different distances.

- ***Don't play peek a boo!*** If you can see the target… chances are the target can see you! Keep in the best Cover you can and expose your self only when necessary, never from the same place twice and when doing so move if possible.

  Don't be predictable… don't pop your head up to shoot where an enemy last saw you shoot from. They will have their sights zeroed in on that area waiting for your head to show so they can ventilate it. Don't look around Cover from the same position twice.

- ***Learn Low Light Shooting.*** Keeping your night vision is keeping your eyes adjusted to the dark. Stay away from lighted places when on duty at night. If you have to use a flashlight to read something, use a red or green filter. This keeps your night vision from adjusting back to white light condition and as a bonus you don't compromise your position.

  Keep your eyes in low light condition so you can hit what you're shooting at. Before moving from a light area into a dark area don't stop before you enter. While in Cover close your *strong* eye to dilate that eye for the dark. This allows you to see better when you move into the dark.

  Then *quickly* move into the dark area immediately backing yourself into an area out of the silhouette of back light and scan quickly right to left with your weapon. Keep from rubbing your gear against anything which will reveal your position by noise.

  Your eyes will become fully accustomed to the dark minimizing your chances of not being able to accurately fire at the enemy. Getting killed is another way your eyes become accustomed to the dark.

- ***Remember night time gun battle muzzle flash.*** When firing your weapon your muzzle flash will reveal your position in the dark. When fighting at night or low light conditions, move away from the last position you fired from, immediately after you fire. An enemy will return fire to where they last saw your muzzle flash.

  Conversely… aim for your enemy's last known muzzle flash when firing because they probably haven't read this book so they don't know this tactic.

  Know that at night a burning cigarette can be seen from 1 mile away. This will reveal your position just as a flashlight can reveal your position. Cigarette smoke can reveal your position by smell or sight.

  Flashlights combined with or on weapons for night time searching is a whole separate issue which we're not going to go into. The Authors believe that when fighting at night… learn to fight in the dark… make the darkness your friend, your buddy and your helper… not your enemy.

- ***Firing from a door, window or Cover.*** Firing to the left out a window or doorway or from behind Cover exposes less of the body for a right handed shooter than firing out the right side of the window or doorway. If you're right handed and have to fire out of the right side of a door or window or from the right side of Cover, switch your weapon to your weak hand to expose less of yourself.

  Never hang out a window or expose yourself or your weapon to the enemy on the ground. Set your window firing positions back from the window at an angle to conceal yourself from outside view. Wet the area in front of your weapon to prevent your position being revealed by your weapon muzzle blast.

  You should always be 'In the Shadows' to observe and be firing from 'In the Shadows' as seen from outside the building.

- ***Use hollow point bullets.*** Neither Author wants to get shot with *any* caliber or bullet… and especially not with a hollow point bullet. Simply put, a hollow point bullet expands when it hits because it has an indentation or 'hollow' spot at its point that causes it to get bigger when it hits the target.

  A crude example would be the difference in getting hit in the back of the head with a half inch tree branch versus getting hit with a 2 x 4. One would smart but the other would knock you out cold or kill you.

  By the Geneva Convention this type of ammunition is not allowed to be used in warfare, but law enforcement and civilian self defense use is allowed.

  Most hollow point ammunition such as the type used by law enforcement has tremendous expansion. A 9MM hollow point round… which is about .35 inch or a little more than one third of an inch… recently tested by one of the Authors expanded to the diameter of over one inch. Not all hollow points are the same, so inquire or test before you stock up on these.

- ***Learn to single hand reload your weapon with either hand.*** You must be able to take the safety off your firearm with one hand easily and reload with one hand competently… learn to do this safely using either hand with your pistol, rifle and shotgun… under time constraints. Remember… *training under time constraints simulates the real threat.*

- ***Learn weak hand shooting.*** If you're right handed… learn to shoot and hit the target with your left hand. If you're left handed… learn to shoot with your right hand. You should learn to shoot with your right hand as your dominant hand as we recommended before.

- ***Know how your weapon works in the dark.*** Blindfold yourself and carry out all the mechanical functions of your weapon including reloading it in the dark. Know by feel, not by sight, where your magazine pouches and holster are. Practice reloading from magazine pouches as if the night is pitch black and you can't see your fingers in front of your nose.

- ***Shooting through glass.*** Know that when shooting through glass that it is anyone's guess where the bullet will go after it passes through the glass. Some snipers have mistakenly killed hostages close to kidnappers when shooting through glass even though they had the cross hairs of their sniper rifle trained dead square on the kidnapper's noggin.

  Whether this is a plate glass 'store front' window, an apartment window or the glass of a door, single, double or triple pane glass, where the bullet will go is generally unpredictable. Some types of bullets will disintegrate hitting glass causing a 'shotgun' effect and others will have little effect on the enemy's side of the glass.

  It is not just the angle the bullet strikes the glass. There is a complex set of ballistic dynamics involved with this. Shooting through the windshield of a car brings the same result so if you're shooting to kill the driver you have to put a number of shots at your target through the windshield.

- ***Use of night sights.*** Use of night sights on pistols and long guns is recommended if your *NPP* can afford this equipment. This can give your Group Members 'that little extra edge' in observation or may give you the advantage to win a gun battle in the dark. Remember to move positions each time after you fire your weapon. Move from Cover to Cover.

- ***Learn Close Quarters Combat techniques or some basic Hand to Hand Combat.*** Never let anyone you don't know or trust *within one and a half arms length of you.* If you do get into a position closer than that and it becomes combative these are some quick ways to get far enough away to bring your firearm back into play to deal with the attacker.

  Palm Strike. If you're walking with your pistol in a holstered position and an attacker approaches you from the front or rear, quickly *clamp down on your pistol* with your strong hand and turn your pistol side away from them. With your weak hand, quickly make several palm strikes with your palm flat open to the attacker's nose. Break away… leading with your pistol side the furthest from the attacker… draw and engage the attacker with your firearm.

  Push away or jab them in the eye. You may just simply push the attacker away or jab them in an eye with your fingers together like a knife to get enough room between them and you… then use your weapon.

Improvise. You and your adrenaline will come up with other ways to distance yourself if too close a contact occurs in a combat situation. A Hand to Hand Combat situation in the word of Unarmed Combat Instructors becomes *"Up Close and Personal."* Don't unnecessarily let it get *Up Close and Personal* where you can't use your firearm or weapon.

Be alert and *avoid* creating the situation. Remember... *"It's not the dog in the fight... but it's the fight in the dog!"* We've seen some small people kick butt of big people.

- ***Wear Body Armor or bullet resistant vests.*** These are not truly bullet or knife proof. They are designed for different levels of protection. The higher the level indicator... the more protection.

  These give protection to Center Mass vital organs against *most* pistol bullets. They *will not stop large caliber or high velocity rifle bullets* unless they have ballistic ceramic plates in them.

  In *A Failure of Civility*, *Intruders* will eventually have body armor and bullet resistant vests. They will get theirs from Armories and from law enforcement and SWAT teams they have taken down.

- ***Don't Trust.*** Do not trust any *Outsider* until you know they're disarmed... even if they're smiling and whether they're a child of 6 or a man of 95 years... or wounded and surrendering. Remember never let your guard down. *Consider all unknowns as a threat until you are absolutely certain... that they are not a threat.*

Always keep your eye on the Intruder or Outsider's hands.

The eyes don't kill... the hands will kill you.

On your Entry/Exit Control Point there should be two Group Members... one as the Cover Group Member and the other as the *approach* Group Member. One Group Member should approach and talk to the *Outsider*. That approach Group Member must never allow the *Outsider* to get within his defensive space... one and a half arm lengths *or more*.

The *approach* Group Member converses, inspects and watches the unknown for any strange behavior... remember *JDLR!* The *approach* Group Member's secondary role is to *keep his peripheral vision on the back drop area while keeping the Outsider's hands in view.*

The Cover Group Member is basically the security for the approach Group Member. His primary concern is the area behind the *Outsider*. He keeps a watch on all areas where a hidden threat could be. Remember both approach and cover Group Members should conduct their business from Cover if possible.

- ***Learn to use the SAS pistol close cover technique.*** A pistol is heavy and becomes much more difficult to hold upright with an extended arm the longer you hold it.

  One of the Authors learned this from a former British SAS Instructor. If you are aiming a pistol to cover a Group Member who is searching an *Outsider* or *Intruder* or you are detaining them for a long period of time, this is the rest position that will not fatigue your arm.

  Extend your strong arm with the pistol out and canted sideways like a gang banger shoots his. Prop your elbow against your side with your hand supporting your strong arm elbow. This in essence allows you to 'rest' your pistol arm on your weak side arm and body.

  This position of covering with a pistol shouldn't be used for over 10 yards because of accuracy issues.

- ***Use the Skipping Rounds technique.*** This turns a rifled weapon projectile or bullet into a shotgun effect from bullet fragmentation and debris splatter from ground strikes.

  Aim at the ground *slightly in front* of your target. Using this technique will make your enemy wish he'd gone to church instead of showing up at your place on Sunday.

  This photo shows the effect of 5 bullets fired from a 7.62 mm rifle just in front of the target. There are over 100 holes through this relatively heavy cardboard. From impact, rounds will travel as much as 2" to 12" off the ground.

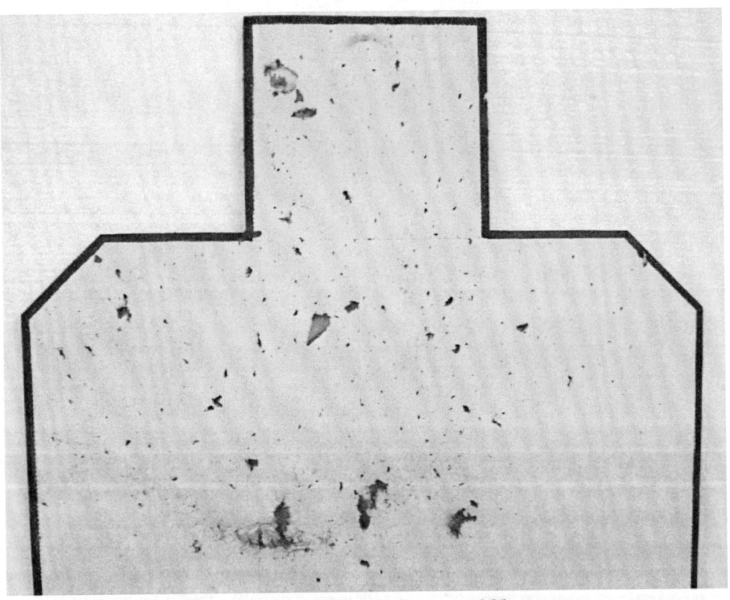

Skipping Rounds effect on a silhouette target from 5 bullets… over 100 holes.

> *We're not promoting Skipping Rounds over basic marksmanship and firing at Center Mass. Shoot to Stop the Threat and aim for Center Mass. Skipping Rounds is a great technique to use when circumstances warrant it.*

Even though this target was in a gravel and sand area it has propelled a lot of rock and sand debris into the target along with the bullet. Hard surface such as concrete or asphalt will not have as much fragmentation effect but will still create secondary debris strikes.

Skipping Rounds will most likely cause lower extremity hits in standing targets or fatal hits on prone or crouching targets.

On dirt, gravel or sand it will create a shotgun effect throwing penetrating debris in your target's eyes and face if they're in a prone position. On concrete and asphalt it's also deadly.

This technique can also be used when only feet or lower legs are visible to you. Skipping Rounds is very lethal when firing under a vehicle slightly in front of targets taking Cover behind vehicles.

A historical illustration of the lethality of Skipping Rounds...

In an operation code named Operation Nifty Package, which would have normally been assigned to the Army Rangers, the elite Navy SEALS needlessly lost men.

Their causalities were mostly from the result of poorly aimed enemy semi automatic and automatic weapons fire during an assault on Panamanian strongman Manuel Noriega's Aircraft hanger in the Panama Invasion. The operation's purpose was to deny Noriega a means of escape and was successful in doing so.

However, after sinking Noriega's boat, the SEALS assaulted across the concrete and blacktop runway and aircraft taxi areas. The SEALS are one of the best Special Operation units in the world, but the officer planning this mission didn't listen to others and take the danger of assaulting across this runway seriously into account when planning this mission. It resulted in the needless death of four SEALs' killed and nine wounded.

Other factors were also responsible for this loss. The SEALs' were *silhouetted by the lights of the city* and *were enveloped in an enemy crossfire.* But the number of dead or wounded would likely have been no where near this number if they had not assaulted across this runway. *Skipping Rounds* reportedly were responsible for most of the killed and wounded… and we say prayer for those brave men.

- ***Use camouflage.*** *Camouflage* not only prevents the enemy from seeing you under ideal conditions… it diminishes their ability to focus on you as a target and improves your chance of surviving shots fired at you. When most people think of *camouflage…* they think of clothing.

*Remember to conceal or paint any thing **reflective or shiny.*** These items make you stick out… like a big pile of cow dung in the middle of your Thanksgiving dinner table would.

*Camouflage **everything***. Paint, *camouflage* or at the minimum choose a solid color matching that of the majority of the color of the environment you are operating in. This goes for weapons, webbing, boots, hats, clothing… everything!

> *When you paint clothing and other items as camouflage... make the colors and schemes standard throughout your NPP. This helps keep Friendly Fire Incidents from occurring.*

Camouflage paint your face, hands and neck… any skin that shows. Use military face paint kits… they're like makeup and they're cheap. Yes Virginia… there is a Christmas… and you *can* camouflage your clothing with paint if you can't afford *camouflage* clothing!

- ***Learn quick reaction shooting to overcome your hesitation in taking life.*** One of the ways to overcome the paralyzing thought of taking another's life is quick reaction target practice… learning to use time constraints that make your shooting a quick reaction… a knee jerk reaction. An instructor times you with a stop watch from the moment you take your weapon from the holster or the ready position… to shooting a target a measured number of times.

  This can also be done as a 'Jungle Lane' routine. A Jungle Lane is a path that's walked that has hidden targets that flip out from each side controlled by a person in Cover pulling them into your view with twine or string.

  Quick reaction shooting must be done with targets stationary… moving… and with multiple targets. When this is done over, over and over again… it becomes a knee jerk reaction.

> ***Do not look into your enemy's eyes** when shooting... the eyes won't kill you... **the hands will.** Focus on the Center Mass that you're going to fire into and watch the hands with your peripheral vision. Fire two or more shots into Center Mass.*

  Quick reaction shooting gives you the ability to stop the threat to you literally without the thought of moral consequence delaying or preventing your action. You'll have to sort out the moral consequences afterwards… but you'll be alive to deal with those moral issues and to further protect yourself and your family.

- ***Be cool under fire… Learn to simulate pressure by training under pressure.*** As much as TV has taught us the 'quick draw,' rapid fire and canting your handgun sideways like a gang banger when the good or bad guys are shooting it out is the way it's done... ***that's hogwash.***

We best describe this part of how to fire under pressure by comparing it to the duels of the 18th Century. The duelers, intent on killing each other because one insulted the other's wife and his honor in doing so, picked a booger out of his nose at the dinner table, or whatever they so foolishly fought over, stood back to back... then walked 10 paces. At ten paces they turned and fired only one shot at each other... since most handguns of the day were not repeat firing handguns.

The winner was usually the man who took careful aim and squeezed off his one and only shot while the other dueler fired first out of nervousness... and because he so wildly missed his opponent... he was then shot dead by his opponent who calmly took careful aim... and fired. Most of the time, the shooter who took his time was the winner.

The gunfighters of the Old West did not draw as quickly as TV would make their contests seem. Most used their sights and took aim. However, they learned to aim quickly. So the point is to reach a compromise with accuracy and speed achieving the best with both to the greatest of your ability.

This is part of having a Survival Mentality. Practice this through training exercises... concentrate on feeling slightly tense and confidence... and going over in your mind your every movement *before* you make that move. Understand, that unless an opponent is right up close to you... your odds of being hit during a gun battle are not as high as you think.

Learn to put your wife, family, friends and everything you love about living life totally out of your mind during a gun battle. Focus on and keep your mind occupied with what you and your opponent are doing.

It's natural to be afraid and feel fear, but if you're paralyzed with the fear of death for one split second... *the Grim Reaper will come snatch the soul right out of your body.*

Remember that you're the hunter and the enemy is the prey! *Overcome your fear with training.*

- ***Get inside your enemy's mind.*** As you progress through stages of combat, believe it or not, your mind will become more comfortable with it. Enough so to where you can think about your enemy's actions in the frequent lulls between shooting.

  During an extended gun battle your enemy, by his actions and movements... tells a story. Like every story, there is a beginning... a middle... and an end. It's the same with a gunfight. Think about your enemy's actions and movements. Predict what his next action or movement will be... and make *the end of him*... the end of that story.

- ***Don't be too cool under fire.*** After a number of gun battles you begin to think that you're invincible… *that mortal man cannot kill you with their puny weapons…* and that's when it happens… and you find yourself playing a game of checkers with Elvis.

  Be as controlled and calm as you can… but not too calm or relaxed. We've had most friends and comrades get hit because they 'forgot the rules'. In other words… they got lazy, careless or over-confident during combat operations.

  Your clothes will be soaked with sweat even in frigid weather… not only from exertion… but from the sweat of fear. *Overcome this fear with training.*

> *The secret to winning a gunfight is…* ***taking your time in a hurry****.*

My God, you ask! How do I do that?

The military has used simulation drill exercises for centuries… training exercises. They do their tactical movement exercises and shooting exercises *over, over, over and over again against the clock* so when the real thing happens their reactions take over naturally.

You become proficient with accuracy and speed by going to a shooting range and simulating the experience by putting yourself under a *time constraint… safely!*

You shoot and reload with yourself up against the clock. Just like the previous *Safety/Threat Evaluation Time Check*, shooting and movement under the pressure of the clock simulates a real gun battle the best that it can be done. *Training under time constraints simulates the real threat.*

Shooting at multiple targets, reloading and shooting again against the clock, maybe with some distractions thrown in like a malfunction of your handgun or having someone unexpectedly set some firecrackers off, fire another firearm in a safe direction or blow an aerosol air horn as noise distractions during your simulation… is great training and lots of fun.

Be safe when doing these training exercises!

10-Other firearms advice

Zero in your firearms. Each of your pistols and rifles should be 'zeroed in.' This is done by adjusting the sights so the bullet will hit where the sights are aimed. Rifles should be zeroed in at 100 yards and pistols zeroed in at 15 yards.

Use Hearing Protection. Other than the 'kick,' what puts most people off shooting a firearm is the noise. What will absolutely damage anyone's hearing is the noise from a powerful firearm shot.

Actually it damages your ability to understand the spoken word. Once your hearing is damaged by high decibel acoustical trauma, your hearing and understanding of others is gone forever… and you have a constant ringing in your ears called 'tinnitus!'

> *Don't be* ***macho stupid*** *about damage to your hearing... wear hearing protection! Repetitive firearm noise will damage your hearing.*

Hearing Aids won't correct this damage… because they're just that… hearing *aids*… not hearing *restoration devices.* They haven't invented those yet. Your hearing will exponentially worsen as you get older. We know.

Along with good ear protection goes eye protection. Talk to your Instructor or the people at your gun store about this. You also want to protect against damaged eye sight from a firing mishap.

Americans think their combat soldiers wear sunglasses more to 'look cool' than to minimize the brutal sunlight of the combat zones they're in. But, have the wind or an explosion blow sand or debris in your eyes or a blast of hot firearm gases hit you in your baby blues without eye protection and you'll 'want to look cool too' every time you fire a weapon.

Have plenty of everything. The Authors both relate that one of the reasons they're still alive is that they always carried *"One more knife, one more grenade, 10 more magazines and one more pistol"* than the guy next to them carried into combat situations.

Weapons are tools and they break just like any tool. Carry spare tools with you. Have plenty of extra loaded magazines for each of your weapons. Remember that a semi-automatic weapon is simply a single shot weapon without a magazine… reloading your magazines in the heat of an action *is out of the question.*

You should use the rule of thumb to have 10 magazines for each long gun and 5 magazines for each pistol. We carried more. You should have holsters, magazine pouches and a heavy belt to hold them or webbing.

Have spare parts for your weapon. Your firearm has parts that can break. Have plenty extra of these parts. Remember to get cleaning equipment and cleaning solutions, lubricants, spare springs and firing pins, screws and any other gizmo that can break or fall off your firearm.

> *Get spare parts for your firearms from your sporting goods store and don't put this off. A broken or malfunctioning firearm has only one other use... as a club.*

Keep your weapon dry. The Authors believe that an excessively oiled and lubricated firearm is a disaster waiting to happen. Keep key moving parts lubricated… the rest of the firearm and magazines completely dry.

Simply keep your weapon clean and lubricate the mechanical surfaces that move against each other. Oil and grease attract dirt, sand and dust more than it protects your weapon or makes it function better.

Keep the inside of the chamber, barrel and bolt face, your magazines and anywhere your cartridges are stored on the firearm absolutely dry. Oil from these areas will seep into many types of cartridges and diminish their power.

In dusty or dry conditions and climates, graphite is a better lubricant. If you use WD-40, oil or the like make certain you remove the excess… or it will attract dirt and dust, gum up, seep into the chamber and eventually wick into the cartridges… diminishing their power or completely ruining them.

This was *"The Luck of the Irish"* for one of our friends… he was shot at close range… in fact at a point blank range of less than one foot with a large caliber pistol. The bullet left the pistol barrel but bounced off his sternum.

He bled all over the place but otherwise was unharmed. Other shots fired from the pistol did the same thing, confirming lubricant had penetrated the pistol cartridges and totally reduced their killing power… and our friend still prays to give thanks.

10-Concealment and Cover characteristics

Examples of various things that you should have between you and your enemy for Concealment and Cover…

Examples of Concealment. These things aid or give protection from being seen…

- Tall grass and bushes.
- Vehicle or open vehicle door.
- Interior house and building doors.
- Being 'In the Shadows' from sunlight.
- Dim light and darkness.

Examples of Cover. These things aid or give various degrees of protection from small arms fire…

- Ravines and gullies.

- A thick brick wall.
- Large rocks.
- Vehicle engine block.
- The Cover side of a brick building corner.
- Sandbags
- Concrete walls
- A fire hydrant.
- A street curb.
- Trees 18 inches or thicker.
- Body armor with ceramic ballistic plates.

The below chart will give you a ***rough*** idea of the protection that common materials give you against the two most presently used U.S. Military small arms cartridges… the 5.56 mm M-16/M4/AR-15 rifle and M-249 Squad Automatic Weapon (SAW) cartridge and the 7.62 mm NATO cartridge which is also called the .308 Winchester and is popular in some assault rifles and bolt action long guns. The 7.62 mm cartridge is used in the American M-240 medium machine gun.

Cartridge	Firearm Type	8" Reinforced Concrete	24" Double Sandbag	16" Tree Trunk or Log wall	3/8" Mild Steel Door	9" Double Brick	12" Cinder Block filled sand
5.56 X 45 mm	M-16, M-4, AR 15 Rifle Cartridge	35	220	1 to 3	1	70	35
7.62 X 51 mm	.308 NATO Cartridge	100	110	1	1	18	18

U.S. Army Chart of Small Arms Cartridge Penetration against Common Materials
(The number of bullet strikes in the same vicinity that are needed to penetrate these materials)

The above chart is vague in explaining the factors taken into account in this study. So much for the military and their tests. Barrel length, distance from target, bullet type and weight, air temperature and a host of other issues come into play.

A quirk of ballistics that makes it hard for most people to understand is that the effectiveness of these cartridges is greater at longer distances than at short distances to up to a point. The 7.62mm NATO round has a greater kinetic impact at 600 yards... much greater than at 50 yards. The 5.56mm cartridge also has a similar kinetic curve… being much more damaging at 300 yards than at 50 yards.

The Authors wouldn't want to stand behind any of these items when they tested them… so for God's sake don't be a jack@$$ and stand behind a 16 inch tree to try this out for real and think that you're safe! In a real life shootout get as much bullet resistant Cover between you and the person firing at you as possible!

The best is to have a combination of Concealment and Cover where you can't be seen and it is hard for the enemy to hit you with small arms fire. If the enemy doesn't know you're there… they most likely won't be shooting at you.

It's also best to know what's at your back and to have Cover there… as long as you don't position yourself so that the enemy can corner you and you have no retreat.

When you've been in combat you instinctively learn to walk from Cover to Cover rather than walk in a straight line from point 'A' to point 'B.' Learn to do this even during *Normal Civility*.

Another tip on surviving a gun battle… pray earnestly to your God or a Higher Power.

In combat, the Authors have frantically said prayers something like this, while they were digging slit trenches with their eyelashes…

"Oh God! If you let me out of this one alive I promise I'll never do anything as stupid as this again! Yes, I know I'm a dumbs#!t...but I mean it this time! Honestly! I'll stop using foul language too! I'll even quit chewing tobacco... I promise!"

Chapter 11
Planned or Emergency NPP Relocation, Convoys and *Security in Motion*

In this Chapter we describe…

- **11- *Planned NPP Relocation***
- **11-During a move… you don't have it… they do.**
- **11-SERE Principles**
- **11-*Security in Motion***
- **11-Making the decision to evacuate your *NPP***
- **11-Questions to consider before making a *Planned NPP Relocation...***
- **11-*Planned NPP Relocation* to your *Secondary NPP Location.***
- **11- *Emergency NPP Relocation***
- **11-*Get the hell out of the Kill Zone***
- **11-Planning for those traveling to your *NPP***

11- *Planned NPP Relocation*

During riots of the last decades in America and European countries, fire was a primary danger. Fires spread uncontrolled because fire departments could not respond to fires in some areas due to the severity of the rioting and the danger to firemen from rioters. This will be a danger to your *NPP* if *A Failure of Civility* occurs.

After some *Catastrophic Events*, fire fighting water sources may not be available and even if fire departments could respond to your area their ability to extinguish a fire would be next to impossible. In a case such as your neighborhood being burned down, you would have to move.

Your only option for your *NPP's* long term survival will be to quickly move your equipment and supplies and then abandon everything else to the fire.

There are other situations that could force a move such as your potable water source being polluted or disappearing… a pandemic or other issues that would make your *NPP* unsustainable where it is.

In this situation Group Members will take as many firearms and as much ammunition as possible for each of those firearms.

One of your Secondary NPP Locations must be close enough to travel to on foot.

If vehicles are operable, you'll have to load your convoy vehicles with as much necessary and practical equipment and supplies as you can, particularly food and water treatment equipment. Retrieve your other supplies from your buried cache later.

11-During a move... you don't have it... they do.

Your *Neighborhood Protection Plan* gives you The Force Multiplier Effect and Economy of Force. This effect made your smaller defensive force much more powerful than the offensive or attacking force because you, as defenders of your *NPP*, are in a stationary position with prepared fortifications of Cover and Concealment.

If you have a *Planned NPP Relocation* or an *Emergency NPP Relocation* the *roles are reversed* and you will lose much... if not all... of the Force Multiplier Effect when you're moving outside your *NPP*. You are prone to ambush whenever you are outside of your *NPP*.

Whether or not the enemy ambushing you is in sophisticated defensive positions or simply on High Ground, they... not you... will have the totality of The Force Multiplier Effect over you and your Group Members.

If traveling by vehicle, you must avoid being caught in an ambush area without the ability to drive past that area. If you're stopped... it may mean the certain destruction of your group. When moving outside your *NPP*, try to take routes that are less prone to ambush and always keep your eye out for emergency protective Cover that you and your group can move into quickly.

You must use *Flanker Group Members.* These are Group Members traveling slightly ahead and on each side of your column to protect against attacks from the side. Further, use *Advance Group Members* traveling about a quarter to a half mile ahead of your main group on your intended path of travel to detect ambushes before your main group gets there. Use these, even if this slows your movement to a crawl.

The U.S. Calvary of the Old West referred to the *Flanker Group Members* as *Out Riders* and the *Advance Group Members* as *Scouts*. The purpose of the *Out Riders* was to protect the main column from sudden attacks on their flanks and for the *Scouts* to track the Cavalry's enemy and to discover ambushes before the main column rode into them.

11-SERE Principles

Survival Evasion Resistance Escape (SERE). By gosh and by golly the military sure love acronyms! They've got acronyms for *everything*! One is SERE. SERE is the acronym for Survival, Evasion, Resistance and Escape. It's required training for all Special Operations Soldiers and American Military Pilots.

Your knowledge of SERE doesn't have to have the complexity of understanding that a Special Forces 'A' Team has or be as sophisticated, but there may be situations where Survival, Escape, Resistance and Evasion come into play.

Unless it's an *Emergency NPP Relocation* where you are effectively 'hastily abandoning your *NPP*'... you will not be in essence *"Escaping and Evading."* Regardless, some of the principles of SERE apply.

Most SERE training focuses mainly on survival and evasion of the enemy. The Resistance part concentrates on teaching those captured to reveal to the enemy as little information as possible while being 'interrogated'... as put pleasantly... or tortured as the reality would be.

SERE Principles.

- Survival
- Escape
- Resistance
- Evasion

Survival. Survival skills taught include woodcraft and wilderness survival in all types of climate. This includes emergency first aid, land navigation, camouflage techniques, communication procedures and how to make improvised tools and weapons.

The word S.U.R.V.I.V.A.L. is used to emphasize the following...

'S' stands for **"Size up the Situation."**

1. Security.
2. Scene.
3. Surroundings.
4. Physical Conditions.
5. Inventory.
6. Planning.

'U' stands for **"Undue Haste Makes Waste."**

'R' stands for **"Remember Where You Are."**

1. Location of the enemy.
2. Location of the Group Members.
3. Location of Water Sources.
4. Location of Cover and Concealment.

'V' stands for **"Vanquish Fear and Panic."**

'I' stands for **"Improvise."**

1. Tools.

2. Equipment.

'V' stands for "**Value of Living.**"

'A' stands for "**Act like a Native.**"

1. Adapt.
2. Observe.
3. Respect.

'L' stands for "**Learn Basic Skills.**"

1. Knowledge.
2. Training.

The word C.O.L.D. is used to emphasize the following for Cold Weather…

'C' stands for **keep your clothing *"Clean."***

'O' stands for ***"Overheating"*… avoid it!**

'L' stands for **wear clothing *"Loose and In Layers."***

'D' stands for **keep your clothing *"Dry."***

A key note… your body needs *2 to 3 quarts of water per day* in 60 degree Fahrenheit weather *with no physical exertion* to maintain the proper hydration of your body.

Evasion. *This will be particularly useful if a large number of people have to make an emergency escape from the NPP.*

If you do get captured, escape and are pursued or get separated from your group you have to evade your enemy. You then become the 'Quarry' if your captors pursue you or you may become Quarry to others outside your group that you'd come across while traveling.

Some suggestions to evade those following you…

- ***Stay off the beaten path.*** Unless your pursuers are trained in Man Tracking, stay off the beaten path. If you have a tracker on your trail, you sometimes use the 'beaten path' to lose your foot prints amongst the others… and if the other footprints are actually hoof prints you're in luck.

  Cattle, horse, human and animal prints on a well travelled path make it very difficult to follow individual footprints. The animals traveling on the same path help to hide or totally erase your foot traffic in these areas. It's actually easier to follow a person in most 'bush' areas than down a well traveled path.

Remember humans are like animals and like to follow the path of least resistance, such as a well worn trail… this is also predictable. He'll pursue you down that trail… but send others ahead to lay in wait for you.

- ***'Rock Hop' and back track.*** If your area has hard surfaces like rocks… carefully move across the rocks for as long a distance as you can. When you're on a surface it is hard to detect footprints. But remember this takes more time, so you have to measure getting out of the area versus not being followed.

One simple way to determine if you are being followed is simply use high ground to observe the area you have just came through. Watch if the bad guys are following you and how they are moving professionally versus a gaggle walk. This is one indication if they are trained trackers or 'Joe Bob,' who likes to hunt, is in the group! There is a big difference between a combat trained tracker and the average outdoorsman.

- ***Avoid 'Track Traps.'*** A Track Trap is an area that clearly shows footprints… it makes your trail like a dotted line showing your direction of travel. All a pursuer has to do is connect the 'dots' in the Track Traps and they can follow you. Some are so telling that your pursuer can also tell the approximate number of people traveling with you.

Stay on the pine needles and hard surfaces. Your foot prints are not that easily detectable walking on rock, pine needles or clear ice, etc. Change your direction ninety degrees from these areas and you'll probably lose your pursuer.

- ***Camouflage yourself.*** Fit into the dominant color scheme of your environment. Do your best to camouflage yourself. Rub mud on your face and exposed skin parts. Put bright or light colored clothes on the inside of darker ones.

Turn jackets inside out if the lining is a less obvious color. Rub mud on bright colored clothes. Poke twigs and branches into holes in your clothing. Use your imagination until you can think with delight… *"Ha ha! I'm camouflaged... you can't see me now!"*

- ***Don't reflect.*** Remove or cover *anything* that is shinny. Take your eye glasses off. The metal clip from an ink pen, wrist watches or a nickel or chrome plated button can reflect enough sun to give your position away.
- ***Move in Concealment.*** Minimize your movement in open areas. Stay in the bush or forest and walk in Concealment areas. Stay away from populated areas. Stay in the shadows when moving.
- ***Get inside your tracker's mind.*** Your hunter will reveal his actions to you if you have time to study them without getting caught first. Don't be predictable to him. Think like an animal… because that's what you'll have to become to elude the animals after you.
- ***Know how to get to where your Group Members are.*** You have to know your Group Members' position, where they're going or where their *NPP Location* is. The sun rises in the *East*. If you put your back to it early in the morning you are facing *West*.

Stick you right arm straight out from your side and you're pointing roughly to the *North*. Your left side is facing *South*. We're not going into finding your direction by the constellations… that would take another book… so read about it and learn how to do it. Get compasses for all Group Members.

The Authors teach Combat Tactical Courses to civilian groups and Combat Man Tracking and Tactical courses to law enforcement and military personnel. Both these courses involve portions that deal with detecting and following an *individual or group of persons* known as the 'Quarry.'

After teaching hundreds of these courses, the number of times the 'Quarry' make obvious and stupid mistakes when we teach pursuing them continually astounds us… some of the Quarry are even seasoned military people.

Resistance. We focus on Evasion, Survival and Escape… because in *A Failure of Civility,* there probably won't be much resistance training needed. If you're caught by a band of the lawless, you'll probably just be beaten and tortured, raped, then killed and left to rot or killed and eaten.

Group Members captured should give the cover story that the *NPP* has… *"Just been traveling around to find another location…"*

Advise them not to give numbers or stocks of supplies the *NPP* has but, *realize… if a Group Member is captured they sooner or later will reveal all that they know. Your NPP must be prepared to have Intruders coming after what you have.*

Escape. You must never allow yourself to fear your captors so much that you lose the desire to escape. Most people will progressively endure increasing amounts of suffering and hunger when in captivity to the point that if they wanted to escape they end up being too weak to do so.

Some people actually start to bond with and become fond of their captors… it's called the Stockholm Syndrome. Don't be a fool… get away when the opportunity presents itself and get to your people.

Escape or end it quickly trying to escape. The best time to escape is just after your capture because the longer time they have you the more secure they're going to make your captivity.

Look for a ravine or hillside to jump or roll into that isn't easy for your captors to pursue you through. Run serpentine, zig zag, never run in a straight line.

The same principles you learned when shooting… apply to you as a target because they're probably going to be shooting at you.

Remember, a moving target is harder to hit…especially for them because they probably haven't read this book. Run in a serpentine movement and pray they didn't read this book.

Consider that if you're not eaten immediately by your captors… sooner or later they'll be looking at you as more than just a 'person'. Look, they're hungry… that's why they were after your group in the first place… *they're hungry for food.*

11-*Security in Motion*

Once the decision to move out is made, you are conducting *Security in Motion.* This is adapting the best security you can to a moving group or column of people or vehicles.

Everyone must stay calm, orderly and move in one controlled flow. You must take into account the route you are travelling to your objective and the distance you can travel on the amount of fuel your *NPP* has on hand.

If you're leaving by vehicle, heavier vehicles must be in front and rear. The lead vehicle's job is to ram obstacles and the rear vehicle's job is to push disabled vehicles out of the Field of Fire of an ambush.

> ***Dictionary Definition***
> ***Security***
> *(Noun) Freedom from risk or danger… safety… Freedom from doubt, anxiety, or fear… confidence… Something that gives or assures safety.*

Anytime you go outside your *NPP* for a task other than patrol or reconnaissance you must provide the people performing that task with a 'Guard Element' whose job is specifically to provide security for those going to fill cars with gasoline, forage food, hunt for game, etc.

11-Making the decision to evacuate your *NPP*

The decision to leave your area and move your *NPP* must be determined by what stage your *Crisis* is in. Again… reevaluate the stage your *Crisis* is in before going on to make a decision to move from your *Primary NPP Location.*

The decision to evacuate your *NPP* and Group Members must then be determined by what circumstances are making your Primary *Neighborhood Protection Plan* unsustainable.

Is your water source is polluted or unreliable, is there is an epidemic of disease in your area that your *NPP* is threatened by or are your food stocks becoming depleted?

Whatever the issue, if no resolution can be found to sustain the *Primary NPP Location,* you must move to your *Secondary NPP Location…* but only if your move will create a solution to the problem at hand.

If there are other *NPPs* in your area, they're probably experiencing the same issues you are. Attempt to coordinate an evacuation with them and make your move jointly.

Remember Strength through Numbers.

This is the balance to your loss of The Force Multiplier Effect of prepared stationary defensive positions.

To determine if a Crisis is turning into a Long Term Crisis or is leading to A Failure of Civility, your must observe and verify the following...

- Is your law enforcement unable to respond to citizen calls for help?
- Is law enforcement unable to maintain order?
- Have you attempted to contact law enforcement outside your local law enforcement's jurisdiction?
- Have local government services broken down leaving your *NPP* as the only effective maintenance of *Normal Civility* in your neighborhood?
- Has Martial Law or a State of Emergency been declared?
- If there is a pandemic or other threatening issue… have you confirmed this… are you certain that this is not just rumor.

In past riots some of these guidelines did not apply. Law enforcement phone centers still answered calls and there was a limited response by law enforcement to citizen requests for assistance. However, law enforcement became so inundated with calls for service that there weren't enough officers to handle them.

The looting of larger commercial stores happened first but then the violence and looting turned quickly to surrounding neighborhoods and subdivisions. Eventually law enforcement was so overwhelmed that they could not respond to *any* neighborhood calls.

If you wait to long, you may be trapped or have difficulty moving your *NPP*. Your objective is to get as many armed people and vehicles as possible in your convoy to be successful against ambushes.

You cannot move simply because you think the grass will be greener at your Secondary *NPP* Location. You have to reconnoiter and know. If you have time and can get a couple of *Advance Group Members* to check out your Secondary *NPP* Locations do that first.

Remember that a move will be costly... it exposes your group to ambush and will deplete your NPP resources quicker.

11-Questions to consider before making a *Planned NPP Relocation...*

Questions to consider before making a *Planned NPP Relocation...*

- Can our *NPP* merge with another *NPP* in our immediate area instead of relocating and solve the problem that is forcing the *NPP* move?
- **If no… you have to ask yourself these questions...**
- What is the cause of your relocation? Will the threat of an epidemic, lack of water or too many armed *Intruders* end up being the same issue at our *Secondary NPP Location?*
- Can we get current intelligence on the condition of the *Secondary NPP Location* by sending *Advance Group Members* to reconnoiter, such as the safety of the route to this location and the situation in the area around the location?
- Is there an extreme danger from people or armed bands along the route we will travel?
- Are roads and bridges on the route we will travel passable?
- Are there water sources along the way?

11-*Planned NPP Relocation* to your *Secondary NPP Location.*

In your preplanning phase of organizing your *NPP*, you should have had at least one, but we recommend *three*, *Secondary NPP Locations* at different distances picked out and at least *three different routes* to each of those locations. This of course depends on you and your particular situation.

This is where real intelligence gathering comes into play before your move…

- ***By monitoring your emergency radio channels*** during a *Crisis* after most *Catastrophic Events*, a State, County or Federal Government emergency agency may relay information on safe locations. This information may describe areas which are affected by the *Crisis* and that are unsafe. *A list of Emergency Radio Frequencies is listed in the back of this book. Be aware that the government may change these during an emergency.*
- ***There may be government camps*** offering a secure location for refugees during a *Crisis*. This would not be the Authors first choice to move to. One reason is that you can count on being required to surrender all firearms *and* weapons for entry. If you are in *A Failure of Civility*, you've probably witnessed the necessity of your firearms and weapons. The Authors would never surrender their means of self defense and certainly wouldn't rely on the government for protection when the government was unable to provide it in the first place.
- ***If your Secondary NPP Locations are not sustainable*** stop and think. Is there another location, such as a secure former work place, a warehouse building, area with cabins, or

another type of building which can offer shelter, security, has a water source and is defensible?

- ***Reconnaissance of your Secondary NPP Location.*** If you must move to your *Secondary NPP Location*, reconnaissance is a necessity before you pack up to move if you have the time.
- ***What to take.*** Weapons and ammo are always the first things to be taken. Next are food and water, then first aid and medical items and equipment.
- ***Heavy vehicles*** should be at the front and rear during convoy movement.
- ***Advance Group Members should travel ahead of the convoy.*** This is critical to prevent attacks and ambushes on your travel route.
- ***Flanker Group Members should travel each side*** of the route slightly ahead of the convoy but slightly behind the *Advance Group Members*.
- ***Have different routes for your move.*** The mode of travel will determine how much you can bring and how far you'll be able to travel. If it's by vehicle, how much fuel do you have? For security purposes, you should make one trip if possible.
- ***Keep current maps of your local area and regional area.*** One should be posted in your Watch Center so the little old lady listening to your radio can immediately mark a map while listening to an emergency radio broadcast that is important.
- ***Once relocated,*** you evaluate your new area and implement the same procedures you had at your *Primary NPP Location*. If this is one of your *Secondary NPP Locations*, you should have a map of the building and the surrounding area.
- ***This is the value of thoroughly organizing your NPP.*** All you have to do is refer to your updated files and all the information you need is there. It sounds overwhelming at first, but the beauty of it is when all Group Members contribute bits and pieces, it creates teamwork and brings overall success to the *Neighborhood Protection Plan* concept.

  This again is why the *Chain of Leadership* is so vital and cooperation and *Strength through Numbers* verses the individual will contribute to your success. The old saying is… *"Piss poor planning leads to piss poor performance."* Plan thoroughly with *everyone* involved with your *NPP*.
- ***Moving.*** Water is heavy. Locate useable water sources between *NPPs*. Beware of contact there. Just as animals frequently visit water sources, humans will also. They may not be friendly and you may attract an enemy to your encampment.

If vehicles are drivable, you will be able to transport more of your supplies than if you have to move on foot.

Advance Group Members travel about a one half a mile ahead of your convoy to prevent ambushes. Radio contact between the main convoy and your *Advance Group Members* must be maintained. Should your *Advance Group Members* be ambushed, your convoy must immediately and quickly pull off the road or path, encamp, set up a hasty defensive perimeter and send your *Response Guardians* to flank attack and defeat the ambushers.

A *Planned NPP Relocation* to a *Secondary NPP Location* is dependent on your Group Member's ability to move the distance of whichever *Secondary NPP Location* you choose. That will be determined by your mode of transportation, the amount of fuel that you have to make the move, how many Group Members you have, Group Members physical and mental condition and what supplies, equipment and provisions you are moving.

You must analyze the *Crisis* that is forcing your move, have up to date intelligence of the physical situation of the *Secondary NPP Location*, the terrain you will travel, the potential of armed encounters between your *Primary NPP Location* and the *Secondary NPP Location* and the *mental and physical condition* of your Group Members.

11- *Emergency NPP Relocation*

It is a last ditch decision… to continue to fight or to be chased out of your *NPP*. Fight like a SOB because if you have to do an *Emergency NPP Relocation* you will lose most of your resources and the advantages of your *NPP* built up defensive fortifications. Unless you can replace these… *you will most likely become like the people you have been fighting off.*

Remember that an *Emergency NPP Relocation* is just that… *for extreme emergency.* If you organize your *NPP* properly, have properly trained and prepared your Group Members, this situation should be unlikely to happen.

You must have escape points around your *NPP* and SERE supplies prepared to take along. Your most likely option for long term survival will be to quickly load your escape vehicle with your *Emergency NPP Relocation Bags* and as much of your additional supplies as possible… then abandon everything else.

Remember what you did to set up Fatal Funnels and Kill Zones. The reason this must be in your noggin is that that's what you may be walking into when your use your escape exits from your *NPP*. Have more than one escape exit and check them out before you rush out the Protective Perimeter into them and get shot to pieces.

In this situation most people will have preselected one rifle, one pistol, and at least 1,000 rounds of ammunition for each of those firearms. They will load their escape vehicles with as much other practical equipment and supplies as they can, depending on the amount of time they have available and then drive to a *Secondary NPP Location.*

You must assume that you most likely will be doing your *Emergency NPP Relocation* on foot. This will drastically reduce the amount of supplies you will be able to take and you will have to leave the rest behind. The majority should have been in a hidden cache as per your initial *NPP* organizing plan.

If going by foot, you need an Emergency NPP Relocation Bag or preferably military style long range reconnaissance back packs. Try to keep the weigh of these packs to around 45 pounds each as you may have to fight on the move. Attempt to have the following…

- You need a 'Camel Pack' water carrier. One for every two people and one bottle of water for each individual not carrying a Camel Pack.
- One bicyclist's water purifying kit and tablets.
- Energy Bars or concentrated foods.
- Bivy tarp.
- Ponchos to protect from rain.
- Duct tape.
- A good survival knife and a skinning knife with a small sharpening stone.
- A folding saw and shovel.
- A lightweight hatchet.
- Wind-up (crank) flashlight/am-fm radio. A small task force flashlight and extra batteries.
- Compass.
- Binoculars.
- Gun/Ammo.
- Maps in Zip lock bags. Have coded marked meeting points and different ways to get to your destination.
- A hat.
- Mosquito net to cover face and neck.
- Cash bills, silver and gold coin.
- No Doze pills or Quick Energy drinks.
- A flask of alcohol whiskey.
- Vitamin supplements.
- Food for three days.
- Copies of all-important paperwork such as passport, driver's license and credit card information unless *A Failure of Civility* is permanent.
- Take your supply inventory documentation if you have to evacuate.

In your pre planning phase of your *NPP* you should have had a location selected to hide or bury your excess supplies beforehand to retrieve at a later date.

11-*Get the hell out of the Kill Zone*

You ***must not*** stop or get out of your vehicle for anyone whose vehicle has been disabled during an ambush, or you simply risk losing more people and other vehicles. The same goes for being ambushed when walking. This is easier said than done if it's your family caught in the Kill Zone… but you have to do it.

> ***If you're traveling by vehicle or on foot and your group or convoy is ambushed…***
>
> ***Get the hell out of the Kill Zone!!!***

Use your heaviest vehicles as a battering ram and punch through any obstacle or push lighter vehicles aside. This is why heavier vehicles are in the front and rear of the convoy… they're battering rams to break through obstructions that create the Kill Zone and to push disabled vehicles aside or through the Kill Zone.

A better solution is to get through the Kill Zone and regroup, out flank the attackers if you have lost a vehicle in the Kill Zone and then recover the people in that vehicle. If all vehicles make it through and your attackers are not pursuing your convoy, don't stop to fight… get out of range of your attacker's weapons and pull over to take account of damage and wounded if that is the case.

Then proceed the hell out of the area continuing to travel to your destination. If your *Advance Group Members* had been through this ambush area on the route ahead of you, this was probably a roving band setting up a hasty and random ambush.

11-Planning for those traveling to your *NPP*

Extended Family and Friends. We are including information on travel for *Extended Family and Friends* to your *NPP* also, because the principles of *Security in Motion* must be understood by them also.

Those who have to travel distances must be prepared to do so in a *Crisis*. Be realistic about them traveling to your *NPP*. If one of your children lives in New York City and plans to travel during a *Long Term Crisis* or *A Failure of Civility* to Helena, Montana… that's unrealistic.

> *If your Extended Family and Friends cannot walk to your NPP from where they are its probably too far to your NPP.*
>
> *It would be better that they find like minded people to join or become a Group Member of another Neighborhood Protection Plan in or outside of their city.*

That's why the Authors are so adamant and believe strongly that you must *Stand in Place.* Unless you have armored vehicles, travel after a *Crisis* has begun is dangerous if not impossible.

You will not have the *Strength through Numbers* advantage if you travel, unless you travel with numbers of people in a convoy. Even then, this is a disadvantage in being able to defend yourself as The Force Multiplier Effect *is not yours…* it belongs to any group that decides to ambush or attack you along your route.

Your Extended Family and Friends need to have all people involved, their NPP Leaders and themselves in planning the following…

- ***Gathering Points.*** Hopefully your family won't be scattered to the four corners of the earth when an emergency strikes, because there's a good possibility cell phones and other forms of communication won't work… and maybe vehicles. It's prudent to plan a meeting location after a disaster.

  If they're some distance from you but live in close proximity to each other, a 'Gathering Point' is one location where they can meet and from which they can all proceed to your *NPP*. Safety is Strength though Numbers while traveling during a *Crisis*.

  The first choice for a Gathering Point is one of their homes. Depending on the nature of the disaster, it might not be realistic to meet there. Establish several alternate Gathering Points with instructions about which one is to be used depending upon circumstances.

  Good places for alternative locations include... A church, school or prominent building in the community… A significant landmark… or a relative's home within a few hours walk.

- ***Stay off the easy and most traveled paths.*** Avoid travel through 'Ghetto' and 'Barrio' areas, metropolitan centers and stay away from government resettlement areas when traveling… you may be forced to stay there.

- ***Leave messages.*** If you're late to a meeting place and other family members leave or you leave before all family members arrive and you're unable to contact those family members, leave a note at that location indicating your destination.

  You need to keep your destination from *Outsiders…* establish code words for your destination and have a weatherproof zip lock bag to put your message in and a hiding place that all are aware of at each of your Gathering Points.

  The key is to make a plan that covers all the scenarios you can think of and to make sure all your family members are well versed in the plan.

- ***Travel back road routes from their area to your NPP.*** Considering the average American has between one quarter and one half a tank of fuel in their vehicle at most times, the major highways will soon be parking lots from vehicles breaking down and running out of fuel, let alone from the congestion of everyone trying to flee a metropolitan area at once.

A number of alternative routes using rarely traveled roads to your *NPP* destination should be drawn up… *test driven* and maps kept in *Extended Family and Friends* member's vehicles or travel bags. There should be at least *three* alternate routes.

- ***Emergency Fuel Reserves.*** Fuel stocks of enough for the entire trip from their location to your *NPP* should be kept at each member's house or at the Gathering Point. Fuel should be stored in containers that transport safely. StaBil must be added to prolong fuel life and the containers stored *outside* homes and garages in safe areas. Rotate these fuel stocks yearly by using them.

StaBil will keep fuel combustible for more than one year, however, be on the safe side and add your reserve fuel to an almost full vehicle tank yearly. Immediately replace and add StaBil to this emergency fuel. Members should have a fuel siphon along. Don't count on any gas stations being open for business.

- ***Dependable Vehicles.*** *Extended Family and Friends* must realistically evaluate the weather conditions and the reliability of their vehicles in regards to the distance they have to travel. A good reason to travel in vehicle convoys is if one vehicle breaks down, the group can still travel onwards.

- ***What Extended Family and Friends should bring along.*** They should bring their most valuable possessions... documents, identification but certainly above all else protection weapons, ammunition, food and water. These are the most important to bring along *and* backpacks if you need to walk. Food should be compact high caloric protein bars or survival biscuits.

If you have to abandon your vehicles… and depending on your new mode of travel… you're going to have to decide... whether to go back, proceed or find another *NPP* or destination. Regardless, carry as much ammunition for your weapons, all weapons, food and water as you can possible carry. You'll never have enough.

- ***When to leave?*** This is one of the most difficult of all issues. When is a *Crisis* going to end and when do *Extended Family and Friends* begin their trip? All we can do is refer you to *the same simple guidelines that we listed on* ***Making the decision to activate your NPP in Chapter 5****.*

If the decision to travel is final, this chapter must be used to brief *Extended Family and Friends* on travel procedures.

If your vehicles are damaged, disabled or break down. If your vehicle is damaged or disabled, that's one thing… but if one or more of your vehicles breakdown, you shouldn't have made the plan to travel anyway.

Until you decide what to do, pull off the beaten path to a secluded area. *"Circle the Wagons"* as they did in the Old West because of the threat of attack, which will be a major concern. At this point you may have to walk.

Chapter 12
Medical Aid, Hygiene and Items needed for a successful *NPP*

In this Chapter we describe…

- **12-What's needed and what priority are they?**
- **12-Weapons and ammunition**
- **12-Water**
- **12-Emergency foods**
- **12-Communications**
- **12-Sanitation and Hygiene**
- **12-Centralized area for medical aid**
- **12-Get a *Ring Bound* version of the *Special Operations Forces Medical Handbook***
- **12-Medical aid and medicines**
- **12- *Jointly…* what your Group Members will have to buy for the *Communal* *NPP equipment and supplies…***
- **12-*Individually…* what each Group Member must have… per each Group Member…**
- **12-Alternative electrical power**
- **12-Specialized Items needed for certain *Catastrophic Events***
- **12-What will happen if *A Failure of Civility* is prolonged or permanent?**
- **12-Vehicles and fuel**
- **12-Preparing your *NPP* with supplies and equipment.**
- **12-Sharing food and provisions to maintain cohesion of *NPP***
- **12-After the storm**

12-What's needed and what priority are they?

So what equipment and supplies do you need for your *Neighborhood Protection Plan* to work? What 'Katunda' do you need? Katunda!? That's an African Mashona word that encompasses *every conceivable item* needed for a task.

The following are broad categories of items that you *must* have… far from everything conceivable. Your climate and circumstances may dictate other items… such as warm clothing and blankets.

There's virtually no end to what you can imagine and the amount of those items needed for a *Crisis, a Long Term Crisis* and *A Failure of Civility,* especially if they're protracted. We wrote this book for John and Joan Q Citizen and their neighbors who don't have a lot of money to spend… so let's start with the basics… then we'll put down a few optional costly items.

We're not going to go into detail on some of these because they're self explanatory or we have previously covered them.

For a Crisis you <u>must</u> have…

- Weapons and Ammunition.
- Water stored and a water source.
- Emergency Food.
- Communications.
- Sanitation.
- Shelter.
- Fire and a source of fuel for cooking and heating.
- Medical aid and medicines.
- Night lighting including red or green filter lights.
- Prepared fortifications and Protective Perimeter alert and security.
- Fire fighting equipment.

For a Long Term Crisis or A Failure of Civility you <u>should</u> have these additional items…

- Alternative electrical power.
- Specialized Items needed for certain *Catastrophic Events* listed further in this chapter.
- Vehicles and reserve fuel.
- More food and ammunition… and then some more food and ammunition.

Now, we've read and heard arguments as to the correct priority each of these items. This is a conflict amongst many people. We believe that some basic form of each of these items is necessary to have an effective *NPP*.

Without weapons you can't keep others from taking everything… your food, water and in the process probably killing you and everyone in your *NPP*. Without food and water you won't survive to use your weapons to defend your *NPP*.

Without shelter in some climates, it would be difficult if not impossible, to survive. We've listed some items with an 'asterisk' which would cost more money but would certainly enhance your joint *NPP* effort. These can cost some serious money.

Have back ups for each item. A version of Murphy's Law comes into play here… the saying amongst preparedness people is that *"3 of an item is really 2 of that item, 2 of an item is really one of the item, and one of the items is really none!"*

Learn to *not* throw anything away unless it is *studied* and deemed worthless. Can the plastic wrap be reversed and used for something else… the tin can be fashioned into a candle holder… the paper packaging burned for heat or used in a cooking fire?

As time passes you may discover a very practical use for each of these items… items you thought were 'trash' and 'garbage' before *A Failure of Civility.*

The Authors are putting a time frame of six months duration for a Crisis. During this time you and your *Neighborhood Protection Plan* need to be *Self Dependent.* You can outfit your *NPP* more to fit your needs and for a longer period of *Self Dependency* down the road and as finances permit, but these categories are the basic items… and you must have enough of each item for a *six month period…*

12-Weapons and Ammunition

We've covered this issue. The basics are that your ideal situation would be that each person has a *primary weapon…* a rifle or shotgun… and a *secondary weapon…* a pistol. At minimum you need at least one long gun, either a rifle or a shotgun per person.

Go for the shotguns. We advise you to lean towards more shotguns in your *NPP* depending on the firearms proficiency of your Group Members.

Your *NPP* should have at least two or more telescopically fitted large caliber rifles and people who know how to use them accurately.

We cannot over emphasize that you'll never have enough ammunition. The longer a *Crisis*, the more you'll realize this. *Realize it now.* Ammunition will be your life blood as water and food will be. *You need to have 500 to 1000 rounds per weapon… more if you can afford it.*

12-Water

Dictionary Definition
Potable *(From the Latin Potare… to drink)*
(Adjective) Water that is fit to drink.

If a real *The S#!t Hits The Fan* scenario develops and potable water sources shut off… people will be drinking from ditches, mud puddles, rivers and lakes without treating this water… many will die within days.

Potable Water means safe drinking water. In *all* areas, water has to be treated. Water has to be filtered to take out sediment, treated with chemicals or distilled or boiled to kill microbes and water borne organisms dangerous to your health.

You must have a water supply source, assuming that the potable… safe to drink… to hydrate foods with… cook and bathe in water source you currently have… may not be available. Again, *your water source must be within one mile of your NPP.* Is there a private well that can be run on emergency power, can you dig a water bore hole or an open well… is there a river, lake, reservoir, or stream nearby? Are they polluted… or will they be in your estimation?

If you live in an area with sufficient rainfall, use your home's roof surface or extend tarps to catch rainwater. If you don't have gutters on your home, get them installed.

In some areas where the water table is close to the surface, a simple 'bore hole' well or open well can be dug. The Authors have seen areas in the arid desert where water will start to accumulate in a hole dug one foot into the ground.

Dig down 8 to 20 feet inside your subdivision and you'll most likely have a water source. You can use a pail and rope to fetch water or buy a hand pump to draw it out of this well. We strongly suggest that you explore digging a well in your neighborhood as your water source.

Hand Dug Water Bore Hole or Open Well

Digging a water bore hole or open well in the basement of a High Rise Building is also a possibility if you have the means to get through concrete and to ground soil. This water will most likely be heavily polluted and will need to be boiled or distilled to make it potable.

This is a dicey situation in some buildings as this can permanently flood your basement. Some High Rise Buildings have such a problem with water seeping into their basements that they have to install a sump pump to pump water out and into a drain.

Storage of enough water for extended periods of time, unlike food, is difficult. There is also clean potable water for a few days in your water heater and your toilet tanks. If you have swimming pools you're in luck. Other than that, it is critical that your *NPP* have a water source that is reliable and fairly secure to access. If not… again… you must look at relocating your *NPP*.

Whatever your source, water in addition to food, is critical in your *NPP* succeeding. Most people can go without food for up to two weeks, however, lack of water under the best of conditions, will incapacitate most people after a few days and all certainly within one week.

Keep in mind also that in addition to drinking water, you will need water for cooking, hydrating food and bathing. You won't be able to eat the dehydrated food you are storing, keep yourself hydrated, wash dishes or clean yourself without water.

Water... The Triple-One Rule of Thumb. This rule of water use will give each person in your *NPP drinking, minimal cooking and bathing water of* ***One Gallon*** *for* ***One Person*** *for* ***One Day***. This depends, obviously on the time of year, your climate, and individual needs. But this rule will generally keep all Group Members functioning adequately.

Have chlorine or water purification tablets of some type on hand to keep this water drinkable. You need to add only one drop of chlorine per two liter bottle... that's about two quarts of water. If *A Failure of Civility* occurs remember to ***immediately*** fill everything you have in your home with water... bath tubs, sinks, containers, bowls, glasses, buckets etc. When the electricity goes out... the water will soon stop flowing.

Save every plastic bottle and jar that has a screw on top and fill every container that will hold water with water while your present water system is functioning.

Save at least one case of bottled water in the 16 ounce or 20 ounce plastic bottles. Keep the empty bottles and the screw on caps. Refill the water bottles with water for personal consumption and they will allow you to keep track of how much water each person is drinking each day.

You make potable water by doing the following...

- ***Filter*** the water **and,**
- ***Boil*** the water ***OR,***
- ***Distill*** the water ***OR,***
- ***Chemically Treat*** the water

Water Treatment Rules of Thumb. In order to live, we must have clean, potable, bacteria-free drinking, cooking, food hydration and bathing water.

Water from streams and other sources of 'unprocessed' water can contain contaminants from sewer systems, bacteria, crop nitrates run-off and animal urine. Contaminated water *will* be hazardous to your health... it can kill you.

Filter the Water. You must filter the water through fine mesh material or coffee filters.

Filtered water can also be dangerous if you use a carbon or paper filters and the filters are not changed on a regular basis. Bacteria can grow within these filters themselves. Some solid substances can be removed with filters, but no filter can remove viruses, bacteria, pathogens, radioactive or chemical compounds and completely soluble pollutants. For that you have to boil, distill or chemically treat the water.

Boiling Water. This is the easiest way to purify water if you have the fuel for a fire. Filter or strain the water before boiling by placing a coffee filter, dishtowel or finely woven cloth over a container and pour the water into the container through the dishcloth. Boiling will not remove dissolved chemicals or radioactive particles... distillation will remove radioactive particles and most chemicals.

To put some taste back into boiled water, pour it back and forth between containers to aerate.

Distilling Water. This will give you the absolute cleanest and safest water if you have the fuel for a fire. In distillation of water, water is turned into steam and collected in another container.

This method requires distillation equipment but it must be non electrical. There are scores of water distillation survival systems on the market. Solar powered and every other type of heating system. Search the internet or if you have a store that carries survival equipment visit them.

Distillation will not only kill bacteria and viruses, but distilling removes almost all heavy metals and chemicals. Filter or strain the water before distilling the same as for all other methods.

Treating Water with chemicals. You can use chlorine bleach and other bacteria killers to attack anaerobes and detoxify harmful elements. All of these additives will have a chemical taste to them.

Inexpensive bicyclist's water purifying hand pumps and water purification tablets are available, but these systems are painfully slow to produce any volume of water. Your *NPP* would have to have one of these for every two people. These are incredible systems though... you can literally filter muddy water through these and have clean drinking water.

Chlorine bleach or pool shock chemicals available at most Walmart and Costco Stores will kill the majority of organisms and contaminants after filtering the water and boiling or distilling it and will keep the water bacteria free for a week or so.

The prolonged use of any of these chemical bacteria and organism killers can be harmful. Follow directions closely to avoid negative side effects.

Storage of water. There are gazillions of container systems for water storage and transportation on the internet and in stores that sell survival equipment. In a pinch *use house hold containers that didn't contain chemicals. If you wouldn't drink the contents of a container... don't use it for water storage.*

Start rinsing out and saving 2 liter soda bottles. Milk jugs are designed to biodegrade but will last for three or four months... the problem is that the milk permeates the plastic and will contaminate the water... *don't use milk jugs. All containers must be rinsed and free of residue of what they contained.* At the first sign of trouble fill them with water.

12-Emergency foods

One important issue must be kept in mind...

Most survival type foods such as the following can make people sick if your diet changes suddenly from Mainstream Foods... the foods you eat daily... to a diet of 'Survival Foods.'

You may or may not receive food in the near future depending on what the *Catastrophic Event* was and what its intensity and effect was. Don't bet your life and the lives of your family members on a promise or 'rumor' that lots of food is on its way. Until you have the food *in your possession* you should not gamble your life on something you anticipate being there. Continue to ration food.

We will list different types of foods that some call Survival Foods. We prefer to call them *Emergency Foods.*

Depending on the duration of a *Crisis,* these foods will sustain life until the *Crisis* ends and *Normal Civility* is restored or until a replacement food supply of less processed origin is found or created by you, such as by gardening, fishing and hunting.

You cannot expect to live for years off of *Emergency Foods* without some physical side effects and you *must* have a supply of *good multi-vitamins* to take with them.

Your Emergency Supplies must include Metamucil or a gentle laxative. You must drink plenty of water with Emergency Food meals.

Store nutrient dense foods. Nutrient dense food is the single most important factor to ensure you have reliable food reserves. It's efficient food because dollar for dollar... pound for pound... ounce for ounce and fork full compared to fork full... it has more nutrition, calories, vitamins and trace minerals than other foods.

Compare a dollar spent today on dried fruits and vegetables to a dollar spent on a box of cereal. Obviously the dried fruits and vegetables wins hands down against a processed box of 'The American Super Heroes' multi-colored, sugar coated, and educational learning shapes cereal with the glittering speckles in it. Clark Griswald would be proud of the 'non nutritive food additive varnishes' they're saturated with.

Like ammunition... food should be kept in a cool, dry place.

Eat what you store... Store what you eat. We recommend that you store whatever foods you feel best suited to you and your situation, but *eat from those stocks... eat daily out of rotated food stocks.* Eat the oldest foods and replace those stocks with the newest.

Purchase replacement items for what you remove to eat and replace these foods immediately to the back of the food storage area. *The important point is to incorporate your emergency foods into your diet regularly or store mainstream foods that are your present diet for emergency.*

MREs'... or Meals Ready to Eat... These are a high energy, high caloric and nutritious staple for the U.S. Military for field use or when cooking facilities are not available.

Meals Ready to Eat or 'MRE'

One of the Authors thinks the other is 'sick' because he likes to eat MRE meals. But they actually are very tasty.

MREs have many, many different entrees and types of meals. Various other emergency MRE type compact/low weight/high caloric count foods similar to MREs are also available through the internet or local purchase.

Because of high volume of theft, if MREs are packaged for the U.S. Government or U.S. Military, they are illegal for private citizens to possess. There is a civilian version that is packaged differently but is the exact same meal as U.S. Government and Military MREs. Just like canned foods... don't eat anything out of these if the bag container is swollen... which is a sign of bacteria growth.

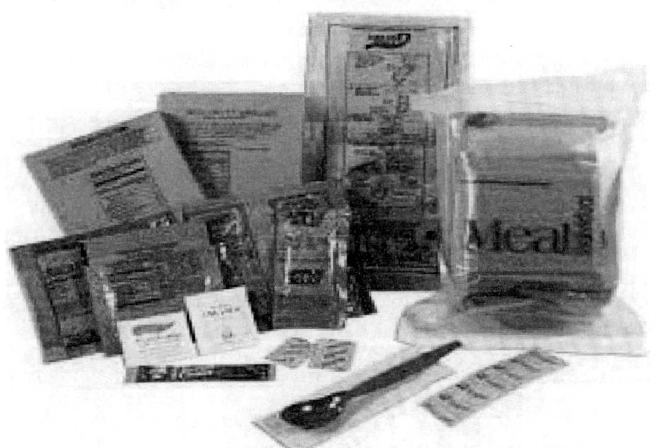

Typical content of a MRE pack

Do not buy military packed MREs off the internet or in surplus stores. MREs have a 'shelf life' of 10 to 15 years from manufacture *if they are kept in a cool dry place.*

Many MREs being sold on the private market

are military and most of these have the majority of their shelf life gone. The longer they were stored in someone's garage in the heat of summer, the less shelf life they have.

If you purchase these, you're buying someone's restaurant waste dumpster garbage packaged nicely… because that's all the value to these there is.

MREs can be purchased freshly manufactured with an optional magnesium/water pouch heater that will warm your main course to 130 Degrees Fahrenheit. That's hot! These magnesium heaters instantly produce heat when water comes in contact with the magnesium. They need very little water to start them heating and have a neat little pouch that you slip the unopened entrée into before adding water.

Be aware that magnesium heaters can be a collateral fire hazard as these will cause a fire to burn more intensely.

MREs' are affectionately known by military personnel by another understanding of the MRE acronym… MRE also stands for *"Meals Refusing to Exit."* One of the Author's sons went through Marine Corps Sniper School and lived on these continuously for a week in the field… and he also never had a bowel movement for that week. We will spare you the ghastly details he conveyed of his eventual bowl movement.

This may sound humorous… however, when it's your butt that's loaded full it's not so funny and can lead to life threatening complications if not attended to. You must drink plenty of water with these meals and we suggest that you consume only a small portion of each meal at one time and have a stock of Metamucil or laxatives if MREs are your mainstream Emergency Foods. Try to integrate MRE type meals with *Mainstream Foods*.

Mainstream Foods. Foods such as Bush's Baked Beans, peanut butter, Spam, soups, canned chicken, canned hams, beef and tuna or similar foods that your intestinal system is accustomed to and that you buy at your grocery store are the simplest way to store *Emergency Foods*. Most canned foods will survive their expiration dates for years if stored in a cool, dry place.

One of the Authors recalls eating a U.S. military ration dated 1959 in 1977. That's 18 year old food. His medic told him it was safe if the can was not distorted or swollen. A bulge in the can would indicate the growth of bacteria. Cook foods over a fire if possible on condition that your fire does not compromise your Protective Perimeter. Smells, noise and smoke will draw hungry people to your area.

Bulk Mainstream Foods can be purchased in lots very cheaply at Walmart, Costco and other stores. A simple method is to buy a few extra cans of each of your Emergency Food items every time you shop at your grocery store. Buy 20 pound bags of rice… they're cheap.

Buy 5 gallon pals with rubber seal lids to store rice and other grains as the rice and grains will not last long term in the original containers. Adding oxygen absorbers or a marble sized piece of dry ice to your pail filled almost full of rice or grain just before you seal the lid will keep these items edible for 20 to 30 years.

If you eat out of stocked food by the method we describe above, you will constantly have fresh food stocks.

Dehydrated and Freeze Dried Foods. These are the best for Emergency Food storage in the Authors opinion and are beginning to be very affordable… actually the price of Dehydrated and Freeze Dried Foods has come steadily down over the years to the point that they are almost as cheap to eat as mainstream foods. These are delicious and close to gourmet when properly prepared.

Dehydrated Foods and Freeze Dried Foods come in complete meals that you just add water to and cook. These are a great investment. You don't have to open four cans of different ingredients to make your favorite recipe.

What's beautiful about the meals is when you need to use food reserves these are convenient and easy to prepare with the minimal amount of heat and fuel.

Dehydrated Foods and Freeze Dried Foods last for 20 or 30 years if stored in a cool, dry area and are fully nutritional when properly reconstituted. Dehydrated Foods take additional water to prepare. If you eat Dehydrated Food without re-hydrating them properly, you'll be certain to get a 'tummy ache'… more like belly cramps.

Dehydrated Foods and Freeze Dried Foods are available for purchase in some sporting goods stores, grocery stores, Walmart, Costco and hundreds of companies make dehydrated foods and sell them on the internet.

Choose to store canned Dehydrated Foods and Freeze Dried Foods such as dried fruits, vegetables, grains and beans.

Dehydrated and Freeze Dried Foods

One can of Dehydrated Food or Freeze Dried Food has a drastically greater nutritional value than the same size can of wet pack food from a grocery store. When storing dehydrated food, it's best to look for the healthiest dried foods available. Get the most for your money.

Vitamins and Trace Minerals. Vitamins supplies are a critical necessity also… especially if *Long Term Crisis* becomes protracted or turns into *A Failure of Civility*. Also, the *trace elements* necessary for healthy maintenance of the body are generally very poor in most Emergency Foods. Long term storage and processing depletes *vitamin content and the amount of trace minerals* in Emergency Foods.

Such diseases as Scurvy, which plagued seafarers in times past, will reoccur if *A Failure of Civility* comes to pass. Scurvy is a simple lack of vitamin C, which the British supplied in the form of limes to their sailors. The British have been known ever since as 'Limeys.' You can get Vitamin C from many fruits and garden vegetables.

Man's best friend and "That Darned Cat." You may be eating them and their food later, but remember to provide for the dog, cat and other pets. Don't count on having enough food to feed them table scraps… *the term 'table scraps' will be an oxymoron.*

Where do I store all this!? You'll be surprised at the space within your home that is unused. You'll be amazed at the odds and ends of unused space you can find to store foods… under stairways, in closets, under beds, out of the way places in your basement… anyplace that's relatively cool and dry.

Do not store foods in your garage, attic or outside sheds. The heat of summer will severely shorten the life of all foods and the below zero temperatures of winter can freeze and burst containers. *Do not buy dented cans* as this increases the probability of the integrity of the can being compromised and being susceptible to spoiling.

Mark your food containers. Use a black permanent felt tip marker to date your cans at the time of purchase in this date format 'P120414'. 'P' is for 'Purchased' the number '12' for the *Year*… the number '04' for the *Month*… the number '14' for the *Day*.

Most containers have a 'Use By' or 'Best if used by' date on them. Again, if the can is not distorted, swollen or does not have any bulges in it… it is generally safe to eat from. The Authors still recommend that you cook any and all foods if possible and when possible before eating.

Slow down! Consume your food as slowly as possible. This may mean that you have to play a mental game with yourself and your family or a literal game to do this. Diversions and games… *again think, improvise and implement.*

The food you consume in one day can keep you alive for six days if you eat only one very small meal every couple of days. This will seem like prolonged torture but it will prolong your life.

You and yours will not be able to eat until you are full to the point of 'appetite gratification' as we do in normal times, because of your limited food stocks. You must stretch your food supply as much as possible.

You will have to *eat slowly* and less than normal. The Japanese have a term "*hara hachi bunme*." It means to *eat slowly and then stop eating when you begin to sense being full…* wait for 10 to 20 minutes and then finish your meal.

This is a rule you should go by even during *Normal Civility*. Consume your food over a *20 minute period of time.* Eat slowly for the first 5 minutes or one half of your meal. Sip on fluids for 10 minutes… this might be a good time to commune with your Higher Power in addition to saying 'Grace' for thanks at the beginning of your meal.

Then consume the remaining half of your food in the last 5 minutes. The mind takes about 20 minutes to sense the stomach has sufficient food in it to curb your urge to eat more. Fluids help to give you a feeling of full satisfaction from a meal.

You don't know when you will receive additional food. This is very difficult to do but learn to go hungry for a day or two before you eat anything. Then eat… but eat only one *very small meal each day*.

Your objective is to stay alive and this method is far better than the semi comatose human being you will become when your body begins to shut down and your mind refuses to function in conscious thought if you're starving.

Starving people the Authors have seen have 'The Thousand Yard Stare,' much like combat veterans suffering from battle fatigue. In the starving, it is a lack of brain neurons firing properly because of the absence of glucose and fluids in the body.

In *A Failure of Civility*, most people will be so filled with fear that their appetite will be that which minimally maintains the body.

Save your containers and cans as they can be used for many, many things in a pinch that neither the Authors nor you can conceive of at the moment.

Eating from rotated stocks of Mainstream Foods and having a 'Survival Weekend' now and then will test the reality of your survival preparations. Have them… they're fun. You'll learn new ways of cooking and it gets the family on the same page.

12-Communications

Your *NPP* needs *one or more* Midland, Motorola or other type of Base Camp Emergency Radio. Everyone should have the same model as your *NPP* Watch Center Radio.

Buy a battery rechargeable, hand crank and alternative 110 volt powered emergency base camp radio with Aircraft, Short Wave, NOAA (National Oceanic and Atmospheric Administration that broadcasts in emergencies), FM and AM channels and bands. These were shown in photos previously.

These radios must be compatible with the *NPP* two-way radios. You need a solar charger for two-way radio batteries and lots of rechargeable batteries.

12-Sanitation and Hygiene

> ***Dictionary Definition***
> ***Hygiene*** *(Greek Mythology)*
> *(Noun) Hygiene is the science and practice of maintaining good health through cleanliness.*

Your *NPP* must operate under the assumption that you will not have water or sewer available for toilets, showers or bath tubs from your municipal or well system.

If your *NPP* has been set up properly, you have a separate Medical Section Sixth Leader that must aggressively enforce hygiene in the *NPP*. Human waste, disposition of the dead and garbage can become a major issue during a *Long Term Crisis* or *A Failure of Civility*.

Failure to properly dispose of human waste can lead to epidemics such as typhoid, dysentery, diarrhea and who knows what. ***The spread of disease is guaranteed unless you take precautions and create and maintain sanitation facilities.***

Human waste… set up an Outhouse or just dig a Latrine. We're not talking about empty MRE packages, Bush's Baked Beans cans and soda cans when we focus on waste here. But, discarded food containers that can't be burned for cooking or heating or used for other purposes must be buried too.

We're talking about p!$$ and s#!t… urine and fecal matter. We guarantee you that you'll be going to the bathroom much less during the first stages if *A Failure of Civility* occurs, but none the less the disposal of human waste is a critical issue to deal with.

It will be critical how you handle this waste. You won't be using the 'throne' in the comfort of your home bathroom. The waste won't be disappearing down that invisible round turd highway to the waste treatment plant either.

Conserve toilet tissue as if it each sheet were a $100 bill that, when used, will be buried never to be seen again. Don't waste your toilet tissue cleaning up spills, removing makeup or for any other purpose except wiping your posterior. Ration toilet paper to kids.

This may sound repulsive, but if held properly, it takes only 4 or 5 sheets of toilet paper to clean your posterior. The Authors have taken dumps in the jungles and out-backs around the world and the few sheets of toilet paper that come in each ration package were sufficient… learn to do this now.

A *latrine* is simply a hole in the ground made for urine and fecal matter. Dig a slit trench three feet or more deep, eighteen inches wide and six feet long to squat over. If you have any feelings of decency left in your *NPP* your carpenter types can build a wooden box with a toilet seat-shaped hole cut out in the top and place it over the hole.

The box should be big enough to cover the trench. If your decency *has* abandoned you, at least cover the hole with boards or a piece of plywood to keep flies down and animals out of it. Tarps or a tent can be used as an enclosure around it for privacy.

If you do have a carpenter type in your *NPP*, you can build a wooden structure as in the photo. Although this seems 'medieval' and is in freezing winter weather as both Authors butts can attest to, it will be the start of your march out of the *"New Dark Ages"* and is a sanitary alternative to endlessly digging and filling latrines. The 'quarter moon' cut in the door is not for laughs… but to vent explosive methane gases.

The Medieval Outhouse

Methane gas from s#!t is harmful to your health, highly flammable and explosive if in a confined area! You must ventilate any enclosure you put around a Latrine or Outhouse. The trenches must be periodically filled in and another one dug to replace it.

Sprinkle lime, borax or laundry detergent, if you have it to spare, on top of the waste daily. This helps keep down the smell and the flies. When the waste is two feet from the surface dig a new *latrine*. Cover the old location and compact the dirt to keep scavengers from digging it up. Mark the center of it with a rock or stake.

Double line your toilet. If you're in a High Rise Building you can also empty the water out of your existing porcelain toilet and put a garbage bag liner in the bowl. Tie the end off after using the toilet and dispose of this waste bag by burying it at least two feet deep if you can find an area to do so or dispose of it away from your building.

A five gallon bucket. A five gallon plastic bucket can be used as a toilet. You can purchase bucket liners or use small garbage bags as liners. You can buy buckets with lids and toilet seats made specifically for emergency toilets… or make them. You use a cheap, thin plastic liner or garbage bag and tie the top of the bag closed as you won't have water to flush or clean this bucket out.

To make your 5 gallon bucket toilet you will need to assemble the following items…

- Five gallon bucket.
- Toilet seat lid.

- Plastic garbage bags to fit the 5-gallon bucket with ties.
- A shovel.

You'll need these things also for your 'bathroom'…

- Toilet paper.
- Baby wipes.
- Anti-bacterial wipes.
- Personal hygiene and feminine products.

Body cleansing. Keeping the body clean during a disaster is important to keep skin sores, transmittable fungus and bacteria from appearing and thriving. If water has to be transported any distance, baths will be out of the question. Water for bathing should be boiled also to prevent bacterial and fungal skin growths.

Tree, Unit shower or Garage Bucket Shower. A shower is the most efficient body cleaning system that uses the least amount of water. A shower can be constructed in an existing High Rise Building unit shower, garage or under a tree big enough to drape a tarp around and hang a bucket high enough with holes punched in the bottom or it. You fill the shower bucket with a water bucket from a ladder.

Take a Spray Bottle Shower. Use a spray water bottle with a small amount of antibacterial soap in it and have another Group Member assist you in 'showering'. Use paper towels or hand wash cloths to scrub down. Water needs to be boiled to bathe in also and obviously let it cool down before putting it in a spray bottle or getting under the bucket.

Wet Wipes 'Pits and Crotch Shower.' This can be refreshing not as satisfying as other ways of cleaning your body. This basic cleaning is necessary to keep rashes, fungus growths and bacteria down. Wet Wipes can be reconstituted with rubbing alcohol if they dry out. Do you see why we recommend you stock all these seemingly 'odd' items?

In America we have become used of modern sewer systems, trash disposal and proper burial of the dead. One of the first modern societies… the Romans knew the danger of disease from ill disposed waste, sewage and from the improperly buried dead and constructed the first modern water aqueducts and sewer systems as a solution to these problems. After the fall of the Roman Empire… humanity de-evolved.

If *A Failure of Civility* becomes prolonged Mankind's environment will de-evolve again. Diseases… most of them unheard of for years… if not centuries… will come back to life. Cholera,

Typhoid Fever, Amoebic Dysentery, Typhus… to name a few will reappear. The mouth foaming and extremely contagious disease called Rabies will proliferate in animals and spread to humans.

The common rat will come back into being quickly… as the result of massive amounts of improperly disposed trash, waste and the abundance of unburied bodies. Diseases like the Bubonic Plague, spread by fleas on rats and animals… may become a reality again.

Again… poor sanitation will be the base cause of resurgence of many of these diseases. Human waste must be disposed of properly and the dead must be buried deeply immediately. This is the responsibility of your Medical Section Sixth Leader with cooperation and assistance from Group Members.

This must be done away from living quarters, being careful that neither contaminates food or water supplies or sources. Bury the dead away from wells to ensure water drainage from burial areas does not flow into your water source. Disease can kill more of your Group Members that any number of *Intruders* will ever kill.

12-Centralized area for medical aid

If your *NPP* has been set up properly, you have a separate Medical Section run by your Sixth Leader. Staff this Section with Group Members who have medical training and experience.

Your Medical Section Sixth Leader should…

- **Ensure all Group Members have personal medications.** It's very important that all Group Members have personal medications in their possession as well as in the Medical Section's supplies and some for each person in the *Emergency NPP Relocation Bags.*

  If you have to evacuate quickly and don't have your necessary medications, it could mean life or death. Most people cannot go more than three days without their medication.

  Each Group Member should talk to their doctor and explain that they need an emergency supply of medication. Some medications expire within a few months so these need to be rotated.
- Oversee the anticipated medical needs of Group Members during *A Failure of Civility.*
- Prepare and inventory necessary medicines, medical equipment and the treatment area.
- Be aware of major disease symptoms and treatment.
- Obtain basic surgical tools and equipment if your *NPP* can afford to spend money on these items. Even a mediocre attempt to save a life is better than none at all if formal medical help is not available during *A Failure of Civility.*

- Read and be familiar with *The Special Operations Forces Medical Handbook.*
- The Medical Section Leader should oversee the processing and storage of potable water jointly with the Supply Section to ensure it's being treated, handled and stored properly.
- The Medical Section Leader should oversee the sanitation and hygiene of the *NPP*. This includes disposal of waste and the burial of the dead.

The Medical Section should be in a room or building in or close to your Watch Center but with enough separation that noise from the wounded does not disrupt the Watch Center operation.

Quarantine facilities and Group Members assigned or volunteered there should be separate away from all other shelters of Group Members.

If your Medical Section Leader is a Paramedic, Certified Nurse Practitioner, Physicians Assistant or doctor your *NPP* is very fortunate.

If not, your Medical Section Leader and assistants can attend many free or low cost community training courses through your fire department, the Red Cross, your local law enforcement Search and Rescue Unit or through hospitals and clinics that teach various degrees of First Aid.

The latter is the minimum training that your Medical Section Leader should have. There is also a wealth of information on medical processes and treatment on the internet and in public libraries.

Read... read... and then read some more... learn.

12-Get a *Ring Bound* version of the *Special Operations Forces Medical Handbook*

We strongly urge you to buy the *Ring Bound* version of the *Special Operations Forces Medic Handbook.* This Medical Handbook covers most major medical and just about every other relevant medical issue.

Almost every Special Forces medic carries one of these on missions. It's one of the best emergency medical reference books available even if you have a real medical doctor as a Group Member of your *Neighborhood Protection Plan* because it *concentrates on medical procedures in the field.*

This medical handbook is a laminated, ring bound at the top, water proof, tear resistance, flip through medical handbook that provides step-by-step illustrated procedures for performance of surgical procedures under hostile and primitive conditions.

It offers alternatives to conventional procedures for solutions to medical problems that can be used in out hospital and non clinic circumstances.

12-Medical aid and medicines

Dictionary Definition
Preparedness
(Noun) The state of being prepared... possession of sufficient armed forces, materiel, supplies for waging war

Depending on your current situation, such as where you live and the skills and special needs of your Group Members, you may need to change the priority or amounts of some of these items. Walgreens, CVS Pharmacies, Rite Aid, Walmart, gun stores, survival stores, military surplus stores, EBay and the internet are sources for all of these items.

Your *NPP* needs a minimal communal First Aid. To make a First Aid kit, collect the items on the following list. You should tailor this kit to fit the needs of your *NPP*. Assemble them into small suitcases or other containers. Ideally, the containers should be waterproof.

In addition, keep all items in sealable bags to keep moisture out and to keep you kit orderly. Once these containers are complete, store them in an easily accessible area of the Group Member's home or unit that will be designated as your Medical Section facility in time of *A Failure of Civility*. You should also make a smaller First Aid Kit as one of your *Emergency NPP Relocation Bags.*

This list is a suggestion for what to store with your Communal NPP Medical Kit. Add extras if you can…

☐ Antibiotics (a must). Penicillin or Amoxicillin for those allergic to Penicillin. We ***do not*** recommend animal antibiotics for human use as some people recommend.

☐ Cold and cough medicine.

☐ Cough medication.

☐ Ibuprofen or equivalent pain reliever.

☐ Tylenol or equivalent pain reliever (Include baby dosages if applicable).

☐ Aleve or equivalent pain reliever.

☐ Aspirin pain reliever and *quick release aspirin* for heart attack.

☐ Antacid.

☐ Syrup of Ipecac to induce vomiting.

☐ Diarrhea remedy.

☐ Constipation medication.

☐ Antibiotic ointment.

☐ Bandages, all sizes (100 count or more each size).

☐ Chemical Instant Cold and Hot Packs.

☐ Sun screen/block.

☐ Lip balm or lip medication.

☐ Vaseline.

☐ Triangular bandages.

☐ Assorted gauze pads.

☐ Sterile gauze roll.

☐ First aid tape. Common grade Duct Tape is a Special Forces medic's alternative tape.

☐ Compression bandages (2 or more) or a supply of feminine pads for major cut, puncture and gunshot wound bandages.

☐ Tourniquets. Each *Alpha and Bravo Guardians* should carry one along with a compression bandage at all times.

☐ Butterfly closures, needles and white thread (non dyed thread).

☐ Super Glue and Liquid Bandage for wound closure.

☐ Cotton balls, swabs and Q Tips.

☐ Small and large scissors to cut tape and clothing.

☐ *Non battery powered* Medical Thermometer.

☐ Large and small tweezers.

☐ Large and Small Splints-Popsicle sticks or tongue suppressers for finger breaks-Precut *flat pieces* of wood for larger bone factures and breaks.

☐ Safety pins.

☐ Multi purpose Swiss type knife or multi tool.

☐ Small flashlight with spare batteries or hand crank flashlight for examination.

☐ Eye protection, masks and medical rubber gloves.

☐ Mucinex or similar type mucus relieving medicine to relieve fluids in the chest to prevent pneumonia in children and adults.

☐ Benadryl or similar anti allergen.

☐ Vicks Vapor Rub.

☐ Sterilization equipment for wounds and cuts as well as for your Medical Section surface areas and surgical instruments. Rubbing alcohol, hydrogen peroxide, Listerine mouth wash, etc. Buy Chlorhexidine for washing wounds, Tincture of Mercurochrome and Iodine. *Hydrogen peroxide comes in different strengths. Buy the 3% over the counter version. Do not use the 35% or anything around that percentage... it will burn your skin and is harmful to ingest.*

☐ 'Tincture of Green Soap.' Cheap. Used to clean and disinfect surgical instruments by hospitals.

☐ Basic surgical instrument kit.

☐ Blood pressure gage.

☐ Buy or make a stretcher.

☐ Old white cotton tee shirts for sterile rags.

☐ High intensity solar powered sidewalk lights for night time medical aid illumination .

This list is a suggestion for hygiene, cleaning products and soaps to store with your Communal NPP supplies...

Keep these items in your Supply Section and in separate 5-gallon buckets or bags as part of your Emergency NPP Relocation Bags...

☐ Lots and lots and lots of *leak proof* plastic garbage bags. At least a 13 gallon size... Like ammunition... you'll never have enough of these.

☐Regular unscented chlorine bleach.

☐ Washboard and tub.

☐ Multi purpose or Pine Tar soap-Can be used body cleansing, washing clothes, etc.

NPP Communal List

12- *Jointly...* what your Group Members will have to buy for the *Communal NPP equipment and supplies...*

This is what each of your NPP Group Members must chip it to buy...

☐ One or more of the same model Watch Center Radios. This must be a battery rechargeable, hand crank and alternative 110 volt powered emergency base camp radio with Aircraft, Short Wave, NOAA, FM and AM channels and bands. This radio must be compatible with the two-way radios and the same radio individual Group Members buy.

Midland Base Camp Emergency Radio

☐ Enough two-way radios *with Microphone/single ear pieces* to have one for each position of guard, roving patrol, Perimeter Patrol, LOP, *Inside* and *Outflanker Marksmen* positions plus spare radios and spare batteries. These must be compatible with the Watch Center Emergency Base Camp Radio for channels and privacy codes. Get 50 channel water resistant models.

☐ One AA battery operated quartz clock and spare batteries that has an alarm and that keeps track of the date, and the day of the week.

☐ High intensity solar powered sidewalk lights for night time Watch Center lighting.

☐ 12 hour chemical light sticks for night time Watch Center lighting.

☐ Green and red filters for night time Watch Center lighting.

☐ Solar charging units. Enough to recharge all radio batteries.

☐ *One or more* good quality compass. The compass should be completely enclosed inside a carrying case that fits on a belt. No battery operated electronic compasses.

☐ Maps of your *Primary and Secondary NPP Locations* and their surrounding areas.

☐ Google or Map Quest photos of your *Primary and Secondary NPP Locations* and surrounding areas.

☐ Maps of a minimum of at least three routes from your *Primary NPP Location* to each or your *Secondary NPP Locations.*

☐ City or County maps of your underground utility passages if you can get them.

☐ Notebooks of paper, ink pens, especially pencils, and a small manual pencil sharpener.

☐ One or more dirt type bicycles and spare tires.

☐ One or more good hand tire pumps for bicycles and vehicles.

☐ Vehicle and bicycle tire repair kits.

A tool kit with hand wood and metal working tools…

- ☐ A Stanley Sharp Tooth type 15-inch wood saw to cut trees and rough lumber with.
- ☐Different types and sizes of pliers.
- ☐Hammers.
- ☐Screw drivers of all types and sizes.
- ☐Files and rasps. All types and sizes of wood files, but mostly metal files.
- ☐Imperial (Inch) and Metric socket sets.
- ☐Different sizes of pipe and crescent wrenches.
- ☐Small axe and Large axe.
- ☐Heavy sledge hammer.
- ☐5 foot pry bar.
- ☐Handyman type jack.

- ☐ Smaller pry bars.
- ☐ Bolt cutters.
- ☐ Simple AC/DC volt meter.
- ☐ Different types and sizes of metal shears.
- ☐ Hand saws.
- ☐ Multiple rolls of black electrical tape.

Additional Items…

- ☐ Water dispensing 5 gallon hand pump back pack fire extinguishers.
- ☐ At least one Emergency Escape Ladder for each ten people in a High Rise Building.
- ☐ Rolls of Vietnam Era trip wire or non glare heavy fish line for perimeter for trip alerts.
- ☐ 1,000 feet of 6# fishing line.
- ☐ Lots of nails and screws. Long ones.
- ☐ ¼" or 3/8" nylon rope-minimum 100 feet. Clothes line, etc.
- ☐ Chlorine bleach and Iodine tablets for disinfecting water.
- ☐ Gallons of treated gasoline as applicable in 5-gallon cans for vehicles.
- ☐ PRI-G, to rejuvenate gasoline in the future.
- ☐ If your *NPP* is a High Rise Building you must have alternative heating and cooking sources, especially if your *NPP* is an individual floor. Have as many 5 gallon propane tanks as possible, a heating and cooking system that functions on kerosene, fuel oil or simply coal. *Beware of fire, carbon monoxide poisoning and oxygen depletion when using these.*
- ☐ If your *NPP* is a High Rise Building you'd better have mucho blankets and good quality sleeping bags for winter weather… many!
- ☐ If your *NPP* consists of individual floors, have lots of food and ammunition. The fools that prevented your entire building being a *NPP* will be at you door after *A Failure of Civility…* you may need a few of them to help you secure the entire building. You can get even by telling *them* what to do.
- ☐ Barbed Wire or Concertina Wire enough to cover your entrances, Kill Zones and other areas of your Protective Perimeter and two pair of gloves to handle it.
- ☐ Enough Clear plastic self sealing sandbags for Guard Posts and other areas they're needed of the Home Depot type.

Buy the following items <u>only if your NPP Group Members can afford them</u>…

☐ A gasoline emergency power generator to run power tools with and for charging batteries. For short periods of time this can be used to run power tools that will enable you to do the work of hand tools in a fraction of the time.

☐ A chain saw and files for sharpening the chain, fuel and two cycle oil supply.

☐ Four or more 5 gallon NATO type fuel cans.

☐ A couple of gallons of PRI fuel treatment. PRI will reconstitute old gasoline.

☐ Manual fluid transfer pumps for fuels and water. Color code these 'White' for human consumables and 'Red' for fuels so they don't get cross used. Have hoses long enough to get to the bottom of the barrel *or to siphon from buried fuel tanks, at least 25 foot in length.*

☐ A four wheel block & tackle with rope.

☐ A good police scanner.

Individual List

12-*Individually*… what <u>each Group Member must have</u>…
per each Group Member…

Firearms, ammunition and accessories…

☐ Preferably a long gun *and* pistol.

☐ 10 magazines per long gun *and* 5 magazines per pistol.

☐ Holsters, duty belt, magazine pouches, webbing and slings.

☐ 500 to 1000 rounds of ammunition *or more* per firearm.

☐ Spare firearms parts.

☐ Firearms cleaning kit.

Water

☐ As much as can be stored in containers… right now.

☐ A dozen 16 ounce or 20 ounce plastic water bottle to ration water with.

☐ Two 5 liter water carriers that can be carried inside a back pack.

☐ A 'Camel Pack' back pack water canteen.

☐ Coffee filters for filtering water.

- [ ] Water chemical treatment.
- [ ] Manual water filter and tablets.
- [ ] Good quality heavy duty tarps in sizes from 8 feet by 10 feet, up to a maximum size of approximately 20 feet by 30 feet for utility but primarily for rainwater collection.
- [ ] Clean barrels and pails or cheap plastic kiddie swimming pools to collect rainwater.

Emergency Food

- [ ] Mainstream Foods, MREs, freeze dried or dehydrated foods.
- [ ] Vitamins-Vitamin C, Vitamin D and a good multiple vitamin.
- [ ] Metamucil and laxatives.
- [ ] Pet foods.

Food Preparation

- [ ] Gallons of Kerosene, Kerosene heaters, lamps and a Kerosene cooking stove.
- [ ] Cooking utensils for open fire.
- [ ] At least one cast iron skillet and an old fashioned Dutch oven.
- [ ] Heating pad gloves to handle open fire cooking utensils.
- [ ] Durable and reusable metal spoon, fork, butter knife eating utensils, metal cup and metal plate.
- [ ] One good quality *100% stainless steel* hand crank can opener.
- [ ] At least two boxes of Reynolds heavy duty aluminum foil.

Clothing and accessories

- [ ] Low key colored loose fitting work clothes.
- [ ] Latex paint to camouflage work clothes. Two to three different colors.
- [ ] Camouflage face and skin cream kits.
- [ ] Winter coats and cold weather gear… gloves, mittens, heavy scarves, ear muffs, stocking caps, balaclavas, thermal underwear.
- [ ] Plenty of underwear, T shirts and extra socks.
- [ ] Cheap but heavy duty work gloves.
- [ ] Plenty of blankets and quilts.

☐ A sleeping bag.

☐ A good pair of work shoes, preferably boots for added support. Waterproof Gortex boots. If you can't afford Gortex boots get a pair of rubber overshoes to go over your regular boots.

Medical Items

☐ Personal prescription medicines preferably a six month supply.

☐ Mosquito spray! Not aerosol cans, but the pump kind.

☐ Two pair of prescription reading glasses and sunglasses in hard cases.

☐ Baby wipes.

☐ Any other medical items you feel you need.

☐ Sun screen.

If you have small children or babies, include baby items such as diapers, diaper rash ointment, and anything else a child would need for a medical emergency.

Sanitation and Hygiene

☐ At least 24 double rolls of toilet tissue for each family member.

☐ Save every phone and lightweight paper book you can collect to use as an alternative for toilet paper when the rolls run out. The glossy pages don't… ah… work very well.

☐ A camping solar shower bag that holds four or five gallons of water.

☐ 100-13 gallon garbage bags.

☐ 50-33 gallon 1 mil garbage bags.

☐ 20-45 gallon 3 mil construction garbage bags.

☐ Supply of feminine products.

☐ Pure 'Dove' or 'Ivory brand soap.

☐ Two toothbrushes.

☐ 4 tubes of toothpaste.

☐ 4 spools of dental floss.

☐ More rolls of toilet paper.

☐ One or more good pair of good scissors.

☐ One or more nail clippers and one or more toe nail scissors.

Communications

☐ The same model emergency base camp radio as the Watch Center Radio. A battery rechargeable, hand crank and alternative 110 volt powered emergency base camp radio with Aircraft, Short Wave, NOAA, FM and AM channels and bands. This radio must be compatible with the two-way radios.

Illumination and fire

☐ Self Powered flashlight.

☐ A hands free headlight.

☐ 12 hour chemical light sticks for night time Watch Center lighting.

☐ Fuel Tablets.

☐ Stick matches that are *"Strike Anywhere"* type matches.

☐ A Zippo type lighter, spare flints and cans of lighter fluid.

☐ 1,000 paper matches.

☐ Lots of butane lighters – buy different brands.

☐ A L.E.D. double AA Mini Maglite or hand crank power type flashlight.

☐ A s#!t load of long burning candles.

☐ High intensity solar powered sidewalk border lights. These can be charged during the day and used for interior lights at night. Most will give up to ten hours light.

Auxiliary items

☐ A surplus military type long range back pack with frame.

☐ Duct tape-rolls of it. This is a Special Forces medic's alternative to medical tape.

☐ 1000 foot of Parachute Cord.

☐ At least 100 feet of nylon or polypropylene braided cord 3/8 inch thick.

☐ Quality Survival/Hunting type Knife with minimum 6 inch blade.

☐ One pair of safety eyeglasses.

☐ Binoculars.

☐ A mosquito head net.

☐ Insect repellent-use Listerine as mosquito repellant.

☐ At least one 3,000 yard spool of sewing thread.

☐ A package of thin hand sewing needles.

- ☐ Package of assorted color threads that also contains needles and a needle threader.
- ☐ A package of thick heavy duty leather type sewing needles.
- ☐ 100 feet of heavy waxed nylon leather type sewing thread.
- ☐ 100 foot long water hose for siphoning.
- ☐ A Leatherman type multi-tool.
- ☐ Board games and Playing cards for entertainment.
- ☐ Rope ladders if you are in a High Rise Building.
- ☐ Garden tools and non-hybrid garden vegetable seeds if you're a gardener.
- ☐ Hunting items such as skinning and meat processing tools.
- ☐ Fishing poles, nets and tackle.
- ☐ 'Tincture of Green Soap'. Cheap. Medical disinfectant but has a dual purpose. It works to environmentally and safely flat-out kill insects that damage a garden if it's washed off afterwards or it will suffocate your plants. Spray it on and wait a half hour… spray clean water to wash it off.

12-Alternative electrical power

You need to have an alternative electrical power source to charge radio batteries and other electrical items. You must assume that *electrical service will be non-existent* during a *Long Term Crisis* or *A Failure of Civility*.

Emergency electrical power is another science unto itself. It's for those more intelligent than us. We'll give you some basics but ***consult someone who knows about emergency electrical power in detail before investing in any emergency electrical items.***

Electrical items… radios, flashlights and batteries *are another item to standardize* in addition to your firearms calibers, magazines and cartridges. Standardize your batteries and voltages of items using these batteries. Standardize your chargers.

Buy equipment with a common voltage and batteries that will work with the same charger and in all items using them. Make this the standard voltage/battery/charger in your *Neighborhood Protection Plan*. If one goes on the blink, then you have others. It makes it much simpler.

Deep Cycle Storage 'Bank' Batteries. The best and most efficient system for emergency electrical power is to have deep cycle batteries as 'storage bank batteries' charged by solar cells or an emergency electrical generator. This is the most efficient way to use the fuel that powers your electrical generator and to store electricity produced by solar cells.

Charge your batteries. You can charge radio or other batteries directly from your *storage battery bank* if they are the same voltage as the batteries you need to charge or you can charge them through a regulator.

An Inverter. From those *storage tank batteries you use a inverter* to turn this stored power back into 110 volt power for *limited* use of tools, limited microwave use and refrigerator or freezer units.

Solar Panel Charger. These have become *very inexpensive* to buy. Solar panels are virtually everywhere now. You can buy basic battery charging units with solar panels built in which are quite small and compact. *Don't invest in one big one...* rather buy a few smaller ones. If your big one goes bad… you're out of luck… but more of the smaller panels give you the odds of continued power from this great source… the sun.

Note where solar panels are on highways and buildings and you can make a crude map with their location on it. Some of these may be destroyed by EMP. However, there is uncertainty of how much, if any, damage will occur with solar panels from EMP.

In a pinch… and this is obviously illegal if you decide to do this… but if *A Failure of Civility* occurs and everything has gone completely to s#!t… 'borrow' these. If *Normal Civility* is restored you'd better get them back up! If you get caught… you're going to be a 'jail bird.'

You'll need a volt meter to determine voltage output if you use unknown panels. Like voltages must be connected in parallel. Consult an electrician or electrical engineer about this before your experiment with these becomes 'shocking.' These will power all your rechargeable batteries.

Gasoline Emergency Power Generator. A gasoline emergency power generator can run power tools and will charge batteries. For short periods of time this generator can be used to run power tools that will enable you to do the same amount of work of hand tools in a fraction of the time.

Fuel supply. Although diesel fuel generally stores better for longer periods of time, we recommend gasoline as the fuel to power you emergency electrical generator. Even though gasoline does not store as well as diesel it is much more common in most metropolitan and suburban areas.

If *A Failure of Civility* occurs, there will be vehicles and underground storage tanks with gasoline that can be drawn from. You must have at least a 25 foot long hose and hand siphon pump.

You must also have *PRI Fuel Additive/Restorer* to add to gasoline for storage and reconstitution. We've not used this but all reports are that this stuff is a miracle worker with gasoline.

Faraday Cage. Named after the British Scientist Michael Faraday... who discovered the principle of electromagnetic induction in the 18th Century. The basic principle of a Faraday Cage is that the metal enclosure totally surrounds, insulates and isolates an electronic object inside it from extremely high 'spike' voltage that permeates the air and floats across the ground. These 'spikes' of voltage will destroy semi conductors and delicate electronics.

Faraday Cage Protection. This generator should be in its own Faraday Cage for the protection of its electronics against EMP damage. We go into this in greater detail in a few pages.

A Faraday Cage for an emergency electrical generator can be made simply by building a frame work of lumber and stapling aluminum screen over this framework. The aluminum screen must cover and overlap at its seams and cover the entire framework including the bottom portion.

We suggest any 'door' be screwed or fastened on, not hinged making certain the aluminum screen is overlapped after the door is screwed on.

Before you put your generator in this Faraday cage, wrap aluminum foil over all of the generator's surfaces including the bottom. Then overlap and tape all foil seams with air conditioning foil tape. Cut sheets of 2 inch Styrofoam for the bottom, all sides and the top of your generator to fit inside your aluminum screen covered, lumber framework Faraday Cage.

The Styrofoam insulates the foil covered generator from touching the aluminum screen on the outside of your Faraday Cage wooden framework. It is critical that the generator, any other equipment stored within and the aluminum foil *not touch* the outside aluminum screen.

When done... holy snikees!... you've built your first Faraday Cage !!!

All other electronic items must be in a Faraday Cage... solar panels, chargers, radios, LED equipment, laptop computers, electronic gun sights... anything with microprocessor or LED displays must be put in a Faraday Cage like the one just described or one like we show next under Electromagnetic Pulse... or EMP *Catastrophic Events.*

If you don't... you and your electronics equipment will be in the *"New Dark Ages"*... like everyone else.

12-Specialized Items needed for certain Catastrophic Events

Most of the *Catastrophic Events* we've listed can be prepared for and combated. *Some cannot.*

The whole purpose of this book as we stated in the beginning was to be an informative source for John and Joan Q Citizen to provide a means of defending themselves, their families and their neighborhood.

Realistically, some of the *Catastrophic Events* listed in our chart are not very probable. However, if they do occur… they are beyond the resources of most Readers this book was intended for… to feasibly prepare against.

Biological, Chemical and Nuclear *Catastrophic Events* would require the resources of the Federal Government to implement. In short… some *Catastrophic Events* are too overwhelming in their effect… which makes them too expensive for you and the Authors to reasonably prepare for. If they do happen… you and the Authors can only pray these will not affect your area.

The following *Catastrophic Events* equipment and solutions may be within your budget… and you *may or may not* want to invest in preparing for them.

Electromagnetic Pulse. One of the most dangerous and probable of the *Catastrophic Events* in the Authors' estimation is the Electromagnetic Pulse or EMP *as it is abbreviated.* This would either be man made as the result of a nuclear bomb detonated high above our atmosphere… or a Solar Flare Coronal Mass Ejection… two different sources.

With the nuclear generated EMP there would most likely be no lingering radioactive danger because to be effective, this type of weapon has to be detonated at extremely high altitude and would be a short duration event. People wouldn't feel it or see it. Your world of modern conveniences would just shut off… like the world's master electrical circuit breaker being thrown off.

The Solar Flare or Coronal Mass Ejection would be natural and could come in waves over days or up to a week or more.

This EMP has the capability to destroy all computers, electronic circuits and the electronics in vehicles, aircraft, ship and train locomotives. All devices that depend on semi conductors. It can also severely damage the electrical power distribution system.

All computers, phone systems, radio equipment, the internet, the food supply sale, processing, growing, storage and transportation systems, water pumping, sewage control, the electrical power system would be damaged or destroyed. *In short… the EMP Catastrophic Event would destroy the modern world as we know it… and you wouldn't know it hit until your power went out.*

The Authors do recommend you have a Faraday Cage to protect your laptop computer, digital cameras and *most importantly your emergency communications equipment.*

The Electromagnetic Pulse (EMP) *Catastrophic Event* that is either from *a Solar Flare* or *Nuclear Generated* requires…

The Faraday Cage. An EMP will destroy all electronic semi conductor, LED and

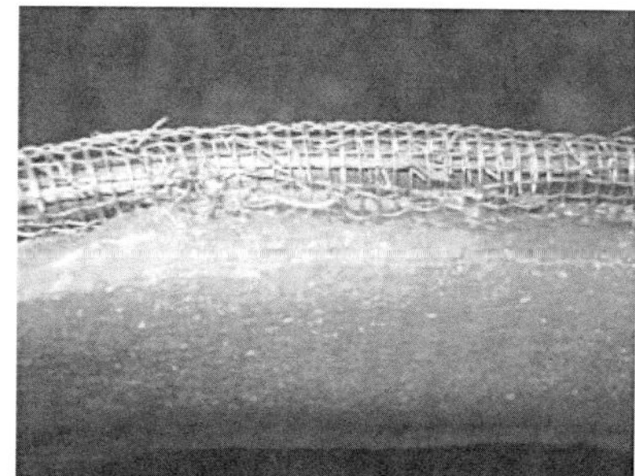

Aluminum screen seal for lid of Faraday Cage

Faraday Cage with cardboard lining in can and lid

Faraday Cage with lid and one of our foil wrapped radios

microprocessor circuitry. A Faraday Cage as the photos illustrate is cheap protection and can be constructed for around $60. We found the plans for ours floating around on the internet. It's simply a galvanized metal garbage can with lid.

We put snap down draw latches on the can to pull the lid down tightly against the aluminum screen in the photo that we put over the lip of the garbage can opening. We lined the can and the lid with cardboard and hot glued everything in place.

We hot glued a strip of foam at the top to keep the aluminum screen from poking fingers. We wrapped our radios in aluminum foil and taped the edges of the foil with air conditioning aluminum foil tape.

EMP voltage 'hangs' around the outside metal of the Faraday Cage, which acts like a 'skin', protecting the electronic objects inside. Eventually, this high voltage dissipates harmlessly. Otherwise it fries all electronics.

A Faraday Cage is for two-way radios, base station emergency radios *and any other LED or electronic equipment.* Back up your computer on a DVD or CD type disk… these are not affected by EMP, but put one laptop computer in your Faraday Cage with all your applications and data on it.

Do not ground a Faraday Cage… let it 'stand alone' preferably a couple of feet off the floor of where you store it. *Anyone who tells you to ground a Faraday Cage to a water pipe or an earth ground is full of bulls#!t.*

Grounding a Faraday Cage can actually direct more destructive high voltage towards the electronics equipment stored by way of the ground wire to the Faraday Cage channeling more voltage to the item inside the Faraday Cage.

This may do the opposite that the principle of a Faraday Cage is intended to do… isolate electronic components from Electromagnetic Pulse damage. Grounding *can* help but it has to be done properly and this is a science unto itself reserved for those who deal specifically with EMP. ***For you…*** *do not ground your Faraday Cage.*

Because a Solar Flare or Coronal Mass Ejection could come in waves over days or up to a week or more... do not open your Faraday Cage after the first EMP problem... wait. The event may come again in the same or greater intensity over the next few days and destroy your once protected equipment.

***Nuclear.* A nuclear event that is above ground in the immediate atmosphere and that puts radiation in the environment requires…**

- ***Iodine tablets for radioactivity.*** These are a 'band aid' for certain types of radioactive poisoning. If the radioactive levels get too intense there is little you can do. Radioactivity is like thousands of tiny invisible bullets going through your body.
- ***Geiger counter.*** This will tell you how deep the s#!t is that you are standing in… or in scientific terms… the extent of the radioactive levels in your area.

  What good that will do you… the Authors don't know. Maybe it will comfort you to know how long it will be until you and your family members are watching each other fatally bleed from the nose and other body orifices.

  You'd be better off spending the money for more food, ammunition and other items mentioned and preparing for a *Catastrophic Event* that is more probable and survivable.

Chemical and Biological Agents. One of the Authors had extensive military training in NBC… Nuclear, Biological and Chemical Warfare. His knowledge of the complexity of this type of warfare and these types of agents brings us to the following conclusion… you are wasting your money preparing for these types of attacks.

Even though there are many types of 'Gas Masks' and 'Chemical Suits' on the civilian market for sale, you must realize that these are not 'A One Size Fits All' solution…

- One size of these masks does not fit all and especially not small children. Each mask requires an air tight seal to the skin around the face… these will not work for children.
- 'Gas Mask' filters are specific to the type of agent encountered.
- Most people don't realize that a two day growth of beard will affect the proper skin seal around your face.
- 'Chemical Suits' made for the U.S. Military being sold in surplus or sporting goods store are sold to hunters as 'scent blocking' suits. These are charcoal based lined suits that are probably no longer effective for their original purpose as the charcoal lining expires after a period of time.

- Eastern European and Russian made 'Rubber Chemical Suits' are also available on the civilian market. These tear or puncture easily and wearing this type of rubber suit for an extended period of time is an *experience in itself…* like being the object of what's cooking in a slow cooking crock pot.

In a nutshell… preparation for *Catastrophic Events* comes down to "Beans, Bullets, Bandages… and a *Faraday Cage.*"

The common thread for all *Catastrophic Events* is 'Beans, Bullets and Bandages' in all *Catastrophic Events…* have plenty of each of them… *and have a Survival Mentality that you train… train… train with.*

12-What will happen if *A Failure of Civility* is prolonged or permanent?

If *A Failure of Civility* becomes long term or permanent you'll need to begin to live like people did 200 years ago in this country. You'll need to learn every trick the pioneers used to survive.

But in the process, not knowing just one simple thing of thousands of issues that our ancestors dealt with daily can quickly kill you and your family.

Incorporating this lifestyle of *Self Dependence* into you modern lifestyle is something you need to do *now*. It can't be learned overnight and you won't have the luxury of time to learn these methods. You and your family will most likely endure extreme suffering or die before you can learn the methods by which our ancestors were *Self Dependent… start now!*

We'll give you a couple of 'for instances'…

One… Did you know that you can catch or shoot and cook rabbits and eat them until you're constantly so full that you want to puke… *and starve to death in the process?* It's called 'Rabbit Starvation' and it's a fact. Unless you have other animal or fruit and nut fats, you'll literally starve to death very painfully trying to subsist on rabbit meat alone.

Two… That's if you don't get deathly ill from 'Rabbit Spotted Liver Disease.' The Authors know that if you kill, skin, gut and cook a rabbit to eat… you'd better be gosh darned certain the rabbit's liver is not mottled or spotted. This is a serious disease that will incapacitate and kill humans.

There's waaaaaay too much to go into to advise you how to live like our ancestors did 200 years ago. We'll just say that if this is more of your concern than preparing for a ***6 month*** *Long Term Crisis* or *A Failure of Civility* that returns to *Normal Civility* which we've given you a checklist of survival supplies and equipment for… go a step further. Read, learn… *and slowly integrate living like this into the reality of your life.*

Get as many books as you can on *"Back to the Basics"* regarding living *Self Dependently*. Plant a garden, harvest and preserve your crops… learn hunting, processing and storing the meat from your kills… learn to fish and forage in the forests for edibles… learn to incorporate living *Self Dependently* 'off the power grid' like our ancestors did. Incorporate this slowly into your present modern lifestyle.

Read everything you can in books on hunting, fishing, gardening *and do those things.* This is not only grand fun and entertainment… *it will save you tons of money and give your family tremendous learning experiences and fun.* It's the best of both worlds. We have all the modern conveniences and yet ***we do it****… so you can do it.*

A few things that may help if *A Failure of Civility* becomes long term or permanent…

Unless you have Group Members who are active and knowledgeable gardeners, from the Authors' experience we can tell you that it will take you 2 to 3 years to *learn* to grow a garden productive enough to feed your family.

You won't have artificial fertilizers… remember how the American Indian caught fish… not to eat but to plant by the base of their crops as fertilizer.

A garden productive enough to provide you and your family with sustenance you will find is by God's good grace and the cooperation of the weather. It will also take you time to learn how to hunt and fish to provide enough food for you and your family.

That's if you have the fertile land, the water, the seeds and the knowhow and *A Failure of Civility* has subsided to a manageable level that your *NPP* is not spending most of its man power for defensive tasks.

We encourage you to have much more of food to sustain each person in the NPP than six months.

You'll need SALT. Salt is cheap, cheap, cheap! Stock pile 20 pound bags of it now! Do not add any salt to commercially processed food because that food already contains an adequate or an excess amount of salt.

If *A Failure of Civility* becomes long term or becomes permanent exhausting your stored food stocks… you will have to begin to live off the land… and for one thing… you will need salt.

You'll not be able to immediately step back 200 years in your lifestyle. We all live with too many technological items that we're dependent upon.

To help you transition… a few present day items and issues will help. If all goes to hell in a hand basket you can also use some of this information…

- Get a copy of the Special Forces Survival Manual. You can literally live off the land with this manual and a few basic tools forever if you have the *Survival Mentality.*
- Buy a *"Back to the Basics"* book… then buy another… and another. Read them and make the information in them a reality by doing what the book describes. You can do a lot of things in these books even if you live in a metropolitan area.
- High proof alcohol is worthwhile for storage and trading. Build up stocks of it.
- Have gallons and gallons of Kerosene, Kerosene heaters and lamps and a Kerosene cooking stove. You must have fresh air ventilation in rooms that you use these or you can die from carbon monoxide poisoning or oxygen depletion.
- Bags of silver, mostly in junk pre-1965 coins, as well as gold one ounce coins will give you something to buy with. These are easier to carry and put up less of a struggle than the chickens and pigs you're lugging around under your arms when going to trade for something you need. The Authors would rather have this value in ammunition. That can be used… and traded too.
- Have packets of all kinds of vegetable seeds. Hybrid seeds for 5 years of gardening until you know what you're doing. Heirloom and non hybrid seeds to continue gardening when you've got your 'green thumb' act together.

It will take a long time for you to learn to do without these and replace them with self sustaining substitutes. If *A Failure of Civility* that long term or permanent is your concern… start preparing for it now.

12-Vehicles and fuel

Your vehicles may not be operable after some Catastrophic Events such as an intense Electromagnetic Pulse or the fact that gasoline is not obtainable and you have no reserve fuel supply. Considering vehicles operate, you must designate vehicles that can be used by your *NPP* if you have to make a *Planned NPP Relocation.*

You should have two of the largest pickup trucks or heavy suburban vehicles as your lead and rear vehicles. If things really go to 'hell in a hand basket,' 'borrow' a transit bus or ready mix truck. They'll ram through about anything.

Have your vehicles filled with fuel as soon as trouble starts. You should make a habit of not letting your fuel tank get below one half full. You should have a minimum of 20 gallons of extra gas stored per vehicle once you form your *NPP*. If you store fuel, it should be stored outside your garage away from your house for safety.

You must keep gasoline fresh. Most gasoline, regardless of how high an octane it is, will become unusable within one year. You must add Stabil fuel preservative or a similar product to gasoline.

Rotate your gasoline by adding about 25% of it… one 5 gallon can… to a vehicle with the vehicle tank already three fourths full of gas to dilute it so it burns properly. Then refill that container, adding Stabil, to what you just used and put that back into your emergency supply of gasoline.

Your *NPP* Supply Section Leader should take an inventory of all fuel in your neighborhood so a detailed inventory is on hand at the Watch Center. He should also periodically check on each Group Member's reserve fuel supplies.

12-Preparing your *NPP* with supplies and equipment.

Accumulating a list NPP Group Member's individual supplies and equipment. This will be sensitive to most people. Most people will not want anyone outside their immediate family to know what weapons and food they have.

This is natural, however. But it is of utmost importance if the group is to survive as a whole and be an effective defense that *trust* be developed *and kept* between the members.

If this isn't possible, some basic information, such as an assurance from each member that they ***will have*** 'X' number of rounds of ammunition and 'X' number of days of food for each member, will have to be given and honored by *NPP Leaders* in a worst case scenario. *NPP Leaders* must periodically ask each of their Group Members if they have the required supplies.

Use the guidelines in the back of this book to calculate what food and ammunition each Group Member should have. Basic calibers of weapons and the cartridge they use should be known.

The worst you can expect is that the member states they have the bare minimum that this book recommends and that the group as a whole can rely on. Remember, the Authors can't stress this enough… *"Your life and that of your family is in their hands, just as theirs is in your hands."* You will *have* to learn to trust each other.

Each Group Member *needs to earn the trust* of each of the others… your life and that of your family members will rely on this trust if the worst case scenario, *A Failure of Civility* occurs.

If you can't get to a basic position of trust between Group Members, don't bother forming *Neighborhood Protection Plan.*

12-Sharing food and provisions to maintain cohesion of *NPP*

There may come a time in your *NPP* where some members run out of food. Considering that when your group was formed, everyone should have had sufficient food to sustain them for the time period that your *NPP* was designed to exist for… these members were either not truthful or consumed more than they should have in the allotted time period.

This leaves all Group Members to make a decision on what to do. *The decision of what to do in a case like this should be made when the NPP is organized.* If the decision is made during a *Crisis*, the psychological trauma that all are in will affect what you decide. This decision will also set a precedent for each additional person who runs short of food or provisions throughout the duration of the *Crisis*.

You can each chip in part of your food and provisions to that Group Member and ration daily what is given to that Group Member or discuss and vote on other options. Whatever you do, if you don't share, you risk *the beginning of the end of your NPP*. Like all plans in life, organizing your *Neighborhood Protection Plan* will have many holes in it. Unfortunately, you won't see those holes until the reality of a *Crisis* is upon you.

Some members of your *NPP* will not be financially able to have the agreed upon amounts of supplies. If you have Group Members who you know won't be able to buy their required supplies, then all others that are capable of spending money for these things must buy more to compensate for this.

Bags of rice and beans are cheap… considering all the trigger fingers, eyes and ears you will need to survive… what's your life worth?

Remember not to look at Group Members in need as just more people to feed. Each member is part of your *Strength through Numbers* for the *NPP* to survive. You must keep foremost in your thoughts the motto of the Three Musketeers… *"All for One… and One for All !"*

12-After the storm

Well if *'hell visited earth'* by means of *A Failure of Civility* and you're come back to read these words afterwards… you survived it and we're happy for you. We know that *A Failure of Civility* as we described would be worse… something that cannot be expressed in words to depict the sights, smells, sounds and reality of it… but you know it now in your mind.

We hope also that most of your neighbors survived and we hope that the effects of the catastrophe have not become permanent. We hope that America has returned to *Normal Civility* and that mankind has benefited by the trauma of the *Catastrophic Event* to bond together unlike mankind ever has.

We have our doubts, though, as to whether we'll ever all be singing *"We are the World" "Kumbaya"* or any song that epitomizes emotionally warm, fuzzy feelings of human unity. How long any 'human unity' would exist is questionable to us.

Capitalists, collectivists, politicians, bureaucrats, dictators, the religious zealot, special interest groups… and just plain ordinary people… always seem to have more 'enlightened guidance' as to how each of us should live… than we ourselves do.

Mankind has a very short memory… in fact both Authors think the word mankind is an oxymoron. The 'enlightened' of the above want to 'guide you along the path' to their 'paradise' even if it's at gunpoint or with a cattle prod up your posterior.

The Authors don't really know what it will take to get to the level of a 'Star Trek Existence' for mankind. We just know that making decisions by emotion, burying your head in the sand while ignoring the truth, being 'politically correct,' suppressing the spirit of man as some ideologies do and insisting that your minority view of life be forced on the majority… won't get us there.

But until such time as we *do* get to a better understanding and acceptance and learn to live in peace amongst each other… violence… and the defense against it by countering with violence… will be a necessity. We still hope for the best from our species… and it amazes us constantly that in this world of brutality, struggle and suffering… that we see compassion and the basic goodness that exists in most human beings.

That aside, we hope that this book will help Americans. It's an attempt… by two dyslexic, worn soldiers, who are hard of hearing and have atrocious grammar and spelling… to convey information from their training and experiences that may help others survive a disaster.

We hope that no event happens, but we also hope that you guide your lifestyle by some of the issues we've written about in this book even during *Normal Civility*. Become *Self Dependent*… but if *A Failure of Civility* does occur we hope you help build a better society afterwards for your children… *for at that moment... they are the sole evidence of you and your ancestors' existence.*

What will your fate and that of your family's be...?

There are three possible futures for your family if *A Failure of Civility* takes place...

1. You and your family would perish.

2. You and your family would suffer but survive for an extended period of time existing like animals day to day.

3. You and your family could survive with some degree of comfort and safety compared to the masses of people.

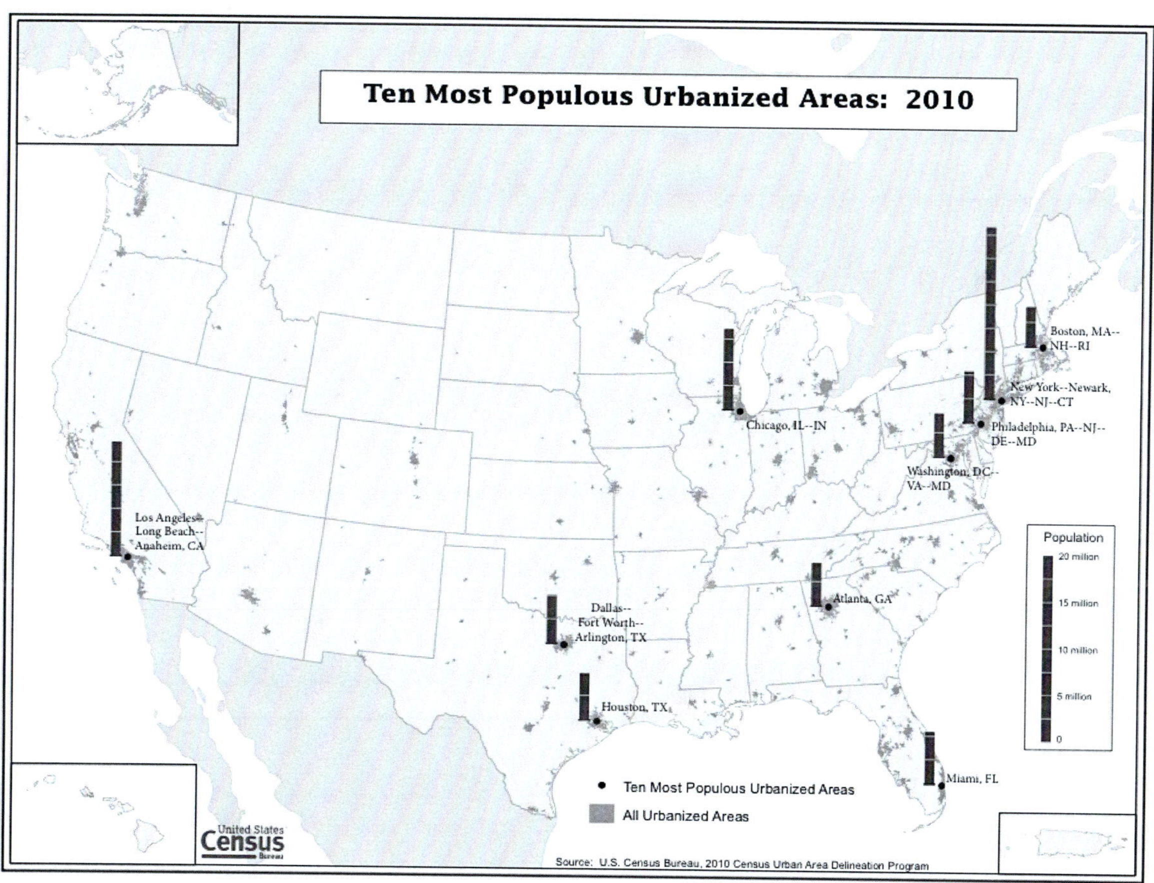

Preparation is the key... this includes developing a *Survival Mentality*, storing food and having a water source, having weapons with lots of ammunition and conducting *training exercises* and *more training exercises* and *then training some more* after reading the information in this book.

You must have *Strength through Numbers. If you don't you're doomed to failure surviving any disaster.* Regardless of how much money you have to store food and equip your

Neighborhood Protection Plan, there is no way you can protect your family from everything. Learn to cooperate and work together as a group.

The Authors pray none of the *Catastrophic Events* of this book will ever happen to the people of this country or the world.

Parents owe a responsibility to their children for their well being and as future citizens to keep this country strong. Our hope is that if a catastrophe does occur that there will be so many *Neighborhood Protection Plans* in place that the charity of human compassion and ingenuity can keep suffering and death to a minimum and promoting *A Triumph of Civility.*

We've given you the information … it's up to **you** to decide what to do...

Our Website… **AFailureOfCivility.com**

Emergency Radio Frequencies

After a *Catastrophic Event* a radio could be the only method of communication. Knowing what frequencies to use becomes vital. If you listen or transmit on frequencies that others are not using… obviously no one will be contacting you.

You need to know what frequencies to use after a *Catastrophic Event*. ***Be aware that the government may change these during an emergency.***

This is a list of the primary frequencies on all bands that could be useful after a *Catastrophic Event.*

Frequency MHz	**Commonly used and Emergency Calling Frequencies**
1.8100	Ham HF QRP CW Calling (QRP = Low Power Transmitter 5 watts or less output)
1.9100	Ham HF QRP SSB Calling (HF = High Frequency)
2.1820	Ham HF International Maritime Distress Frequency
3.5600	Ham HF QRP CW Calling
3.5800	Ham HF QRP CW Calling
3.8850	Ham HF AM Calling
3.9850	Ham HF QRP SSB Calling
7.0300	Ham HF QRP DX CW Calling
7.0400	Ham HF QRP CW Calling
7.2850	Ham HF QRP SSB Calling
7.2900	Ham HF AM Calling
10.1060	Ham HF QRP CW Calling
14.0250	Ham HF CW DX Calling
14.0600	Ham HF QRP CW Calling
14.1950	Ham HF DX Calling
14.2850	Ham HF QRP SSB Calling
14.2860	Ham HF AM Calling
21.0600	Ham HF QRP CW Calling

21.2950	Ham HF DX Calling
21.3850	Ham HF QRP SSB Calling
27.0650	CB AM Ch-9 Emergency Channel
27.1850	CB AM Ch-19 Unofficial Highway Channel
27.3850	CB AM Ch-38 LSB, National calling frequency
28.0600	Ham HF QRP CW Calling
28.3850	Ham HF QRP SSB Calling
28.4000	Ham HF CW Calling
29.0000	Ham HF AM Calling
29.6000	Ham HF FM simplex
<u>34.9000</u>	<u>Used nationwide by the National Guard during emergencies.</u>
<u>39.4600</u>	<u>Used for inter-department emergency communications by local and state police forces.</u>
47.4200	Used across the United States by the Red Cross for relief operations.
50.1100	Ham 6 Meter DX Calling
50.1250	Ham 6 Meter SSB Calling
50.4000	Ham 6 Meter AM Calling
52.5250	Ham 6 Meter FM Calling
<u>121.5000</u>	<u>International Aviation Emergency Frequency</u>
<u>138.2250</u>	<u>Prime disaster relief operations channel used by the Federal Emergency Management Agency</u>
144.0500	Ham 2 Meter DX CW (Europe)
144.2000	Ham 2 Meter CW and SSB common Calling
144.3000	Ham 2 Meter DX CW/SSB (Europe)
144.5000	Ham 2 Meter FM Calling (Europe)
146.5200	Ham 2 Meter Ham FM General calling and emergency and wilderness protocol
146.5500	Ham 2 Meter Ham FM Simplex National Emergency Frequency
151.6250	Used by "itinerant" businesses, or those that travel about the country.
<u>154.2800</u>	<u>Used for inter-department emergency communications by local fire departments... 154.265 and 154.295 also used.</u>
154.5700	Used itinerant business channel. Circuses, exhibitions, trade shows, sports teams. 154.600 also used.
<u>155.1600</u>	<u>Used for inter-department emergency communications by local and state agencies during search and rescue operations.</u>
<u>155.4750</u>	<u>Used for inter-department emergency communications by local and state police forces.</u>

156.4500	Ch-9 The boater calling channel.
156.8000	Ch-16 International maritime distress, calling, and safety channel. Heavily used on rivers, lakes also.
162.4000	Used for NOAA weather broadcasts and bulletins.
162.4250	Used for NOAA weather broadcasts and bulletins.
162.4500	Used for NOAA weather broadcasts and bulletins.
162.4750	Used for NOAA weather broadcasts and bulletins.
162.5000	Used for NOAA weather broadcasts and bulletins.
162.5250	Used for NOAA weather broadcasts and bulletins.
162.5500	Used for NOAA weather broadcasts and bulletins.
163.2750	Used for NOAA weather broadcasts and bulletins.
163.4875	Used nationwide by the National Guard during emergencies.
163.5125	The national disaster preparedness frequency used jointly by the armed forces.
168.5500	The national channel used by civilian agencies of the Federal Government for communications during emergencies and disasters.
222.1000	Ham CW and SSB USA Calling
223.5000	Ham FM USA Calling
243.0000	Used during military aviation emergencies.
259.7000	Used by the Space Shuttle during re-entry and landing.
296.8000	Used by the Space Shuttle during re-entry and landing.
311.0000	An active in-flight channel used by the U.S. Air Force.
317.7000	An active channel used by U.S. Coast Guard aviation.
317.8000	An active channel used by U.S. Coast Guard aviation.
319.4000	An active in-flight channel used by the U.S. Air Force.
340.2000	An active channel used by U.S. Navy aviators.
409.6250	National communications channel for the Department of State.
432.1000	Ham CW and SSB USA Calling
446.0000	Ham FM Simplex USA Calling
462.5625	Citizens FRS/GMRS Ch-1 commonly used Calling Frequency
462.6750	Citizens GMRS Ch-20 Emergency Communications and Traveler Assistance
902.1000	Ham SSB USA Calling (weak-signal)
1294.5000	Ham FM USA Calling
1296.1000	Ham SSB USA Calling
2304.1000	Ham USA calling
2305.2000	Ham FM Simplex USA calling

DO NOT TRANSMIT ON THE ABOVE UNDERLINED FREQUENCIES. You can listen to these but do not transmit on them during times of emergency.

The lower the frequency the further the distance it can be heard. Use whatever frequencies your radio equipment is capable of.

A low cost, low-power radio frequency scanner can be programmed with these frequencies to do the monitoring. It also may be advantageous to scan other frequencies once you know what the locals are using. Program a scanner, test, and get familiar with your equipment before a *Catastrophic Event*.

A good operating practice is to move off channel keeping the calling channel clear. After a *Catastrophic Event* you may want to stay on the calling frequency so that others have the possibility of hearing and joining in conversation.

Have the person monitoring the emergency frequency every 10 minutes or so say… *"This is station XXX listening"*.

Remember that when you transmit through a radio, your location can be triangulated. In other words… those with sophisticated enough equipment can pinpoint your exact location.

The Military Phonetic Alphabet

Radio transmissions can sound garbled and letters and numbers can be mistaken when transmitting by radio or speaking. To reduce this confusion, the **military phonetic alphabet** was created.

Each letter of the alphabet has an assigned word. When speaking or transmitting an important message the words that represent each letter are spoken in succession.

For example, if you wish to transmit the phrase '2 vehicles', you would say these words in succession...

"Two (pause), Victor-Echo-Hotel-India-Charlie-Lima-Echo-Sierra"
OR
"Two, I repeat… Two, Victor-Echo-Hotel-India-Charlie-Lima-Echo-Sierra"

The Chart representing the military phonetic alphabet...
A – Alpha
B – Bravo
C – Charlie
D – Delta

E – Echo
F – Foxtrot
G – Golf
H – Hotel
I – India
J – Juliet
K – Kilo
L – Lima
M – Mike
N – November
O – Oscar
P – Papa
Q – Quebec
R – Romeo
S – Sierra
T – Tango
U – Uniform
V – Victor
W – Whiskey
X - X- Ray
Y – Yankee
Z – Zulu

The first ten digits representing Military Phonetic Numeric...
0 – Zeero
1 – Wun
2 – Too
3 – Tree
4 – Fower
5 – Fife
6 – Siks
7 – Seven
8 – Ait
9 – Niner

The number 9 is pronounced *"Nine-er"* in the Military Phonetic Numeric as the German word for *"NO"* is *"Nein"* which sounds like the English pronunciation of 9 and can cause confusion.

Good luck !!

Calculation of Water, Food and Provisions for EACH PERSON

Each person will consume and should have the minimum of the following items: Food, water, a firearm, ammunition for that firearm, clothing for all seasons. The best way to ensure you have everything is to gather your household members and *Extended Family and Friends* and 'brainstorm.' Talk about it!

Speak out loud and visualize what you each will need for all seasons of the year. This must include simple things like cooking fuel per person. Have one or two members act as 'recorders' and put everything thought of down on paper. Make a list and distribute and then be persistent until each person has these items.

Water… The Triple-One Rule of Thumb. This rule of water use will give each person in your *NPP drinking, minimal cooking and bathing water of* ***One Gallon*** *for* ***One Person*** *for* ***One Day***. This depends, obviously on the time of year, your climate, and individual needs. But this rule will generally keep all Group Members functioning adequately. You should have as much water in storage as possible and your *NPP* should have an identified renewable water source.

'Calories of Emergency Food Stored.' A simple rule of thumb is to calculate **2000 calories of food requirement per day for each person.** This number '2000' will be used below to calculate your ***'Number of Days of Emergency Food Stored.'*** There is a Calorie Chart at the bottom of the next page that you can reference for a more detailed calculation of individual food needs in calories. Use the form on the next page to list and calculate your 'Calories of Emergency Food Stored' from all the items of Emergency Food you have.

To calculate the 'Calories of Emergency Food Stored' you have to…

1. Multiply the *'Calories per Serving'* times the *'Servings per Container'* in each container.
2. Multiply that times the number of *identical sized containers* you have.
3. Perform this calculation for each of your food items for a *Calories Subtotal.*
4. Then add up Calories Subtotal column of all food items to get your Total number for ***'Calories of Emergency Food Stored'.***

'Number of Days of Emergency Food Stored.' This will tell you *how many days of Emergency Food your household will have* to live on.

1. To calculate take the *Total Number* of *'Calories of Emergency Food Stored'* from your form below.
2. Divide that by the *Number of Persons* (household members and *Extended Family and Friends*) that will be eating out of these Emergency Food stores.
3. That number will be the *Number of Calories of Emergency Food for each Person.*
4. Divide that number by 2000 (Or by the *Individual Calorie Needs* using the Calorie Chart below.)
5. This will give you the ***'Number of Days of Emergency Food Stored'*** for your household.

Individual Calorie Needs. Calculate a more precise individual calorie consumption amount by using the Calorie Chart.

You do this by calculating the consumption per day of calories per individual by age, gender and activity level…

Then total all of those daily individual calories amounts…

Then divide that total by the number of persons.

This will give you an *average amount per person per day* which will be more accurate. It will reflect age, gender and activity level of your household members, but if your household has younger or older members it will be more accurate.

Estimated Calorie Requirements (in Kilocalories) for Each Gender and Age Group at Three Levels of Physical Activity[a]

Gender	Age (years)	Activity Level[b,c,d]		
		Sedentary[b]	Moderately Active[c]	Active[d]
Child	2–3	1,000	1,000–1,400[e]	1,000–1,400[e]
Female	4–8	1,200	1,400–1,600	1,400–1,800
	9–13	1,600	1,600–2,000	1,800–2,200
	14–18	1,800	2,000	2,400
	19–30	2,000	2,000–2,200	2,400
	31–50	1,800	2,000	2,200
	51+	1,600	1,800	2,000–2,200
Male	4–8	1,400	1,400–1,600	1,600–2,000
	9–13	1,800	1,800–2,200	2,000–2,600
	14–18	2,200	2,400–2,800	2,800–3,200
	19–30	2,400	2,600–2,800	3,000
	31–50	2,200	2,400–2,600	2,800–3,000
	51+	2,000	2,200–2,400	2,400–2,800

Source: HHS/USDA Dietary Guidelines for Americans, 2005

Calorie Chart by Age, Gender and Activity Level

Food Item Description	Calories Per Serving		Servings Per Container		Number of Containers		Calories Subtotal
1. ______	______	times	______	times	______	Equals	______
2. ______	______	times	______	times	______	Equals	______
3. ______	______	times	______	times	______	Equals	______
4. ______	______	times	______	times	______	Equals	______
5. ______	______	times	______	times	______	Equals	______
6. ______	______	times	______	times	______	Equals	______
7. ______	______	times	______	times	______	Equals	______
8. ______	______	times	______	times	______	Equals	______
9. ______	______	times	______	times	______	Equals	______
10. ______	______	times	______	times	______	Equals	______
11. ______	______	times	______	times	______	Equals	______
12. ______	______	times	______	times	______	Equals	______

Total Number 'Calories of Emergency Food Stored' ______

Add and subtract from this total number when you add foods to your emergency foods or subtract from this number if you eat out of your emergency foods.

NPP Survey Questionnaire and Address Checklist

"I live in this area and I'm your neighbor. We're having a neighborhood meeting about protecting our neighborhood against fire and protecting it by whatever means necessary against criminals, rioters and looters in support of our Fire and Police Departments if an emergency or a disaster strikes and they are unable to respond."

"I'm not in charge of this, but I'm helping others organize.

We're going to vote to elect two experienced people to lead our group at our meeting and we'll answer all your questions there.

Would you be willing to help the rest of us and come to our meeting?"

1. Name: ____________________ Address: ________________________ ☐Yes ☐No
2. Name: ____________________ Address: ________________________ ☐Yes ☐No
3. Name: ____________________ Address: ________________________ ☐Yes ☐No
4. Name: ____________________ Address: ________________________ ☐Yes ☐No
5. Name: ____________________ Address: ________________________ ☐Yes ☐No
6. Name: ____________________ Address: ________________________ ☐Yes ☐No
7. Name: ____________________ Address: ________________________ ☐Yes ☐No
8. Name: ____________________ Address: ________________________ ☐Yes ☐No
9. Name: ____________________ Address: ________________________ ☐Yes ☐No
10. Name: ____________________ Address: ________________________ ☐Yes ☐No
11. Name: ____________________ Address: ________________________ ☐Yes ☐No
12. Name: ____________________ Address: ________________________ ☐Yes ☐No
13. Name: ____________________ Address: ________________________ ☐Yes ☐No
14. Name: ____________________ Address: ________________________ ☐Yes ☐No
15. Name: ____________________ Address: ________________________ ☐Yes ☐No

Notes: ____

____

NPP Survey Questionnaire and Address Checklist

Our Neighborhood Protection Plan Statement of Purpose

This Neighborhood Protection Plan is intended to PROTECT OUR NEIGHBORHOOD area in times of emergency, civil unrest and disaster.

Our objective is to PROTECT OUR NEIGHBORHOOD against fire if our area fire department is unable to respond timely.

Our objective is to PROTECT OUR NEIGHBORHOOD against looters and criminals if law enforcement is unable to respond timely or unable maintain order during a disaster.

Our NPP is being formed and when organized is for the sole purposes above and each member is acting as a Neighborhood Guardian to promote and secure this purpose.

You, as a Group Member of our NPP, agree that we are not a 'Militia' that has been authorized or deputized by any city, county, State or Federal Government entity or law enforcement agency to carry out law enforcement and you agree to conduct yourself accordingly.

Each Group Member will act responsibly and respectfully towards all people within and outside our neighborhood to the best of their ability. Each Group Member agrees to refrain from vigilante actions and will use force in defense and only as a last resort in protecting our neighborhood.

Write any questions you have on the back of this paper.

NPP Group Member Information

This Information is voluntary and will be held in the strictest of confidence by our Neighborhood Protection Plan Leadership and Council. You've expressed a desire to become a member of our Neighborhood Protection Plan. This information is voluntary, however for our Neighborhood Protection Plan to be effective, leadership has to have some basic information about you and your capabilities to enable you to help us to the maximum of your abilities.

Name: ________________________ **Email:** _______________ @ ___________ . ______

Address: ____

Home Phone: (____) _____ - ________ Cellular Phone: (____) _____ - ________

Check the following areas if you have any training or expertise in them...

- ☐ Military training
- ☐ Law enforcement training
- ☐ Firearms training
- ☐ Medical training
- ☐ Radio communications, electronics or electrical training
- ☐ Fire Fighting and Prevention
- ☐ Food storage and preparations training
- ☐ Construction experience
- ☐ Nutrition and cooking expertise
- ☐ Gardening-fishing-hunting knowledge
- ☐ Vehicle repair knowledge
- ☐ Chemistry training or education

Information about your health and fitness:

Age: _____ Health issues: ____

____

What would you prefer to do to help with protecting your neighborhood and neighbors?

____

____